SAQQARA

S. Skinner-Young

SAQQARA

Copyright © 2022 S. Skinner-Young

All rights reserved.

This book or parts thereof may not be reproduced in any form, stored in a retrieval system, or transmitted by any means–electronic, mechanical, photocopy, recording, or otherwise, without prior written permission of the publisher, except as provided by the United States of America copyright law.

ISBN: 979-8-9868754-9-1

Scripture quotations unless otherwise noted are taken from the (NASB®) New American Standard Bible®, Copyright © 1960, 1971, 1977, 1995, 2020 by The Lockman Foundation. Used by permission. All rights reserved. www.lockman.org.

DISCLAIMER:

This book is a work of fiction. However, the author provides a sense of authenticity by referencing real people, events, establishments, organizations, or locals factiously. She draws all other characters, incidents, and dialogue from her imagination or experience. Therefore, any character resemblance to an actual person, living or dead, is entirely coincidental. The word satan intentionally is not capitalized; that entity deserves no honor.

Cover artwork "God in My Veins" by Dinah Rau

Edited by MarJean Peters

Book design and formatting – Kim Gardell

SPD Publishing

Contact information to purchase:
saqqara-book.com
acaciaministries.com

DEDICATION

I dedicate this book to those who survived severe trauma and overcame the dissociation that resulted from it.

To survive a horrific act is different than to heal from it. Surviving could mean you are still living the nightmare, but [if] you do not let it define who you truly are or who you will become... that's what it means to be saved and free.

Reaksmey Haas (survivor and abolitionist)

ACKNOWLEDGMENTS

My sincere thanks to Fatima and Annie, who begged this book.

I am indebted to the clients who taught me about dissociation.

Gratitude goes to Bethany, who listened to the raw substance and offered wisdom for changes. I am so grateful to Majority, Brilliance, Carlotta, Pam, Kay, Debora and espcially the A.C.A.C.I.A. team's prayers and encouragement which supported the long work.

Certainly, I am indebted to my Christian parents and, most of all, Jesus Christ of Nazareth for His healing power.

INTRODUCTION

Many of my thousand or more clients pled with tearful eyes and wrenching entreaty that I write a manual to help the tens of thousands who cannot access the help they received. So, ten years ago, I started the manual.

Still, after serious deliberation, I realized relatively few people go to the bookstore and buy a manual, but they purchase fictional novels. Hence *Saqqara* [pronounced suh·kaa·ruh] is a book about living with hidden trauma, healing, and hope for the promised abundant life.

TABLE of CONTENTS

Dedication iii
Acknowledgments iv
Introduction v
Prologue viii

PART I

1. Awakening 1
2. California Seminar 6
3. More Meds 26
4. Capacity 29
5. Nadine Helps 41
6. Anger Out 43
7. The Book Club 53
8. Hello Wives 61
9. Packing for Europe 69
10. The Request 74

PART II

11. Up, Up, and Away 79
12. Hidden Trauma Detective 85
13. Leaving and Touring 99
14. Office Weirdness 103
15. Lebensborn Man 106
16. Deliverance 114
17. The Temp 123
18. Quarry and Erotica 126
19. Tabea's Sleep 134
20. Den Hague Farewell 137
21. Train to Kassel 140
22. Naysa's Offer 146
23. The Hike 148
24. Stranger than Fiction Conference 152
25. Train to Leipzig 185
26. Destabilization 188
27. Introspection 192

28 Leipzig Appeal 194
29 Sowing and Reaping 198
30 Triune Mother's Day 202
31 Celebrate Away 206
32 Home Sweet Home 208

PART III

33 Hello Spokane 213
34 The Encounter 217
35 World Views 262
36 Chicago, My Wonderful Town 272
37 Short Trip 276
38 Wives Unveiled 279
39 The Wedding 286
40 The Last Straw 288
41 Desmond's Visit 290
42 The Move 294
43 The 9th of July 298
44 Uba 306
45 Seth and Clarice 310
46 Vacations 313
47 Runner 321
48 Gone 323
49 Evtwin 326
50 Magic 329
51 Absolution 331
52 Unfinished Business 337
53 Hope 339

Glossary 341
Major Characters in the Book 343
Resources 345
About the Author 349
A.C.A.C.I.A. Institute Vision 350

PROLOGUE

Before you embark on this reading journey, I provide the following historical profile to lay a foundation and address some references you shall encounter. There is also an example of burden-bearing.

Respectfully, Sandra

The mystery religions of ancient Babylon, Egypt, India, and Greece helped lay the foundation for occultism. The *Egyptian Book of the Dead* is one of humanity's earliest writings. It describes rituals for torture and intimidation for bringing an individual to complete submission. satanism employed these measures throughout the ages.

One of the best ways to control the world is to limit people's thinking. In 1882, the first recorded Behavioral Science Research began in England. In Germany, the Kaiser Wilhelm Institute conducted early medical and psychiatric techniques involved in mind control.

In the 19th century, the primary geographic areas of Illuminati control resided in Great Britain and Germany. The hierarchy of

Prologue

what we know as the Masonic Order decree Lucifer as their God when they take the thirty-third degree.

In 1921, the Tavistock Institute of Human Relations in London studied humans' "breaking point." In 1932, Kurt Lewin, a German psychologist, became the director of the Tavistock Institute about the same time Nazi Germany increased its research into neuro-psychology, parapsychology, and multi-generational occultism. A progressive exchange of scientific ideas took place between England and Germany, most notably in eugenics: the movement devoted to "improving" the human species through the control of hereditary factors in mating. The nefarious union between the two countries bonded partly through the Order of the Golden Dawn, a secret society that consisted mainly of English royalty, high-ranking Nazi Party members, and aristocracy.

After WW II, Project **PAPERCLIP**, the U.S. Department of Defense program code name, secretly imported some 5,000 top German Nazi and Italian Fascist scientists and spies into the United States via South America and the Vatican for rocketry and mind control. Of course, Canada, Russia, and other countries did similar things.

In 1947, Hitler's former chief of intelligence against Russia, General Reinhard Gehlen, initiated the Central Intelligence Group (CIA) and the National Security Council.

The National Security Council spawned the National Security Act, signed by President Truman on July 26, 1947. It protected an unconscionable number of illegal governmental activities, including clandestine mind control programs. Did you ever have questions about the Black Ops Budget or wonder why a single screw should cost $400.00?

The CIA recruited Dr. Joseph Mengele, whose brutality scarred the souls of survivors from Auschwitz and countless victims throughout the world. He worked primarily out of Brazil.

In 1947 the U.S. Navy instigated the brain-washing program, "Project Chatter," using the Soviet's brainchild "truth drugs" for interrogations.

It officially stopped in 1953 but continued as Operation Artichoke, later called **MK Ultra**. You may have heard of this mind control program. To keep MK Ultra from being easily detected, the CIA segmented its subprojects into specialized fields of research and development at major universities, prisons, private laboratories, and hospitals. The CIA well subsidized all of them for their co-operation.

Perhaps the most famous split-personality courier is MK Ultra victim Cathy O'Brian. I recommend her book, *Trance Formation of America,* co-authored by her rescuer Mark Phillips, a former electronics subcontractor for the Department of Defense. Phillips was privy to some top-secret mind control activities perpetrated by the U.S. government. Names of other mind control programs were **Monarch or Marionette, Montauk, and Bluebird.**

I wish to honor the people who bravely sought to confront this evil, many of them have been murdered. Domestic and international people are doing a valiant job of freeing some of these survivors. I heartily commend the groups that are actively confronting human trafficking. I encourage you to join one. These groups are aware of the sex slave trade and worker slavery, but I wonder if they are remotely mindful of the extent of horror and complexity of some of it.

Prologue

Burden Bearing Example

I believe God creates people with the gifts they need to accomplish their destiny. One of my most valuable gifts is burden-bearing or an empathic sense. In this book the counselor protagonist, Lydia, possesses this gift: Lydia pondered, *but most women thrill at the prospect of shopping. Not me! I can still feel my legs at the mall as heavy wooden stumps. I just wanted to leave. Fairs are the worst. It felt as if I soaked up the atmosphere. Neither the taffy nor delectable waffles made it worth the drudge. Thank goodness I finally learned about burden-bearing and how to manage it, but... it's not always so easy to recognize.*

I remember that morning while showering, suddenly symptoms of a heart attack drew me to the floor in a streaming bonnet of shampoo. Once nausea ebbed and the pain waned, as nurses are prone to minimize their symptoms, I dismissed the coronary event as likely due to stress or a strained muscle. Instead, I pulled myself up and got back into the tub with streaming water.

Immediately, a firm mid-sternal pressure swayed me to the side and down again. At least the swoon threw me under the water spray so that most of the shampoo rinsed away. Finally convinced I should maybe go to the emergency room (ER), they drew the usual labs and hooked me up to an electrocardiogram (EKG) for a long time. Having no insurance, every minute in the ER meant a lot of moola. I studied the EKG oscillations, noted the rhythms, and concluded no abnormalities. I felt a bit sneaky as I quickly removed the electrodes, dressed, and said, 'Goodbye.' That same day, I discerned burden-bearing, did the intercession, and the symptoms left.

I hope you enjoy the book and recommend it to someone who needs it. Our hope is Jesus Christ: Justice Exposing Systems, Usurping Senseless Creations of Hegelian Rhetoric Into Sensational Transformation.

PART I

CHAPTER 1

AWAKENING

―•◆✕◆•―

RUN... RUN... RUN! Then, everything stopped abruptly. Pushing through to awareness, she bent low, her hand deeply pressed against her right side. *This grabbing agony is what alerted me!* Relief. A drop of brine from soaked blond hair burned an eye as she straightened. She blankly surveyed the surroundings without any sense of familiarity. After a few hobbled steps, she noticed the five-inch stiletto heel gone from her left shoe. A sickening in her stomach crept up to meet the distant, faint blackness in her brain. Millions of tiny crackling sounds filled her ears. Somehow, she lay down on the front steps of a small cottage.

A warm light streamed from inside a white-framed window onto the icy cement step where she lay. Her velvet ballgown stuck to the step as she pushed herself up to a sitting position, then struggled to stand, and finally stepped up to approach the door.

The cheery doorbell quickly brought a short, stooped woman with bluish-white hair, wearing a long-favored chenille robe. Her pink cheeks faded as she asked in astonishment, "Yes?"

The disheveled stranger asked to use her telephone.

She muttered as she unlocked and opened the screen door, "You won't hurt me, will you? Oh well, what does it matter? I've had a good long life."

The house felt suffocatingly warm. "Sit down, Honey. My, you look frozen," the octogenarian remarked, observing mottled skin turn to red splotches. She then hurried to dig a blue shell afghan from the bottom of the entry closet. "There, wrap yourself in that, and I'll get you some nice hot tea. I just brewed a cup for myself. This old body fights to sleep these days. Oh yes, the phone. I don't own one of that new-fangled educated kind. My old-style phone is for dummies, I guess, but it works," she said.

"I need to call a taxi, please," a shivering voice announced.

"We ain't got no taxi cabs here, Hon. You'll need to look in the Chicago directory for that," she explained with a perplexed frown.

The long wait for the cab to arrive provided enough time for the stranger to get warm, dry, and eat a hot breakfast. Most people make small talk, ask questions, or explain their situation. Strangely, considering the lingering remnants of winter weather and that she arrived without coat, purse, or gloves, the stranger remained reticent. She waited.

The sun rose about two inches above the horizon when the cab finally arrived. The compassionate older woman insisted the afghan go with her guest. She explained she made it for her eleven-year-old daughter, who disappeared years ago, one of the flurries of stories spun at breakfast during the stranger's silence.

Scraggly wisps of gray hair interrupted the driver's wrinkled face. A dingy cap sat precariously on his head. His fare sat quietly and stared out the window at nothing until noisy Chicago traffic required attention. The driver spent the fare money in his mind on the long trip. His gruff voice escalated when it became apparent she carried no payment. He sat impatiently with his arm stretched across the top of the passenger seat, straining to hear.

The afghan-wrapped woman rang her apartment manager and explained she had lost her key. Helga scanned her disheveled

Awakening

tenant, retrieved a key, and with an inconvenienced scowl, led the way to unlock the apartment.

Key in hand, the young woman paid the driver and thought, *I'm glad he didn't charge for waiting, and luckily, I arrived before Helga's dog-walking ritual. The taxi fare would never get paid if silence and looks could kill!*

Back in the apartment, she stood looking into nothing, winced with a headache, then spied the clock, 7:45 AM! Hopefully, enough time remained to make her 9 AM appointment with the prospective client! She threw off the afghan, ran to the bathroom, and whipped off her clothes along the way. Once in the shower, she gave herself the fastest scrub and shampoo ever. The shower steam clouded the mirror, blocking her view as she brushed even white teeth. She toweled a swath of vision and decided she looked good, then styled her shoulder-length hair skimmed back with a black fanned bow. Itsy-bitsy tendrils of hair popped out here and there. The smooth, fair complexion sported a smattering of freckles soon hidden with a swish of the make-up brush. Today azure eyes received no enhancement. Glossy red color swiped across her full lips.

"Great! The headache is gone," the young woman exclaimed. Black tights hid the leg bruises to which the swift washcloth drew attention. A straight skirt enhanced her slim, five-feet-eight figure. The red, black, and beige striped tunic top and large red hoop earrings finished the outfit. As she pulled on black boots to purposefully hide her swollen feet, she found herself wondering what in the world caused it?

Following her mother's socially active example, she kept a fancy bag for party necessities amply supplied for everyday life, complete with an extra set of keys in addition to her purse. Today, the stressed lady, grateful for the habit, grabbed the everyday bag as she buzzed out the door.

She paused to take a deep breath upon arrival minutes before the meeting with the prospective client. She read the bronze office door plaque: Saqqara Alexandria Fain, Event Co-Ordinator/Chief

Project Manager. She ignored the ringing phone until she spied Tiffany's name.

"Where in the world have you been? Are you alright? I tried to reach you all night! You just ran out of the ballroom! I felt clumsy covering for you," Tiffany affectionately chided. "I'll bring your coat and purse to our luncheon meeting today with…"

"Gotta go… meeting with our hopefully new client." Click. The headache returned. *To what was Tiffany referring? Where had I been? I can't think about that now.*

The office manager buzzed to notify her of the client's arrival. Saqqara loved the enticement, the convincing, the dance of engagement, and finalizing the deal with prospective clients. The schedule already bulged, but money flowed. Keeping super busy always proved the sane way to function.

Tiffany, a triple type-A person, steady, methodical, full of charisma with an infectious laugh, seemed to bounce her trim, tall figure around the curved art deco restaurant wall. Her long raven hair framed her heart-shaped face and dramatic almond-shaped eyes. She and Saqqara met in graduate school and quickly became friends. Since they complemented each other and shared the same goals, they formed a corporation. The public considered them the go-to people for "top drawer" events. They recently decided to hire someone to do more footwork due to the thriving business.

"Millie texted to say she won't be able to lunch with us because she broke a tooth and is at the dentist as we speak," Tiffany reported. "It's just as well. We must talk, Saqqara," she whispered. "Mayor's ball? Do you realize how embarrassing it was for me as you raced away like Cinderella? What a scene!" Her hair whipped around her shoulder as she addressed the waiter, "No, we need a few more minutes, but lime for the water, please." Turning back, she spied the package she brought. "Oh, I almost forgot! Here's your coat and purse. Where was I? Oh, yes, the Governor's wife was a real pain, prodding me for explanations."

Cell phone music interrupted. Saqqara scrunched up her face and said, "I must take this, sorry." Her best high school friend waited at O'Hare Airport for lunch. She purposefully booked a long layover so they could visit on her way to a convention in New York. Impossible to reach O'Hare in time for a visit with her friend now, Saqqara apologized profusely. Her friend replied courteously enough, but Saqqara could detect her ire. *How could we double book such a special occasion?*

Saqqara explained the situation to Tiffany. Tiffany took off on a critical litany of Saqqara's recent behavior until her cheeks looked like a clown's. She noted double bookings, missed appointments, unable to recognize clients, dressed inappropriately for meetings, and forgot vital components for events.

Saqqara sat in denial staring in unbelief at this ridiculous, frenzied, once stable co-worker.

They decided to discuss this later in private. Since appetites were nil, they each went their separate ways. The meeting finished, and so was Saqqara. She quit work and took the rest of the day off. Driving to her apartment, she thought about how her sister recently accused her of lying. Saqqara knew she was not a liar. How dare she! That call had not ended well. Afterward, she reflected on times when other people accused her of falsehoods. People could be so fickle and unkind.

While ascending the stairs, Saqqara's right peripheral vision caught a curtain quickly closing in the main floor apartment across from the manager. She vaguely remembered seeing a young woman in a wheelchair there.

Inside her apartment, exhaustion consumed Saqqara. Her legs and feet throbbed. A blue afghan lay on the white love seat. *How did that get there?*

CHAPTER 2

CALIFORNIA SEMINAR

All lights blinked off and on twice, the background music faded, and the din of many voices dwindled to a hush. A venue administrator gave the usual housekeeping instructions to the audience and introduced Birgit Malloy, Director of Survivor Matters. Her willowy, dignified body strode across the platform to the podium. She felt flooded with satisfaction as she noted the capacity-filled room. Her silvery hair looked luminous with the causal rose pantsuit.

She smiled a cheery welcome and announced, "You are in for a seminar to remember. Our guest speaker is Lydia Ouray Voight. She practiced the profession of nursing extensively for years and now comes to us to share twenty-five years' experience as an international expert working with severely traumatized people. We invited you because you too share in this work in one way or another. Lydia is a knowledgeable woman of principle and high standards without compromise. Her healthy boundaries for healing and restoring highly complex issues balance with incredible sensitivity, love, and discernment. So, it is my honor to present not only a gifted teacher but also my friend, Lydia Voight." Birgit clapped and backed away from the podium as Lydia occupied it.

A short asymmetrical hairstyle framed Lydia's oval face in a warm apricot hue. Her strongest beauty feature, vivid green eyes, highlighted a cameo complexion. Her neck accommodated volume earrings that she loved but ensured they accessorized her attire without distraction. She was one of those people who, upon entering a room,—a presence about her. Lydia's thank you quieted the applause.

"My purpose is to help you become aware of perhaps one of the most important covert strategies operating in our world today. From talking with some of you, I know people with crippling dysfunction, physically and mentally, are flooding counseling offices everywhere with complex problems that our usual conventions, psychological or medical, do not seem to help. I trust this information will result in dynamic changes in your leadership and life. Please write any questions as the presentation goes along so as not to forget them. There is much content to cover in the allotted time. I hope for time to answer questions at the end. If you become symptomatic at any time, please feel free to leave the room, take care of yourself, and return."

She paused, briefly surveyed the audience, and emitted a surprised expression to see a more significant number of men in the audience than usual. Then she activated the screen behind her, simultaneously announcing, "Our topic is Dissociative Identity Disorder: A Coping Mechanism. This seminar is merely an introduction to understanding the complex protective coping mechanism known as, Dissociative Identity Disorder, hereafter referred to as DID. This coping style provides a way for young children to survive real or perceived severe trauma and then manage the inner conflicts which arise from it, such as denial of the trauma. We will address diagnostic parameters and sketch how the mind constructs and manages the fractured impact of trauma. We will also provide tips to assist in solving a few common physical problems associated with becoming aware of the brokenness.

"Webster defines coping as: a way to strike, fight or contend successfully. DID is an extreme form of dissociation, commonly considered a problem or alteration in identity, memory, consciousness, and perception, the way we see something. The combination of the ova and sperm carries the genetic material that will determine the individual's uniqueness, plus their spirit. The person God creates at conception is the Original Person or OP. DID involves the dividing, splitting, or shattering the OP's spirit, mind, will, emotions, and physical body.

"Standardized diagnostic tests may be administered. However, a problem occurs when the patient dissociates during the tests without symptoms, making an accurate diagnosis impossible. Many misdiagnoses result. Most of us learned little about this disorder in college or heard it is infrequent or does not exist at all.

"The following information is in your syllabus starting on page four." A shuffle of paper sounded from the audience. "In 1994, the diagnosis label changed from Multiple Personality Disorder, MPD, to Dissociative Identity Disorder, DID. A diagnosis for DID would require the following:

"First, the person must manifest at least two distinct personalities with consistent patterns of perceiving, thinking about, and relating to their environment or themselves. These personalities may present as any age, gender, race, animate or inanimate. They must repeat executive control of the body for an extended time. These changes in identity may be observed by others or self-reported. In some cases, we observe possession-like phenomena.

"Second, all of us forget. For instance, we forget where we put our keys or that it's an important anniversary. However, with DID, there is an extensively overlooking beyond ordinary forgetfulness. This is not due to external influences or drugs. Alcohol is also a drug, you know.

"Third, there are gaps in memory, not only for trauma but everyday life events. For instance: A person bought new tires for the auto yesterday and needs to put them on today, but today no idea about new tires is conscious. These also cannot be due to disease or drug use.

"Fourth, reported intense experiences not due to psychosis, being out of touch with reality.

"Fifth, some individual's conditions may include functional neurological symptoms that account for more varied disorder presentations.

"Severe trauma usually breaks a human being, especially for an infant or child. This breaking in psychological terminology is dissociation.

- Some people, even psychiatric professionals, deny that DID is real.
- Some people say the idea is too preposterous even to consider it valid.
- Medical texts used to say it was so rare that one may never see it in practice.
- In the early 1990s, it was believed only one in 100 cases existed; today, one in ten is more realistic.

"Undoubtedly, some present here today suffered such shattering.

- It could be from a singular event of trauma.
- It could be from repeated childhood dysfunctional family events.
- It could be from cold, calculated technical mind control.

"We will explore mind control in our afternoon segment. I will now demonstrate how I teach this to my clients, rather than a didactic or lecture format presentation. This modality may be more instructive for you," Lydia explained. "People use their dissociative coping mechanism to 'go away' or 'go inside' from the perceived or actual trauma to survive the conflict. Then, at the same time, they create another aspect of themselves to "suffer" or "perform" the life event. In other words, the mind separates one or more of its functions away from its usual stream of consciousness. There is a separation of functions or compartmentalization into altered personality components referred to as other selves, alters, or parts. Individuals often create their terms for themselves.

"Let's look at an illustration." Lydia directed the laser pointer onto the screen. "We see an elementary diagram to illustrate the division of degrees of self-awareness with DID.

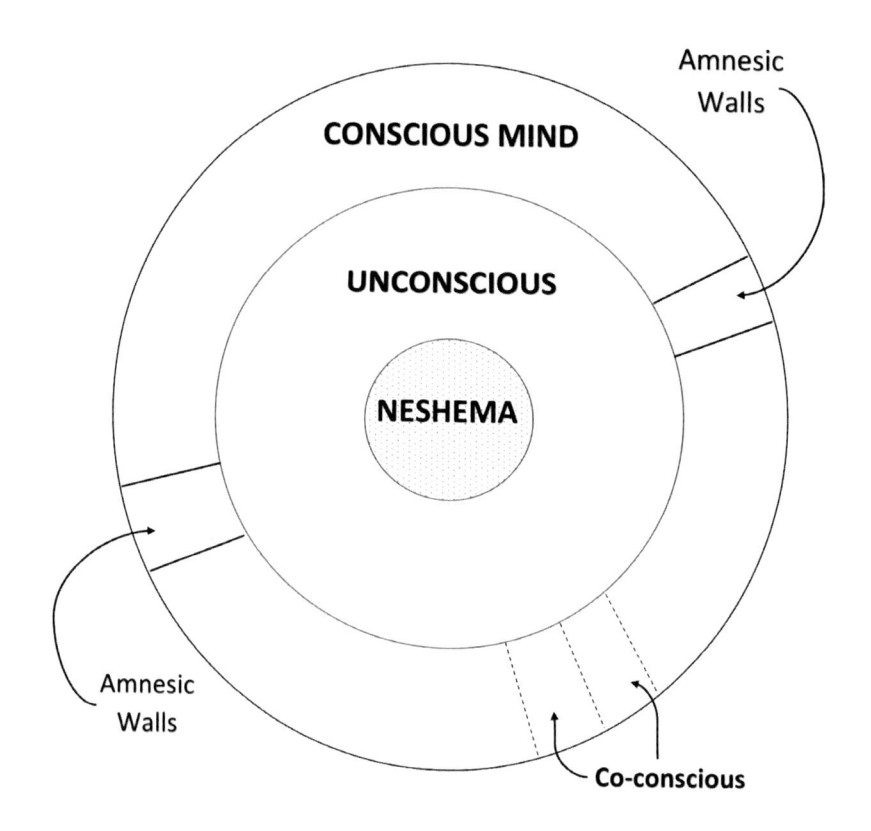

"The outer circle represents the conscious mind. This part of our mind is aware of current life, some past experiences, and imaginations for future life. Notice the lines with open spaces forming little compartments in them. These represent the alters or parts of whom you are aware. We call that co-consciousness. Compartments with solid lines represent the alters or parts of whom you are amnesic. You don't even know they exist. The large inner circle represents the unconscious mind, a huge storehouse of information without our knowledge or access. The center represents your spirit or Neshamah, made in the essence of God himself; it is your life and glory. Job 32:8 tells us, *But it is a* (vital force) *spirit* (of intelligence) *in man, And the breath* (Neshamah) *of the Almighty gives them understanding.* Job 33:4 also says, (It is) *the Spirit of God has made me* (which has stirred me up), *And the breath* (Neshamah) *of the Almighty gives me life* (which inspires me).'

"Some of these parts or alters may only be fragments of the OP (original person) with limited function. It is possible that senses, such as taste, sight, smell, hearing, and touch become separated. People accomplish this by building walls between the separated parts or alters so that a person's component can be unaffected by a certain experience. A normally functioning person integrates these aspects of function. That means they automatically do them all at the same time.

"A highly complex DID mind could separate even into thousands of parts. Easy now," Lydia humorously cautioned. "Do not allow yourself to get overwhelmed by the number count! The number of alters is only an indication of the extent of a trauma you suffered. One traumatic event can produce many fragmented parts before the person creates an alter who can survive the fear, pain, or ability to perform an act reprehensible to the OP.

"Your entire humanity, regardless of fracturing, is YOU, incredible YOU! It is critical to know that all your humanity is the same person irrespective of how many alters or parts there are. All alters begin with the OP.

"Once a person realizes alters exist, they often become afraid they will be overpowered or overwhelmed by them. There is no reason to fear your human alters. They are all you! The only difference is now you know they are there. Maybe you sensed their thoughts or heard their voices, although not all people with DID hear the inner voices. People who are not DID, do not have this kind of noise in their heads. Once a dissociative person is whole again, the noise is gone. People with schizophrenia often report hearing voices outside their heads.

"I take great joy explaining to people with DID they are not insane! I realize you may fear you are crazy. You could have been. Then I say…." Lydia directed the laser pointer onto the screen again.

"**You are not insane. You are not insane. You are not insane!**"

Row after row of wide-eyed stares fixated upon Lydia. Finally, she took a moment to take a sip of water. Then lowering her volume but retaining the intensity, she continued, "I am very proud of you because three choices confronted you: death, insanity, the complete break with reality, and dissociation. You made the best choice. You dissociated!"

Lydia watched different people broadly smile.

"Congratulations!!! You made the best choice! You used the coping mechanism, dissociation, to escape an inescapable situation as-a-way to manage life or to survive. Trauma usually causes dissociation. Infants and little children unequipped with many coping strategies can dissociate. The Creator especially designed dissociation to protect little children powerless to protect themselves."

Lydia noticed several attendees here and there leaving the room. *I wonder how many fractured therapists sought help by studying psychology?*

"A classic example is a puzzle. These examples have different pieces and characteristics, but each is part of the same whole. Be aware that many of the parts or alters of a dissociated person are children. Think of this alter or part stuck in the time of the trauma or frozen in time. Some pain you experience leaks from these alters who continually experience the trauma as if it never ended. Alters never regress or become younger. Some alters age with time, and others stay the same age as when you created them.

"That's right. You created the human alters! Even if instructed by someone else to create a certain type of alter, you still were the only one who could do it! I hope you get this because it **is the foundation of your empowerment for your healing!** If you can create something, you can change it!"

Lydia paused for a long time while surveying the immeasurable impact upon the audience, then concluded with, "Tomorrow, we find out how." Applause, then the shuffle of chairs and clamor of people leaving ensued.

"Wow!" said Birgit as she and Lydia walked to the elevator. "I was blown away with all this amazing new information. Now I remember a host of clients I recognize as dissociated. I feel such remorse

California Seminar

that I didn't see it and failed to give them the help they needed." She added, "You must be exhausted. Lydia, are you hungry?"

"You're such a good hostess. The yogurt and chamomile tea you provided in my room are perfect tonight. A bed also sounds delicious. My flight required my rising at 3:30 AM. I'll meet you here at eight o'clock tomorrow, Birgit," she called as the hotel elevator closed.

Lydia held great admiration for Birgit. Reflections of their relationship filed through her mind on the way to her room. *Birgit came to me for counseling years ago. At that time, she highly functioned as a wife, mother, community servant, and professional but experienced extensive symptoms of the DID amnesic barriers breaking down,* she interrupted that train of thought to note she would teach that tomorrow.

Once inside her room, while still contemplating, Lydia started the hot water for tea, kicked her shoes into the closet, and headed for the shower. She focused on making tea during the refreshing shower, then snatched a yogurt from the small refrigerator and cozied herself into her bed. The smooth peachy yogurt melted in her mouth as Lydia inhaled the fragrance of the tea. Her thinking fled to thankfulness to God for His abundant blessings she enumerated from the day. Finally, sleepy peace closed the door to thought.

Suddenly the cup made an alarming sound as it slid off the saucer. Birgit provided a China cup and saucer in place of the standard hotel mug for tea. She tootled off! "Oh well, dental hygiene is calling anyway," she mumbled while clumsily making her way off the bed to her toothbrush.

Waving her hands in an artistic flair, Lydia detailed her breakfast experience to Birgit as they walked to the seminar staff room. The humble steel-cut oats, butter, nuts, brown sugar, and cream served in a silver combo set delighted her. The coffee tasted incredibly bold and satisfying. Freshly pressed orange juice arrived in a stemmed goblet. She described the spacious room décor as definitely Californian, with high ceilings and open spaces softened with voluptuous urns of fresh flowers.

Birgit beamed at Lydia's pleasure as she reminded her, "We are royalty, you know."

"Lydia animatedly asked, "Birgit, I meditated on our history last night. It occurred to me I can teach, but how much more exciting and powerful would the segment on Lebensborn be if you gave your testimony?"

Birgit stopped in her tracks. Surprised eyes sparkled while a duet of delight and "I, I, I uh, I's," followed.

"You are an accomplished orator. Think of the authority to be delivered!" coaxed her friend. "Consider it and let me know your decision at lunch. Here's a copy of my notes."

They discussed the day's scheduled plans, prayed, and started the day on the dot. Lydia's strong sense of honoring people included respecting their time. Some did not share her opinion because many empty seats faced her, or were many seminar participants dissociative? That wasn't unusual.

Once, a former client invited her to do a seminar for small group leaders in the church. These leaders needed help understanding people who showed up with behaviors and needs they did not understand. Before the symposium began, the pastor told Lydia he did not recognize eighty percent of the attendees. So during the break, she made a point of talking to many people. To her surprise, a large number were therapists.

"Good morning, everyone!" Birgit said. "Did you have a good night's sleep, or were you too wound up for slumber? Most of us were amazed by the provocative material we received last night. Well, put on your seat belts. Here's Lydia! Welcome back. I understand you will help us understand that dissociation is all about denying the conflict," Birgit announced with enthusiasm as Lydia took her place at the podium.

This morning wide gold earrings and a red, gold, and black scarf draping a chartreuse jacket created a completely different look for

Lydia as she warmly welcomed the audience. She began, "Once the child learns to dissociate with life's troubles, they will usually continue to use that coping skill even in non-traumatic situations. **Dissociation works for the child but proves to be a problem in adulthood.** The amnesic walls usually start to disintegrate or break down in women in their late thirties or early forties."

Lydia scanned the audience with an apologetic expression on her face. "I need to apologize to you men for teaching that the female human brain is much more complex than the males."

One gentleman shouted out, "We already knew that!" Almost all attendees laughed uproariously at his comment, which gave momentary relief from the serious topic.

"Dissociative men usually experience disintegration in the early or mid-thirties. The breaking down of these walls produces nightmares, flashbacks, and erratic behavior.

"The healing goal is to bring all the human alters into the OP to function as one according to the original design. Once the trauma resolves, the opportunity exists for conflict resolution or the need for the separation, and a coming together, merging, fusion, or integration becomes possible. For example, if four parts exist before one part's trauma is resolved, after the integration, instead of four different opinions about what to order at the restaurant, there are now only three."

Lydia watched the people's reactions as they chatted together and chuckled. "That may sound funny, but decision making with a dissociated mind can be exhausting and is a primary indicator!"

Placing her hand at the base of the back of her head and turning around, Lydia demonstrated. "As you may know, trauma is stored in the occipital lobe... here. Clients often put their hands at the back of their heads and complain of discomfort during prayer counseling when traumatic memories are coming forth. I tell them, 'You may experience physical discomfort in certain places when something reminds you of some bad event.' For dissociative persons, we might also describe this as an alter triggered or cued to do their job.

"As incredible as it sounds, magnetic resonance imaging, MRI's, can visualize which alter is active. A person's x-ray with an illness, for instance, bronchitis, will picture the inflammation of the bronchi in the lungs. The bronchitis person in executive control of the body can switch to another alter, whose x-ray demonstrates no disease.

"I often hear clients report during prayer counseling sessions that they are feeling movement in their heads or other parts of their body. This feeling is because they are experiencing the alters. At other times, they report a head or cranial sensation when Jesus heals them by creating new neural pathways to reconnect the person or integrate them with other alters or the OP. I am telling you this mainly so you will understand there are excellent reasons why you struggled so-o-o-o-o much all this time.

"As Psalm 139:13-18 (KJV) says:

> *For Thou hast possessed my reins; Thou hast covered my mother's womb. I will praise thee; for I am fearfully and wonderfully made; marvelous are Thy works; and that my soul knoweth right well. My substance was not hid from thee, when I was made in secret, and curiously wrought in the lowest parts of the earth. Thine eyes did see my substance, yet being unperfect; and in thy book all my members were written, which in continuance were fashioned, when as yet there was none of them. How precious also are Thy thoughts unto me, O God! How great is the sum of them! If I should count them, they are more in number than the sand: when I awake, I am still with thee."*

Lydia nodded to Birgit to take over for the fifteen-minute break. An agitated quality permeated the conversations as attendees rushed to restrooms or indulged in the break offerings.

Fifteen minutes passed quickly. Lydia began on the dot. "Welcome back. People who primarily use the coping mechanism of dissociation include DENIAL to cope. The joke goes, 'Denial is not just a river in Egypt,'" Lydia laughed with the audience. "No, it is a way to fool oneself into accepting a lie or disbelieving a truth. They may want to deny a way of thinking, a behavior, or an event in their life or sometimes another's life. The person wants to disbelieve the truth because they perceive that knowing it would be too painful or overwhelming.

"In some cases, they believe acknowledging it requires potentially dangerous confrontations on their part. For others, they may think to do so would activate internal or external danger for themselves or others. Yes, it could be any combination or all the above as well. In other words, the victim in pain, trying to deny its cause results in great confusion.

"Dissociation, or shattering, usually happens following repeated trauma before age six. It may result from prenatal /womb life trauma such as an attempted abortion, birth trauma, occult activity, or perpetrated acts of violence or serious accidents. Evil-intentioned groups or family members cause dissociation through calculated and highly technical torture and mind control. However, the family is not always the source of the trauma.

"It's possible some of you feel yourself fade away or are unable to make sense of my words. This feeling is typical of dissociation. Experiencing pain in your forehead or behind your eyes or blurred or double vision could be an alter. Some aspect of yourself is trying very hard to come out and take executive control of the body. You may know, or be co-conscious with that part of you, or maybe not. So, you are amnesic to that alter. The blurred vision could be due to more than one of you trying to peer out.

"Many of my clients reported it is like being inside a big murky window. They see the sunshine outside but cannot feel the warmth. They view the beautiful snow, but they cannot smell the clean fragrance or feel the crisp air. They may see the hot dog vendor but cannot smell the aroma of the food. They know the puppy is barking along with the laughing children, but they cannot hear the cute little bark or laughter.

"I cannot remember any clients who weren't troubled with headaches. Some received a diagnosis of migraines and prescriptions for heavy medications. If you get a headache or blurred or double vision, I recommend before reaching for drugs to simply ask, 'Could you please step back?' and 'Who is there? My head is hurting.' With that instruction, you usually experience a significant event. Usually, the symptoms vanish, and a fantastic sense of awareness occurs. Some people experience a flash of anxiety. Be at peace. You are just embarking upon a journey of healing through self-management. If there is a relief, good, then if convenient, it is expedient to continue a conversation with that alter.

"When this happens in my office, the client often says something like, 'I feel really weird doing this!' I respond, 'I know; everyone does at first.'

"It is essential to take good care of yourself. You may want to take a break now and return to this material later via the conference recording, so you will not miss anything."

Not immediately, but soon after the encouragement to attend to personal needs, Lydia observed ten to fifteen people departing but trying to be inconspicuous.

"The alters may just be curious. On the other hand, they may be doing their job. Some alters want to stop you from continuing with this information because they believe it is dangerous for you to know it. Such an alter is a protector. There are predictable categories of alters. The purpose of all alters is the protection of the OP. You and I may not think what they do is protective. Protector alters interrupt other alters or the OP and do their job, which in their mind is a protective measure."

Frowning, Lydia said, "I will not be able to address all categories during this seminar, but you can get much of that information on my website. My business cards, books, DVDs, and other products are available at noon and the seminar's conclusion."

Lydia noticed more vacant seats, and most of the audience looked a bit dazed. "Do you feel like continuing, or should we take a break?" she asked. It was as if suddenly they woke up, and most urged her to continue.

California Seminar

"People with DID need a physician, therapist, or prayer counselor experienced in dissociative disorders. I believe it is imperative they must be skilled in spiritual matters. Clients often receive misdiagnoses such as schizophrenia, borderline, bipolar, et cetera. Many tolerated institutionalizations. Others ingested ineffective medications because DID is not a biochemical imbalance of the brain. This condition is trauma-based and is usually curable. However, it is also possible for a dissociative person to receive an accurate diagnosis for a demonstrated chemically imbalanced psychiatric disorder. Some people are frightened or ashamed of Dissociative Identity Disorder diagnosis. They do not understand how creative their mind is to survive such horror.

"Guess what? That same creativity will help them heal more completely than someone whose mind retained all the trauma and did not separate. Many of my clients are extraordinary artists, poets, musicians, thinkers, scientists, strategists, and theologians, who function in moderately stressful life situations. But some are unable to function productively in society," Lydia concluded.

Birgit announced a movie to educate clients and the community to show in the Tamarack Room during the lunch break. The next session would begin at two-thirty.

Lydia slipped away to her room after lunch at the hotel with Birgit and some old friends. After elevating her feet, she activated her empathic gift of burden-bearing prayers for those in attendance. She sensed and felt some of what the people experienced as she taught. Perhaps her best advantage, this gift functioned to maximize effectiveness in the counseling. Before she learned about burden-bearing, she found it exasperating and exhausting. Over time, however, she came to understand it to be a God-given tool to help her reach deeper into the hearts and minds of her shattered clients.

After her reverie, she returned to prayer. Still, she was startled when her timer alerted her to shoe on and leave to present the afternoon program. She checked herself in the mirror for any stray locks of hair or other imperfections, then returned to the auditorium. She remembered from previous seminars that this portion proved difficult for the audience to believe.

The elevator yawned open. Lydia met a pleasantly eager Birgit, determined to accept the invitation. Lydia quietly shrieked with delight and gave Birgit a quick hug and a highlighted Lebensborn material copy of her talk. Birgit looked at her watch. "Two-thirty, we are on, dear Lydia." She strode to the microphone, amused to see most everyone arrived on time. She called attention to the yellow Q&A form and gave instructions for getting it completed and returned. As Lydia came to take her place, she adjusted the lapel-clip microphone she chose for more freedom of movement. As they passed each other, their microphones encountered each other with an ear-wrenching screech. People grabbed pained ears. "Well, I guess we are off to a screeching start," Birgit covered.

After the chuckles died away, Lydia said, "I hope all of you enjoyed a substantial lunch since we used plenty of energy to keep our focus today. You may realize that a significant amount of spiritual warfare comes against a seminar of this nature. I hope you like history because that is the topic for this segment.

"The occult, or hidden knowledge, religions of ancient Babylon, India, Egypt, and Greece laid the foundation for occultism. One of humanity's earliest writings to reference occultism is the *Egyptian Book of the Dead*. It is a compilation of rituals to control people's minds. It explicitly describes methods for torturing and intimidating people and the use of potions or drugs to create trauma. satanism utilized these ingredients of occultism throughout the ages.

"One of the best ways to control the world is to control people's thinking. In 1882, England established the first recorded Behavioral Science research. In Germany, the Kaiser Wilhelm Institute pioneered early medical and psychiatric techniques involved in mind control.

California Seminar

In 1921, Kurt Lewin, a German psychologist, began to study the human 'breaking point' in London at the Tavistock Institute of Human Relations. He became the director of the institute in 1932, about the same time Nazi Germany increased its research into neuropsychology, parapsychology, and multi-generational occultism.

"In 1935, Nazi SS leader, Heinrich Himmler, founded the Lebensborn Project. We are fortunate today because a product of that project graciously agreed to share her testimony. Please welcome, Birgit Malloy." Amazed glances shot around the room as people clapped.

Birgit stepped to the podium and said, "Thank you. Lebensborn means fount or spring of life. Women of pure blood, who could prove their Aryan ancestry to their grandparents, were viewed as racially pure. My mother qualified. The expectation loomed for those blond, blue-eyed women to give birth to as many children as possible with Hitler's elite Nazi officers of pure blood who were married or not. Forget any morality.

"Women who produced the most children received The Iron Cross. My mother birthed six children and died in a Berlin bombing. I am number six, born in 1943. I do not know who sired me. Special homes staffed with nurses provided care and nutrition for me and other babies and children. Regimented diaper changing and care for babies occurred on assembly line conveyor belts.

"In 1939, the Nazis started kidnapping children regarded as "looking like Aryans" from Poland, Yugoslavia, Russia, Ukraine, Romania, Czechoslovakia, Estonia, Latvia, and Norway. Germany estimated 8,000 babies and 12,000 in Norway. After the war, an American soldier stationed in Germany and his wife adopted me. I am proud to be a German American.

"In my early forties, my seemingly normal productive life unraveled. I spent several weeks a year counseling for several years to uncover the dissociated memories with Lydia. Together we traveled to a professional de-programmer, hoping to speed the discovery and healing process. That was in the early nineties, the embryonic stage of DID counseling. Lydia said counselors learned more from their clients than from common counseling knowledge. I plan to write a book, so be on the lookout for it. Thank you for your attention." Birgit concluded, looking a bit shaken, and took her seat.

Lydia whispered, "Are you alright?" When the applause quieted, she thanked Birgit. She continued the lecture, satisfied all was well.

"During World War II, Joseph Mengele conducted much preliminary experimentation concerning genetic engineering and behavior at Auschwitz. He purposed to create a super-race—Aryans, with total allegiance to the cause of the Third Reich or New World Order. But of course, you may already know that. But did you know his ultimate goal was to discover the genetic formula to create the master race? And, at the same time, complete a slave race to do the menial, less glamorous tasks?

"Mengele included experimentation with twins to remove defective or inferior genes and replaced them with superior genes and visa-versa. George Estabrooks of Colgate University conducted parallel research. Estabrooks is said to occasionally 'slip' and discussed his work involving the creation of hypno-programmed couriers and hypnotically-induced split personalities.

"After WW II, Project PAPERCLIP, the U.S. Department of Defense program code name, secretly imported some 5,000 of the top German Nazi and Italian Fascist scientists and spies into the United States via South America and the Vatican for rocketry and mind control. Of course, Canada, Russia, and other countries did similar things.

"Joseph Mengele and a Jewish doctor named Dr. Grünbaum, who supposedly collaborated with the Nazis during WWII, were recruited by the CIA at the end of the war. Although he worked primarily out of Brazil, some of my clients and colleagues reported being with these two men, often referring to Dr. Grünbaum as Dr. Green.

"Research requires subjects. Researchers shortened sentences for prison inmates and made free education deals, especially with medical students. Frustrated, they found adults do not fracture as easily as children. So, school programs for gifted children and especially health programs for underprivileged children began.

California Seminar

They were desperate. Researchers snatched about one million 'missing children' per year. They held them in iron cages stacked floor to ceiling in abandoned factories in Chicago, on piers of the Port of Los Angeles, and on military bases. Do you remember all the faces of missing children on our milk cartons or pictures of missing children in the post offices? Adoptions also made for easy access." Lydia's voice became solemn. She finished by announcing a fifteen-minute break.

The room buzzed. People became so engrossed in their conversations that many never left the room. Lydia could feel the negative energy fueled by the denial and unbelief of the audience. Still, she decided years ago to accept this 'call.' She only desired to obey God's call, regardless of people's thoughts. It was her design, her assignment, and her destiny. After a snack of mixed nuts and water, Lydia began the final segment of the seminar, hoping for enough time to answer the group's questions.

"Many victims of these projects sought help from us. Maximum security required for the "final product" of mind-controlled human beings usually occurs on military installations and bases: referred to as re-programming centers or near-death trauma centers.

"In 1995, President Clinton signed executive order #12958, which required classified documents twenty-five years and older to be automatically declassified by April 2003, with a few exceptions. President Bush later extended the three-year deadline to December 3, 2006, due to the Deep State's cries of 'impossible.'

"Just one released "top secret'" mind control program's final reports numbered 186,000 pages. I arranged for helpers to carry forty-seven copy paper boxes to represent that number of pages. At the same time, I explained this at another seminar. Helpers stacked them high in front of the room. The evidence represents just one program of our country. One country. What about the other countries?

"Time prohibits honoring the people who bravely sought to confront this evil. Many of them were murdered. However, the names and locations of some major institutions and people involved in mind control programming and experimentation are at the back of your syllabus. You will also find a list of domestic and international people and their contact information who are doing a valiant job of freeing these survivors from slavery," Lydia stopped to allow the audience to absorb the impact.

Lydia trembled inside, leaned heavily over the podium, and felt the rounded wood as her hands gripped each side for support. Tears flooded her green eyes as she looked at each person individually. Then in a trembling voice, she spoke, "Ridiculous? Impossible? Disgusting? Yes! Remember, all it takes for evil to thrive is for good people to do nothing."

Deafening silence followed.

Lydia sipped her water and stepped back, taking a yellow paper from the podium. She walked to the front of the platform and warmly said, "Thank you for attending and may God bless and protect you always." Then, looking at her watch, she said, "I see fifteen minutes remain to answer some of your questions."

Before she finished, the audience broke out with applause, many rising to their feet. Hooting resounded. Tears streamed down faces. Some people remained sitting like statues, staring ahead. The brief question and answer period concluded the seminar, at which time Birgit reminded everyone to search out Lydia's website. She went on to say that a more in-depth conference would be held in Kassel, Germany, in three weeks and challenged anyone who was able to attend to do so. Finally, Lydia signed her books, giving warm words of encouragement along the way to those with whom she spoke.

As they drove to the airport, the sparse conversation found Lydia recollecting her friendship with Birgit. *A year is required to pass before starting a friendship with a client. That practice allowed them to return for more help if needed. It's not appropriate for a counselor to befriend a client because the counselor's objectivity may be lost, and the effectiveness jeopardized. When that year passed, Birgit asked me to be a consultant for her counseling center. Birgit, a born administrator, created a thriving prayer counseling center complete with educational opportunities for her staff and community, such as she provided today.*

"Sorry, I couldn't be a better conversationalist," Birgit sweetly smiled after turning into the departing flight area. "I must fully concentrate on the terrible traffic. It seems airport drivers usually drive too fast or are distracted. It's so good to be with you again. Did you ever think this little Lebensborn Gal would be your friend and heal other Lebensborn kids?"

Hugging Birgit goodbye, Lydia said, "You're an inspiration and walking evidence of healing for the hopeless. I am so proud of you! I'm very thankful to participate and now I'm not only your colleague but a friend as well. Thank you for inviting me. Everything was top drawer. I may need to consult with you regarding our mutual Lebensborn client in Den Hague while working with him but promise to only call during your daytime."

CHAPTER 3

MORE MEDS

The sun warmed the brisk spring breeze. Pigeons hopped on the physician's building to leave white splashes on the old gray stone as reminders of their presence. Chrome-supported leather chairs lined the walls of the busy waiting room. The doctor's office mailed papers to be completed and brought to the appointment. Saqqara forgot.

Here I sit on these hard chairs to complete all these forms. I need to recall my surgeries, accidents, allergies, current medications, and childhood illnesses. I can't re—mem—ber. I don't like that oversized modern painting. The angles are too sharp and the colors gaudy! Tiffany insisted I see 'someone' because of all the forgetting. Maybe I forgot the papers because I waited two months to get in!

A plump medical assistant uniformed in a cartoon print smock interrupted Saqqara's reverie. "Ms. Fain, Dr. Chenoweth will see you now. My name is Megan", she said as she wrapped the blood pressure cuff around Saqqara's arm. Then, after taking other vital signs, she positioned herself at the computer to ask most questions on the forms which Saqqara had just handed to her.

The only magazine available to fill the cold wait focused on health for seniors. Saqqara had just finished the exciting article about constipation when she heard a man's voice in the hall, followed by a door swoosh. Dr. Chenoweth roughly adjusted the wheeled stool in front of the computer and sat down, briefly glanced at her with a smile, then fully attended to the computer screen. "What brings you here today?"

A flash of irritation pricked her mind. After a deep sigh, she repeated the written information on the form and reiterated to Megan. Again, she spoke of the unaccounted-for physical marks, recounted nightmares, forgetfulness of important events, and insomnia.

All the while, he perused her health record on the screen. Finally, he raised his eyebrows above tortoise-shell rimmed glasses and said, "It sounds like you need some help sleeping and to reduce your stress. I'll prescribe just the ticket, and you can pick it up at our pharmacy on your way out. Give it two weeks and if that doesn't help, make another appointment." He left.

On the walk to her car, Saqqara tried to figure out how to pronounce the name of the prescription. *It must be new. None of the others ever worked. It didn't take long before the side effects were almost worse than the problem. Whew! That took longer than I thought. Better get to work.* She tossed the prescription onto the passenger seat along with her purse and drove to the office.

The elevator opened. Saqqara's eyes met Nadine's, one of those senior forever-young women. The petite paralegal worked for the prestigious law firm, which occupied an entire floor above Saqqara's office. They occasionally ate lunch together.

Nadine pulled her steel gray hair away from the heavily lashed brown eyes. Her welcoming smile configured to a frown as she asked, "Still having trouble sleeping? I hope you don't mind me asking, but you look tired."

"Between you and Tiffany, I had no choice but to see an M.D. So now I get to take another drug. Thank you for your concern," Saqqara snipped as the elevator door closed. Usually, she worked late but decided to go home considering the "reduce stress" admonition. Saqqara savored a glass of wine, got into her blue satin jammies, started the new medication, and went to bed.

A scream!

Saqqara bolted upright. Instantly, rapid panting punctuated the air. She slammed the covers aside and threw her legs over the bedside while wildly looking side-to-side through the darkness. She jumped to her feet, ran toward the bedroom door, then abruptly stopped. Perspiration streamed down her face. Satin clung to her. *I must have had another nightmare, or maybe it is a side effect of the new medication.* The clock's green LED showed three-fifteen. She dried off, shivered into fresh jammies, and snuggled back under the covers.

CHAPTER 4

CAPACITY

It felt good to be counseling again. Lydia rested the Sunday after the California seminar, filled Monday with office work, caught up, and detailed the next two weeks. The deep care and compassion which developed in her heart for most of her clients always amazed her. However, some came on assignment by people who mind control them, to learn precisely what Lydia did and how she did it. After counseling sessions, they reported to programmers who tried to use the data to undo the freedom any of their programmed slaves obtained. She found it fascinating she could not connect with them, try as she might. They soon found an excuse to leave or discontinue work with Lydia, especially after she explained she used no method other than dependence on and obedience to the Holy Spirit since everyone is different.

Experience demonstrated the traditional fifty-minute counseling appointment inadequate for DID clients due to the time needed to prepare for deep memory recall. Many clients traveled long distances and preferred longer sessions. Two hours constituted a minimum session. American clients far from her office in Spokane, Washington, and international clients often scheduled a week or more.

The morning flew by. Lydia looked forward to the afternoon Canadian client whose parents agreed to receive $10,000 from a famous Canadian university on the pretense of entering their daughter in a child development study. Lydia served several such clients. Hopefully, the parents were oblivious to the consequences of the agreement or better-stated sale. The parent's attention was piqued when informed their child possessed special talents or gifts. True enough. Often the 'hook' to agree originated from pride to say their offspring participated in such a prestigious program.

The reality for these children resulted in years of development through extreme torture, all types of abuse, and experimentation, which resulted in a shattered being. Marley Cosmescu, being of Romanian descent, interested her programmers due to the mystical gypsy heritage. Prime child candidates for the mind control programs demonstrated paranormal or spiritual giftings.

Unlike many other victims, Marley didn't function well in everyday life. She suffered great pain from severe fibromyalgia. However, pain significantly diminished with the healing of traumatic memories. **Once a memory is recovered and its conflict resolved, the part of the body which held the trauma heals.**

"I can't do it… I can't do it," Marley gushed, her anorexic frame collapsed into heavy weeping. "I can't journal. The alters won't talk with me. There's just silence unless screaming starts when I'm not trying to speak with them. I can't speak to anyone; nobody understands! Sleep is still a fight, and I'm in constant pain. I shouldn't have come. I'm too weak and tired of this whole thing. I just want to be well. I just want it to be over and this cold too! Achoo, achoo!"

The minute she arrived and flopped on the couch a string of negative statements flowed out of her mouth. Her stringy dishwater blond hair fell onto the pale complexion. The ruby nose diminished sunken eyes.

Moved by her condition, Lydia asked permission to sit next to her and touch her shoulder to express empathy. From experience, she knew Marley would flatly deny any offer to forego the session and return to the hotel to rest due to the hardship of travel, lodging, food, and counseling expenses.

Marley's sobs came to a jerky halt. "I value your sensitivity to ask permission to sit close or touch me... achoo, achoo... but that isn't necessary anymore," she said, wiping her eyes with the same tissue used to blow her nose. "I trust you, and safe touch is healing! Can we pray now?"

Lydia explained that even though the Marley she spoke with may trust her, some parts may not, and she never wanted to put stress on them. She returned to her chair and prayed.

> "Dearest Lord Jesus, thank You for being strong when we are weak. We are grateful that You are patient with us and desire us to depend on You. Please lift off the pain and fatigue from Marley. Properly align her spirit, soul, and body by strengthening her spirit to rule one with Your Spirit. We ask for the means to increase her capacity for healing. I command all evil entities to be totally impotent for the duration of this intensive, in the authority of the blood and name of the Lord Jesus Christ. Thank You for anointing us to receive knowledge, understanding, and wisdom to accomplish Your will in this time. May the words of my mouth and meditations of my heart be acceptable to You. Thank You for what You are about to do. We give You all the glory, Amen."

After the prayer, Lydia offered water and a box of tissues. She consoled Marley with encouraging facts regarding her journey of healing. "When you began this counseling, you were hopeless, in burnout, and completely ignorant of your history or why you were in the condition in which you found yourself. Consider where you are now. You equip yourself with knowledge of DID and the power that truth brings, a safe support system at home, understanding of anorexia as related to the need to control and eliminate most prescription drugs. How admirable! You accomplished difficult memory retrieval despite the degree of burnout and purposed to do the homework, even though it seemed impossible. It is difficult to see the positive when we feel bad, but it's necessary to fight to see it and declare it. So, in response to your 'I can't do it!' I say, "Yes, with capacity."

"Achoo, achoo." Several loud sheesh sounds from nose blowing accompanied a faint smile. "What do you mean by capacity?"

Lydia popped an elderberry lozenge as she studied Marley. She drank the remaining coffee from her favorite cup and began, "If we expect to do anything, we must first have the capacity to do it. If a person wants to heal, they need the capacity. I hear you. Today you don't have the strength or reserves to do the difficult memory retrieval task. Therefore, we'll work to build capacity so that your capacity quotient will be higher in the days to come. Here is a simple example. We cannot reach a distant destination in an auto on a small supply of fuel." Lydia watched Marley's shoulders crowd her torso and discomfort paint her face. "Why don't you elevate the footrest… it's there on the right side of your seat; here is a soft fleece in case you get chilled. Just relax. I'll explain how we get more capacity," Lydia said, "and today, whenever you get too tired to listen, let me know, and we will stop for the day to attack that cold, okay?"

Marley's stick figure disappeared under the fleece and evidenced a shoulder shrug and a forced smile.

Lydia began. "For teaching purposes, I will use the word **soul** to refer to your **mind, will, and emotions**. All humans consist of personal spirit, soul, and body. We will not be able to function in various areas of life, respond fully to Jesus Christ, or experience dominion in the Kingdom of God until the **spirit awakens, matures, and rules our lives.** Science informs us that a singular severe traumatic event can change our brain chemistry. If this is true of our body, could it also be true of our spirit? Many people resolved psychological and physical traumas but not their spiritual trauma. Some of us are oblivious to our personal spirit. **The human spirit thrives with hope when confident of its identity, loving acceptance, and purpose.** The desired result only occurs in a particular order.

"A good campfire needs dry wood, tinder, and a source of fire. We waste lit matches without gathered wood. To stack the wood and tinder but never light the match will not torch the marshmallows the way I like them or even get them brown! Western Culture usually refers to our body, soul, and spirit in that order. We spend a lot of time caring for and developing our bodies and souls. Greek thought greatly influenced Western Culture, which valued the mind and physical fitness over spiritual development.

"According to the Holy Bible, the Triune God (Father, Son, and Holy Spirit) created us in His image to be His family. God's order is spirit, soul, body. We communicate with God, Spirit to spirit. The book of John tells us, *God is spirit, and those who worship Him must worship in spirit and truth* (John 4:24). Because we experience the Holy Spirit in such a magnificent way, we try not to think about other things that distract our spirit from communing with God's Spirit when we worship Him.

"When we go into our heads or minds, our soul takes charge, and our spirit is not the one communing. Water and oil don't mix because they are different. There is a change from one to the other. I own a book where the author doggedly encourages us to keep on, develop our spiritual connection with Holy Spirit, and offers practical ways to accomplish this.

"This is God's proper alignment for our lives:

The Holy Spirit rules

_____ our spirit which rules

_____ our soul (mind, will, emotions),

_____ which rules our body.

"If we know that Creator God is perfect, holy, created us to be loved and only wants what is best for us, it is wise to agree with Him. How good it is! Our minds do not judge others with vindictiveness, competition, jealousy, evil, and rivalry. Godly values and decisions compromise our will. Emanated emotions of love, peace, and joy make the body bloom in health. But of course, other factors can cause illness.

"I was born into a Sunday church-attending family who said the same grace for each meal and the *Now I Lay Me Down to Sleep* prayer at bedtimes. In our Bible, which I often dusted, photos and "treasured papers" stored there fascinated me. However, I never remember reading it. My childhood Presbyterian church experience equipped me with the most popular Children's Bible Stories and the love of Jesus. As an Evangelical United Brethren teenager, I learned a lot about Paul's journeys and heard that we needed an altar experience.

"My grandmother gifted me with a Bible at high school graduation. At college, I rarely opened it. I married a Lutheran and became a pillar of my church. I grew to love the deep meaning of liturgical church and still long for that environment of reverence. But liturgy can also become a habit of meaningless rhetoric. The extraordinary education of church history, love of God, and the sacrifice Jesus paid to cover our sins impressed me greatly. I knew about Father and Son but wondered about the third Holy in the hymn, 'Holy, Holy, Holy.'"

Marley shifted her position, blew her nose, and said, "Me too! How did you discover more?"

Lydia began, "I had a friend who stored the Word in her heart. She took me on as her assignment and inspired me to embrace the Word of God also. She and her husband invited my husband and me to house meetings during the early seventy's Charismatic Movement. In that environment, I learned about the third Holy.

"Even though I had met the Holy Spirit, I never considered that I possessed **a personal spirit** despite all the teaching and reading about the spirit. When I attended a prayer counseling school, I first encountered the idea of me having an individual spirit. Perhaps I thought a person got one when they died! Strange how a person can miss something like that, and then God finally reveals the truth to us.

"Several places in the *Holy Bible* allude to the idea that our spirit was with God before He knit our physical substance together in our mother's womb. Other scriptures inform us that saved spirits return to God and spend eternity with Him. I realize this may rankle some people's theology. I am not trying to be problematic, just relating what scripture says.

"When the female human egg, ovum, and the male human seed, sperm, unite into the zygote or first cell of the human being, Creator God breathes life into it. This life is our spirit. The person does not yet have a developed brain, a heart, lungs, et cetera; however, it seems that their spirit is somewhat mature.

"At eighteen months of age, the control center of brain development completes. Abstract thinking develops around age twelve. Ever wonder why we don't do algebra until then? Finally, our brain develops to maturity when we reach twenty-five. Maybe we should consider that with military service, voting, and drinking laws. I digress, sorry!" Aware of exhaustion from burden-bearing Marley's fatigue, Lydia rose from her chair. "This feels like a choice time for a break. What do you think?" Lydia offered.

"I love the stories. I think it's interesting about the mature spirit because I read scientists are teaching languages to babies in the womb. Sure, a ten-minute break? But I can finish my scheduled time," she assured Lydia while gathering a handful of fresh tissues.

Lydia had enough time to check messages, refresh herself and load up on echinacea and a giant-sized OJ before resuming the session with a revitalized Marley. As they settled in, she asked, "Is this starting to make sense?"

"I'm the same as you. I didn't know I possessed a personal spirit, and I thought I only became a spirit after death. I didn't study or read the Bible with a religious upbringing or spiritual instruction but believed I needed to be perfect. I think my body ruled me because since I could not control most of my environment, I could at least control my body," Marley responded.

"A few public health clients suffered anorexia. My medical understanding begged to know the spiritual blockage to heal. I asked, and the Lord led me to: Leviticus 19:4 *Do not turn to idols or make for yourselves molten gods; I am the Lord your God. Now when you offer a sacrifice of peace offering to the Lord, you shall offer it so that you may be accepted.* The application is this: Instead of trusting the Holy Spirit to rule, anorexics idolize themselves. To absolve that idolatry, one needs to be aware and ask forgiveness for freedom.

Marley's red-rimmed eyes widened to ask, "Did it work?"

"Yes. Rightful alignment paved the way to identify and work on other blockages successfully. We may hear and even know the laws of sowing and reaping and the healing process in our minds. **There is a difference between knowing and understanding something.** The Bible says: *But it is the spirit in man. And the breath of the Almighty gives them understanding.* (Job 32:8)

"A considered genius in spiritual research believes that God gave us all the time of pregnancy, usually nine months, plus eighteen months after birth, to develop our spirit so that our spirit will always be more mature and rule over our soul. He produced a collection of CDs with spiritual blessings to read to babies to develop their spirits in the womb and after birth. He recommends playing them while the child sleeps since our spirit is more available then.

"Grandparents who purchased them decided to try them out. The change in themselves amazed them. So, it is never too late to develop our spirit. There are wonderfully inspiring books of spiritual blessings created to build capacity. I'll lend one to you to read this week.

"Did you know that Mary, the mother of Jesus, lived in a time when the Hebrew culture provided a pregnant woman to be relieved of most of her duties in the early months of gestation? She usually stayed with a mature female relative who could nurture her and provide a loving environment. Mary went to stay with her cousin,

Elizabeth. This tradition freed the expectant mother to spend her days speaking scripture, singing prayers and blessings into the spirit of the developing new life. This way, its spirit developed before the brain; appropriate if it's to rule, don't you think?"

"Wouldn't women love that!" Marley exclaimed, "But great for the little person too, of course."

"When I first attended prayer counseling school, most of the same psychological conditions studied in nursing presented with different names, i.e., biblical slumbering spirit represented sociopathic psychological behavior. It was refreshing to realize that it brilliantly reduced hundreds of psychological labels to a shortlist of categories. It soon becomes confusing as one reads psychological diagnostic symptomatology because many listed symptoms apply to many conditions.

"However, there was only one exception for which I could find no parallel, spiritual captivity. Today I believe that term to be the psychological label, Dissociative Identity Disorder. However, it includes the personal spirit, soul, body, and other dimensions. *But a natural man does not accept the things of the Spirit of God; for they are foolishness to him, and he cannot understand them, because they are spiritually appraised* (I Corinthians 2:14).

"The scientific community tells us there are at least ten different dimensions and probably more. We are most aware of only four; height, depth, width, and time. Quantum physics enabled us to contemplate previously conceived mysteries with a new sense of understanding. The *Bible* mentions the words: Sheol, hell, land of forgetfulness, miry pit, and shadow of death. Unfortunately, we often read scripture and treat these words simply as metaphors or something other than real. These are different dimensions where **demonic forces can captively torment parts of a person's spirit.**

"Our spirit may be awake at the beginning of our lives, yet, through suffering trauma, chooses to hide or go away—dissociate. Parts of our spirit can be held captive in these dimensions where torment by demonic forces occurs. This spiritual captivity which accounts for some of the unaccountable pain, perhaps some of your pain, Marley."

"So, my physical body experiences the results of unhealed spiritual wounds too?" A brighter Marley asked as she drew her legs under the cover, then continued, "I remember a proverb I learned in Sunday School: *A joyful heart is good medicine. But a broken spirit dries up the bones.*"

"Yes, according to Proverbs 17:22, human beings are astoundingly resilient! Every hurt is contrary to our nature. The coping mechanism of dissociation helps humanity to survive. Study history. Look at museums of the Jewish People in Nazi death camps. Aleksandr Solzhenitsyn's, *The Gulag Archipelago*, a treatise of communist Stalin's ruthless reign of terror, exemplifies resilience. Listen to current news reports of people enduring wars, terrorist attacks, famines, tsunamis, and rising criminal activity.

"Human beings are spirit, soul, and body. Our spirit needs to be developed and fed. We need proper spiritual alignment, so our spirit rules our soul, and our soul rules our body. If our spirit is not mature and liberated to rule our lives, we will not fully function. Our spirit can be traumatized, the same as our physical body. Our spirit can be captive or hidden, slumbering or underdeveloped. How many of us received spiritual input and environments without trauma? NONE. To some degree, most of us function with a hardened heart in our spirit. Our bodies, souls (minds, wills, emotions) can be overwhelmed, but a spirit aligned with the Holy Spirit will keep us afloat even in the worst times.

"Scientists used to say we have no memories possible before the age of three. Now research is realizing that something is functioning. I believe it is our spirit. Marley, you have endured my teaching very well, considering how miserable you must feel. Shall we stop now and continue tomorrow?" Lydia sweetly asked as she leaned forward and offered her hand.

Marley pled with red, watery eyes, "A few more minutes remain; how about another story?"

Capacity

"I don't want to tire you. How about one more short story about a wonderfully anointed colleague who did a practicum for her master's degree?"

Marley sneezed three more times, carefully dabbed her tender protuberance, then nodded and snuggled into readjustments of the downy fleece.

"One day, she stood before a group of around thirty elderly people. Her deep blue eyes grieved and filled with mercy as they observed a sorrowful display of sleepers in wheelchairs, others zoning out into space, some busily having conversations with themselves, and a few who kindly smiled at her and seemed attentive. Even though difficult, she persevered. When she got to the part of her lesson about personal spirits, she compassionately invited their personal spirits to attention. WOW!!! Immediately, as if on cue, all jolted alert and looked at her in a very deliberate way! Her eyes sparkled with surprised joy. She experienced the same situation each time she invited the group's spirits to attention. All shared a precious time as she lovingly blessed their spirits."

"What a grand finale! You're a good storyteller!" Marley exclaimed, throwing off the cover to scoot herself to the edge of the leather couch.

"There is no homework today except to listen to this CD. I would encourage you to take advantage of the hotel sauna, drink lots of fluids and get to bed very early. The next session at 1:00 PM tomorrow will allow you to sleep in for maximum healing. Our body heals while we sleep, you know. Shall we pray?

> "In the name of our Blessed Lord Jesus, I invite your spirit to attention. You are eternal and precious in the eyes of your Creator. Your life is not an accident. God planned your life on this earth before earth's foundations were laid. You have a rich spiritual heritage available to you as you receive the grace and mercy of God through forgiveness

> and cleansing of generational iniquity. You are beloved, and the Lord desires only good for your life and purposes a future, not of calamity, but intimacy. We thank You, Lord, for Your plans for Marley and Your healing. Amen."

Marley gathered tissues on the couch and those which fell on the floor to throw them into the wastebasket. "Despite this cold, I feel better. Thank you so much. See you tomorrow at one."

As soon as the office door closed, Lydia put on gloves and sprayed disinfectant on the couch and floor, wiped surfaces, and door handles, opened the window for fresh air, and bagged the waste for disposal. The environment needed to be pleasant and safe for the next appointment.

Lydia felt the pressure build. Only two weeks remained before the European tour. It always amazed her how much catch-up is required even after an absence of only a few days. Nevertheless, the California Seminar pleased her. All products sold indicate a genuine interest in the topic. She filed the sign-up sheet of people who wanted more in-depth seminars like the one coming up in Kassel, Germany.

Finally, she attended to the phone messages. The spring days lengthened, and streams of late afternoon sun spotlighted the telephone as Lydia plunked into her swivel chair, spun around with feet following, and punched the message button with a flourish.

"Hello, I am Clarice's husband, Seth," he forcefully declared in a controlled voice. I think you are helping Clarice. Since working with you, she has displayed fewer meltdowns, but I need help. Can I make an appointment?"

Lydia scanned the schedule. She noted the Wednesday schedule included Julie, a woman she mentored. The opportunity to learn interventions with the extended family of clients offers a vital learning experience. She called Seth to schedule the first appointment on Wednesday. *I wonder what is so urgent.*

CHAPTER 5

NADINE HELPS

———◆◆◆———

Saqqara pondered; *What a terrifying night! I sensed a presence and felt raped! I hope the double application of eye erase to cover my dark circles doesn't noticeably cake. The throbbing fatigue is taking its toll.*

"Top of the morning! So nice to see you again," Nadine sang as she twirled in, carrying the usual massive stack of legal files. "What say we lunch today in the cafeteria at twelve-thirty?"

"It's lunch. See you then," Saqqara replied as the staccato of her black heels echoed on the glassy marble floors toward her office.

The pleasant décor and comfort of the building cafeteria offered excellent soups with an extensive salad bar. Nadine and Saqqara indulged in the Crab Louis Salad, a pre-seasonal offering.

"I've been off carbs for a month, but it is hard to pass these scrumptious yeast rolls. So, I thought only one would be a treat today," Nadine giggled. "How is your health recently?"

Saqqara sipped her coffee before speaking. "I called Dr. Chenoweth's office. Either the medication is not working, or its side effects are as troubling as the problem. He told me to try it for two weeks and make another appointment if it didn't work. It looks like August is his next opening!" A surge of hot resentment rose in her cheeks as she struggled to control her voice, "I asked if he could call me or take a message. They transferred my call to voicemail. Nothing until the next evening when his physician's assistant returned it. He agreed to give my message to the doctor. With a fierce poke, I turned off the phone, slumped, studied the swirl design in the carpet, and dreaded the coming night." She looked away from Nadine and angrily forked the crab.

"I am so sorry, Saqqara. I know how frustrating the current medical system can be at times. You've suffered so long and tried so hard to find a solution," Nadine cooed.

"I could try that naturopathic doctor again. She was nice. No, not all those horse pills and capsules! After I took all that stuff, stomach food space nearly disappeared!" Saqqara expounded.

"I've known you for eight years. I enjoy lunches shared in this cafeteria and value our conversations. It seems you consulted many people for help, tried many medications, worked all those diets, and even went to the hospital a few times. Perhaps conventional medicine is not the answer. One of my relatives who suffered similar symptoms to yours received amazing help from a woman in Washington State. May I get the contact information and e-mail it to you for consideration?" Nadine asked.

"That is so kind of you, Nadine, yes... sure, that will be helpful, thank you very much," Saqqara smiled as she offered Nadine another golden-brown roll.

Lunch over, the two women boarded the elevator. As Saqqara exited, Nadine called, "I'll e-mail that resource information for that problem."

Saqqara automatically walked towards the office suite, lost in her thoughts. *Nadine and a host of other people seem friendly, but I need to keep them at a distance. You can't trust anyone. I've been hurt enough by well-meaning people.* She picked up mail at the reception desk and sorted it as she meandered to her office. An e-mail alert greeted her. Nadine's resource information beat her to the office.

CHAPTER 6

ANGER OUT

Julie Wiseman, the mentee, arrived one hour before Seth's appointment for pre-session, which provided:

- A review of the case
- Planning for the session
- Spiritual preparation for all concerned.

One of Lydia Voight's main professional objectives purposed to train other counselors on the interventions effective for DID. She established a mentoring program that required the applicant's completion of Christian Inner Healing Education and at least one year of general counseling experience. In addition, three required specified references validate the applicant's maturity and capability for such demanding work—the mentoring program comprised three competency-based components. No specific timelines exist, which offered convenience for established counselors to progress at their speed.

The first component involved observing prayer counseling sessions without communication with the client, other than a cordial greeting or goodbye. However, they wrote notes about their senses, observations, thoughts, and questions. Lydia and the student reviewed the client file before each session, referred to as pre-session. After the client left, they checked the session's content, referred to as posting. A review of the student's notes and additional teaching occurred during the posting. Homework assignments concluded at that time.

The second phase included the mentee in the session as a co-counselor. This role increased as the student became more proficient. In this phase, the student passed notes to Lydia with their insights, et cetera.

The third component consisted of recorded or observed independent prayer counseling sessions critiqued and evaluated by Lydia. Once the student demonstrated knowledge and skills for each element, they progressed to the next.

Julie came highly recommended as a seasoned school counselor. However, she became overwhelmed by the number of children of all ages with attention deficit disorder (ADD), the many forms of autism, obesity, eating disorders, depression, cutting, drug addictions, and suicides.

A friend recommended Lydia as someone who deals with everything and anything. "Although her specialty is severe trauma, she is also called upon to do interventions for troubled organizations, so she can certainly help you," the friend encouraged. She had counseled together with Lydia previously.

Incredibly impressed with her prayer counseling experience, Julie enrolled in inner healing classes. During that season, a growing desire to enter the mentoring program began.

Julie is now in her second phase. Since she had never worked with these clients before, Lydia reviewed the family history with her.

"Clarice first saw me six months ago. Her pastor attended one of my severe trauma seminars and later augmented that information with my website's professional resources. She then talked with Clarice and Seth to recommend that they spend some time on the website. Eventually, Clarice made an appointment for prayer counseling with me.

"Clarice is making great progress and faithfully journals and encounters some of her other selves. She overcame the temptation to deny that they were parts of her personality. She decided to accept her alters and is getting acquainted. Now they are sharing their memories with her. In our last session, she recovered memories of continued incest by her stepfather. I instructed her about anger management," Lydia concluded, handing Julie a fresh stack of paper notes. "Any questions?"

"Seth. Is. Her. Husband," accompanied each new direction into which she pulled and secured her brindled hair onto the top of her head. "Is he also a client? We cannot talk with him about Clarice due to confidentiality. How will we conduct this session?" looking to Lydia now, Julie squinted her hazel eyes to a question mark.

"Right! I apologize. I forgot to mention Clarice signed a release to disclose her information to Seth. Yes, he is a client. Note that it is common for DID people to marry dissociative people, although I did not find that to be true with Seth," Lydia explained and added, "It is important to be sure you groom before arrival. Are you ready?" Lydia asked with a mixture of fondness and irritation stirring inside.

Seth, a middle-aged, medium height businessman with sandy hair, wore a light brown sports jacket, khaki slacks, a mint green shirt open at the neck, and metal-framed glasses. He sported a forced smile as he entered the office. Florid cheeks shone as he proceeded to tell his story.

"I am doing what you said to do when she wakes up with the nightmares. You're right. She sounds and acts like a little girl. I quietly slip out of bed and turn on the soft light we installed. I stand far away from her and softly talk with her. I tell her she is safe, and it will be okay. It weirds me out a bit to see her frightened young face seem to enlarge to become Clarice's questioning face. I stand like a statue until she recognizes me. I immediately tried to comfort her in the past, and she went ballistic and fought at times. After Clarice settled, I encouraged her to write in her bedside journal.

"She is getting multiple insights and relief and told me that you and she discussed the journal entries with great revelation resulting in understanding. It's hard on the children too.

I just wanted you to know that it is going better. My wife is starting to understand the source of her dysfunction," he reported.

"Clarice is fortunate to have a caring, devoted husband such as you, Seth. Many of my clients have no one. Your presence in her life will speed her recovery. Be assured that your sacrifices will be greatly rewarded. I know this is not easy," Lydia consoled. "Some people try to help without the benefit of education and actually harm as they try to help."

"I am so relieved that Clarice signed a release so that you can freely talk with me to help our situation. It is hard to be in the dark, especially with so many... a... well... a... well, I need to share something. After Clarice's last appointment with you last week, she came home not really in a good place. I suggested she go to bed, and I would do dinner and the kids. When I went to bed, she was asleep. I left early for a morning meeting before she got up. I came home earlier than usual and found her in the kitchen with a meat cleaver in her hand. Two packages of hot dogs lay on the island butcher board. Our larger family requires two packages for a meal. I ... I don't think she saw me. She let out war whoops with each loud chop of the cleaver onto the hot dogs. I don't think she was fixing a casserole. I found myself covering my privates with my hands. Excuse me; I don't mean to be vulgar," Seth whined.

"No problem, Seth—continue," Lydia said.

"She screamed profanities as if someone else were there. I never heard Clarice swear before. I feel embarrassed to admit it, but I gathered the two kids at home and ran like a coward," he croaked with shoulders gently shaking and tears spotting his shirt. A respectful silence followed.

"You were not a coward but very courageous. You did exactly the most needed action at that time. You protected your children and yourself. You granted Clarice the privacy to vent her rage.

"I strongly encourage my clients to find a safe method to vent their anger. Anger holds enormous energy. Clarice received treatment for depression for years, but most depression is rooted in repressed anger. Anger is about injustice. Emotions are messengers that tell us something is going on. Unfortunately, the 'something' is not always accurate for that specific time. The 'something' is not fair but requires address.

"Some secular therapists instruct their clients to use ball bats to strike blow-up figures, representing people toward whom they harbor bad feelings. They are to say anything they want and imagine hurting the designated person. This way, the energy is evacuated, and a resolution is supposed to happen. I strongly warn my clients never to do anything like this. Why? Because it is a big-time sin. Do you remember that Jesus said… *but I say to you, that everyone who looks on a woman to lust for her has committed adultery with her in his heart*? (Matthew 5:28)

"The principle applies. Most people do not want to curse, harm, or murder another person, but that exercise promotes a spiritual plane. I am not here to judge those methods, but I do responsibly equip my clients with tools to process their anger in a spiritually safe manner. I instruct them to find a way of venting which is not harmful to themselves, any people, or any worthwhile structures.

"One client bought old couch cushions and an old wooden tennis racket at the thrift store. She kept them in a certain part of the home, stacked up with the racket beside them. Whenever triggered with the rage, she knelt before the cushions, raised the racket, and prayed: 'Lord, help me release this fury and not sin.' Then she beat the daylights out of the cushions. When exhaustion and peace which follows came, the client lay on the bed and thanked God for taking the rage. Then they waited and focused on the Holy Spirit to remind them of the triggered trauma. They learned that whatever it resembled was almost exactly whatever just happened or was about to happen. The journaling of the experiences and revelations proved invaluable for healing.

"This is also a profound way to realize the actual existence of a living Savior who wants us healed more than we do. The Wonderful

Counselor is on the job 24/7. Isn't it mind-boggling to realize the Holy Spirit knows every detail of every person's life, past, present, and future! What a Mighty God we serve!

"Unexpressed emotions cause harm to others and many physical and emotional diseases. Every emotion gets expressed one way or another. It's best to learn how to appropriately express them by talking about them with people who will compassionately listen in a non-judgmental way. It is also helpful if they offer wisdom when requested.

"In the last session, Clarice found decades-old memories of plundering by her stepfather. The rage is also legitimate towards her mother, who did not protect her. That is why she was not doing well Monday night. She experienced numerous abreactions during the session that day. Abreactions are returning memories that seem to happen at the moment. Your consideration of offering her to retire early expressed great understanding.

"Abreactions are very tiring," Lydia said as Julie nodded with a sympathetic frown.

"By plundering her, do you mean that she remembers her stepdad had sex with her?" queried Seth.

"God calls it defiling an innocent child with incest, and the law calls it a punishable crime. It might well account for sexual problems in your marriage."

"I can't believe Lyle is a pervert. He used to drink a lot, but he's been dry for a long time!" he said while his glasses slid further down the ridge of his nose. Then, after processing a long time, he continued. "This is all too much! He looked up alarmed, a quick shake of his head, then frowned and thoughtfully said, "That is what the little girl with the nightmares cried, "No, no, Poppy." Clarice called her stepdad Poppy as a child. I didn't get it before, but now it is clear who she meant! Oh," sobs interrupted.

"Seth, I want you to tell Jesus your honest thoughts right now. He already knows them, of course, but He wants you to invite Him into your pain and to share your heart. He wants you to be aware of

His presence and caring now. You do not have to carry this alone," Lydia encouraged.

"You mean just talk out loud like I talk to you?"

Lydia's serene green eyes blinked a yes.

"Well, here I am, God. How can such evil things happen in this world if you are a loving God? I need your grace right now because I am disappointed in You. Who can a person trust? What a mess! Did he hurt my kids? Anger, confusion, hatred, and revenge consume me. He is responsible for all our marriage problems and stole our pleasure together. I just want to hit something!" Seth scowled with clenched teeth. Two thick brown pillows were moved towards Seth and rested on the couch beside him.

"What... what are these for?" Seth asked while lifting his head and unfolding his hands.

"You said you wanted to hit something. Remember, you are just releasing the energy of emotions and not thinking or saying negative things about anyone. Go for it!"

Scanning the room, he noticed the French windows framed a gently swaying evergreen. Sure no one was looking, he sheepishly lifted a fist and let it fall on a pillow.

Lydia waited. Julie screwed up her face, lifted her shoulders, and then let them fall in a flop. Seth's facial expression suddenly mirrored hers. Fingernails dug into the palms of his tightly formed fists which pummeled the pillows. Running sweat and heatwaves coursing from his collar jolted him away from the total weight on his hands deeply embedded in the cushions' fullness.

"Good work, Seth. Now, ask Jesus what He wants you to know," Lydia gently urged enthusiastically.

"What do you want me to know now, Jesus?" he dutifully asked, looking somewhat blank for a while. Hot alligator tears, not sweat, now streamed down his face as he listened. He reached for a nearby tissue, methodically removed his glasses to dab his swollen eyes, replaced the glasses, and smiled widely.

"Guess my time is up," he said.

"Do you care to share what He said?" Julie hurriedly asked.

Seth shared, "The Son of God appeared for this purpose, that He might destroy the works of the devil. I know the plans I have for you, plans for your welfare and not for harm to give you a future with hope."

Lydia said, "God is not the cause of evil in the world. It is the result of decisions people make. God understands your disappointment. I can't imagine how disappointed God must be in human beings. Your father-in-law is not the cause of all your marriage problems. Seth, I would like to say a prayer for you to lift off these heavy burdens."

> "Father, it's a comfort to know that You know our suffering, fears, and burdens. What is even more comforting is that You truly care and not only want to but can help us. Please lift off the weight of the shocking trauma of this knowledge, any fear, and deliver Seth of any demonic entities which want to take advantage of him now. Fill him with your peace and the confidence that his job is to be a loving and supportive husband. You are the Just Vindicator. Empower him with Your pure agape love and wisdom for his life. In Jesus' name, Amen."

"Fortunately, her parents aren't nearby. It would be wise for you and Clarice to create a plan for your family to avoid being with them for now. We need to discover potential dangers and make plans for future safety. I encourage you to make a script that you both can memorize and tell anyone who might question you about your decision. It needs to be something like this, but in your own words: **'We are in a busy season and not in a position for visiting. Thank you for being so understanding.'** Keep it short and respectful, and repeat it if they pry more. You know, be assertive.

Anger Out

We need to find out what is safe. Okay? Be sure not to lie. Lying opens the door to a demonic attack.

"I want to encourage you to join our trauma support group. Here is the information. These are family or friends of dissociated people and others full of compassion for broken people and their families. They offer practical value to you on this journey of healing for your family," Lydia said.

"Okay, even though difficult, somehow, I feel lighter and more capable of dealing with this. Thank you so much," Seth kindly expressed as he left.

"Please feel free to call with any questions. Be sure to leave a message to return your call if I do not answer. There is only one stupid question. That one is the answer you already know. Good work, Seth. Goodbye," Lydia called.

POSTING

"Clarice came up with an interesting way to vent her anger! Who do you think did the chopping?" Julie asked in a joking manner.

"Julie, we will find out next time. There is much to teach Seth and Clarice. We need to help them to nurture and manage their children through this journey."

"Did I read somewhere that children of dissociative parents often develop dissociative behaviors too, simply because children mirror their parent's behavior?"

"Yes, that is so. We also must keep in mind that some part of the client may be hurting the children, and in that case, the child is dissociative due to trauma. There may be a time when Clarice will need to be relieved of her current duties to allow for more concentration on the healing," Lydia added.

Hoping to impress Lydia, Julie suggested, "An intensive week enables total focus on healing when alone and away from home and responsibilities."

"Clarice is a wife, manages a home, albeit, according to her it is a disaster area. She mothers two teens and two elementary children whom she also homeschools and deals with the chaos of dissociative identity disorder. That is amazing! Psalm 139 describes us wonderfully made. Let's call it a day," said Lydia in a tired voice. "Let's pray."

> "Dearest Heavenly Father, we thank You for the privilege of ministering to those whom You so deeply love and desire to be whole. We release them fully into Your care now. You are the counselor who is always 'on call' and present to them. We request to be disconnected from our clients to now focus fully on our personal lives. Refresh us and come with Your holy consuming fire to cleanse all defilement in us and on this property. In Jesus' name, Amen."

CHAPTER 7

THE BOOK CLUB

It's a happy day because the first Monday of the month is Book Club night! Lydia quickly locked up the client files, office and headed to the corner deli, where she grabbed a main dish salad. Her crossover vehicle automatically headed to downtown Spokane as memories of the beginnings of this cherished group filled her mind.

Anyone who signs up for a twelve-hour summer college quarter needs their head examined if they simultaneously manage responsibility for husband, children, home, garden, food preservation, nursing practice, and a visiting mother-in-law. I desired to get the degree out of the way. Universities are infamous for requiring courses that seem irrelevant to students; another required statistics course mystified me. The scuttlebutt around campus informed me to get into a psychological statistics course that involved less super hard math. I guessed there might be a good side to gossip after all. Well, just a tiny bit. Class composition greatly varies in student types, ages, and academic disciplines.

That extra hot summer class provided a visiting professor from back east. She impressed me with a fantastic wardrobe of two pantsuits, navy and dove gray, an artsy multicolored skirt, white or yellow blouses, and an array of beautiful scarves twisted and tied like jewelry. She always looked well-attired and professional, yet the same clothes mixed and matched all summer long! What an excellent model for one who traveled a lot! Short thinning white hair covered her rounded head. Spirited eyes squinted with delight as she taught. When she turned towards the board, her body gently swayed as prominent rounded shoulders gave a rhythmic lift and settled with each determined, heavily planted step. Looking towards her feet with arms hanging at her side, one could imagine a little munchkin. Lydia smiled as she turned into the underground parking garage.

The Book Club changed meeting sites throughout its eight-year life span. Personal home meetings were fraught with interruptions by pets, kids, phones, spouses, or unacceptable due to allergies, unequal travel distances, smoke, or food odors. It helped when a wealthy member offered a luxurious meeting room and underground free parking right downtown. What a deal! It became "home" to the group.

Yacov, a successful jeweler, joyfully opened his business suite for the 6:30 PM to 8:30 PM event. The seven faithfully prioritized the time. Even if someone traveled and the time frames worked, they would still join via smartphones, et cetera.

Lydia took the cherry-paneled elevator to the top floor. Ceiling to floor windows framed the Spokane River winding its way through the one-hundred-acre Riverfront Park. The land, an ugly discarded train yard, a blight on the city's image became transformed by transferred ownership and the creation of the 1974 Environmental World's Fair, the first of its' kind, thanks to sophisticated negotiations with the Great Northern Railroad. Afterward, the park became the beautiful heart of Spokane, crowned by the Spokane Falls.

Everyone welcomed Lydia back. She presented a seminar in Texas during the last meeting time. "It is good to be back! I missed all of you." While hugging everyone, she said, "On the way here, I thought about how our club originated. Do you remember Professor Kimber Trost? She knew her stuff, but the class soon discovered we could divert her focus to lively discussions of—BOOKS! Her passion burned in literature. Two-thirds of the class grade relied on completing a statistical analysis of a given subject conducted by a team. She chose the ten-person teams and posted the proposed study topics.

"Natroya, you urged us to ask Professor Trost for permission to conduct a study about literature and not one of the posted options," Yacov offered. "We elected you to approach her with the idea. Little did we know then how brilliant you are in human psychology."

"Yes! At first, she hesitantly considered the idea," Natroya responded. "Three deep furrows appeared between her widely set eyes. Suddenly she pulled her hands away from the stack of books on her desk to lift her arms to clap in glee. Quickly, she gained her composure and, without emotion, gave a little lecture on the immensity of the topic."

"A definite shoo-in!" Viviana cheered mischievously.

"Maybe, but not easy," Cavanaugh rebutted. "The library needed more study rooms."

"Even though I loved my mother-in-law, to study, I escaped to our rental duplex. That venue became perfect for our long sessions of research, banter, group composition, and conflict!" Lydia added. Laughing sarcastically, she exclaimed, "We were trauma bonded!" Everyone chuckled in agreement while making faces of different feelings at each other.

"I wonder what happened to the others," pondered Desmond. "Ten comprised a group. Remember that guy, Yin, from South Korea?"

"No, Yin's Chinese," corrected Thi. "A lot of Asian students attended that summer."

"North Korea is a real problem internationally and especially for the US. So in my news prep, I wade through and process."

"Viviana, remember our rule? Only information directly related to our personal lives and the books we agree to read for discussion use our time." Cavanaugh gently stopped her with his southern drawl. Yet, at the same time, smile lines appeared around his deep blue eyes.

Viviana developed a genius for constant talk. Sometimes one could feel themselves hurling down a roller coaster with her constant chatter. It probably served her well in her television world of news and glamor. Lydia wondered if the continual chatter provided a defense mechanism from her childhood; poor thing, probably experienced no chance to talk or feared questions. A good block against honest communication. A lot of contemplation about Viviana's negative traits buzzed in all their heads.

Finally, Desmond wagged his head and praised her for the unending flow of "yummies" she showered upon them. They shared reputations as gourmet cooks.

"Nostalgia can be fun, but a book review awaits," Natroya directed with a cup in hand towards the high-backed leather chairs. "Considering all the terrorist attacks worldwide last week, we are right on target with this one. Grab your refreshments, and let's get started." In her usual administrative mode, she presented the epitome of strength, authority, Zulu height, a warrior, and head of a university social justice department. Her creamy brown complexion and piercing ebony eyes could be captivating. Each book review was assigned a leader. Natroya led the discussion for *God's War on Terror* by Walid Shoebat. "This was work... a thick book. So let's go around the table to present what most impressed you. Thi?" she smiled.

Thi interpreted the American Forces as a young man before evacuation from Vietnam in 1975. Families in Spokane sponsored him for orientation to American culture. His high intellect and proficiency in languages served the Federal Bureau of Investigation (FBI) until retirement, then he returned home to Spokane. Thi began, "I'm impressed that he was a dug-in terrorist for sixteen years in Chicago before being caught and sent to prison. Wow, someone was not on the job!" Furrows in his forehead formed and ebbed as he looked around the table. His bottom lip thrust beyond the upper in a determined manner. "The terrorists planned a mosque in every American town with a population of five hundred or more, and they accomplished it in less time than planned. That made me envious. Why can't we as a nation be more proficient

The Book Club

with our plans?" he patriotically asked, pursing his lips; he nodded to Desmond.

Desmond, or "Mr. GQ," affectionately nicknamed by the club, owned his own drama company. His theater group became known as more than amateur. He enjoyed painting in watercolors and demonstrated proficiency with several instruments. "No wonder these people succeed. Think of Wahid's commitment. His famous Imam grandfather required him to study the Koran, not just like any Muslim, I mean thoroughly study it in and out! Without a desire to follow in his grandfather's footsteps, he committed to studying the Koran," he dramatically expounded.

Yacov reported next. Yacov's ancestors immigrated to Canada to escape the plight of their homelands. Life in Europe from mid to the late 1800s became increasingly difficult for Jews. Land ownership did not exist as a dream there, but they took advantage of Canada's Sifton Plan. It offered ownership of land to those who would settle and farm it. The Sifton term characterized early immigrants as able to survive harsh climates. Some Jewish people, not the best farmers, quickly transitioned to what they do best—commerce. They developed towns and businesses. Yacov brought those genes to Spokane when he immigrated to the United States.

Stroking his full black beard, he began. "Wahid studied the Bible and superbly documented evidence that the Koran borrowed much content from the *Holy Bible* but sometimes adjusted it a bit. This Muslim scholar testified to many astute documentaries and books written on the topic. Ancient writings and archaeological data attest that the *Holy Bible* led God's people many years before the *Koran* existed. Perhaps the most provocative part for me involved his adamant persuasion that the anti-Christ will come from Islam." He smugly smiled his conclusion toward Viviana.

Viviana offered a surprised look. Then broadly smiled, straightened, thrust her generous bosom forward, and began, "I thought his wife had balls to make such a dangerous wager."

"What wager?" Desmond interrupted.

"Did you read the book? Viviana sarcastically snipped. "He married an American Christian woman and harassed her to convert to Islam. Finally, probably worn down, she made a wager with him. If he would study the *Holy Bible* from front to back as diligently as he studied *Koran* and still wanted her to convert, she would. He took on the wager, saw contradictions and outright plagiarism of the *Holy Bible* in the *Koran*."

"I'm reminded of a scripture in Hosea 4:6 *My people are destroyed for lack of knowledge,*" Yacob added.

Vivian's and Desmond's frequent squabbles intrigued Lydia. But if Viviana held romantic interest, she faced disappointment. Desmond's interests did not include women.

Natroya expressed her admiration for the bold man, Wahid, traveling extensively to educate the populace of the serious evil inherent in Islamic Doctrine. "He and his family received death threats. I feel sorry for good Islamic people who lack education of the fullness of their doctrine. It reminds me of the celebrity Mormons who complain to talk show hosts that people accuse them of not being Christians. Those Mormons do not know their professed religion either. If they knew their doctrine, they would realize they are not Christians," she said.

"My turn?" Cavanaugh asked, breaking a weighty silence. "I concur. Nice, moderate, professing Islamists are ignorant of what the entire Koran instructs, or they could not condemn their jihadist Muslims. However, they are like many professing Christians who warm pews and sing songs in church, may attend a Bible study, and sometimes pray but know no intimate relationship with Jesus Christ and do not know what the *Bible* teaches in full.

"*Koran* **requires** people to convert to its doctrine, or their head comes off. The Holy Bible **invites** people to accept Jesus Christ as their Savior. People are free to reject or accept that doctrine, and that profound difference impacted me the most.

The Book Club

"Wahid's impact led to his conversion to Christianity. His wife professed great faith in the powerful authority of the Word of God to take such a treacherous risk."

Lydia jumped in. "Maybe that wasn't such a risk. The elite-controlled mainstream media would never report this. Still, there are numerous current credible reports of Jesus appearing to tribal Imams in dreams and visions that evangelize their villages. Jesus appears on their school buses resulting in conversions. The *Koran* acknowledges Jesus as a great teacher and prophet, but not as God come in the flesh and as Savior of humanity," Lydia shared. "I assess the book brilliantly written without condemnation but factual. I hope this book will reach many to wake up the confused."

"I'm not a religious person," Desmond declared, "but this book provoked my ignorance about world views. What would you think about reviewing a book that lays out world views with an unbiased, objective perspective?" he inquired.

The group tossed around the pros and cons of the idea. Finally, Cavanaugh remembered hearing about a best seller on that topic and agreed to research it for the group. He planned to email the book information to the others so each could get their copy.

"Thank you, Cavanaugh. I see our time is up. It was a weighty review, to say the least. Lydia, would you like to lead our next book review?" Natroya asked.

"Thank you, but I'll be in Europe. But unfortunately, the nine-hour time difference means it would be three-thirty in the morning, so I may not be joining you," she lamented.

"We will miss you. How about you, Thi?" Natroya inquired.

Thi raised his eyebrows with an affirmative smile.

Lydia sidled up to Cavanaugh as they exited the elevator. "How are you doing? Did you look into the grief support group?" she inquired quietly.

"This is the worst part, Lydia. Going home to an empty house, she is there everywhere I look. No, I did nothing much or went anywhere other than the book club, grocery store, of course… but you know what I mean. We were married thirty-five years! It feels like half of me is dead too," he groveled.

"Try not to be impatient with yourself. It's only been six months. Healing is a process, and grieving is one part. Grieving is all about loss. The Hispanic culture taught me how to grieve. They wail without inhibition. I would encourage you to try it. I know the grief support group will breathe new life in you when you are ready. I'm here through Thursday. Call anytime," Lydia offered. "Good night."

CHAPTER 8

HELLO WIVES

"I hate life! Nobody understands. I want off this planet. I don't trust anyone. There's no one to support me. I can't stand this pain!" the angry voice screamed on the other end of the phone. Lydia's announcement of her month-long European tour probably precipitated the outburst.

Lydia consoled her anguished client one more time, "Remember the two-month business trip? I returned from that one, and this is only one month. I did not abandon you then, nor will I this time. When you first came to see me, you signed a disclaimer agreement that states I work internationally and often travel. She referred the client to the provided contact information in an emergency.

Clients seemed fine with the idea of their prayer counselor traveling on paper, but when it happened, most found it extremely difficult. Even when not traveling, the answering machine recorded many client calls to hear her voice. Lydia considered making a CD of her voice, talking to her clients with encouragement and reminders of tools for healing to give contentment and help when she is not available. This call reminded her of all the good things she should get around to doing someday.

Julie arrived excited about today's appointment with Clarice. "You're in the co-counseling phase, so I expect to hear from you in the session. You barely said a word in the session with Seth, Julie," Lydia reminded. They reviewed Clarice's last session and prayed for direction and wisdom before the meeting.

"Clarice, you look so bright today. Not just because you are causing that lemon yellow sports outfit to look stunning, but your eyes are not as sad! What a delight to be with you! You bring us sunshine. Thank you," Lydia chimed.

After the opening prayer, Julie requested Clarice summarize the time since the last prayer counseling time together. Clarice all but sparkled telling how Seth came home after his prayer counseling and asked her to go for a walk. He shared his previous concern about her activities in the kitchen when he saw her chopping hot dogs. Then thanked her for sharing about DID after her first three sessions and the signed release form. Finally, he exhibited excitement about joining a recommended group for supporters of DID people.

Clarice fussed with her scarf, removed it, and dug into her oversized bag until she found a baggie with a delicately bejeweled necklace. She demurely smiled as she put it on. She ran a hand through her hair. A relaxed curl fell, partially covering her left eye.

> "Now, I feel like me!" smiled Bride. Seth was so tender and protective when he told us he knew about the incest and that it didn't change his respect and love for us. He assured us that we are not alone in this journey of healing and that Jesus can and will heal as we rely upon Him," she shared while tears of gratitude dripped from her square, determined jaw.

The voice strained.

Clarice's eyebrows seemed set higher. Then the tossed curl disappeared, gray eyes indignant, hands-on-hips, she sat forward and spewed criticisms until breathless.

> "Enough of this starry-eyed rhetoric about the knight in shining armor malarkey," a brisk officious voice commanded. "He is useless, never at home, always

at meetings, at the business, or some philanthropic organization. I work and slave day and night to keep a decently ordered house. Do those kids help? No! What kind of a father allows his kids to be lazy bums? All Mother does is drive them all over creation to one practice or another. She sets up homeschool for those little rats to waste time and make bigger messes for me or coddles them with stories and helps with homework ad nauseam. I do all the shopping, cooking, dishes, cleaning, washing, yard work, gardening, cleaning the toilet, and cleaning out the drains! What do I get? No recognition. No credit because the place is still a chaotic disaster. The brats don't even hang up their clothes. Plates, even with food, are left wherever by all of them!"

"It's so nice to meet you," Lydia said sweetly. I'm sorry you are so upset and feel unappreciated, but thank you for sharing with Julie and me. I'm glad you heard Clarice share. When made, how old was the body?" Lydia asked matter-of-factly.

"Clarice was five. Her mom worked all sorts of hours. Undone chores made her furious when she got home. She daily ranted how Clarice would never amount to anything and never did anything right. She claimed her daughter made a bigger mess cleaning up than when she began. Well, her dad was her stepdad; her real dad was never in the picture. He was usually out with his drinking buddies or a super slob when home. He took food anywhere in the house and just left the garbage for the ants. The stink hit you in the face when you opened the door. I did all the housework because no one taught her. Did it well too! I always came out when the mom came home so Clarice wouldn't get her heart crushed every-time she heard what a failure she was."

"You showed great compassion," Julie said while handing her a water bottle. Do you have a name?"

"Of course I do! It's Cinderella... duh!" she said haughtily.

Julie flinched, "How silly of us not to figure that out. Forgive us. It is so nice to get to know you,"

Lydia contritely said. "You worked diligently to protect her feelings all these years. Do you realize that you are a crucial part of Clarice?" she inquired.

"We heard you tell Clarice about that confusion, denial, and pain stuff. I'm not in denial. I help Clarice every day of my life. My problem is that man and all those kids. I'm getting exhausted trying to keep up. Since she started coming here, Clarice told me I am married to that guy. He better not do any of that goo-goo gaa-gaa stuff with me, or I'll whack him upside of the head with my mop! Then there's that starry-eyed one, always putting me in the wrong place with him. Well, I go inside and leave them to do their shenanigans. She isn't as much a problem as Mother."

"Mother?" inquired Julie.

"You know, the other wife!" Cinderella rebuked.

Julie replied, "We honor rules to respect all parts of a person with whom we speak. Perhaps you were not listening during Clarice's first appointment."

"This place is all tidy. Why clean here?" she asked in a puzzled tone. "Clarice suffered so much mixed-up pain today, I decided to come out to help," Cinderella clarified.

Julie empathetically offered, "I'm so glad you did. Thank you for the compliment, Cinderella. We purpose to offer our clients a healthy, safe, and beautiful environment. One of our rules restrict talking for another part, or telling their story unless given permission. Tattle-telling is never allowed. Express only your own opinions. The other parts or alters tell their own stories when ready. Do go on and offer your opinions about Mother."

> "She and the man make a lot of plans for the kids. She only has eyes for the kids. They consume her time with none left to help me. We waste a lot of time hiking, swimming, and doing all those useless things. I seem to be getting sick a lot."

"It sounds like you could be in a stage of burnout and require some vacation time. I will see what we can do to help you get more rest when I talk with Clarice."

"What is a vacation?" she asked.

Julie's shocked eyes quickly darted in unbelief toward Lydia.

Lydia jumped in, "It is something restful and fun. I want to talk again and tell you about other wonderful things you never experienced. You see, all you experienced is doing your job of keeping house to protect Clarice from getting into trouble and hurt feelings. You did a wonderful job. It worked for the child, Clarice, but your help poses a problem as an adult. You seem worn out! Please plan to pay attention to all Clarice does. That will build what we call co-consciousness."

> "I can't believe you understand and seem genuine about caring that I am so tired! It feels terrific!" she exclaimed.

"Would you like to ask Mother if she wants to talk with us?" Cinderella gave a forty-five-degree body turn to her right, dropped her head, and then spritely lifted it. Julie passed a note to Lydia: was that a switch maneuver?

> "Cinderella goes on and on in that negative vein. It is so unhealthy for the children. I teach them the power of positive thinking and always do their best. No one is perfect, but we can aspire to excellence and do our best, whether in academics, sports, or the arts. I think outdoor activities are essential for child development, but books are also a staple in our household. Seth and I strive to provide the best opportunities for our children.
>
> "I homeschooled the two older girls through middle school and home school the two younger boys now. We read parenting books, and I studied education in college. However, Clarice proves too dysfunctional to free me to hold a teaching position. I keep the children busy and away from home as much as possible to avoid a negative impact from Clarice. Seth expresses great confidence in me. He paid for doctors and expensive medications all these years and stood by her in and out of the hospital those two times she tried to kill herself; he showed himself quite a trooper. You may call me Mother."

She sat comfortably in a dignified manner, with her ankles crossed and hands neatly folded in her lap. Her demeanor projected intelligence and kindness.

"Thank you so much for talking with Julie and me. I see our time is nearly finished. Please purpose to stay close to Clarice all the time as much as possible. May I speak with Clarice?"

"Seth has three wives!" Clarice clasped her hand over her mouth. "Or maybe... four!" she giggled.

"Clarice, this is exciting to see that you are co-conscious with those parts or alters," complimented Julie.

Lydia looked up from her notes. "This is your homework, Clarice. Use twenty minutes in quiet privacy with journaling and the Wonderful Counselor, four times a week, minimum, to get to know if they are the only wives. Do not be dismayed, if you find more. Remember, they are all wonderful you, doing their individual jobs. I am so proud of you. What an excellent worker you are. Wisdom dictates not to share this information with Seth just yet. Let us get the full picture first. Then we can call him in to do some work with you. We will look forward to being with you next time," Lydia affirmed as Clarice left.

POSTING

"Is this unusual? All these wives? "Julie comically scrunched her face.

"Not at all. I'll not be surprised if we find Clarice's mom personified in an alter. That may be who she constantly hears, calling her derogatory names. Julie, this is a fine example of a sorely traumatized person but not severely fragmented. I doubt there is any occult or governmental mind control in this case. She has a good prognosis; I can see her integrated before long. Do you remember the main principles for healing?" her mentor asked.

"Oh, no, a test! Well, first they must want to be healed," Julie nodded and looked at Lydia for confirmation. "Second, they need a safe environment. They need to find a competent counselor with experience in dissociation. I say competent because my experience indicates these people can get complete healing with supernatural interventions of the Holy Spirit. Much of this wounding involves the human spirit. Psychological therapies or only renewing their minds cannot accomplish healing. Maybe I should say a Christian counselor rather than competent."

"Keep the competency. It is important to remember that probably thousands of Christian counselors do secular counseling. They might open or close a session with prayer. Still, the prayer counseling we do is an ongoing modality of interaction with the Holy Spirit. We are dependent upon Him.

"Can you believe there is a group of powerful and influential people who want to change the professional mental health manual to formalize child sexual activity as normal? Their basis is that human beings are sexual beings, so they should be involved in sexual activity at any age. If accomplished, can you imagine the ramifications of such insanity? People like Clarice are hard factual evidence that child sexual involvement is very damaging. Proponents might argue that the only reason is due to indoctrination by people in their lives who condemned certain ages, genders or marital statuses against sexual involvement. That does not stand! Thousands of clients sustain trauma from sexual involvement in infancy and very young ages before such indoctrination would be possible. Even those born into families who sexually initiate their children at birth hold trauma from those experiences.

"By the way, you passed the test. You offered good co-conscious confirmation to Clarice today. You get a gold star."

"Thank you, Lydia. Enough about sick sex for a while. How about some sexy food for lunch?" Julie offered playfully.

Later that day, Cavanaugh dropped by the office to deliver the Book Club's new study book so Lydia could keep up and to wish her well on tour. Her heart gladdened as his long-time invisible smile wrinkles reappeared with his report of the Grief Support Group attendance. He planned to go again next week. Lydia mused the sweetness of love between old friends is a treasure as they hugged goodbye. The week flew by. Lydia felt thrilled with the thought of travel.

CHAPTER 9

PACKING FOR EUROPE

———◆※◆———

The alluring aroma of freshly brewed coffee filled the air of Lydia's Voight's office. She audibly checked off the international packing list she created years ago to minimize travel stress:

- Set phone messages.
- Pay bills in advance.
- Notify banks and credit card companies.
- Send clients resource information and itineraries to family, hosts, and officials.

Okay, I completed these two weeks ago before the California Seminar. "Now for the carry-on briefcase: seminar thumb drives, mumh, mump, mumh, prescription medications in original pharmacy bottles, make-up kit, inflatable neck pillow, and a bag of raw almonds. Good! Now the money belt: Euros, dollars, credit cards," she enumerated, then startled from her concentration as the phone rang.

"Hi, Neil Blake told me he did all he can, and now I need you," a shaky female voice resentfully announced. "He said you're an expert in ritual abuse cases. I'm sure I attended satanic rituals as a kid. Night terrors always ruin my sleep, and I never hold a job. Doctors gave me all kinds of diagnoses. The time spent in psych wards and mental hospitals, years with different counselors, and the tons of drugs I take never help. There is a problem. I'm not a Christian. I gave up on God a long time ago, but I realize you're a Christian Prayer Counselor, so now what do I do?"

"I am so sorry to hear of your struggles. Thank you for calling. I've heard many similar stories from Christians and non-Christians with whom I work. When Jesus walked the earth two thousand years ago, He did not require the people He healed to be Christian. He is alive and well today and still maintains the same policy. Would you care to tell me your name, and do you know what a Christian prayer counselor does?" Lydia sweetly inquired.

The voice relaxed, "Not really. Oh! Sure, my name is Nancy."

"Prayer counseling differs from a therapist, psychologist, psychiatrist, or a Christian who does secular counseling. We do utilize principles of psychology that come from Biblical principles. Christian prayer counselors do not use hypnosis or guided visualization but use prayer and depend upon the Holy Spirit for guidance. Healing results from confronting the lies believed and replacing them with truth, based on God's Word and in the love and forgiveness available in the person of Jesus Christ. This new way of thinking is how the Holy Spirit transforms all our degradations to glory, weakness to strength, deserts to gardens of blessing, and ashes to beauty. satan wins no victories this way. Those who love and obey God find He causes everything to work for their good.

"For us to work together, you need to be comfortable joining me as I talk to my God and let Him help us. I am not the Wonderful Counselor; He is. So, I happily get to help by coaching," Lydia explained until interrupted.

"Okay, okay I get it. Desperate people do desperate things. So how do I get an appointment? Do I need any forms or medical histories, look at a website or send money?" Nancy asked.

"I sense you are anxious to do this. I regret to tell you that I leave for an international business tour tomorrow. Why don't you give this more thought to ensure this is a fit for you? Meanwhile, answers to most questions are on my website and many helpful resources. If you still want an appointment, you can download the life history, complete it, and e-mail it back to me. I will review it and pray into it to be sure I am to work with you. Then in May, if we are both on board, to say, you can confirm an appointment with a deposit as soon as you want to schedule. How do you feel about that?" Lydia asked.

Nancy's disappointed voice agreed, "What's your e-mail address?"

They finished the necessary details. To end the phone call, Lydia commended Nancy for her determination for healing. She asked that she please give her regards to Neil for his excellent work and referral.

Lydia mournfully yelled, "Another victim of hideous abuse! God, how many thousands or tens of thousands are there? Where was I? Oh yes, the money belt contents are contact information for the USA embassy, passport, birth certificate copies, Eurail tickets, and itinerary." She whooped as the last two items went into the money belt.

Ring, ring! A grunting sigh read the 4:57 PM LED—not yet 5:00 PM closing time. The very professional and somewhat sophisticated-sounding woman identified herself as Saqqara Fain. Remembering her coffee, as whispering swishes expired from the leather chair, Lydia sank and took her cup in one hand and pen in the other.

Saqqara's story resembled the caller's minutes before. Only, Saqqara seemed very high functioning or was. She double-booked her work, suffered bizarre physical symptoms her doctor could not diagnose, and insomnia. As she answered more of Lydia's questions, she suddenly reported a severe migraine, so she could not think and needed to call back later.

Lydia raised her voice with a quick, "Wait! I want you to try something. I want you to say to yourself, 'Please step back.'"

It was Saqqara's turn to sink into her soft white loveseat. "Okay. Please step back," her eyes rolled, trying to discern something.

"Oh, my gosh! The headache is gone! What in the world was that?" she gasped in delightful surprise.

Lydia had remained on the line, "It is a tool that may save money on headache medicine. Your friend, Nadine, who referred you, did an excellent job of explaining how I work. We appropriate gifts of the Holy Spirit. The ministry also includes administering holy water, anointing with oil, laying on of hands, offering Holy Communion, music, worship, and praise. We are not problem-centered, nor do we attempt or want to change life's history. But we allow the Holy Spirit to change history's effect on us, so we can cherish all areas of our lives and fulfill our created destiny," Lydia tutored.

"I have a Catholic or limited Catholic background, so I understand those things," Saqqara informed.

"You have requested an intensive week of counseling. That could be four days of three, four, or six hours per day, depending upon your stamina and finances. I regret to tell you that I leave for an international business tour tomorrow. Meanwhile, answers to most questions are on my website and many helpful resources. Download the life history, complete it, and e-mail it back to me. I will review it and pray into it to be sure I am to work with you. Then in May, if we are both still interested, we can schedule an appointment. How do you feel about that?" Lydia asked.

"No, that won't work for me. My schedule is hectic. I need to arrange with my colleague now so I can be away," Saqqara anxiously quipped.

"I can pencil you in, but I need to be sure I am to work with you after reviewing your life history form. If that is a go, I could send my decision via e-mail. Receipt of your non-refundable deposit confirms the penciled-in appointment. Then, I will e-mail directions to the office, lodging information, and a confirmation letter. Deposits apply to the session fee for honored appointments." Lydia explained. A cordial closing followed.

Initial interviews take a lot of time! Lydia noted. "Lord, I thank you for the privilege of assisting You to heal these people. Please

Packing for Europe

guide her and provide the resources she needs. Now, please help me get out of this office, get home, and go to the airport tomorrow. *Extended business trips are a lot of work,*" she deeply sighed.

At home, she accomplished the final drill of setting the furnace and alarm systems, then gifted neighbors with refrigerator contents which always brought happy smiles of appreciation.

Travel decorated her condo with only silk plants. At last, the luggage scale completed packing.

CHAPTER 10

THE REQUEST

"Do you believe in alien abductions?" Saqqara asked Tiffany. "You are the closest person to me, and I hope you don't think I'm crazy, but I must talk to someone! Last Friday night, I awakened to a familiar sensation. I've never told this to anyone." Her eyes filled with fear and her voice and hands trembled. "I floated above my bed... honestly floated... that isn't the biggie, but the walls closing in on me and knowing soon I'd be sucked out through them was the terrible part. I glanced at the familiar 'worker bee Grays' with their black almond eyes as I searched for the clock. It glowed 2:00 AM. I don't remember what happened, but I returned at 5:00 AM."

Tiffany's doe eyes searched Saqqara's face as she reached out and took Saqqara's hand, "What I believe is that you are suffering and losing grip on life. I am so sorry, Saqqara. I wish I could help more. My brother is a sci-fi guy who talked about the high-level military and scientific whistle-blowers. They reported the Roswell Area 51 event not as the reported weather balloon event but as an actual alien spacecraft crash. Wright Patterson Air Force Base, near Dayton, Ohio, received the transported craft aliens. The government quickly shut down all investigations, and locals were hushed. There are stories and movies about alien abductions. I don't think you are crazy. I don't know what to think."

The Request

Saqqara gathered Tiffany's hand, held hers, and squeezed while she choked back unpermitted tears and then pulled away. "Tiffany, you knew I went to the doctor and started on a new medication. Well, it didn't help. Nadine is also concerned and offered a non-traditional resource which she claims has good results. I talked with the person, and if she accepts me as a client, I will need time off to do a week of intensive counseling May 15-19."

"May!" Tiffany exclaimed. "Oh Saqqara, even with Millie helping, you know how busy we are servicing May Day and Mother's Day as well as all those graduation parties. It's one of our busiest months. A whole week!" Tiffany's frown disappeared as her raven hair veiled her lowered face.

"I realize this is difficult for you. Quite frankly, Tiffany, I think you would benefit if I'm not here doing all the messing up you tell me about every day. May is the earliest she could see me, but she may decide not to as well. I send a life history for evaluation. If she is willing to take on the case, I will receive a confirmation. I downloaded the document. It's a challenge to think about the questions and I struggle to address them, but I purpose to send it to her this week."

"My mother called me shortly after I spoke to the lady to make the appointment. Isn't that interesting? You know we are not close, and really, I still don't know why she called. Weird."

After a long silence, Tiffany released a giant sigh. "Okay, be patient with me. I'm trying to get my bearings. Can we afford to hire a temp for May? That way, you could orient them for a couple of weeks, and they can help me the rest of the month."

"I think that's a great idea," Saqqara smiled in relief. "I'll personally select the person who best fits my role."

PART II

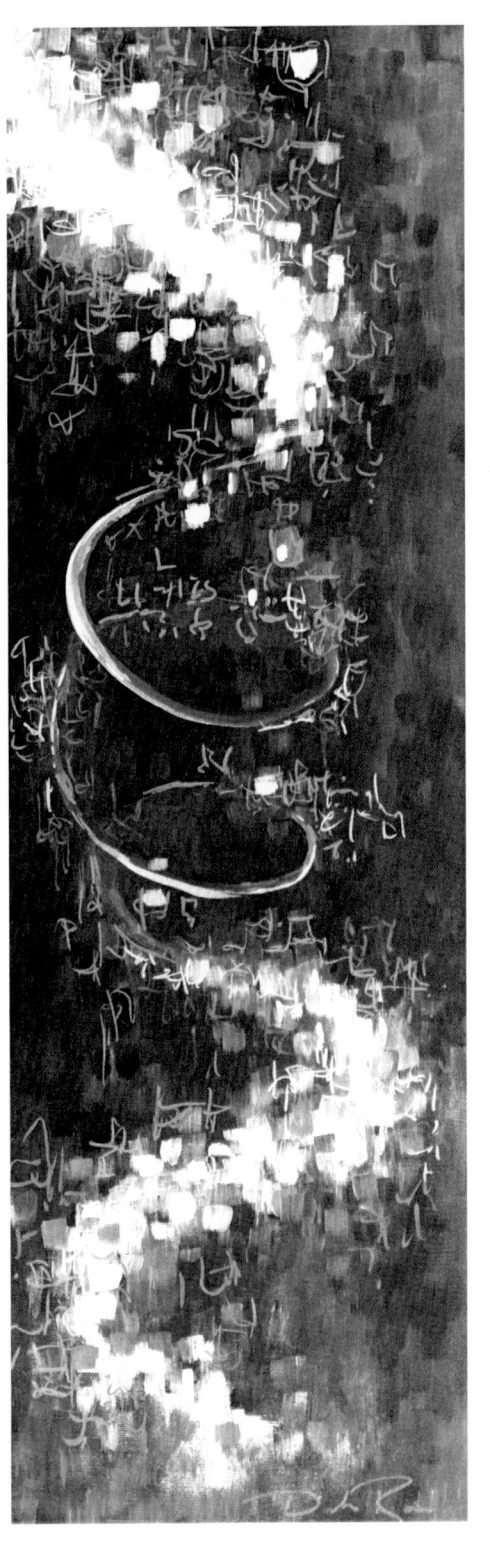

CHAPTER 11

UP, UP, AND AWAY

It only took thirty-five minutes to fly from Spokane to Seattle. Lydia usually saved approximately a hundred dollars by flying out of Seattle to international locations. She appreciated the small carrier with the passport, credit card, and tickets/boarding passes for quick access. It perfectly fit her inside jacket pocket. It hung from around her neck with a small black leather purse that held her phone and most crucial lipstick, and personal items needed for the nine-and-a-half-hour flight.

She checked in two huge bags for Romanian orphans, her Pullman, and a smaller suitcase. Her wheeled backpack loaded with the briefcase on top made a comical clickety-clack cadence traversing the long concourses. She noticed heightened security. Wise money management, always important to Lydia, prohibited paying a thousand plus dollars for a seat when she saved hundreds of dollars riding coach. Now the great mystery. Would she be lucky with nobody beside her window seat, or who in the world would be her traveling companion?

A trained observer, Lydia enjoyed people-watching. A chorus of different languages accompanied the varied shapes, sizes, ages, odors, and attires of passengers. Their heads bobbed up and down as they looked for their seats and hoisted their usually oversized carry-on luggage high over the seats into the baggage compartments. A couple with a tiny baby shared the five seated center block behind the partition between business class and coach. A doting flight attendant demonstrated the apparatus for the baby's bed.

The muffled thud sound of boarding stopped. The purser welcomed all on board in three languages. English often issued forth first, but the first spoken tended to be the tongue of the plane's nationality. *Yea! I got a seat to myself!* Counseling requires intimacy. Lydia liked people but needed a break. Unlike some friends, she did not see sitting next to someone for a long time as the ideal time to evangelize them. Although she traveled for years, she never lost the thrill of going up, up, and away into the sky.

The plane taxied, and once in the air circled over Puget Sound, where gigantic lift-locks taking freight off ships now looked miniature. The eastern Cascade Range's Mount Rainier quickly replaced Hurricane Ridge Mountain Range in the west. Rainier's snow-capped majesty seemed in awe of Mount Saint Helen's missing north face. Lydia promptly gave in to the seductive somnolence she often experienced shortly after take-off. She rarely slept on a plane but could dose a bit.

Over Canada now, the flight crew hustled to help passengers and offer water which they frequently do since flying dehydrates. She put thick wool socks over her shoes. If she took off her shoes, they might not fit at the end of the flight due to common flight edema or swelling. Flights often get nippy, and socks feel cozy. She ate a delicious seafood lunch at Sea-Tac Airport, so the mini-sized dinner offering augmented by a glass of wine sufficed. She organized her area to easily find everything after stewards turned off the lights after dinner.

Lydia almost chuckled aloud as she marveled at a couple's ritual across the aisle. The man sat very still and straight. The woman posted a hot pink paper message *'DO NOT WAKEN'* on the aisle side of her seat. She handed the man a pill he took and then put up his seat tray. Next, she gave him a blanket which he draped over his knees. Then she did the same for herself. Eye masks followed earplugs. Then, as if on cue, they simultaneously adjusted their seats back to the farthest reclining position. Lydia foresaw trouble for another passenger to climb over them to get out of the long row of seats.

Available choices of movies, music, and TV shows abound. Even exercise clips help passengers stay limber while sitting. Many people sleep. Lydia preferred to get up and walk the track, as she called it. She walked as far forward as possible, crossed to the other aisle, and walked back as far as possible to stand and stretch in the open spaces. Lydia enjoyed chats with the crew. The flight provided an ideal time just to be or meditate, watch movies, and review her upcoming talks.

A favorite part of trans-oceanic flights occurs shortly before breakfast when steaming hot white cloths arrive to refresh one's face and prepare hands for eating. Shortly before arrival, bustling activity surged with grooming, wafting perfumes, chatter, and children shrieking with excitement. At the same time, some men exchanged business suits for mid- eastern white traditional robes or *thobes* and headdresses called *ghutra* to finalize their voyage.

Lydia jerked away from her raised window blind as the orange sunrise on the horizon blinded her eyes. Then adjusting to the light, she scanned for the expansive fields of multicolored tulips, which create a panoramic quilt of splendid color on the landscape of the Netherlands this time of year.

In Lydia's opinion, the direct flight route over the Arctic Polar Cap is the fastest and easiest to Europe from the west coast. Leaving at 1:30 PM Pacific Standard Time put her in Amsterdam at 07:30 Central European Time. The purser gave instructions for deplaning to customs and thanked the passengers for traveling with their airline. The long human lines paraded a mix of the weary, excited, impatient, and those in awe of the new experience. Lydia pulled her backpack, queuing and shuffling with the other non-Europeans as she recalled the most stringent customs protocols that occurred in the USA and Israel of all the ports of entry she experienced.

Lydia grabbed a luggage cart and put her backpack into the small area next to the handles. The wait for luggage to appear, if it does, is usually a negative for flying. With little grunts, she hoisted the three Pullman cases and the smaller case from the luggage belt onto the cart.

Amsterdam Airport Schiphol ranks at the top of the best airports in the world. It offers panoramic restaurants, gleaming shopping boulevards, a wedding hub, and even a museum. It felt energizing to walk and exert the effort to maneuver the luggage cart among the bustling cultural diversity after the long sedentary voyage. However, she never found authentic German pretzels to immediately savor as in Frankfurt or Munich. Most important to Lydia, a train at the airport made an easy transition from plane to train to the following desired location. Today she needed the direct train, which frequently ran to the Amsterdam Centraal Station in twenty minutes and Haarlem Station in another nineteen minutes.

Feeling awkward, Lydia wiggled into her backpack, piggybacked the suitcases, and stowed the cart. This train's modern platform-level design made boarding immensely easier than lifting onto high steps. Fortunately, she got a seat next to the door and an area for luggage. She winced at the morning glare of the windows as the train whizzed along.

In no time, she exited Haarlem Station. Cool air kissed her cheeks. Suddenly a waft of cigarette smoke made her nose search for fresh air. Finally, she stepped out of the shadow of the station. Brilliant light streams blinded her as they glanced off a sea of bicycles left at the station. Being awake long hours, straining to read with a pencil light, and watching movies weakened her eyes. Nevertheless, the sun aided their recovery from the jet lag, and she welcomed it.

A rendezvous at a famous pancake house with Kirsten Grundman, her Dutch hostess, and Tirza Piltz, Lydia's mentee, beaconed. Tirza had followed Lydia all over Europe for several years. This tour plan included teaching her the ropes of public speaking, fielding seminar questions, teaching tools for healing, working equipment, PowerPoint, formatting recordings, and speaking agreements for legal purposes. She made a wide swath in her path as she pulled the two piggybacked suitcases. Small booths with vividly colored tulips for sale lined the narrow water canals. *I wish I could buy some for*

Up, Up, and Away

my hostess but how could I carry them? I'm amazed there is already a long line of tourists at the old brick Corrie ten Boom house with the 'hiding place' when it doesn't open for two hours. Lydia found herself smiling and remembering that she and her precious staff videographer also waited in the queue two years earlier. They made the stop on the way to do a conference.

At last, the quaint pancake house came into view. Tirza ran to greet her and quickly relieved Lydia of one piggyback. She arrived from Germany an hour earlier. Kirsten warmly hugged Lydia at the reserved table next to a lace cafe-curtained window. While Lydia shed her backpack and coat, the two ladies stowed all the luggage out of the way.

The discomfort in Lydia's shoulders from the pack weight yelled as she tried to focus on the cozy warmth and delicious aromas filling the crowded eatery. *What should I order? I think I'll forgo water because it is usually not free, nor is a refill of coffee or tea in Europe. Yum, the spiced sausage, apricot, and feta pancake with a cup of coffee sound super.*

The waitress took orders and soon served beverages.

"How was your flight, Lydia? And your train ride, Tirza?" Kirsten asked.

"My wonderful seat to myself offered time to review the seminar, and all the luggage arrived with me," Lydia replied.

Tirza piped up to report that many moms and children were on the train for the spring health spa holiday. A discussion about the severe cut in German health care programs ensued.

Kirsten, ever observant, remarked, "I identified Tirza from your description, Lydia. However, Tirza, your hairstyle is different from the emailed picture, but it is just perfect for you! Lydia, I realize you'll not be eating supper tonight. So, I put food in your room for the middle of the night hunger and enough for breakfast if you sleep in."

"You remembered! Thank you so much," Lydia said. "The nine-hour time difference rings my dinner bell in the middle of Europe's night," Lydia explained, laughed, and leaned towards Tirza. "Kirsten remembered that I need to sleep quite a long time immediately upon arrival after a trans-Atlantic flight. So, we always met up a few days after my arrivals," Lydia continued eyeing the scrumptious pancakes her companions ordered while pushing back to receive hers.

During the meal, Kirsten laid out the plans for their visit, "It's only 63.5 kilometers or around thirty-nine miles to Den Haag or The Hague in English. It will be a short drive, but my dilemma is where to put all the luggage in my small auto. For the rest of today and tomorrow morning, you can rest. We will prepare for the seminar in the afternoon, and then voilá, *The Hidden Trauma Detective Seminar.* After a day of rest, we'll sight-see before counseling your clients."

Thankfully, only a short walk took them to the auto. After multiple adjustments, all luggage fit to allow space for the women. Kirsten exclaimed, "Well, that was nothing short of a miracle!"

Once away from the bustle of autos and bicycle traffic, Kirsten offered a travelogue on the drive. "Den Haag was first mentioned in history in 1242. It is the home of Noordeinde Palace, visible from your combined lodging and venue for the seminar. The horizontal flag of Holland is red on the top, blue on the bottom, and white in the middle. An orange strip flies above the country's flag when royalty visits the castle. This wimple orange denotes the House of Orange-Nassau, Holland's royal family. Waving her hand, she proudly said, "You will see many greenhouses such as we passed, acres of them."

The sleep deprivation, sore muscles, and encroaching ominous clouds lessened Lydia's attention. Her tired eyes studied Tirza as she listened intently to Kirstin's energetic entertainment of her guests. *Thank God we arrived. I don't care about the history right now, just please show me to my room.* Even the cold room did not mitigate quickly getting into bed.

S L E E P.

CHAPTER 12

HIDDEN TRAUMA DETECTIVE

The heavy gray sky drizzled into the nippy day. The antiquated brick venue towered over the narrowly cobbled street as seminar hopefuls made their way closing umbrellas upon entry. It lacked elegance but presented stark, polished, and serviceable. The warmth of the meeting room welcomed them to find their slightly cushioned sets, all the better to stay alert. One could hear some quiet chatter from the more social and those acquainted.

Kirsten Grundman brought a ray of sunshine to the stage. Her cheery smile and friendly voice welcomed everyone to the *Hidden Trauma Detective Seminar.* Her granola choice for the day included green Birkenstocks with thick gray wool socks, a straight brown tweed skirt, and a forest green turtleneck under a thickly woven ivory sweater. Dishwater hair hugged her rosy cheeks and fell on her shoulders as she spoke. She gave venue instructions, followed by a glowing introduction for Lydia.

"Welcome! Thank you, Kirsten, for inviting me to the Netherlands again. It is such an honor to be with and to talk to survivors and overcomers," Lydia enthusiastically greeted. Then, she smiled upward to face the translator, "What a delight to work with you again, Rolf."

An affectionate smile preceded the soft sound of a slight bow wrinkling his fashionable leather attire. Rolf Gehrke translated for Lydia at previous conferences and counseling schools in Germany. *But, sadly, his radio program audiences do not see his handsome, chiseled face and warm chestnut eyes,* Lydia pondered.

Holding up a paper in one hand and a pen in the other, Lydia instructed, "Please write any questions which come to your mind. There will be time to answer questions not answered in the presentation during the last session.

"I understand that you experienced a lot of physical, mental, emotional and spiritual pain for which there seems to be little help or cure. I am sorry that you suffered so long! I feel sad that you took so much medicine that did not help much or worsen things. The agony of decision making and difficulty in relationships, private and in the workplace, need not continue. People should not spend most of their life in counselors' offices. Hospitalization experience in a psychiatric unit can be humiliating and frustrating, especially when another mental illness labels you with little improvement. I believe some things you will learn today are vital enough to make a positive and hopeful change to your life."

Lydia paused as Rolf translated. Translation time cuts a message time almost in half. It is necessary to use simple English spoken slowly for complete understanding by most audiences. Even though English is an offered subject in Europe, everyone is not fluent. Academic teaching is usually high English, even technical, so adjusting can also challenge a speaker.

"I am here now for two reasons. First, to respond to my dear client's pleas to get this information out there so others who suffer as they did will get the help they need and hope to live. Hundreds of them suggested that I talk to you the same way I talk with them.

"The second reason is equally important. My heart aches for the thousands or, more accurately, tens of thousands of people who suffer like you. They never received an accurate diagnosis or were accurately diagnosed but did not receive the kind of interventions or treatments which bring healing."

In her customary manner, Lydia left the lectern walking to one side of the podium to express an idea, then crossing to the opposite side, focusing on another topic. "Sometimes we like to know something about the person who speaks to us. I worked for over thirty-five years with severely traumatized people. As a Registered Nurse, I mainly focused on the physical traumas. In the capacity of a prayer counselor, I mainly focus on the severe mental, emotional, and spiritual traumas people experience. "Of course," she continued, "there are often physical traumas in these cases, but other traumas often cause physical problems. We call those psychosomatic illnesses in medicine. Research tells us that eighty percent of physical illnesses' origins are psychosomatic, not caused by violence, accidents, or microbes we commonly call germs.

"It is instructive to define trauma, so we are all on the same page. But first I want to introduce Tirza Piltz, who will assist me with PowerPoint presentations. I currently mentor her for certification as a prayer counselor for severe trauma. We will travel together throughout this European Tour. She assists with seminars, training other counselors, and counseling. Won't it be great for a capable European to serve?" she smiled approvingly at her.

When the applause ceased and Tirza repositioned herself at the computer, Lydia began the PowerPoint definition and instructions. "Trauma results from a physical injury or a violently produced wound. It is an emotional experience or shock with lasting psychological effects in psychiatry.

"Most of my clients over twenty-five years of age received a diagnosis of fibromyalgia. This disease can be a very debilitating, painful condition. It is a great joy to see pain reduction and increased mobility in people who heal from the recovered or remembered traumatic events.

"Trauma is stored physically as body memories. One client suffered severe shoulder pain resulting in a non-functioning arm. The family doctor found no cause and referred her to a specialist who could not identify the cause of the problem. He suggested exploratory surgery, to which she almost succumbed. Upon learning of the impending surgery, we focused upon any trauma to the shoulder as a priority. Sure enough, as we discovered and processed the trauma, the pain ceased, and function returned without unnecessary surgery."

An emotional flurry filled the atmosphere. So many excited whispers and note taking scratches sounded among the hopeful smiles.

Lydia continued, "Many people go through life with various problems and do not realize these are symptoms of hidden trauma. Now we can be trauma detectives. Here are the clues, symptoms, and indicators." She turned to the screen and introduced the following list:

1. Repeated negative patterns in life
2. Repeated dreams
3. Flashbacks
4. Abreactions [psychological term for reliving an experience by memory]
5. Body memories
6. Overreactions
7. Food reactions
8. Oversensitivity to sound, flashing lights, hand movements
9. Time loss
10. Interrupted thought
11. Unexplained illnesses
12. Inappropriate need to please
13. Problematic need to be in control/authority
14. Inability to remember childhood
15. Sudden changes in mood
16. Use of the pronoun WE about self
17. Headaches or dizziness

18. Secretiveness or refusal to reveal personal experiences
19. Urgency about time
20. Sense of being ripped off.
21. Trouble staying awake during worship / *Bible* teaching
22. Highly developed use of imagery/suggestible
23. Uneven achievement in school
24. Report hearing inner voices
25. Sleep disturbances
26. Denial of actions observed by others
27. Memory loss

"Do you identify with many of these? If you answer 'yes,' you may harbor hidden trauma. I see it is time for a break. We resume in fifteen minutes," Lydia announced.

Rolf hurried off to smoke while Kirsten, Tirza, and Lydia relaxed in a private break room. After enjoying the refreshments, they laughed together as they simultaneously applied lipstick. Lydia's mother initiated the winning tradition with her family females, and now it served as a bonding exercise. Fifteen minutes flew.

"Kirsten treated me to your amazing Dutch pancakes upon my arrival in Amsterdam. I never imagined that delicacy here. Yum! Thank you, staff, for such a delicious break," Lydia laughed as she rubbed her tummy, and the crowd joined in gratitude.

Lydia began, "The wonderful human design enables people to escape to a safe place within their minds. When they experience real or perceived trauma, the mind can simultaneously create a version of themselves that can survive it. We call this escaping or coping mechanism Dissociative Identity Disorder. I shall refer to it as DID from now on. DID often presents with awareness of memory losses such as no remembrance of being somewhere, spending money, or making a commitment. Commonly clients complain of others accusing them of saying something they don't think they said, acting childishly or differently, which they strongly deny.

"We best understand dissociation as a continuum. We all dissociate. Young children easily dissociate. There are degrees of increasing separations from self. Normal is on one end of the continuum, not the setting on your clothes drier. On the other end, we might even find the inability to know what a part or alter, a dissociated aspect of the person, is doing. This inability is known as an amnesic state or lack of co-consciousness. The most significant degree of separation is DID.

DISSOCIATION CONTINUUM

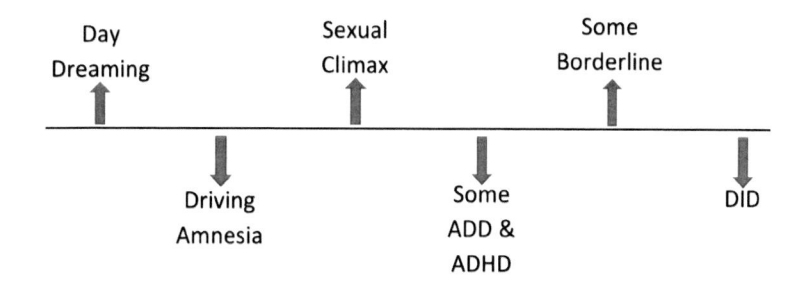

Day Dreaming ↑		Sexual Climax ↑		Some Borderline ↑	
	↓ Driving Amnesia		↓ Some ADD & ADHD		↓ DID

"My design of this continuum includes a condition called borderline personality. An internationally renowned author and prayer counselor once described this condition as hemophilia of emotions. Just as the blood disorder, hemophilia lacks the clotting mechanism for stopping bleeding, borderline personality disorder lacks regulation or stopping mechanisms for the emotions. I think this condition is a dissociated part of the person whose job is to contain only emotions. I believe this because I "called out" another part or alter, and the undesirable emotional state stopped. Although this result may not be actual for all people diagnosed as borderline, it certainly is for many.

"Likewise, I believe that many cases, not all, of attention deficit disorder (ADD) and attention deficit hyperactive disorder (ADHD) are a forms of dissociation. In these cases, the lack of focus or concentration is due to the interruption of other alters or parts trying to do their function or jobs."

A fervor of conversation rose in the room. Lydia patiently waited for attention to return.

"A woman in her early forties came for prayer counseling. She still lived with her very critical mother. Her part-time bakery job provided her only friends. Although intelligent and creative, she was labeled ADD in elementary school and could not focus long enough to get higher education for a better job. Nevertheless, she managed to move to her bachelorette apartment away from her mother's destructive control, resolved the trauma, attended, and graduated from a community college to secure a fulfilling career, and developed healthy relationships.

"I also believe that some forms, not all, of autism are the result of extensive dissociation in the womb or prenatal period of development. I found autistic alters within people."

A rustle of activity and chatting stirred. Lydia waited.

"Why am I telling you this? Because too many people wear inaccurate life-long hopeless labels complete with harmful medications. Dissociation can heal without drugs," Lydia almost shouted. "I believe that some conditions mentioned above are actually DID. Instead of putting children and adults on drugs, we should first resolve severe trauma."

Lydia pointed to the screen, "Other forms of dissociation exist. For example, have you heard about someone away from home who can't remember their past or identity? This type of dissociation is called a *dissociative fugue*. Some intriguing literature and movies become constructed upon this type.

"Many episodes of *Dissociative amnesia* with the inability to remember personal information is due to trauma and not simple forgetfulness.

Another form is called *depersonalization disorder.* One's body or mind feels persistently or recurrently detached from the experience. It is like a dream, but the reality is still intact.

"Many different opinions exist about how common this condition is. In 1990 estimates quoted two and one half million people were victims of satanic ritual abuse alone. satanic abuse is highly traumatizing. In 1992, a leading American therapist suggested four and one half million people presented with DID. In1996, a famous Canadian therapist estimated that half of ten and one-half million DID people received an accurate diagnosis. Psychiatric hospital inpatient percentages range from ten to fifty percent. Psychiatry thought this condition extremely rare, which resulted in misdiagnoses. The psychiatric community only recently began to treat DID.

"There are highly respected psychiatrists today who tell you DID does not exist. I sincerely question their intentions. Most university texts of psychology mainly describe DID as extremely rare and only give it a short paragraph. Thousands of people are seeking help around the world for this condition. Thankfully, with the appropriate interventions, the service from people who understand dissociation, and the know-how, the cure rate is 80-90%. Why only 80-90 percent? The cure rate and speed of healing depend upon many factors.

"The most important is the desire for healing. Sadly, some people develop the comfort of being the victim. People do not essentially enjoy this victim mentality, but they are used to it. Human beings are creatures of habit. Moving out of co-dependence feels too challenging to accomplish.

"As a public health nurse, I labored to arrange resources for a victim of domestic violence and her abused children to escape. Often, the victim sabotages the plan at the last minute because she thinks it will be too demanding on her own. But of course, it is not since many do escape by finally believing in who they are. They learn assertiveness, and good communication coping skills in place of destructive coping mechanisms or dissociation.

"They may depend on governmental funding for living expenses and do not want to give that up. Some people like to punish their family for the abuse and do so by being a dependent burden. A healthy adult citizen is independent of such subsidies.

"Perhaps the strongest deterrent is fear. Many DID people experienced evil cults who performed unthinkable rituals. Victims of governmental or conspiratorial groups suffered clinically performed procedures to induce dissociation for mind control. There are many threats regarding 'telling' or retrieving the memories in all these situations. Their observations of the persons who threaten them lead them to believe such threats are possible. If they ever divulge the secrets, they, a family member, friend, pet, counselor, et cetera, will be harmed or killed. I hold no interest in the secrets, just the client's freedom," Lydia concluded as she reorganized her notes.

Kirsten swept onto the stage and asked, "Is anyone as hungry as I? Lunchtime! Enjoy!

There are lists of restaurants and maps in your packet. We resume at 14:00."

Rolf, Kirsten, Tirza, and Lydia spent the subsequent half-hour debriefing. They sat in an austere yet immaculate dining room in the facility. The Catholic nuns who ran the venue in Den Hauge served their lunch later. Being leaders in the Catholic Renewal Movement, Kirsten and her husband, Günther, retained the venue for the seminar. Frequently attendees requested counseling even though the registration forms clearly stated that none would be available. This desperate need felt extracting for Lydia, but now she must focus on awakening and educating.

Standing for hours and the strain of being translated called for a rest. The chilly dining room urged Lydia to return to the break room, kick off her heels and snuggle in a blanket with a hot cup of herbal tea. She liked her own company. Shortly before 14:00, Rolf, Kirsten, and Tirza joined Lydia to pray for the afternoon session. Giggling at a high pitch while Rolf rolled his eyes and shook his head, the three ninety women ended lunchtime with their lipstick tradition.

Kirsten announced a ninety-minute teaching time followed by a fifteen-minute Q&A period. Lydia began with, "I hope you delighted in a refreshing lunchtime. If any of this material is disturbing, I encourage you to leave this area until you recover before you return. There is no provision for counseling at this seminar.

"I am often asked, 'How long will the healing take?' The standard length for working through complex DID in a secular counseling environment is around ten years. It is around three years or less with Christian Prayer Counseling. These figures assume there are no interruptions in the process.

"I trained many intern and resident prayer counselors. They usually remarked that my style was unique in that I taught during the prayer counseling. I firmly believe in teaching clients how to fish rather than only giving them a fish. Dedication to the process is primary. A motivated person can do much healing work outside of the counseling office. Some of my clients soar through the memory work once they learn the tools.

"A survivor must accomplish memory work of trauma to heal. It is not easy, but it is some of the best work a person will ever do for themselves. Now it will be less arduous and less fearful. Unfortunately, life happens despite dedication to the process and a sincere desire for healing. Some clients endured healing interruptions due to illness, unemployment, surgery, divorce, or the death of a loved one.

"It is not wise to do trauma work during pregnancy due to possible adverse effects upon the little person in the womb. Thoughts and feelings are electrochemical. The mother's electrochemical thoughts and feelings pass through the placental membrane to the baby's fetal bloodstream. So, if mommy is sad, the baby is sad. If mommy is thinking disturbing thoughts, the baby is disturbed. You can probably see now how trauma occurs in the womb. So if a client becomes pregnant, we mainly work on life skills, ensuring the baby's mother will deliver the infant without interruption from other aspects of her personality.

"Once, I worked with a group of clients who all progressed very well. Then, suddenly, one of the women's healing significantly slowed. Finally, after much prodding, I discovered her abusive alcoholic husband. We only heal when we are safe.

"It may be necessary to move to obtain safety. One client began her healing journey at sixty and realized she could not stay in her home. Her husband, fifteen years older than she, resembled the mostly old men abusers! He was extremely gracious during her time away. Once her memories of the sexual abuse from older men healed, she safely returned to her husband and home. The old man image was a "trigger" of previous trauma.

"Even though the desire for healing may be passionate, the ability to trust may be non-existent due to many repeated traumas and betrayals in a person's life. Distrust is especially pervasive if the people supposed to protect and provide for them perpetrated the abuse. Trust is necessary for building rapport or a working relationship with someone, certainly with a therapist, physician, or prayer counselor. Trust is earned, which may take a long time.

"In conclusion, we looked at indicators of trauma and learned that many people hold hidden trauma which continually causes problems in their daily lives. Unremembered trauma often accounts for physical pain for which there seems to be no medical basis or treatment. Tens of thousands of people worldwide suffer from subconscious trauma, misdiagnoses, and wrong treatments. Severe trauma often results in a condition known as dissociation. There are different types and degrees of dissociation; the most extensive is DID. Since DID is not biochemically based, 80-90% of the cases are curable. Recovery rate depends on the healing desired, environmental safety, minimal interruptions, courage to do memory recall, and willingness to examine belief systems (since lies we believe cause our pain). The trauma victim must risk building trust with a capable person who understands the condition and can offer appropriate treatments or interventions.

"I see it is 15:30, and I smell the coffee. Some of you may need it," Lydia teased.

Taking the microphone, Kirsten said, "Some of you asked about resources. I'll give instructions for purchasing DVDs and CDs for this seminar at the book table after Lydia concludes with your questions. Enjoy your fifteen-minute break."

Elevating herself onto a stool next to Rolf's, Lydia asked for the first question. A young woman in her thirties asked if it were possible for Lydia to diagnose her quickly. "I am not a licensed diagnostician. That means, I cannot give a diagnosis to a person. Some people who come to me for prayer counseling received a diagnosis of DID from a licensed diagnostician.

Others self-diagnosed and some learned that the interventions I practice proved successful with someone with DID and the same problems they are experiencing.

"The focus of work with my clients is not a diagnosis or label but what they believe. We discover the belief systems and then analyze them to find truth. Reality is not necessarily the truth. What a surprise to learn that! The person then decides to keep the old belief or change. We never get a different result if we keep thinking and doing the same things. The lies we believe cause most of our pain. Sometimes, after a client works with their brokenness, they may want to verify it with a diagnosis. I encourage them to do so. The only problem is that DID people can sometimes fool even the most astute psychological tests. That is one reason why getting an accurate diagnosis of DID is often so difficult. Next question?"

A distinguished-looking gentleman asked his question in excellent English, causing Rolf to startle as he transitioned to Dutch. "Do you work alone, or what exactly is your model of therapy?" he asked.

"I believe a team approach is essential. Through the years, I greatly appreciated and respected the physicians, nurses, therapists, nutritionists, social workers, other prayer counselors, clergy, dedicated support people from many walks of life, and certainly the family and friends. They coordinated their services and assistance with my work. A popular adage states, 'It takes a community to rear a child'. I believe it also takes a community to heal a person. Thank you for your question."

"The woman next to the oval window; what is your question?" Lydia asked.

"I relate to most of what you taught. I am wondering, since you are a Christian and I am not if you could help me?" she queried as she adjusted the hijab on her shiny ebony hair.

"Chances are that many victims are of different beliefs and orientations. Some of you may be Agnostics, Atheists, Buddhists, Catholics, Cultists, Christians, satanists, et cetera. I minister to people of many religions and orientations. I usually work with an intercessor and depend on the leading and insights that Jesus Christ of Nazareth provides. Some of you may know He lived over 2000 years ago. He served an amazing ministry of healing and miracles for about three and a half years while living on earth. Jesus Christ never required that a person become a Christian to heal them. That did not change. He overcame death and is alive and active today via His Holy Spirit. His enormous love for all people and desire for them to live abundantly healthy free lives is constant.

"He is the only Person I know who is aware of all details of every person's life, as well as their ancestry. What a terrific resource when one cannot remember what trauma happened to them! He also has authority over evil spiritual forces which often capture and harass victims of trauma."

Lydia's face beamed as she said, "I am extremely grateful to work with such a Great Physician and Wonderful Counselor as Jesus Christ of Nazareth. My statistics show that to date, we have helped approximately a thousand severely traumatized, fragmented people from around the globe to become unified as created and set free from terrible bondage. It has been a pleasure talking to you. For more information, check the website listed on my card for many teaching articles about DID, its history, causes, the effects upon people and society, other resources, as well as the store."

"I want to thank Rolf sincerely. A great job, Rolf—so fluid!" Lydia crooned. Rolf offered a mischievous smile as he stood and waved a hand toward Tirza. The people stood and extended applause to Lydia's following expression of gratitude.

"I also want to thank Kirsten and this facility for making this time together possible. May the Creator richly bless you and yours. Thank you!"

Kirsten handed a profuse bouquet to Lydia, saying, "We want to thank you, Lydia, for your dedication, sharing your experience, knowledge, and love. Thank you, everyone, for the other great questions we did not address today, such as satanic ritual abuse, governmental mind control, differences between schizophrenia and DID, and the reality of demons. These frequently asked questions are on Lydia's website. She will be addressing some of them in Kassel, Germany, at the *Stranger Than Fiction Conference* noted in your packet. Details are available at the book table. The standing ovation resumed, faded, and then the room was alone.

Lydia felt energized talking with attendees from many countries at the book table; however, deciphering the numerous accented English conversations proved draining with a headache. Rolf needed to hurry back home to Germany. Tirza, Kirsten, and Lydia found a quaint family restaurant for dinner. The soft lighting hummed along with the tune of voices embracing good friends, relaxation, and satisfied palates. Sleep promised sweet regeneration tonight, but little did they know what tomorrow would bring.

CHAPTER 13

LEAVING AND TOURING

KNOCK, KNOCK, KNOCK,... KNOCK, KNOCK, KNOCK, KNOCK, KNOCK! "Wake up, Lydia," Tirza's demanding voice finally connected with Lydia's consciousness. They had planned for all to sleep in, hang out and relax after the full-day seminar. Although Lydia was tired, she wasn't sleepy and began to read the new Book Club assignment brought to her by Cavanaugh. She didn't know how late or early she went to sleep, but it evidenced sweet until now. She alerted herself upright and threw on a robe while calling, "I'm coming, I'm coming."

Seas of blue overflowing onto flushed cheeks met her eyes. Tirza shook and stammered. Lydia gathered her into her arms and encouraged her to weep. When the sounds of anguish subsided, Tirza's cheek lifted the saturated fabric of Lydia's robe as she straightened to explain herself.

"My brother's phone call from a hospital awakened me. My mother fell down a flight of stairs; you know her curved marble stairway. She suffered a concussion and broke her right hip. She is unconscious, and they suspect a stroke too, so plan more tests. I need to be there! I checked before coming to you. A flight can get me there in an hour and a half if I quickly catch a plane at The Hague Airport in Rotterdam. It is only 16.4 kilometers away, but

I need to leave in twenty minutes to make it. Oh, Lydia, I am so sorry to disappoint you and leave you stranded like this. You know how much and how long I looked forward to this tour. I'll join you as soon as I can, but I know you understand that I must go!"

"Absolutely. Don't give that another thought. God is not surprised and has everything needed in place, but we need to find His provision. What can I do now to help?" Lydia asked.

"You can grab some cheese, bread, and water for me to take along. Could you bring it to my room and help with packing? I'm not as neat as you. I need everything with me, and my things are strewn everywhere."

Kirsten arrived in Tirza's doorway with a questioning expression and robe flying behind, resembling a super-hero in pajamas. She asked, "What is going on? Günther and I proceeded with our devotions when I felt an urgency to come here."

"I'll explain later. Can you please take this suitcase to the elevator and hold it for us?" Lydia responded.

Tirza's cab arrived and left on time to meet the plane. Lydia reported the events to Kirsten and Günther as all three savored cups of aromatic tea, still attired in their robes. They prayed for Tirza's situation and thanked Jesus for direction and provision for the coming tour days. The relaxation highlighted the stress of the morning, so they warmed themselves with another cup of tea. At the same time, Günther gave a short travel log in preparation for tomorrow's sightseeing.

Kirsten's eyes searched her husband's face in communication known to married couples. She smiled and then asked, "Lydia, would it be appropriate for me to intercede for the prayer counseling scheduled here? I know how you function in sessions. I seriously doubt Tirza will be able to rejoin you soon, and counseling begins the day after tomorrow. Günther and I discussed this experience possibility in the past, and he encouraged me."

Feeling stunned, Lydia paused, then broadly smiled a deep sigh. She briskly flung little streams of gratitude away from her chin and said, "He's a speedy guy, our Jehovah Jireh—the Lord will provide. I am honored you requested to do this with and for the client and me. Yes. Thank you so much. This absence posed my main concern since Tirza left. I always feel strongly about the Bible's mandate: 'They go two by two'. The immense spiritual warfare involved with DID counseling screams for knowledgeable experienced prayer intercession. My staff at home prays for us, but there is no substitute for support at hand. Of course, we need to make time today or tomorrow to orient you to the procedures. Could we do that after lunch to be sure we are well prepared and not mix pleasure with business tomorrow?"

"I would prefer after dinner since it is already close to lunchtime. I haven't even dressed yet, let alone done errands in preparation for tomorrow," Kirsten chuckled.

Lydia used the day to review client files, prepare an outline for Kirsten's benefit and strengthen herself for the upcoming counseling session.

The next day's weather proved discouraging. An overcast sky sent chilling winds. Nevertheless, the excitement among the three early birds spawned an atmosphere for fun. Lydia related being in Germany some years ago and driving to France for a holiday on a miserable rainy day. Some of the women complained. Another shared the teaching about our mandate 'to have dominion over the earth.' She declared, "It will not rain on us!" The others scoffed, but every time they left the auto to walk to a restaurant, cathedral, et cetera., it stopped raining. By the end of the long day, their faith enlarged. "We could do that declaration!" Lydia offered.

Günther said, "That would be a stretch for me, but when we visit Madurodam this afternoon, I will welcome warm sunshine because it requires a lot of outdoor time. I thought to visit Keukenhof first because it is farthest, and hours can fly by drinking its beauty. It also provides pavilions for shelter." He beamed love-filled regret to Kirsten, "Kirsten prepared a lovely picnic for us. If rain continues, there is a fine restaurant there for whenever we get hungry."

Awe filled their time at the enormous Keukenhof Pavilions. Each exclaimed amazement at the innumerable varieties of tulips, hyacinths, and daffodils. Keukenhof receives credit as the largest and most famous flower park globally. More than seven million flowers adorn the grounds in the spring. It is located a half-hour from Den Haag and not far from Amsterdam. One of the many pavilion rest areas provided a comfortable site to enjoy the tasty picnic that Kirsten specially prepared. Whenever precipitation slowed, they umbrellaed their way into the vast 32 hectares of color and intoxicating fragrances, which temporarily lifted them from troubled earth to heaven.

It was 14:30 when they started back to the Scheveningen district of Den Haag to visit Madurodam Park. It displays scale model replicas of some of the most famous Dutch castles, public buildings, and industrial projects. It offers interactive activities for tourists. Since opening on July 2, 1952, it has wowed more than fifty million visitors. Originally built to honor resistance hero George Maduro, its revenues go to the Madurodam Support Fund Society for children in need. Kirsten delighted in Steden Rijk, featuring old town centers. They marveled at the Wereldkijker, a globe replica that pointed out Dutch accomplishments. What a marvel considering the country's small size. Lydia delighted in one of the many interactive, hands-on experiences by helping a plane take off from Schipol Airport. Günther prevented a flood by operating the Oosterscheldekering storm surge barrier. Perhaps the epitome of the tour occurred at one of the three themed areas, the 'Wadden Sea.' They realized children shrieked with glee as they splashed diamonds into the bright warm sunshine.

CHAPTER 14

OFFICE WEIRDNESS

"How crazy difficult to find a replacement for one week! That's the fifteenth temp I've interviewed," Saqqara snarled aloud to herself. She looked up from her desk. Hot embarrassment agitated her to see an important-looking woman poised with a smug, dignified smile inside her office doorway. *Who is she?*

"Maybe you underestimate your extraordinary ability and value. I easily comprehend the impossibility of replacing you even for one hour, my Dear. May I?" Her left hand pointed to the plush green and white striped channel-backed chair, and she spoke as she settled herself. "I need to apologize for this unscheduled appearance, but I just lunched with a leading member of the Cultural Foundation! Last fall, I praised your work with me for the Mergecco League's homecoming gala. To make a long story short, you will be getting a call very soon," Adriana Byerson cooed with great aplomb.

"Yes, excuse me, do make yourself comfortable. May I get you anything?" Saqqara widely gestured.

"Thank you. Actually, I'm engaged soon, Dear. Still, I wanted you to get the good news straight from me. Also, since we share history, could we consider a standing fall contract? I know calendars fill up quickly."

A shift with recognition of the client brought relief and soothed Saqqara's being, "That's exciting news. Thank you so much for your influential recommendation. I'll inform Tiffany of your request and get back to you."

Adriana Byerson dove into her Fendi Selleria purse and grandly surfaced to offer a card, naming the caller. Then, she excused herself and exited the elaborate doorway. Her bag floated from her outstretched arm like a merchant presenting a product.

The next day Tiffany received the prospect of a standing contract with one of Chicago's most prestigious historic clubs. She eagerly anticipated what offer they would get from the foundation in ecstasy. But when Tiffany learned Saqqara had not yet hired a temp, her excitement cooled. While shooting arrows with her ebony eyes, she said, "We must hire someone by the end of the week! I need to be comfortable with this person too!"

Two hopefuls filled Saqqara's mind by the end of the twelve-hour day. First, she met a friendly young woman in a wheelchair when entering the apartment building. Her engaging face reminded her of the woman in a window the day she arrived home in the taxi—deep dimples presented along with an inviting smile. "I hoped to meet you someday. You are famous, you know, a popular event manager for high society. I read the newspapers. My name is Naysa Wallace," she said, offering her velvety soft hand. "I moved to Chicago from Wheaton four months ago for upscale physical therapy—nasty biking accident."

"It's a pleasure to meet you, Naysa. What a lovely and unusual name," Saqqara responded. *There's something so alluring about her personality.*

"Jewish for a miracle of God. I guess my parents were prophetic considering I should be dead," she winked. "Would you like to come in for a latte or cool one?"

Saqqara chuckled. "Thank you very much. A day with no end squeezed into these spiked shoes calls for rest. Maybe another time. It's nice to talk with you," she kindly replied and departed, thankful for the elevator. *Tonight, I must finish the life history and get it e-mailed to Ms. Voight. Why do I get such headaches or blurred vision every time I work on it?*

Saqqara massaged one barefoot with the other. She supported her aching head on the one hand and struggled to see well enough to finish the life history to send it. Finally, exhausted from the long day's work, she fell into bed, grateful to close her eyes from blurred vision.

In Saqqara's apartment, mobile phone music sounds, "Hello? Wrong number," a deep voice croaked.

The phone sounds again, "Good morning. You dialed the wrong number," a child's voice sings.

More mobile music. "Saqqara, this is Tiffany! Stop this nonsense. An applicant here says you scheduled an appointment with us this morning... you never told me... are you there... are you there? Saqqara, answer me!"

CHAPTER 15

LEBENSBORN MAN

Dear Lydia,

Answer me only when you have a chance. I know you are very busy now. I trust you found an intercessor. Please thank Kirsten and Guenter for their incredible hospitality. It didn't even enter my mind as I left. I'll send a note soon.

Now for die Mutter. She is unconscious and in the intensive care unit. Tests continue, and many are not back yet. My brother returns on the weekend. Maybe this is an opportunity to mend our hostilities over der Vater's will. Even though he always lived in cities, my brother got the family farm. My husband and I worked the land for twenty years, which is stereotypical of generational injustice here. The chief is coming. I've got to go, but I'll keep you posted.

Blessings, Tirza

Lydia deftly closed her e-mail and computer. She had been too tired to check it after the delightful day of sightseeing. A glance at her watch hurried her to breakfast.

The first client is due at 08:30. She and Kirsten reached the counseling room at the same time when Lydia recounted Tirza's e-mail. She then gave last-minute details to work with Bernhard Fährmann, now in his seventies but one of the thousands of Lebensborn babies.

"We need to mature and heal all life-long. I worked with people in their 80's," Lydia shared. "I first saw him and his faithful support gentleman twelve years ago. He presented himself as dependent, morbidly obese, severely withdrawn, and painfully fearful of just about anything. It took two years for Johannes and his family to gain limited trust despite housing, transporting, providing meals and clothing for him. At that time, we did a week-long intensive and removed many basic mind-control programs. He sat motionless most of the time. Occasionally triggered, his body thrust up and sat on the back of the chair, frantically hugging a blanket to his chest, all the while glaring emptily. My mentee worried that he might be violent and wanted me to stop meeting with him.

"Those same riveting eyes smiled with contentment the next time I worked with him… two years later, I think. He capably moved into an apartment and held a part-time job, menial but respectable employment. He continued to improve and tried to meet with me whenever I worked in Europe. I think you may remember Birgit, who traveled here with me four years ago. She and I worked with him in Belgium, where he lives. Being a Lebensborn baby also, he identified with her and routinely called her for what he called a 'check-up'. Any questions? Ready?" Lydia smiled with raised eyebrows.

Bernhard Fährmann entered radiant with tears swelling as he quickly strode across the room and extended his hand to Lydia. Their eyes locked in mutual joy and great admiration. His stocky build was supple for his age. His deeply waved silver hair gave him an air of importance. He discovered he was fluent in English, so he no longer needed a translator for prayer counseling sessions. To his amazement, he found fluency in four other languages as well.

"Where would you like me to sit?" he asked, looking about the uninteresting room. Yellow, violet, and pink orchid blossoms on scraggly plants adorned the tall window ledge. Bright orange blooms covered a well-leafed pot, a stark contrast to winter's resilience.

"I know, wherever I am most comfortable," he mimicked and settled into a well-worn leather chair.

"I want you to meet my intercessor, Kirsten Grundman. Please catch us up. What happened since we last met and what brings you here today?" Lydia asked.

"Could we pray first? With what happened, we need it," Bernhard asked with a forced smile. The usual opening prayers of thanksgiving, protection,, and requests for anointing and direction followed. Next, Lydia asked Bernhard if he wanted to permit whatever the Holy Spirit wanted to do in the session. That done, Kirsten poured cups of coffee.

"Well, as you can see, I maintained a healthy weight. The secondary diabetes is gone, although I admit to a powerful temptation by any candy on a stick." Scooting to the edge of the chair, he laughed and said, "In my old age, I am going uphill instead of downhill. Strangely though, that is why I am here. You knew I contacted Birgit early in 2013 after viewing *Die Tribute Von Panem—The Hunger Games* movie. The triggers in it destabilized me for several months."

"I remember that movie well; calls swamped my office, and I made a point to see it," Lydia interjected.

"Birgit helped me get back to normal, but we never accessed any alter trauma then. Perhaps you are aware… I'm sure you are in the work you do, of the trials in the recent past in Brussels at the International Common Law Court of Justice. Well, I followed those trials as often as possible by various modalities. There are documents of over ten million Catholic priest child sex cases as of 2013. More than 350,000 are suspected to be in Catholic child mass grave sites in Ireland, Spain, and Canada. But the part I want to get to, is the 2014 Leopold's Against Church Terror Survivors Network, which headed a witness delegation. It prosecuted global elite members of the Ninth Circle satanic Child Sacrifice Cult.

"At least eight witnesses testified that Pope Francis, former Pope Ratzinger, or Panchon were present at child sacrifices. The court received evidence that the Vatican used covert means to interrupt the trials. Panchon stepped down. Ratzinger resigned on February 29, 2013, a few days after being found guilty of crimes against humanity. Six hundred years have passed since another pope did so.

"You know, most of the royals, government ministers of Belgium and England, cardinals, judges…," Bernhard Fährmann's entire body shaking released the bitter tears. Then, in a furious voice, he looked up and shouted, "God, how can such evil hide as the Church?"

Kirsten silently prayed in her spiritual language. Pale vertical lines striped Lydia's rouge as she reached out and took Bernhard's hand.

"Ahem, ahem," cleared the way to the point. I know that I participated in some of the elite's games. I also remember some well-known royals, cardinals, and big wigs. Sure, one might accuse me of making that up based on the stories I just heard. I recognized one of the women who testified.

"Since seeing *The Hunger Games* movie, I have experienced nightmares about being chased nude and dodging bullets. I also experienced weird symptoms since I started to follow the trials. That is why we are here today," pushing back into the chair, he turned to Kirsten and asked for a warm-up."

Lydia observed Kirsten's noticeable distress. "Perhaps this is an excellent time to take a short break." When Bernhard left the room, Lydia closed the door and walked to Kirsten's side to burden-bare her anguish.

"I'm a Catholic. Working with the Catholic Renewal, I know hundreds of Catholics are true believers in Christ and do not do satanic rituals. I don't know how I missed all that news, and I don't want to believe it anyway!" Kirsten sobbed.

After a while, Lydia offered, "Owners of the mainline newspapers and media strangled the majesty of pure journalism long ago. The New Testament warned that even the elect could be deceived in the last days. Some of my closest friends are Catholics who live their faith in Jesus, not Mariolatry, satanism, or superficial religion. Tragically some Catholics, Protestants, and others are guilty of such heinous crimes."

"Is the break over?" could be heard from the other side of the door. The ladies dabbed their eyes. Kirsten shook her head in the affirmative, and both found smiles in greeting their client.

"What are some of the symptoms you are experiencing?" Lydia inquired.

"Weird sensations in different parts of my body, especially at night. It feels like sharp pricks. I get achy muscles for no reason, bad headaches, or sores on my head. I sometimes see strange things, but whatever it was is gone when I blink. When I first started seeing you, alters caused trouble because they thought you were dangerous? Similar stuff occurred before this appointment, which completely stopped a long time ago."

Lydia repositioned and then focused on her notes, "Have you had any eye surgeries? Have you been in a hospital recently or gotten the many recommended immunizations?"

"I got the flu shot last fall and a cataract operation… come to think about it, the strange pictures occur in that eye."

Lydia opened a book, "I feel led to use a special prayer of protection. I highly recommend this book for your library." Holding it up for Bernhard and Kirsten to see, she explained, "The author and intercessor teams do spiritual research and then formulate these prayers. The book is like a second Bible for me, but, as you know, I am fairly direct and find the prayers a bit lengthy and often reconstruct them for my purposes. A timely prayer, for now, is dealing with powers. I always require you to preview the material before agreeing to it. So, after reviewing it, if you agree, do you want to read it aloud or give a verbal, "I agree" after I read it?"

"I know the power of declaration, but I also know faith comes by hearing. My faith needs strengthening today, so I'll repeat after you if that's okay?" he answered, reaching for the abbreviated prayer. After reading through it, he handed it back to Lydia, who read short portions as follows, followed by Bernhard, who declared, "I agree!"

"I declare that I once slaved under the elemental spirits of this world. God the Father sent His Son, Jesus, to be born of a virgin, under the law to redeem me from the law. God sent the spirit of His Son into my heart. He adopted me into His family with the full rights of a son. I am no longer a slave but an heir of the Father."

"I renounce and ask forgiveness for myself along with my ancestors for belief in and practice of all ungodly philosophies, traditions, and religious reliance on the law and ungodly magical beliefs in the four elements of creation fire, water, air, and earth."

"I command that all magnets, cylinders, tubing, capacitors, implants, antennas, and any other devices placed in or on me be deactivated. If possible, I command them to leave along with all ungodly powers and to go straight to the feet of Jesus. Lord, place me on Your frequency and bring all magnetic fields influencing me into correct alignment and balance."

"Father, remove all dominions, thrones, and rulers aligned with these powers. Send Your holy fire to consume all evil associated with these powers."

"Thank you for returning all the enemy stole from me and my generations. I thank you for releasing me into my personal and generational birthright."

"I declare that I am seated with Christ in heavenly places with the enemy under my feet. Father, thank you for free will!"

Bernhard sat open-mouthed; eyes closed with arms raised. Presently, his eyes fluttered, and he stirred to relax, "Whew, what was that? After almost every declaration, I felt movement in different parts of my body."

"Remember things in the spirit parallel the physical. Spiritual devices, even weapons, can be found in or on a person's body due to witchcraft, curses, et cetera. Things such as nanochips are so small they can be inserted into our bodies with a large needle or deposited under our skin. A remaining scar is almost invisible, resembling a cosmetic dermatological operation. Millions of people are now chipped and probably with more than one chip. They are not new because the enemy elite uses most technologies at least twenty years before commoners even know they exist. The rapidity of knowledge of neurotechnology is growing exponentially. It can control a person by inducing pain or introjected thoughts microscopically.

"You have no doubt heard of the USA school shootings. Police investigations of the shooters almost always find satanic involvement evidence and a history of what we might refer to as anti-social behavior. The elite uses these mind-controlled enslaved people to inflame compassion to motivate demand for more gun control. Programmed, sick, or chipped people who kill are at fault, not guns. Most people with guns are not human killers. If people let their emotions rule, fail to get the facts, and allow the right to defend themselves to be lost, they will be more enslaved and or slaughtered.

"The prayer requested that devices be deactivated and, if possible, to leave. Almighty God can do anything, but if He chooses not to remove all possible implants, we need to do something. Do you still journal?"

Bernhard's teeth sparkled, "Oh yes! Maybe not daily, but journaling is a lifesaver for me, especially when my alters robbed me of time. Why do you ask?"

"For homework, I want you to go back into your journals and look for the symptom, time of day, week, year, and location when you noticed it.

"Wait, wait," he interrupted. "I need to write this down." Kirsten held up a paper and assured him that she was scribing for him.

Continuing, Lydia listed "duration, people you were around at the time, and any changes at your apartment. Touch the areas where the symptoms seem to occur most often to see if you can

Lebensborn Man

palpate, feel, any structure. Now, I am going to offer a silly-sounding suggestion. Wrap your head in aluminum foil tonight!"

Bernhard guffawed, "Aluminum foil—you want me to be the Tinman?" Laughter filled the room. Then Lydia penned a name on one of her cards.

"You can put your computer genius to work for yourself now by going online and reading some material of this particle physicist. She also sponsors interviews on YouTube. Ask the Holy Spirit to highlight what you need to know and take notes. Any questions?"

"It's always a trip to be with you, Lydia. Thank you so much. I get it! A pleasure to meet you, Kirsten. Thank you for the coffee. Same time tomorrow?"

"Same time… shall we pray?" Lydia offered.

> "Dearest Heavenly Father, thank You for this divine appointment. Thank You for all-knowing and leading us to the resources we need. It is comforting to know as Bernhard leaves, You are with him to guide and protect him. As he learns more about nanotechnology and its nefarious evil uses, I ask he will not be overwhelmed nor allow the spirit of fear to visit. He does not have a spirit of fear but a strong mind and power in love. I bless him with strength and courage. May any anger be righteous, and its energy directed to what he can do about the situation. Thank You for answering our prayers. In the name of Jesus of Nazareth, Amen."

After Bernhard left, Lydia explained that the renouncements were for females or males because all Christians are sons and brides: a Christian mystery. Then Lydia and Kirsten tidied up the office and enjoyed a hearty midday meal. One of Lydia's previous clients, a psychologist, would bring the next client.

CHAPTER 16

DELIVERANCE

Sunshine flooded the small, tiled entryway as Lydia warmly greeted Brunhilde Hetz, Ph.D., a former client who introduced her patient, Tabea Schichan. The pale thirtyish woman's eyes sunk in purple sadness. She shyly offered her hand as her tall frame withdrew. Her clothes hung limply as Lydia ushered them into the counseling room and proceeded to introduce Kirsten.

Dr. Hetz seated herself and then retrieved her notes from her briefcase for reference and Lydia's release of information form. "We apologize for the life history lack of completion. Tabea reserves little energy, and you know how that document starts things in motion," she said.

Lydia noticed Tabea glancing at a mirror on the wall and asked, "Is there something distracting about the mirror?"

Tabea straightened. Wide eyes stared in response. Dr. Hetz reached out, touched her arm, and explained that demonic appearances in mirrors often terrorize Tabea. Kirsten immediately removed the mirror and laid it on its' face.

"Thank you," said Dr. Hetz as Tabea relaxed.

Lydia queried, "Cell phones? Please do not bring phones or remove the batteries for security's sake.

Deliverance

"Oh, I forgot to tell you, Tabea," apologized Dr. Hetz. Then with eyes darting around the room and in alarm, Tabea plucked her mobile from the worn backpack and removed the batteries with help from Kirsten.

Opening prayers over, the client gave her permission to the Holy Spirit. "I thought it best if I give a summary," explained Dr. Hetz, glancing at Tabea, who stared steadfastly back at her. "Her husband is an extremely controlling man who is physically, emotionally, mentally, sexually and spiritually abusive. We now suspect him to be or to have been her handler. He often travels and leaves her destitute, but his absence allows us to schedule counseling. He requires coitus at least five to six times a day when he is home and ignores her the rest of the time. That much sex is totally off the grid and demoralizes Tabea to say nothing of the physical cost."

Lydia noticed Kirsten's shocked reaction to the required sex. She considered how Brunhilde's suffering enlarged her mercy quotient resulting in her practice of taking on pro bono patients.

Dr. Hetz continued, "We recovered memories of her being tightly swaddled and hung upside down with a butcher hook attached to a metal swivel on the rafters of a castle chamber. She remembers the baron's boisterous glee as he spun her along with other toddlers and babies in the same situation. The dissociation from the traumatic spinning produced available alters programmed after age two, old enough to give consent. We dealt with the memory associated with dismantling the spin program …."

Suddenly a screeching chair toppled, and a chaotic form flailed onto the floor. Dr. Hetz, Lydia, and Kirsten sat immobilized as they helplessly watched Tabea violently assault her private parts with masturbation. At times, the violence bounced her whole body off the parquet floor as her hair flopped about her torqued face and her black eyes gawked. Agonized moans escaped.

Quickly, after what seemed a long time, Lydia stood and proclaimed, "You unclean spirit, are bound to be totally impotent in the name and blood of Jesus Christ!"

Instantly, Tabea jerked like someone released at the shoulders, let out a final groan, and crumpled backward just in time for Dr. Hetz to catch her head and gently lower it to the floor. It was then she noticed Tabea voided during the manifestation of the demon.

Embarrassed, Dr. Hetz's stood over her patient, perplexed about what to do next. Tabea appeared to be asleep or unconscious.

Lydia reached out to lead her out of the room and reassuringly said, "She may need to rest a bit. Kirsten, could you find something to pillow Tabea's head and cover her? I'll take care of this, Brunhilde. There is a rest area next door. We understand these things, don't we? It's not unusual for the client to need time to rest after such an experience."

While Kirsten shared refreshments with Brunhilde in an adjoining room, Lydia looked for cleaning materials. Instead, she found a nun who refused to let her clean up the area alone. As Lydia sopped and mopped around Tabea, satisfying feelings enveloped her as she considered the promise of Ephesians Chapter 1. True Christians who know their identity and inheritance in Jesus Christ and routinely take advantage of God's grace to forgive their sins, have safe power over the demonic. The promise excited her spirit for the rest of the session. After freshening up, she joined the two ladies while the dear nun hurried off to get clothes from the Needy Closet.

About a half-hour later, Tabea stirred. Kirsten decided she would assist her needs by providing professional distance from the psychologist and the prayer counselor.

They reassembled in another room. Lydia reassured Tabea, "There is no reason to feel embarrassed or ashamed. Our bodies, spirit, and soul are one. You were under a spiritual attack, so your precious body also suffered duress. If you remember, we prayed to bind all the demonic at the beginning. That works unless the Lord wants to reveal or get some entity out for good. In that case, He identifies it by letting it show off."

Tabea weakly offered, "Well then, the Lord let it show off for years, especially when my husband is away."

Deliverance

Lydia spoke up, "To clarify, I meant that a Christian could bind the demonic. Have you tried to bind it?"

Looking at Dr. Hetz, Tabea apologized for not telling her about the masturbation. Then she explained that she wasn't allowed to read the Bible or engage in the activities to educate her more about a Christ-like life due to her programming.

Lydia asked Dr. Hetz if they covered sowing and reaping, generational sins, and The Healing Process.

"Actually no, due to many interruptions with cognitive therapy, but as I started to say, we finished the alter integration of the spinning program, and since then, interruptions have been minimal. She requires safety to heal, so I am working with a social worker to explore options for a safe house, but we need to be sure the saboteur alters are healed before that could even have a chance."

"Are you aware of any part of you who is a Christian? Or any part who bitterly hates God, Tabea?" asked Lydia. "If so, it will be important to identify them. I have CDs and DVDs and website teachings on sowing and reaping. I think you must understand those principles for healing. If it is too dangerous to view at home, do you think it would be possible to view them at Dr. Hetz's office?"

She turned to Dr. Hetz, who agreeably nodded to everyone. Lydia expressed her appreciation and then displayed a chart on her computer for all to see. Lydia read, "Once we know the bitter root of a problem, we can resolve it with **The Healing Process**:

- The first step in the process is **awareness** which admits that trauma or wound exists and stops denying it."
- Second, we agree or **confess** to God that sin or an ungodly belief or action exists in relationship to the trauma or wound.
- Step three is **forgiveness.**

"It is often misunderstood. True forgiveness is a decision to give up my right to get even with those I know or perceive hurt me and entrust vengeance to a perfect Holy Judge of Righteousness. Forgiveness," Lydia elaborated, "is the GREAT TRADE—all our chaos and pain for joy and peace. **Forgiveness is not a feeling**, and none is required. It is a **decision** to obey a loving Savior so he may forgive me. In Psalms 94:1, David calls upon the God of vengeance. Verses 21-23 tell us ... *the righteous are tried, and innocent men condemned to death, but the Lord has been his high tower and rock of refuge; God requites the wicked for their injustice and silences them for their misdeeds.*

"There are **two parts** to forgiveness. One, **I forgive** whomever or whatever hurt me. Two, **I ask forgiveness** for my wrong thinking or actions relating to the issue. Those you perceived or know hurt you could be God, others, nature, the spiritual realm, or even yourself. **Forgiveness is the key to freedom**. It is no wonder that satan, all humanity's arch-enemy, works so hard to confuse the understanding of forgiveness.

"I highly recommend you lend Tabea the book on forgiveness I sent to you, Dr. Hetz, it so excellently describes all the wrong ideas about forgiveness.

- Step four is **absolution**.

"That is a fancy word that means you are not guilty anymore. Absolution is spoken and ideally to you by Christians who understand they are priests of the Most High God. They say, 'You are forgiven in Jesus' Name. Receive full release of penalty for your sin and be free.' If there is no one, you can remind yourself, and speaking out aloud is most helpful. This Psalm is comforting: *He has not dealt with us according to our sins, Nor rewarded us according to our iniquities. For as high as the heavens are high above the earth, so great is His steadfast our transgressions from us.* (Psalm 103:10-12).

"Did you see the movie *Braveheart*? It feels like that great ending when Wallace shouts 'FREEDOM!!!!!!!!!!!!!!!!!!'. The similarity in his death is the same as our sin in us gets put to death, and the difference is we are now free to live a more abundant life. There

Deliverance

is often a sense of feeling lighter. The evil entity must leave when no legal right (an ungodly/sinful thought or action) is left. We call that deliverance. Sure, we can exorcise or drive out a demon, but we must remove the legal right, or the demon may come back with more, according to Matthew 12:24. Evil spirits want to reside in humans. Our authority comes from God, Jesus promised, *Truly I say to you, whatever you shall bind on earth shall be bound in heaven; and whatever you loose on earth shall be loosed in heaven.* (Matthew 18:18).

- Step five is **repentance**."

Lydia further taught, "Repentance means to turn away from the old way of thinking or acting. Do a 180! This process is not magic. Most of the time, it is a process and requires your will to change. The good news is that now you can effect changes. Previously you were unaware of the judgments or powerful vows of sowing and reaping. Their bondages keep you from consistent success in developing new healthy holy habits. A vow is a special kind of negative conclusion or judgment, a promise to oneself. It usually sounds like vowing 'I'll never' or 'I'll always.'

"I'm sure you are tired, Tabea. But before you leave, I want to pray trauma off you.

> "Dearest Lord Jesus, we are so grateful that You cherish us so much that You wanted to share Your tremendous power and authority with us. You came to earth to overcome evil. We thank You that we, too, can overcome the evil in ourselves by Your Holy Blood. We are asking for restraining orders from Your Holy Court against all spirits with legal rights which harassed Tabea. Lift the shock, fear, and trauma from her body. Remove the effect of the traumatic memories down to the cellular level. We call upon Living Waters to cleanse her from all sexual defilement. Jesus, You died to take our shame. Thank You."

A draft blew through the room. "Roses…where are the roses?" shining-faced Tabea asked, scanning the austere room noticeably devoid of any flowers or room fresheners. "Oh… it's so…" deeply inhaling the essence, her radiant eyes closed on warm living waters.

Flushed, Kirsten furiously hand fanned herself between pulling off her wool cardigan and apologizing for her menopausal episode. She then looked around to see everybody florid and Lydia's hair wet on the ends.

Euphoria filled Dr. Hetz as she explained they had just witnessed a supernatural personal visit from The Rose of Sharon. Then seeing Tabea frown, she clarified that it is one of many names for Jesus.

Lydia added, "We empathize with your change of life symptoms, Kirsten, but the heat probably emanated from healing. Thank you, everyone, for your patience and endurance on an unforgettable day. Tabea, more happened than we will probably ever know. Have you ever luxuriated in a hot bath of healing Epsom Salts?"

"Dr. Hetz, your counseling priority now is to identify the root for the entity's entrance to close the door permanently. See you tomorrow, same time?"

Gathering personal belongings after their guests left, Kirsten exclaimed, "What an extracting day; it feels like a week! How in the world do you manage to do this all the time? I've never even imagined such stuff."

"Reverend John Sandford once told me that, 'People who do this work tread the sewers of mankind.' I've concluded God made me for this. God equipped me with all the gifts necessary. He continually pours His love through me for people I seriously doubt my carnal self would give the time of day," Lydia commented.

Kirsten dreamily said, "That's something to think about," then quickly changed the subject to inquire about Lydia's comfort.

"It felt uncomfortably cold again last night. I'll run now to buy a sleeping hat and see you at dinner," Lydia told Kirsten.

So good to be outside. Crisp air brushed her cheeks while she inhaled the food aromas tantalizing her hunger. She located

Deliverance

a department store with soft, snuggly hats only a square away. Although she owned many scarves, one long, unusually wide scarf enchanted her.

A dinner invitation from Kirsten for the following night, their last evening together, enhanced the evening meal of cold cuts, bread, and tea. On the way to her room, Lydia calculated that it was close to 10:00 AM in California, the time Birgit usually took a break. Lydia felt anxious to share Bernhard's session with her and finally open her e-mails.

Birgit sounded fascinated with the report. She then shed some light on the flashbacks of one of his alters, Quarry, from her last talk with him. She promised to intercede and send a text if she received anything timely.

Lydia donned her flannel pajamas and wool socks and smiled at the mirror as she noticed the cap matched her PJs. *Now my heat will stay with me and not warm the room.* She climbed into bed with her computer and a cup of tea from the kitchen. She opened e-mails to find many new junk mails, regular updates, and the life history of Saqqara Fain. Then she further scanned for news from family and friends, although they usually texted. Nancy sent a message without any attachments, so she opened it.

Dear Ms. Voight,

I called before you left for your business trip and requested you counsel me. I told my family, and they wanted me to forget about it. They think counseling is nonsense. That is why I never talked about Neil. I looked at your website like you said. It's nice. It costs a lot of money to come there too. I hope you aren't mad at me for taking up your time.

Nancy

What satanic family would ever want their child to leave the cult? Heaviness filled Lydia's heart for Nancy as she typed back, telling her that she felt privileged to meet her, and not angry. She encouraged her to visit the website as often as she could, and to contact her again if she changed her mind. She added a spiritual blessing prayer with one of her favorite Bible verses at the end.

Lydia's fatigue negated adequate concentration on Saqqara's life history form, so she postponed it to the train to Kassel. Instead, she contentedly wiggled warm toes as she snuggled under the covers and drifted off, praying in the spirit for her family and Nancy.

CHAPTER 17

THE TEMP

Tiffany's ire at Saqqara ebbed as she smoothed her jacket on the way to the waiting room. She looked stunning in her hot pink designer suit. The applicant also posed a striking figure in a royal blue suit trimmed in white piping with imposing white buttons. Triangular white and royal blue earrings matched the spectator pumps. Elaborate African braids crowned her beautiful Nubian face. Tiffany immediately recognized her as a former competitor.

Jillian Woodard submitted an impressive resume'. She founded *Exuberance,* a luxuriant-styled event business in Chicago. Pregnant, Jillian married, and nine months after the birth of a son gave birth to twin daughters. A devoted mother, she closed the popular business to be a full-time parent for six years before signing on as a temp.

"It's so nice to be with you. I am so sorry that Saqqara cannot be with us, but she is regretfully indisposed. However, we can still conduct the interview," Tiffany gushed to open the meeting. They discussed the job description and exchanged questions and answers.

Jillian straightened herself in the chair and leaned forward with a smile that displayed perfect dentition. She cooed, "Your company inspired my former company and challenged it as a stiff competitor. So, I consider it a high privilege for the opportunity to be associated with it."

"That is very gracious of you, Jillian. Your exceptional experience is fortunate for us. Moreover, it appears your skillset is similar to Saqqara's, so you will be a perfect fit in her absence. Done then!" Tiffany triumphantly announced, reaching to shake hands. "Saqqara will meet you in the waiting room on Monday at 8:00 AM for orientation and introduce you to our assistant Millie, who will be your right-hand person. It was a pleasure to be with you again, Jillian, and I look forward to working together. Thank you for your time. I will contact the temp agency to finalize the contract immediately."

Saqqara arrived in the office an hour later. The receptionist's expression warned friction was in the air. Saqqara entered Tiffany's office and asked, "Where's Jillian? I thought she would be the ticket."

Tiffany flowed her raven hair to the side, gave Saqqara a grave look, and snarled, "I interviewed and hired her a week later than planned! Therefore, you must be here promptly at eight Monday morning to meet her in the waiting room to begin orientation and introduce her to Millie. FYI, you were indisposed today and regrettably unable to keep your appointment!

Caustic words of criticism, blame, demand, and not measuring up burned hot to deafen Saqqara's ears. A vague feeling of going away encompassed her.

Tiffany snipped, "By the way, this morning, I scheduled the senator's wedding for the middle of June. That uppity agency in New York double-booked if you can believe that. They contracted eight months ago — well, anyway, we get it. Heaven, help us! We'll contract for mega top dollar, considering the last-minute request. Because of that, I took the liberty of employing Jillian through the middle of June and trust you won't wig out again. I'm busy. I work here!" She refocused on the computer screen.

Stupefied for a while Saqqara sweetly asked again, "Where is Jillian?"

The Temp

Tiffany's eyes widened in utter confoundment. But then her expression mellowed to bewilderment, "Didn't you hear or understand a word I just said?"

"What do you mean?" Saqqara asked with a frown.

Tiffany rose from her chair, walked to embrace her, looked into her eyes, and said, "Saqqara, you forgot an interview this morning. You didn't show. I called you three times. I know your number. The answering voices were... strange. You've got to get help! I need you! I'm wearing thin!"

CHAPTER 18

QUARRY AND EROTICA

Bernhard Fährmann arrived in high spirits and announced, "The tin man experienced almost no interesting phenomena last night. But definitely felt stupid wearing his new bonnet."

Kirsten and Lydia joined his laughter and imagined his appearance. He then produced several pages of his journal research listing symptomatic patterns. He offered a prayer of thanksgiving, after which all examined the patterns. Bernhard identified patterns with two particular men, Jewish holidays, solstices, mid-October to mid-November, and the Easter season with a little less intense Christmas.

Symptoms exacerbated significantly with anticipated or actual contact with his family. He had found it almost impossible to stay in church with Johannes's family at the beginning of their relationship, but that practically stopped since seeing Lydia the first time. He identified a similar pattern whenever he tried to do prayer counseling homework and whenever he scheduled appointments with Lydia or Birgit.

Smiling as Kirsten served him coffee, he said, "To be honest, I got so intrigued with the particle physicist's material that I didn't get to bed till late."

After picking up Bernhard's file and sipping her coffee, Lydia said, "I'm pleased when clients do their homework because I know it will be greatly beneficial. I will consult an expert when I return home and get back with you about the next step...other than wearing your new bonnet. Today, I discern we need to find and free any alters associated with quarry. Are you up to that?"

Straightening with a severe expression, he agreed, then quickly warned Kirsten that he might do or say something bizarre or offensive. "I know it's okay, though, because it's part of the process. I apologize for any defilement or anxiety my behavior might cause you." He then relaxed, closed his eyes, and folded his hands in his lap.

Lydia waved her hand to stop Kirsten, who started to respond and then reminded Bernhard that she and Kirsten were not important now, only the Holy Spirit. He would hear her questions but listen for the answers from Him. She reminded her client that everything he immediately thought, saw, felt, smelled, heard, and tasted was critical to report, no matter how strange, silly, or unimportant it might seem. Fight to stay co-conscious. He nodded his head.

Lydia prayed to bind all lying spirits and loosed the Seven Spirits of God. Then, gently said, "Bernhard wants to help anyone naked, who must run fast, and is afraid. He is sad that he did not know you were there until recently. He did not know how to help you in the past, but today he does and wants to."

Nothing.

Lydia didn't seem bothered at all. She sat there and calmly prayed in her spiritual language in a hushed voice. Kirsten shot a concerned look. Bernhard repositioned. Then Lydia's and Kirsten's eyes widened as his chair appeared to enlarge, or did he shrink? Kirsten's open-mouthed glance at Lydia begged, can this be happening?

Time went by.

He changed position and looked around the room as if unfamiliar with it. A much younger appearing Bernhard finally said,

"We're inside now. Is it time for the orgy?"

Wonder popped off Lydia's face. Realizing that Bernhard switched to a child alter, she then quickly intoned as if to a child, "Hi. I'm glad you're here. It's good to be with you, but it's not time for the orgy. We don't have orgies here."

"I'm here cause I'm a fast naked. Other naked kids run fast too, but if they got bright colored circles on their backs and don't win, they get eaten by some big people at the feast. Us winners get all the lollipops and suckers we want at the orgy."

A lower lip protruded while a small hand smashed a single tear.

"I won. How come there's no candy? They promised!"

Before Lydia could respond, Bernhard leaned forward with an indignant chin in a feminine voice and said,

"He's such a wimp. He doesn't even know what an orgy is. The first time some john poked his bitsy butt, he went ballistic and got the puddin beat out of him. Quarry wins hunts, but I'm Erotica, and I get all the candy I can take."

Focused, Lydia greeted Erotica and asked the body's age when she first came to help Quarry. *"Four."* Then she asked her age. The answer "seven."

Erotica proudly offered,

"I can suck any sucker to hell and back. That's what one of the movie stars told me, and the women go crazy with hilarious giggles when I lick their lollipops."

"It sounds as if Quarry and you are very good at your jobs. I'm just curious. Are you naked too?" asked Lydia.

She frowned and looked down at her body, then replied,

"Yeah. Of course, unless they command us to wear the leather, spikes, or chain stuff... sometimes a costume. We always wear makeup and heels. Are you blind?"

Lydia asked the question because she knew stripping one naked is the first step to demoralizing a person. She visually searched the room for a blanket or anything to offer for cover. Then she saw herself in the spirit wrapping her client in the new scarf she happened to wear that day. "May I walk over to you and cover you?" Lydia asked.

As Erotica nodded, she closed her eyes; tears swam between her lips. Lydia gently draped the scarf over Bernhard's shoulders, arms, and shoes. Erotica abruptly opened her eyes, saw the scarf, and flung it away.

"What are you doing? she shouted.

Lydia flinched, then realized the Lord went before her. "Erotica, you are part of a beloved child of Creator God Jesus. A God who covers our nakedness and lifts our head in honor," Lydia said as she put her scarf back on. Psalm3:3 says, *But Thou, O Lord, art a shield about me, My glory and the One who lifts my head."*

"How'd you know he did that?" Erotica's face flooded with shocked question marks. *"We've heard Bernhard pleading to know us for years, but we were mad at him because he never let us go to the*

hunts and orgies. So, nobody wanted us, and he's ashamed of us anyway!"

Lydia said, "I want you and Quarry to look at your hands. What do you see?"

First, Quarry exclaimed, **"Dem's really big, huh!"**

Hesitating, not wanting to face the truth, Erotica turned the hands over and back again until she tilted her head and said,

"They aren't my hands."

Lydia motioned to Kirsten to get the mirror for her. She held it in front of Bernhard and asked, "Whom do you see?"

Staring at the image, not a child but a furious man gritting his teeth as he slammed his left fist into his right palm. Maroon faced, ready to explode, Bernhard lifted his head, looked at the women, and cried aloud, "God have mercy on the children! I ran for my life at four and acclimated to prostitution by seven. Dear Jesus, I pray I didn't eat the feast. I can hear the gregarious noise and loud boasting over the world-class wines."

Profuse tears of remorse, shame, guilt, disgust, and relief finally cleared any past confusion as Bernhard embraced the identities of Quarry and Erotica as himself and their thoughts and behavior as his own. Exhausted from weeping, he asked for a break.

Bernhard reviewed, "I managed to escape the horror of childhood with the coping skill, dissociation. I created Quarry, the runner to survive the hunters when he became petrified and Erotica, a girl, to protect my male dignity when sexually plundered and humiliated. They would not want to shoot a valuable Lebensborn, hence no target on my back."

Quarry and Erotica

"May I ask a question?" Kirsten inquired.

"Of course, and add any wisdom you may have too," a recovered Bernhard replied.

"I understand the defeated Nazi regime intended the Lebensborn babies for the ruling Aryan class, but what happened to the babies after the war? Who are these monsters continuing these practices? Why subject such gifted children to such evil?

Lydia explained, "We will need to discuss this more at another time. Many were placed in orphanages or adopted. Be sure that the Third Reich remnant, now Fourth Reich, salvages all possible. These monsters, as you call them, are some of the various conspiratorial groups hoping to rule the New World Order served by mind-controlled enslaved people. They subjugate children to the terror of a hunt and attendance at cannibalistic feasts. They use sexual abuse to whittle away the child's natural self-esteem, which blocks blind obedience.

"Bernard, you may have been a sex slave at an early age. I can see that you were probably a darling, but when the programmers realized your brilliance, the plan changed. That explains some of your memories of the computer stations. They kept you essentially disabled during the day and enslaved at night working on quantum computing. Quarry and Erotica were unresolved trauma in you not being active and lay dormant. You struggled to accept such a hideous past. Sexual abuse probably continued because it negatively impacts the spirit. You recovered your memory of being sodomized as a teen. Love your inner children for all they suffered so that you could survive."

From past experiences like this session, he knew that he could be totally justified: just as if it never happened. Memories are his history. These things happened. But the justification made possible the exchange of Christ's Holy Blood for the trauma, guilt, fear, and condemnation for joy and peace. First, he would confess ungodly acts and thoughts such as judgments, vows, and belief in lies about himself and what happened to him. Then he needed to give up his right to get even with his persecutors to the Almighty Judge by forgiving them. To get even levels one equal with the offenders. It's impossible anyway because some offenders would be dead and others unable to be found. Bernhard worked on the healing process for the next hour.

Lydia offered cleansing prayers and absolution. Finally, the three enjoyed Holy Communion to celebrate his justification and new-found freedom.

"I see that we ran over time," Bernhard noted and hurried to say, "thank you for solving runner triggers. Birgit will be interested to know what we found. I feel well-equipped to deal with any more implants from the knowledge gained last night, and the identified patterns pointed out the triggers, which I know can lead me to more traumatic memories. Hey, whew, we did it! Thank you, Kirsten, for your support. Any homework?"

"It sounds like you just gave it. Instead of me, why don't you tell Birgit about the session? I'll be home in May. Please e-mail then with convenient times for a follow-up session with me. The relief you experienced last night with the bonnet suggests nanotechnology interfacing. I will consult an expert when I get home and get back to you regarding the next step-other than wearing a bonnet. It's a crime that you won't get the monetary benefit nor credit for your contributions to quantum computing, but the Lord knows.

"I bless you with this psalm to sustain you and give you hope. You may want to memorize all of it:

> *Keep me, O Lord, from the hands of the wicked; Preserve me from violent men, Who have purposed to trip up my feet. The proud have hidden a trap for me and cords; They have spread a net by the wayside; They have set snares for me. [Selah]. I said to the Lord, 'Thou art my God; Give ear, O Lord, to the voice of my supplications. O God the Lord, the strength of my salvation, Thou hast covered my head in the day of battle. Do not grant, O Lord, the desires of the wicked; Do not promote his evil device, lest they be exalted. (Psalms 140:4-8)"*

After paying for the sessions, which Lydia referred to as 'high finance,' Bernhard left, and Kirsten marveled at the difference between him, and the client scheduled this afternoon.

"Our lives are never the same once we know the power of knowledge of the truth," Lydia whimsically sang as she grabbed Kirsten's arm to whisk her off to lunch.

CHAPTER 19

TABEA'S SLEEP

Lydia hardly recognized her client without haunting dark circles under her eyes. Dr. Hetz and Tabea ecstatically competed to report a first remembered whole night's sleep.

Tabea elaborated, "I bought Epsom Salts on the way home and soaked in a bath with them. After I went to bed, I slept twelve hours!"

"Tabea spent this morning in my office viewing DVDs about principles of sowing and reaping," reported Dr. Hetz.

Tabea added, "I see the principles like the cliché of what goes around comes around."

Lydia agreed and said, "Yes, what we sow, we reap." She then proceeded to join them and Kirsten in opening prayers of thanksgiving and petitions for the session. "I want to offer tools for protection. Kirsten, please scribe for Tabea so she can fully attend. Do you know any spirit-filled Christian who is discerning of spirits?" Tabea looked blank, but Dr. Hetz knew someone for a referral.

"Great," Lydia said. "First of all, you and the referral person go through your apartment room by room, asking Holy Spirit if anything needs to be spiritually cleansed or destroyed. Sometimes the area or an object, even jewelry, will feel cold due to a demonic presence, or you may feel uneasy. The uneasiness is a function of

Tabea's Sleep

your spirit discerning evil. Handing off a pamphlet, she continued, "Apply holy oil to cleanse the object and pray the prayers in this. If you sense the object needs to be destroyed, do not put it in the trash. Utterly destroy it by crushing or, ideally, by fire. If your husband objects, plead a Holy Blood Barrier around it and apply oil. But if oil damages it, apply holy water to the object.

Specifically, regarding your husband's arrival home, bind all demonic spirits operating in him using the Name of Jesus mentally or away from his hearing. Also, pray the Holy Spirit will be a spiritual barrier between him and you in times of marital intimacy to block demonic or other spirits from crossing from him to you. This way, you are protected and still honor your husband. In addition, you will probably find the sexual demands to lessen greatly."

Rocking with eyes expectant, Tabea folded her hands and asked Lydia to pray the barrier prayer now. She would repeat it after her.

"Lydia began:

> "Dearest God our Fortress and Protector, we choose to trust Your words in Psalm 18:2&3, *The Lord is my rock and my fortress and my deliverer. My God, my rock, in whom I take refuge; my shield and the horn of my salvation, my stronghold.* I ask You to be a shield of protection about me. I especially ask that a spiritual barrier shield be placed between my husband and me in our intimate union to block any transference of all spirits. I call upon the Lord, who is worthy of praise. Thank You for saving me from my enemies. In the name of Jesus, Amen."

Tabea repeated and, in the end, gushed thankfulness for the help.

Lydia explained, "Even though much trauma remains for Tabea to work through, it is best to begin at the beginning. Evilly intentioned people build upon the fodder of foundational wounds at early ages from parents or caregivers. Once belief systems from the foundational wounds heal, much of the later trauma from specific perpetrators and new beliefs reduce dramatically. I'm sure Dr. Hetz will effectively work through that with you," Lydia assured. "So, tell me about your family history."

The extensive family history with Dr. Hetz taking extensive notes ended the session. Kirsten escorted Tabea into another room for refreshments. At the same time Dr. Hetz consulted with Lydia about the previous two sessions and follow-up plans. Lydia stressed the importance of baptism for Tabea if she could not remember receiving the sacrament. "If slight improvement resulted after spiritually cleansing her apartment, it may be necessary to spiritually cleanse the land on which Tabea lives." She referred her to a book and website for assistance if required. Lydia prayed blessings for Brunhilde before they departed.

Post-counseling cleansing prayers are effective; however, the lengthy soothing shower before the dinner engagement invigorated Lydia. She loved to dress fancy and looked forward to the fun. It created a healthy balance for the intensity of her work.

CHAPTER 20

DEN HAGUE FAREWELL

At 19:00, Lydia stopped in front of the full-length mirror, turned side to side, fluffed the apricot coiffure, and smiled approvingly. She patted her tummy and congratulated herself on being hungry. *I'm ready to join Kirsten and Günther for a night on the town.*

They only drove a short distance when Kirsten bent low and impassionedly pointed out the orange stripe on the palace flagpole, "Royalty is in residence. I wonder who it is?"

"Please excuse my wife. Her interest in Royalty baffles me," said Günther. "I thought since we are on the North Sea Coast that you might enjoy prime seafood so, I reserved a table at our favorite restaurant.

"We need to talk about your departure plans. Kirsten told me about the suitcases for the Romanian orphans. Loading and unloading all that luggage without Tirza's help will be very strenuous and stressful when times between trains are short. I realize you can use your Eurail pass with almost any train at any time. Perhaps travel plans are made, but I've done some research. Most trains to Kassel-Wilhelmshöhe from Den Haag take up to seven hours with two or more transfers. I found a train that takes five hours and forty-five minutes with one transfer but departs from Amsterdam Centraal. It leaves at 14:38 and arrives at 20:23. I hope that isn't too late for arrival, but fewer trains run on the weekend. To leave by noon allows adequate time for travel and lunch. I'm happy to drive you to Amsterdam and help load the first train. Kirsten works all day. If you choose to do that, I'll reserve a seat for you as soon as we get to the restaurant."

"That is so thoughtful of you, Günther. I planned to do that after our outing tonight but be my guest. *Vielen Danke*!

Kristen added, "You'll have all morning to finish packing, and we can stay out as late as we want."

Seagulls danced above and occasionally landed on the wet sidewalk as if to lead the way and announce the restaurant. Aromas of succulent ocean fare filled the air. The chic hostess noted the reservation with a deferent smile, directed coat check, and led the party to their table view overlooking the harbor. Kirsten led the party and turned to be seated. Affected with sudden surprise, she threw up her hands in delight and said, "My, Lydia, you are gorgeous in that copper sequin top. You certainly know how to select colors that accentuate your natural beauty. I could take a few lessons from you."

"You do look lovely tonight, Lydia," turning to Kirsten, "so do you, Wife. You always appear beautiful to me," Günther extended with a smile of endearment. "You know what I want, Kirsten, please order for me while I make Lydia's train reservations."

An evening of delicious prime seafood, fine wine, and superior ambiance conducive to conversation followed. Bright orange lobsters nested in brilliant green parsley accompanied by glistening ebony clamshells, accented jumbo shrimp with savory butter, and plump cream scallops. Riotous laughter and subdued whispers escaped their table during memory lane stories, especially how they met at the seminar house in Biburg, Germany, years before.

They departed the sumptuous environment and cozy warmth in favor of a salt air stroll along the harbor. A starry sky fashioned cherished memories among friends as they shared current life and dreams. The perfectly satisfying event ended with joyful tears of farewell between the ladies.

The sleeping hat worked. Another good night's sleep and Lydia rose to finish packing after breakfast. At least she didn't fret over the weight of the suitcases as when she flew. Günther insisted on loading the luggage. On the way, they discussed Catholic Renewal plans and European immigration issues.

"Thank you for allowing Kirsten to sit in with you. The experience offered new possibilities for her and equipped us for future ministry. Please be cautious traveling alone, Lydia. There are reports of marauding gangs of immigrants who rob, beat and rape people all over Germany and other countries as well," warned Günther.

"Thank you for your care. My dear friend who lives near Fürth told me she is now reluctant to shop alone in broad daylight."

After a yummy lunch, they arrived at the train station with plenty of time to load and still chat more. Before detraining, Günther indicated on the training brochure where he reserved seats closest to the exit door near the luggage area. "Hopefully, there will be enough space, so you won't need to hoist heavy bags above your seat."

A quick hug from her friend followed with him backing away, voicing a blessing before detraining. They waved until a sea of new faces replaced his.

CHAPTER 21

TRAIN TO KASSEL

Lydia hung her coat and hat on the hook next to the window seat. As she started to unload her backpack, she was surprised to find a bagged meal and several bottled beverages packed on the top. The attached note said, "Abendessen (German evening meal) blessings, Kirsten." Smiling thankfully, she placed her computer and opened the briefcase on the table in front of her. *This segment of the journey is three hours and forty minutes. Now would be the best time to work. Frankfurt's generous twenty-seven-minute transfer allows time to buy a German pretzel.* She salivated, imaging the sparkly salt crystals atop the shiny brown twists.

She opened an e-mail to Saqqara's life history form. As she read the lengthy document, certain information seemed to jump out, which she highlighted in yellow. Finished, she closed the computer, sat back, closed her eyes, and asked the Holy Spirit if this person was an assignment for her. As usual, during these communication times, deep relaxation and invigoration emerged. Saqqara's phone conversation floated through her mind without red flags.

She waited a few minutes, knowing God always answers prayers. After hearing nothing, she understood the decision belonged to her. Reflection upon the proverb about safety in an abundance of counselors inspired her to read phone e-mails from staff intercessors.

She purposefully waited so they could serve as confirmation of her plan or requirement for more deliberation. She asked if she should accept new client #434. Privacy mandated minimal information.

The responses sent encouragement and offered prophetic content valuable for future sessions. "Great," she said aloud as she spied a chocolate mouth and peering eyes between the seats in front of her. Peek-a-boo ensued with giggles from both. Then she reopened the computer and replied to Saqqara's e-mail.

Dear Saqqara,

Thank you for sending the completed life history form. I am happy to accept you as a client beginning on May 15-19 at 9:00 AM. I will provide the rest of that week's schedule at your first session.

As soon as I receive your deposit, you will receive a confirmation letter, directions to the office, and discount codes for nearby lodgings. Deposits apply to full payment except when less than a two-week cancellation or 'no show' occurs. We accept payment by check or via my website. Before arrival, please be sure to read the first book listed on my website. If you prefer an easier, less rigorous read, then study the second book listed.

Please be aware that a prayer intercessor is with us in our sessions.

Sincerely,
Lydia O. Voight

When she finished responding to other e-mails, she sent them all off from the table outlet device. She reloaded the pack, threw it on her back, then exercised through other cars, delighting in people watching as was her custom when traveling. When she returned to her seat, she observed the chocolate-faced child taking a nap.

Lydia ate her evening meal watching late afternoon shadows play on the landscape as the train whizzed southeast. She finished, then extracted the outline for next week's conference to study the rest of the way.

The first leg of her journey easily transitioned at Frankfurt Main. She hurried to a German pretzel stand and boarded her train to Kassel. She shoved the larger cases into a luggage area and only needed to hoist her smaller carry-on bag above her seat. Only ninety minutes remained, so she decided to read the club's book and nurse the second beverage while munching on her pretzel.

Darkness clothed the train's arrival into Kassel-Wilhelmshöhe Station. She found it unusually quiet for being the city's most important station. She searched the usual places to meet the scheduled hotel van and many other sites, but no van showed. The hotel didn't answer the phone. She waited to call again, but then the battery died. *On no! I forgot to charge it on the train. They always met me here, but maybe they misunderstood, or it's a new person, or they're waiting in Kassel for me.*

She checked the schedule board. The next train to Kassel HBF was due in thirty minutes. It sounded like one of the old step-high-into trains. Suddenly feeling quite deflated, she reloaded the suitcases and made the wide swath along the walkway to the train's first-class boarding area that Eurail tickets provide. She unhooked the bags to sit flat on the pavement and laid her backpack on top. She rotated her shoulders while looking around; always a relief to take it off. The commotion of voices stopped after the last train pulled out. Odors of oil and fuel filled the air. Across the numerous tracks, an occasional person walked somewhere. She made a striking sight in the flared full-length raincoat, a wide-brimmed hat, alone and flanked by luggage. Occasionally a distant sound like bouncing metal pierced the quiet. The chilly night dropped degrees.

Time dragged. She mentally rehearsed the seminar material to pass the time. Cigarette malodor alerted her to scan. She spied, sauntering in a ribald manner towards her, five middle eastern looking men. One of the older men wearing a black leather jacket approached her, removed the cancer stick from his mouth, and in a friendly accent, asked, "Excuse me, do you know where this train is going?"

Train to Kassel

Red flags flapped wildly in this conversation! Lydia's glance around found only an empty station. Pointing to the schedule board, she answered, "Those boards display all the schedule information." Lydia presented a disinterested demeanor, stepped back, and turned away to distance herself from the man.

"Do you know when it leaves?" continued the fortyish fellow. The other men shuffled their shoes and smirked.

"Soon," she clipped, after which they walked a short distance away to talk among themselves. Then, heart pounding, short of breath, she lifted the backpack to mentally practice how to deliver a painful wallop, which would certainly hurt! *Jesus HELP!* Occasionally, a lecherous laugh expelled from the group as one approached her, stared, and turned to rejoin the others.

Huge relief flooded Lydia when her train broke the haunting scenario. The group doused smokes, shot disgusted glances at her, then walked to the coach car section at the end of the train. While passengers detrained, she donned the pack. She hoisted suitcases up the stairs to the loading platform between the cars, then pulled each into a seating area. She was alone.

On the short jaunt to the next station, a conductor passing her seat tossed his head backward, and on the sly, said, "*die Vorsicht!*"

Caution? She looked to the other end of her car to see the same group of men entering. The train stopped. She tried to ignore them as she exited her seat and readied her luggage for departure. Unloading proved easier. Once all the suitcases were on the platform, Lydia looked around to discover a long hike to the terminal. *The train pulled into the station with coach cars closest to the terminal and first-class farthest away, yet that group of men who boarded coach walked back to my car.*

She was startled to find a tall, blond, American football player-type man with an old bicycle standing next to her. As soon as the group of men saw him, they leaped out of the train and raced away towards the terminal, after which he asked in English, "May I help you?"

Not sure who he might be, she said, "No, thank you. I'm balanced this way." She piggybacked the luggage and began the wide swath.

Following close behind, he asked if he could walk with her. Still, before she could answer, he enthusiastically informed her this was his first trip to Kassel. He embarked on his internship as a medical student. "Are you sure I can't help you with those bags? I have room for the small one in the basket, and I can also pull a big one," he beamed.

There was such a sense of wholesomeness about him that she recanted. She and the blue-eyed companion strolled chatting like old friends. Entering the building, he pointed and said, "Telephones are on the other side of that information board on the left." They stopped beside it and, together again, piggybacked the luggage. Lydia looked toward the telephones and turned back to wish him well. Her panoramic view of empty marble floors stretched in multiple directions. A fluorescent light blinked at the end of a corridor. *Where is he? No one could get away that fast!*

A distant shout interrupted her quandary. She searched in the direction of the sound to see Hannes run walking towards her. "There you are! I'm so sorry, but my van had a flat," he explained. But unfortunately, I forgot my mobile and the other, what do you say... emergency tire?"

"Spare," Lydia said.

"I carefully drove until I found air and finally reached Kassel-Wilhelmshöhn, but I couldn't find you anywhere. I memorized your schedule. We always met there. I looked everywhere then, duh, it occurred to me to ask Jesus where you were. Heh, heh, sure enough, the thought came to me. Since I was not there, you might think I would get you in the city."

As they left the station, Lydia said, "We know God causes all things to work together for good to those who love Him, to those called according to His purpose. If this mix-up did not happen, I might not have met a handsome angel!"

"What? Tell me every detail," Hannes adjured, hunched over the wheel and peered in her direction.

Lydia enjoyed telling her harrowing story and hearing Hannes's comments, especially his question, "Do angels lie"? He said it was his first time to Kassel, yet he knew the location of the telephones, and how did he know you needed a landline?"

Lydia proposed, "It may be more important to overcome evil than never lie."

Hannes quoted, *"Do not neglect to show hospitality to strangers, for by this some have entertained angels without knowing it.* That's in Hebrews 13:12, you know." The half-hour drive to the hotel flurried with pertinent questions about Lydia's flight, work in the Netherlands, and the upcoming conference. The lights of the small village beaconed welcome.

CHAPTER 22

NAYSA'S OFFER

A smile crossed Saqqara's face when she saw Naysa at the window. Since their first meeting, she waited at the window or in the entrance hall to greet Saqqara returning from long workdays and offer dinner, conversation, or both. The short time of their acquaintance seemed like a lifetime. Naysa was an easy conversationalist. Saqqara often felt too tired to cook a decent dinner after a ten or twelve-hour day. Naysa proved an extraordinary cook and prepared nutritious dinners despite the limitations of living in a wheelchair.

While Naysa finished preparing the meal, Saqqara updated her on the upcoming counseling appointment. Previously she received acceptance and mailed the deposit. Today she received the e-mail with the promised documents. "Can you believe this confirmation letter? She wants me to bring someone along for support when I'm not counseling! They can't be offended if I want my space and are not to counsel me but to have fun and pray with me if I want. It sounds like you would be a perfect fit, Naysa!"

Wheeling to the table with a tray of spaghetti, salad, and wine, Naysa regretfully declined due to the rigorous physical therapy schedule to which she committed. "Sounds like she cares about her

Naysa's Offer

clients. I don't remember any of my practitioners even mentioning my private life."

"I don't need support. Anyway, that would be more expensive," Saqqara said.

"Yes, you do; everyone needs support. I can't go, but I'm happy to commit to being with you in spirit. You will never know how much your friendship means to me," Naysa tearfully offered. "What else does it say?"

"Oh, read a book before coming, ask people to pray now and while I'm there, and get this! I can expect things to get worse. That's all I need!"

"You are so busy, I'll get the book, and we can read it together in our spare time. I can ask my Bible study group in Wheaton to join me to support you in prayer."

"Naysa, I don't know which is more amazing, you or this spaghetti!" Saqqara praised as she twisted the second spoonful of pasta onto her fork.

CHAPTER 23

THE HIKE

Melodious church bells awakened Lydia. "What a great alarm clock," Lydia muttered. Using her mobile's flashlight, she navigated through the pitch-black room to the window. She recognized the design and joyfully opened the horizontal Venetian shades inside the glass panes to peep out. Blue skies puffed white clouds to declare the weather. She cranked the window to open in an outward sideways direction to breathe in the fresh air and leaned out to bathe her face in the sunshine. *If I ever build a home, it will install windows like these.* She closed the window to reopen it in an outward upward tilt. Too late for church, but Lydia unloaded her backpack and reloaded it with hiking supplies, then quickly slipped into blue jeans topped by an orange plaid blouse. She pulled on her favorite hiking boots with a grunt, hopped up, and tied sweat-shirt sleeves around her neck as she left her room.

She bought cheese, an orange, and delectable rolls from a quaint bakery. The yeasty sweetness of the bakery followed her up the nearby trail. She enjoyed Germany. But she appreciated its people as intelligent, organized, efficient, industrious and they also valued classical music.

The Hike

Maybe, because its terrain reminded her of home. Many of the same animals zipped through the brush, peeped from under a bush, or frolicked, from branch to branch. The flora was familiar, as well as the birdsong. Her boots churned up the musty odor of decaying fall leaves from under budding deciduous trees. Shades of green confers also lined the trail, and junipers released their pungent fragrance as she passed. Lydia's spirit soared in the worship of her Creator as she drank in the majesty and beauty of her surroundings.

Shrieking voices from two Asian women running downhill towards her interrupted the private service. "Hello, Lydia. We got so excited when we saw you would be teaching again that we took our holiday to be here this week. We arrived yesterday and plan to go to the hot springs this afternoon. Would you like to join us? It's so good to be with you again!"

Lydia recognized the sisters whom she counseled in Singapore some years ago. The two appeared in different countries where she taught. Their smooth rosy cheeks glistened as they excitedly chatted and made plans to meet Lydia after lunch for the hot springs. We hiked to the top and are tired! Hate to go, but if we are to grab a nap before lunch, we must say bye for now," they chorused as they scurried downhill, excitedly chatting out of audible range.

After a three-hour hike, Lydia returned to the hotel and immediately checked her e-mail. Tirza's mother had become alert, progressed to a step-down unit from ICU, and hoped to get a discharge to homecare on Tuesday. On Wednesday, Tirza offered to train to Kassel to continue the original plan or drive to meet Lydia in Leipzig. Although disappointed, Lydia responded that the Leipzig idea seemed best since this conference ended Friday noon. More e-mails. The family is fine but misses her—news from the Club. Natroya's husband suffered a mild heart attack. Thi's campaign for city councilman is strong. Cavanaugh benefits from the grief recovery group, and Desmond has mysterious trouble.

Lydia stopped at the main desk on the way to lunch. Hannes busily poured over the registration packets. "Ninety registered," he said, "and I need to be sure to prepare more for those who 'drop in'... Rolf should arrive tonight. In the morning, staff can meet to organize before the onslaught. Some people are already here, and some will arrive tonight, of course," he reported.

Simultaneously, Heike, Hannes' wife/ head-cook, and Lydia recognized each other. Squeals hurried across the hall and hushed in big hugs. "We eat red cabbage just for you *mittagessen* (German lunch) today," she said in her broken English.

The hilarity and hot water at the hot springs begged a nap before abendessen for Lydia. After rising, she approached the window to shut out the cool breeze. She looked below to recognize Harald and Holger walking to the hotel. Some ten years ago, while on holiday, these Danes and their wives lost their hearts to the orphans in Romania. They returned home to start the Romanian Orphan Ministry, which delivers a truckload of supplies three times a year to supply designated orphanages. Both widowers now, Lydia met them on a train in Austria, and having counseled American families who adopted Romanian orphans, she became inspired.

She contacted a dear past client who created a sewing center where she taught Native American Women to sew layettes and other things for their tribe's use and sale. Two of Lydia's big suitcases bulged with layettes. Once she mailed them, but they never reached the orphanages. Since then, she scheduled a rendezvous with the two men whenever in Europe or Scandinavia to deliver her cargo.

Harald and Holger saved a place for Lydia at their table. It felt like an old home week. Then to make fellowship richer still, Rolf arrived, deposited his luggage outside the dining room, and joined them. "Where's Tirza?" he asked. Lydia filled him in, after which they arranged a meeting tomorrow after breakfast to go over her notes.

After the meal, Harald and Holger accompanied Lydia to her room to relieve her of their precious cargo. They each pulled one suitcase down the hall, thanking her all the way.

Lydia ended her wonderful day by organizing her outfits for the conference week. She learned serious suits at the beginning of an event or with a new client establishes authority. Sadly, some people still misinterpret the Bible and think women shouldn't teach. The correct interpretation of Scripture must consider its context and the day's culture. Saint Paul had no problem with women teaching; in fact, he appointed Pricilla as an apostle. He did restrict the women of Corinth from teaching due to their pagan foundations and understanding. *I can relax the attire later as I deem wise.*

CHAPTER 24

STRANGER THAN FICTION CONFERENCE

DAY 1 – Schizophrenia and False Memory Syndrome

The hotel buzzed with activity after breakfast or *frühstück* (German breakfast). First, Rolf and Lydia practiced audio with the sound techs, selected microphones, then looked over the first day's notes together. Next, Lydia helped to arrange the book table with Gerta, a hotel employee assigned to manage it throughout the week. Then, satisfied all was in order, Lydia followed savory aromas to the buffet. She put her selections on a tray and carried the mittagessen to her room. The diner sat next to the window to enjoy watching the activities below. Dishes stacked; she fluffed her bed pillow, comfortably propped it, and sat to meditate and prepare her spirit for the evening conference.

The social hour began at 15:30 with *kaffee* and *kuchen*. The coffee tasted okay, but Lydia especially enjoyed the cakes because they were not overly sweet as most in the United States. Time for later arrivals to settle in followed kaffee time. Abendessen started at 16:30, and conference presentations started at 19:00.

The original 400-year-old stone hotel building housed the conference room, main lobby, small multi-purpose rooms, and dining room with kitchen facilities. Its multiple high ceiling narrow inset windows had shutters on the outside. Beautiful plants adorned the windowsills. Arched above, wooden beams spanned the room to meet panels of pastel tapestries and paintings of times long ago. Marble floors gleamed. The 100-year-old lodging addition recently got a facelift and renovated kitchen. As people entered, overheard snippets of conversations exclaimed appreciation for the charming ambiance.

Musicians and singers opened the session and enthusiastically received the audience who joined the singing. Hannes encouraged the audience to refer to the syllabus for the week's details. He then introduced Lydia and Rolf. Lydia recognized most of the audience. Many stood as they applauded. This conference required a pre-requisite of attending the Advanced Conference for DID two years prior in Nürnberg or completing an online course with similar content.

Lydia wore a beige suit with an umber turtleneck accented with a multi-stranded topaz and dravite necklace, a gift from an audience in Austria. Brown heels repeated the hue of voluminous earrings. She felt the strength of Rolf's hand meet hers as their eyes met in welcome.

She smiled and then turned towards the audience while nodding her head pointedly in many directions towards people she knew well. "It's such an honor to be with many of you in person again. It's a pleasure to finally meet with you, who completed the online courses and know you are real and not an AI. Welcome!" The audience chuckled, taking their seats.

"You designed *The Stranger Than Fiction Conference.* Unanswered questions from other conferences birthed this one. Some of the questions were: How do schizophrenia and dissociation relate to each other? What is False Memory Syndrome? Are demons real? We received requests for more information about governmental mind control, transhumanism, and satanism. You seek pure scientific evidence and not fake news reports from scientists whose only goal is to preserve funding for their research. Their benefactors are determined to enslave humanity. You asked, 'What is behind all this strategy and highly complex work to alter and control human beings?' I hope to shed light on Telescope Lucifer, new faster healing strategies for DID, and what may be under the earth. You have an extensive bibliography.

"I will not be burdening you with a barrage of dates, many names, or statistical percentages. I intend to summarize my study on these subjects and then ask you to reason together. But, moreover, be good Bereans; you check it out. I am not an authority but a fire starter and provider of resources for the original documents in these matters. Too many people willingly accept convenient information from magazines or newspapers, television, the internet, social media, movies, and educational institutions. It is always wise to form your opinions upon original source documentation. The information I present is from these sources. Please hold your questions for the end of all presentations.

"All of you should now hold a solid foundational knowledge and understanding of how dissociation affects trauma victims and how it functions in society. We will have didactic teaching interspersed with small interest groups, as you can see on the schedule. These groups are assigned a leader well-versed on the topic. I will visit the groups to augment sessions as needed. In addition, we designed long breaks to process the information alone or with other attendees. We want this time to produce new questions to enrich your time here and create content for another conference.

"I am told that all great athletes practice the basics daily. I'm not an athlete, let alone a great one, but the principle can apply here. So, I will briefly review the basics of dissociation for a launching pad.

"Severe trauma usually breaks a human being, especially if one is an infant or child. This breaking in psychological terminology is dissociation. Its most severe degree is known as Dissociative Identity Disorder, DID, "Some psychiatric professionals deny that DID is real. People will say it is too preposterous even to consider it is valid. In the early 1990s, statisticians believed that only one in 100 psychiatric cases existed. Today there are tens of thousands of dissociative people, most of them are not in treatment and if so, are misdiagnosed. DID could be caused by a singular event of trauma. It could be from repeated childhood dysfunctional family events, or it could be from cold, calculated technical mind control."

A mustached man stood and anxiously asked, "Will you be talking about mind control?

Lydia felt a little annoyed that the man ignored her request to hold questions to the end. "Yes, on day three. It is listed on your program." A stir in the audience posed, *Was my answer too curt?*

"Dissociative people usually receive many diagnostic labels, including schizophrenia. Many of you asked, 'What is the difference between dissociation and schizophrenia?' The significant difference is that resolved trauma potentially heals dissociation. Schizophrenia is a biochemical imbalance in the brain treatable with appropriate drugs; there is no cure to date. Lithium is one prescription of choice; however, patients hate its side effects. Efficacy with medications specific to brain chemistry imbalances can satisfy a diagnosis of schizophrenia. Those medications are not helpful for dissociation.

Schizophrenic patients usually report hearing voices outside their heads. Dissociative people say they hear voices inside their heads. Both conditions are possible in one person. I hope that clarifies any confusion on that point," Lydia said as she scanned the audience for question mark expressions.

"Next, I would like to address the False Memory Syndrome or FMS. This term surfaced in 1992 when a non-profit foundation by this name resulted from allegations of sexual abuse in a family. The adult child recovered memories of the abuse during therapy. The named abuser denied the allegations. Loosely, the organization's stated purpose is to offer support and assistance to people accused of abuse.

"Soon after that, many other court cases surfaced due to accessed repressed memories involving sexual abuse, incest, and pedophilia. A flurry of concern arose regarding the validity of repressed memories. The accused sued therapists for suggesting false memories to patients. Abuse victims doubted themselves and their counselor's credibility. Pedophiles championed and capitalized on the foundation.

"Psychology researchers presented the latest brain findings to explain if a false memory is possible or if recovered memories are actual reality results. A significant contention regarding the accuracy of a recovered memory was how it could be false with exact details. A notable study tried to answer that question with their concept, and I will try to explain it as I understand it in simple terms. Their theory explained that our brains store information or memories in two forms independent of each other; one catalogues general information and the other detailed information. They theorized a story or therapist's suggestion could cue the area of the brain with exact detail and therefore make it seem authentic. In other words, memory is a reconstructive thing; accordingly, there could be false memories."

Murmurs drifted about the room. People shook their heads in confusion.

"Therapists afraid of being sued and people who disbelieved so much abuse existed under their noses embraced the new information. This fear and disbelief resulted in many victims never getting healed nor getting justice. Perhaps needy people could drift into such confabulation. None of us are so naive as to believe embittered, hateful people would hesitate to make up a story to get revenge. None of those stories would be false memories. They would be fabrications. Memory is genuine, never false. If something is a memory, it must have truth even though there can be distortion."

Disturbed facial expressions relaxed before her.

"I respect research, but their research proves incomplete. It's always important to address an issue in the whole context. If we ignore past research findings, we are on a slippery slope. We should always take science into context. Our brains are like a computer with different components with unique functions. Our hippocampus is like a super file cabinet collecting all the data in our lives and saving it for a time. It deletes obsolete data. You know, 'Use it or lose It.' Simultaneously, the amygdala snatches away pertinent data such as trauma for safekeeping. It includes content from all the senses.

"Dr. James G. Friesen, a clinical psychologist, wrote *The Truth About False Memory Syndrome* in 1995 to discredit the propaganda of the FMS movement. He presented established explicit scientific data in a neutral attitude, unlike the extreme examples and inflammatory ridicule from FMS supporters. He explained the facts as detailed information so the readers could conclude.

"There is a significant difference between repressed memories and dissociated memories. The two words false and memory contradict each other. Unfortunately, that fact gets left out of the debate. If there is distortion, it is crucial to reduce distortion in therapy to find the accuracy within the memory. Repression aims to improve things, not worsen, and increases distortion over time.

"On the other hand, dissociation prevents further distortion over time. It is perceived by the brain to be overwhelming to the person and logged in the brain differently. Dissociative memories tend to come back suddenly and succinctly, while repressed memories are more gradual in recovery. The precision of the event prevents tricking."

Lydia lifted his book high, "This is Dr. Friesen's contribution to the dilemma. It will equip you with facts to explain the fallacy of FMS to others. Enjoy the read.

"It is critical to remember that the primary directive for work with clients does not require anyone to prove the realities of memories or to litigate. The objective of therapy is to help the client resolve conflicts which eliminates need for dissociation and enables connection with themselves or integration." Rolf finished translating, then he and Lydia stepped back.

Shaking their hands, Hannes thanked Lydia and Rolf, then announced, "Many of you traveled far and are ready to call it a day. We will convene tomorrow at 09:00. Thank you."

Lydia opened the e-mail, organized the next day's notes, and laid out tomorrow's outfits when a knock on her door interrupted. The aroma of chamomile tea greeted her before the endearing expression on Heike's face. "I taut you might like dis," she said, handing the tray to Lydia. She backed away and vanished before Lydia said more than, "Vielen dank."

DAY 2 — Demons, Alters, and New Interventions

The initial full day of the conference began with singing and some jovial play between Rolf and Lydia. Rolf liked to tease her about speeding on the autobahn. Then, head down, eyes peering over the top of her glasses, she gave him a 'that's enough look' followed by a wide grin and a twirl to face the audience.

"Demons are mentioned at least seventy-five times in the Greek New Testament and called devils in the King James Version of the Bible. Jesus commanded Christians to cast out or exorcise demons, the same as He. You may be reflecting on situations in which attempting to rid a person of a demon did not work.

"A few reasons exist. First, I believe these entities sense if a person knows they are authorized to oust them. But if a person is unsure, nothing happens, or the demon will jeer and humiliate that person.

"Familiar spirits or demons follow a family line for generations and know its iniquity. They initially access a child by asking if they want a friend or helper. If the child consents, the invited demon receives the legal right to stay even if the exorcist experienced great success in the past. In these cases, the person must disinvite the familiar.

"Other instances occur in which even the most seasoned exorcist fails. The reason is that the entity is not a demon, which is another topic.

"On the other hand, this principle is of value to us who are invited somewhere and find nastiness. We own the legal right to take authority over evil in a place if we are a guest, whether by invitation or payment for the area. **DO NOT** cast out because the legal rights involved are not yet eliminated but bind the spirits in the name of Jesus to be totally impotent for the duration of your visit. The people there will notice a different atmosphere, especially children. Remember Matthew 12:44? Look it up in the small groups.

"Scripture tells us demons don't like dry places, are earthbound and seek habitation. Your pets may need an exorcism!" Lydia teased wide-eyed, nodded yes, leaned toward the audience, and said, "Really, honestly!" The listeners momentarily became avid speakers among themselves.

Lydia straightened and continued, "There is a growing agreement that demons are the spirits of Nephilim, the offspring of fallen angels and human women as recorded in Genesis six. More about Nephilim later in the week."

"Please focus your attention on the PowerPoint chart. You will see three categories, OPI, alters, and demons. The OPI represents the O for the original God-created human. The PI for the primary identities understood to be functioning expressions of the original person identified as denial, pain, and confusion."

The day began calm and sunny. As Lydia turned to point at the screen again, foreboding clouds heaving and twisting their sinister substance in the distance caught her eye. Trees bordering the hotel's distant periphery bent low. Willow branches whipped furiously. Suddenly, a shutter crash banged against a window frame, then another and another. The din of howling wind almost drowned out the audience's agitation while objects were jettisoned by the windows. Expressions of fear and frenzy focused on Lydia. Turning to Rolf, she asked, "Were severe weather warnings issued for today?"

He anxiously responded, "My information forecasts are sunny and clear."

Lydia called for attention. When the audience quieted, she asked for a show of hands of those who attended her seminars or other classes about dominion over the earth. About thirty people raised their hands. She then asked how many of the thirty practiced what they learned? Now twelve hands raised. Lydia directed all but the twelve to please be seated. Then she said, "Demons are real! According to the first chapter of Ephesians, Jesus Christ received an inheritance of all authority in heaven and earth. He chose to share that inheritance with people who accept Him as Savior and Lord." She prayed.

> "Almighty God, we come before you as children in need. As priest and king of Your Kingdom of Light, I declare forgiveness for all our collective sins here in this building today. We thank you for trusting us with Your power."

Then she instructed the standing twelve to extend their right hand and loudly declare authority over the storm just as Jesus calmed the battery on the Sea of Galilee. They did. Immediately a shutter shot its last calamitous bang, then hung fixed midair. Quiet. The sun's rays burst through the dissipating darkness. Trees swerved to motionless. The gagged audience choked out utterances, stirred, and wrongly began to credit Lydia for the deliverance. She quickly shut it down, "Demons are real. Moreover, Almighty God is real and active and deserves our thankfulness. As children of God made in His image, we are highly privileged to participate with Him in overcoming evil. Let us give Him the glory due!"

A vibrant time of praise and worship followed. In due time, Lydia announced that it was wise to take a half-hour break, but first, she wanted to pray for Holy Spirit to lift off shock, fear, or trauma resultant of the storm from everyone. Whispered sighs of relief filled the room after the prayer.

Rolf and other smokers quickly exited. Heike hurried her staff to prepare the break refreshments earlier than planned. Hannes inspected the building for damage but found none. Lydia e-mailed her team and intercessors to seek God's face for understanding the attack. She asked if open doors in participants or hotel staff provided legal rights to allow the attack. She then lay down, propped her feet, and meditated.

"How is everyone doing?" Lydia inquired of the assembly. Positive comments rang through the hall. "Some of you are asking, 'Why did God let that happen to us?' That is an excellent question for you to discuss in your small groups today." Grumbling abounded.

Smiling sympathetically, Lydia said, "Okay then, let's continue comparing the OPI, alters, and demons. The OPI is usually not far from the presenter, although they may live "behind" alters. Like a marionette show, they project the alters or push them out. The OPI presents a strong sense of self, can age regress, is usually life-aware, and expresses personal preferences from their center of personal identity. EKGs show them firing from the frontal orbital cortex, front of the brain.

"Alters, however, feel different and separate from the OPI with a drastically different self-perception from the OPI, such as gender or morals. Often fear, rivalry, or even aggression occurs among them. They are stuck at the age created to be or older but cannot regress. In counseling, it is important to learn the body's age when the OP created the alter to isolate that trauma for healing. Remember, an evilly intentioned programmer can bring a person to the point of dissociation with torture, et cetera, but only **the OP creates the alter**. Yes, the programmer may give the script for the new alter to the victim, but only the victim creates an alter."

Rolf's ardent translation immediately followed Lydia's voice escalating in speed and volume, "This is their God-given power! This power heals! Our job is to convince them they have it!" Lydia fervently shouted, waving clenched fists. Rolf's supportive expression lingered upon Lydia as he mimicked with waving fists.

The audience responded with shouts of, "Yes, amen, and preach it, lady!"

Surprised at the robust response, Lydia stepped back, grimacing at Rolf. She raised her eyebrows, shrugged, and returned to the lectern to continue. "Alters are only concerned with doing their jobs, usually protective, with immediate results, not truth. They live from the back of the brain, the occipital lobe. She placed her hand at the back of her head and turned for all to see. "Clients complain of discomfort there when alters are active."

Aiming the pointer, she said, "Here we see the OPI's shift of perspective is imperceptible except for speech content, viewpoint, or body language.

"But an alter's switch is usually more apparent as they reflect the OPI's fears and conflicts, although these subside with therapy. They are motivated and bonded by fear. Some alters may be deeply buried and only surface years after perceived integration. Those are usually alters created by the denial primary identity.

"The OPI resolution yields a "whole" person, while the alter resolution is partial and illusory.

"Now, return your attention to the chart again. Contrast these traits with the demonic identifiers and differentiate between OPI, alters, and demons. When you encounter a demon, there is no connection, no sense of relationship with them. They remain ego-alien or 'outside of self'' in the client's point of view. Demons are arrogant and very self-assured. You may think they have negative-sounding voices. That is true except in some circumstances. They can use the hosts' voice and completely fool you into believing that you are dealing with an alter. Confusion, fear, and lust persist, despite therapy in that perceived alter, who is not an alter, but actually a demon pretending to be an alter.

"Regardless of the sound of the voice, there is no corresponding personality. They often present with foul odors. For instance, a demon of shame often emits a fecal smell. They force unwanted behavior and then blame the alter. An undisguised devil reveals itself when the client's eyes appear black.

"The word demon comes from the Greek word, *daimonion*. It means to enlarge or exaggerate the emotion, thought, or action. Lydia demonstrated this by expressing anger in a normal tone and a sincere facial expression of anger. Then with an ugly expression, she scathingly yelled into the microphone. The volume startled faces, and flinching bodies reacted to the latter. "Do you see?" she asked.

"What are the levels of demonization? Infestation means external demons can temporarily tempt a person to sin. Like my anger example, a demon can be internal or inhabiting but exerts little power. We contrast that level with obsession, a habit in the flesh, sometimes compulsive, serving as a house for demons. Examples of this would be addictions to pornography or physical substances. Possession means the devils are in complete control, with the personality and character of the person entirely suppressed.

"Christians can experience torment by these three levels mentioned but never demonic possession because their Savior purchased and possessed them.

"The accuser uses his devils to bring into reality about whatever you fear or worry. Remember Job saying, *For what I fear comes upon me. And what I dread befalls me.* (Job 3:25)? The word tells us not to worry or fear because we are overcomers as we obey God's will for us. Always ask the Holy Spirit to help you identify your motivations for worry or fear, then go to the trading floors of heaven. Ask forgiveness for your ungodly fears and anxieties, be specific. Then request God to make a trade of all the times you thought, spoke, acted upon, or shared your fears or concerns with others. Ask Him to exchange them for His promises related explicitly to those worries and fears, plus anything else His unfathomable grace would like to offer.

"I trust you are more demon-wise than before and will be able to differentiate between them, alters, and the OPI in the future. Enjoy a lovely mittagessen and perhaps a walk? We reconvene at 15:30 with kaffee and kuchen," Lydia concluded.

Text messages and e-mail alerts greeted Lydia upon returning to her room. The intercessors reported three representatives of a coven attended the conference and conjured the storm, but God allowed it to teach the attendees more about taking dominion. So they prayed that they leave.

Hannes found Lydia between small afternoon groups to say, "I'm sorry to report two men and a woman left the conference; they checked out at noon." Lydia thanked him and walked away with a satisfied knowing smile. *They were on assignment. Thank you, Jesus!*

The evening teaching session came quickly since the small group's subject content vigorously continued into abendessen conversations. Lydia opened the session by sharing the answers from the intercessors and staff with the reunited group. Then, she smiled at Rolf while the buzz of discussions among the audience ensued.

"Our remaining topics are potentially rather disturbing, so I decided to end this evening with good news, a newer approach in prayer counseling for DID.

As you know, when we first discovered DID and integration, we spent a lot of time talking with alters and finding their traumas. Then we found that a shortcut could be made in some cases, not all, by predominantly working with only the primary identities and traumas. Remember that DID is all about the conflict. Resolved conflict deems dissociation unnecessary.

"A new approach is remarkably effective in satanic ritual abuse cases and highly technically induced dissociation that incorporates the same spiritual dynamics. Even in cases of single abuser trauma, there seems to be a common occurrence of the same conflict. I hope you are on the edge of your seat wondering, 'What is the conflict?'" Lydia jested now at the far end of the stage to search faces as she stealthily walked to the opposite end and returned to the podium. satan knows that he needs our permission to do anything. What is the favorite word of darling two-year-old toddlers?

"No!" chorused the crowd as they shared comical stories with their neighbors.

"Correct. That is when the brain develops with power of permission. Once a child is two, or as soon as possible, people responsible for the child's programming will lead the child to Christ. The Holy

Spirit comes into the little one's heart, as we say, and stays. He promises never to leave. This evangelism is accomplished by reading Bible stories and teaching worship songs for little children and talking well of Jesus to the child."

Several women waved anxious hands to announce, "But that is what we do in Sunday School. We are not programmers!"

"You may ponder, this is the usual method of leading a child to Christ, so what? You are right. Now we have a Christian person. However, in these cases, once the child reaches around twelve, the age of accountability, the brain is developed enough to do analytical thinking. Then programmers manufacture a viciously horrific situation to aid the young person in making an accountable decision against God.

"Many clients called upon Jesus or God to help them thousands of times, but in their eyes and the indoctrination of their abusers, He never rescued them. Once they renounce any faith in God, they are offered the power of satan and instructed to invite demonic entities to indwell them. Torture ensues if the youth is not instantly keen on that idea until they comply. Let us call this part the Renouncer.

"So... now we have a major conflict. Two power sources reign within one body. Each set up its throne in the individual—two parts of the person operating according to their respective theology, morality, and conscience. Co-consciousness brings awareness of the two. The Christian is horrified by the presence of the Renouncer and all they stand for and do. The Renouncer hates the Christian and sees them as weak, boring, and pathetic.

"The Word tells us love never fails. Therefore, the counselor's immense task is to convince the Christian to embrace, accept and offer forgiveness to the Renouncer. This agreement forms a loving relationship of encouragement and support from the Christian. Soon, the Renouncer resolves their trauma, accepts Jesus, and integrates with the Christian, eliminating the conflict or need for dissociation. Yes, there may be more traumatic issues, but now as a singular person, an individual owning their past without denial or confusion seeks healing from the pain of trauma.

SAQQARA

"As we talk of this phenomenology, it is easy to forget we are asking someone who suffered unimaginably, to choose to admit they committed all revealed, ask forgiveness, and accept it. Once upon a time, I encouraged clients to forgive themselves. We do not possess the authority to forgive ourselves. We need a Holy Perfect Savior; only Jesus can do that. Jesus commanded us to forgive others to receive forgiveness. We need to ask forgiveness for not accepting all our humanity and His forgiveness."

Lydia walked in front of the podium. She outstretched her arms, beamed, and said, "In conclusion, in rare situations, a miracle occurs, and a child gets rescued. The principles of authority usually explain why this is rare but now is not the time for that teaching. Please understand. Thousands of times during counseling, clients see in the spirit, Jesus is there—helping them survive!"

"Tomorrow, we will learn that in most of these situations, drugs and hypnotism are used extensively in mind control and later how satan hopes to use the unintegrated."

Despite the full day, many gathered around the fireplace with good German beer, wine, and snacks to discuss the day's events. The teacher returned to her room, pulled her large suitcase from under her bed, and reached into a side pocket to fetch an envelope. Just as Lydia sat to open it, she heard a knock. She laid the envelope aside and opened the door.

"I'm sorry to disturb you so late, but I felt compelled to bring this to you," a young woman said and handed a wrapped gift to Lydia. "I made it to give it to you at the end of the conference but convinced by strong urgency; it must be now. Do you understand why?"

Tears filled Lydia's eyes, "Thank you so much for being obedient to the Father's leading. Would you like to come in while I open your gift?" After they were seated, Lydia said, "Yes, I do understand. Today is my birthday."

The guest's eyes widened with amazement as she exclaimed, "Oh my goodness. We didn't celebrate or anything. We didn't know…

but Abba knew and wanted your day to be recognized and special for you!" Lydia agreed, invigorated with delight as she unfolded a white chiffon scarf with hand-painted flowers of lavender, pink, and purple with green leaves. The young woman happily exited after a generous hug from Lydia.

"I will never cease to be amazed at your loving-kindness, Precious Lord. Thank you for such excellent care about things that are important to us. Bless her for being 'skin on' for You today," the birthday woman whispered through gushing tears of gratitude. Turning away from the door, Lydia noticed the envelope. She retrieved it. Her family instructed her not to open it until her birthday, and she almost forgot it or her birthday until the quiet at a full day's end. A beautiful card with loving words and promises of gifts and fun upon return, languished in her hand. A profound emptiness and homesickness engulfed her. Travel extracted its cost.

DAY 3 — Mind Control, satanism, Nephilim

Lydia sported her birthday scarf on a vivid purple sweater and wore black slacks. White pearl earrings completed the outfit. "I see you got the memo," she told Rolf, attired in black pants with a white and purple pinstriped shirt as he joined her for the morning session. Interesting how many times this matching happened, even with mentees and intercessors, without any communication.

"This morning, we focus on mind control methods and components," Lydia began. "The initial process begins with creating dissociation or splitting the mind within the subject. Electroshock therapy (ECT), is often used from birth to about six years of age to produce severe trauma. In many instances, the child is still in the womb. X-rays of victims show scars at the base of the brain.

"Hypnotism, drugs, and virtual reality are used extensively. We need to remember that the elite used technology at least twenty years before the masses even knew it existed. Of course, that duration is much less now that knowledge increases at such an exponential pace. Extensive use of drugs alters certain cerebral functions. They often put drugs into a punch for the children.

"Every imaginable form of sexual abuse, including bestiality and object rape, is used extensively. All sexual activity involves the spirit, which is eternal, and abuse deliberately cripples some of the spirit or imprisons it to some degree in other dimensions. Sodomy or anal sex exquisitely impacts a primary nerve plexus located at the base of the spine. That blow is quickly carried up to the brain to create shattering, producing reserve alters to be programmed later.

An audible stir among the attendees caught Lydia's attention. Some people shivered at the thoughts the message delivered. Several ladies left the room.

"Programmers use a satanic-style parenting plan. It's called a double bind. You are dammed if you do and dammed if you don't. For example, a programmer tells the child, 'Look how pretty you look in that dress, lace topped socks and sparkly shoes, and a bow in your beautiful curls. Then she is placed in front of a mirror to admire herself. After doing so for an adequate time, the caregiver angrily taunts her with, 'You idiot, you aren't pretty. You're the ugliest person on earth.' et cetera. This induced confusion quickly erodes the child's sense of self-confidence in their thinking. In satanic abuse, the child must choose between being harmed or harming another child or killing their pet or being killed. These double binds are the recipes for dissociation. The so-called choices are unconscionable for the child, which overwhelms them. So, the brain automatically protects the child with dissociation by creating an alter or a part of the child who can do the deed. Therefore, the OP can deny responsibility for the act to stay sane.

"A common induced confusion occurs with alters to reverse pleasure/pain perception. Black is white; white is black. Pain is pleasure; pleasure is pain. Sexual encounters frequently adapt this common satanic language."

The same man who interrupted yesterday stood, "What about sensory deprivation?"

"Sensory deprivation is used extensively. The suspended child soaks in water tanks at the same temperature as the human body in darkness and silence for extended periods. The experience greatly disorients any human and readies the child for dissociation. Recreational sensory deprivation businesses exist, but these are not ... or maybe not used exclusively for recreation. Hmm," she said with an index finger at her chin.

"Children are caged or locked up in various ways and places without food or water. This is common practice for transporting slaves. Factories full of caged, deprived children have been discovered, especially in Chicago and Los Angeles. Other countries stock their factories. Human trafficking is quickly becoming the most lucrative business on the planet. Drugs currently hold the number one status, but a drug needs replacement. Slavers use human beings over and over again until they are used up or die."

A shadowy veil slowly dimmed faces as she taught. Finally, Lydia's voice choked, "I am so sorry to be the one to bring such despicable facts, but we cannot be ignorant of the enemy's modus operandi. The realities are more strange and worse than fiction."

"Children are often made to eat and drink as animals to dehumanize them. They may be kept awake for extended periods, especially in dangerous or precarious positions, or places like a high precipice or overhanging the spillway of a dam. Sleep deprivation changes the brain chemistry."

A woman's hand flew up. "A high percentage of western society are sleep deprived. How can we prevent brain chemistry change?"

Lydia stepped in front of the podium to better scan the audience. She pointed from side to side and said, "Better turn off those LEDs in your bedroom, take the T.V. out, throw a towel over the digital clock and keep the mobile in a drawer. Humans require total darkness to obtain adequate rest and healing. Our body heals during sleep. I'll let you consider that lifestyle change during the morning break," she sagaciously smiled. "I realize this is disturbing information, so let's take a thirty-minute break this morning. Go outside, drink in the beauty, smell the roses. See you in thirty."

Lydia left the crowd's warmth and walked into the coolness of long corridors to her room. She unlocked her phone and excitedly moved the cursor to select recent Easter celebration pictures. A dismal weight from the teaching ebbed away as feathery contentment replaced it. One smile faded into a fresh one with each different view. She locked the phone after the encouraging office e-mails uplifted her spirit. Then she joined others on the flagstone patio appointed with prodigious urns of fragrant spring flowers to enjoy the panoramic view and nibble hazelnut tortes.

"How are you feeling?" Lydia began. "Today's information is heavy, and we need to learn to balance ourselves as we encounter such provocative knowledge or people with these histories, lest we become vicariously traumatized. Counselors especially need to be alert for vicarious trauma. Please be sure to leave and take care of yourself if you become disturbed. Once settled, please return to the assembly. Today, most of you represent health care, education, law enforcement, social work, pastoral, and legal professions. Some of you are also victims of such atrocities. You seek help for your personal or professional lives. People perish for lack of knowledge. I pray that the accumulation of knowledge will be augmented with understanding and then acted upon with wisdom. Your design ensures there is no mistake you are here now. You are the chosen to change this evil. History shows how the action of just one person changes the world time and again. Never doubt your impact!

"We looked at some methods used to dissociate a person. The next step is programming. Programs are what we believe. We are all programmed. Hopefully, created and free-style learning disseminates what we believe. **Mind control programming is accomplished via torture and indoctrination with beliefs for the well-being of the one doing the programming at the expense of the one programmed.** The programs automate a person to do assignments.

"The assignments are embedded with compressed detailed commands. Virtual reality optical devices are sometimes used with harmonic generators to project pulsating colored light, subliminal, and split-screen visuals. Together with computer-driven generators, hi-tech headsets that emit inaudible sound waves or harmonics cause our ribonucleic acid (RNA), to converge neural pathways to the subconscious and unconscious mind. Stimulated implanted chips trigger actions, emotions, thoughts, and assignments.

"High voltage electroshock is used for memory dissolution. However, during prayer counseling with these victims, the omniscient Holy Spirit reveals supposedly wiped memories.

"Programming via visual, auditory, and written mediums is updated and reinforced periodically. Some original programming themes included the Wizard of Oz and Alice in Wonderland. Programmers use many recent child-focused movies to desensitize a majority of the population. They use subliminal, neuro-linguistic programming, and deliberately construct specific triggers and keys for base programming of highly impressionable Monarch programmed children."

Raising her arm, Lydia asked, "How many remember hearing news several years ago of many teens in different Japanese cities simultaneously committing suicide? Many of you! That was an example of mass assignment triggering."

"I receive many questions about satanic ritual abuse. In my opinion, all ungodly abuses are satanic, whether in a laboratory, hospital, military base, or in the woods with a blazing bonfire and chanting hooded figures. However, demonized individuals can carry out stereotypical satanic rituals. Therapy often discovers military fathers or small groups of self-styled satanists following the satanic bible. Long-established secret societies honed the skills of torture, programming, debauchery, and collaboration with demons for centuries. They rejoice in sacrificing animals, babies, and other humans as their way of worshiping. In ritual abuse, bloodshed abounds tied with the betrayal of natural affections and denigration of human dignity or worth. Their aspirations are to nothingness, whereas Jesus promises abundance. People are buried alive or kept in animal or human carcasses, then rescued to simulate resurrection. The best satan can ever do is imitate God, and he does this in every possible way because he aspires to be like God. satan holds his holidays at the exact times as Jewish and Christian holidays. satanic victims experience difficulty around those times.

"Some people are born into cults without birth certificates or a normal life, purposed to breed babies for sacrifice or be sacrificed.

"The animal kingdom is defiled by training to interact unnaturally with people. Standard methods for terrorization include enclosing a person in a box of spiders, other insects, snakes, or body parts. Do I need to go on? In other words, if you can imagine the most heinous detestable evil, you barely touch on the unimaginable horror of satanism. It is easy to believe that demonic entities are involved."

Laments burst forth from the audience, "Hideous, God have mercy, heaven help us!"

"Many children in generational satanic families are farmed out to a relative for the "in house" programming. Powerful God-given instincts within parents inhibit the ability to commit the required cruelty to their child. Many adoptive families appear stellar on the outside but are committed to such groups. Please do not get me wrong. I highly honor people who adopt children to love and nurture them.

"satan hopes to use the unhealed. Shattered people who believe they are worthless except to the group who programmed them are like arrows in satan's quiver. So the programmers use and abuse them until they are no longer useful.

"The purpose of this event is to increase general awareness of Dissociative Identity Disorder. This awareness helps us appropriately administer healing, which only comes via the gift of life and forgiveness of our Savior, Jesus Christ. This gift effectively blocks evil infiltration into every walk of our lives.

"Now I ask our Precious Lord and Comforter to lift off any defilement and vicarious wounding from all who learned this information.

"The afternoon workshops begin here at 15:30 to view footage of the *Kandahar Giant*, followed by teaching on the Nephilim. Small groups will meet this evening. Have a refreshing break." Lydia threw kisses with both hands as she said, "Thank you for your attention to such difficult material."

A rustle of activity and animated conversations followed the dismissal for lunch. Excited attendees happily returned to the main conference hall, where drawn drapes darkened the room. Next, Hannes introduced the *Kandahar Giant* film. When the movie ended, the hotel staff quickly opened the weighty drapes. Rolf made large gestures with his arms and legs to give impressions of giantism as he reached the stage, then bent almost to the floor with an infectious laugh at himself. Soon the room filled with gregarious laughter.

"Thank you, Rolf, we needed that!" Lydia said. Feeling a little light-headed from laughing so hard, she grabbed the lectern for balance while she dabbed fun tears and began.

"So, U.S. Special forces encountered a fifteen-foot giant in a cave in a remote region of Kandahar, Afghanistan on August 16, 2016. It killed some of the soldiers, and it required many high-powered weapons to finally bring it down. A military helicopter then transported the giant to somewhere for study. Do you believe this? Maybe it's a conspiracy theory doctored movie to scare us, as reported by some on YouTube? Are there now, or ever been giants on the earth?" Lydia inquired.

"Famed author and researcher L. A. Marzulli found photos in a museum of a skeleton over eight feet long excavated by Glidden from the interior of Catalina Island, twenty-six miles across from Los Angeles.

"Timothy Alberino studied archaeological digs worldwide and found skeletal heads far differently shaped and much larger than current humanoid craniums.

"Recently, researchers gained access to highly restricted areas of the Smithsonian, which houses similar giant skeletons. Steve Quayle's book, *Genesis 6 Giants,* illustrated charts and compiled extensive data.

"Many people viewed the Old Testament God as cruel for ordering a flood to eliminate all but Noah and family from the earth. Later, He ordered the Israelites entering the promised land to kill all men, women, children, and animals in certain areas. Why would He do that? It is not His nature!

"Because all were genetically altered except for Noah's generation. They were not pure Adamic stock made in the image of God to have dominion of this earth. Even plants were genetically modified. Remember the two men who carried gigantic grapes on poles? Genesis 6:1-4 tells us about the fallen angels leaving their first estate by taking human form to procreate with beautiful human women. Their offspring were avatars, a mixture of terrestrial flesh and celestial flesh. They corrupted man and beast, plant life and fish to the point that God said in Genesis 6:5, … *every intent of the thoughts of the heart of man was only evil continually*."

Lydia watched amazed eyes reflect thoughts of reconciliation towards God, grateful understanding, relief, and smiles sent from one to another.

"Giants translated is Nephilim, meaning fallen one from *naphal* according to *Strong's Exhaustive Concordance of the Bible*. Giants are referred to in Deuteronomy 1 as descendants of the Anakim. There were Emim and Zamzummim. King Og of Bashan ruled the Rephaim. David's giant, Goliath, had four brothers, hence five stones if the brothers came after him.

"Genesis covers immense spans of time. Nimrod founded Babel and Nineveh, along with many other great cities. Only a civilization far more advanced than ours would presume to build a Tower of Babel to reach heaven. Ancient writers described advanced Atlantis, and incredible precisional accuracies of the pyramids seem to confirm this. Some theologians suspect Nimrod genetically enhanced himself.

"The disciples asked Jesus to describe the signs of His coming and the end of the age. He said, as in the days of Noah, so shall be the time in the end. You may want to read more in Matthew 24, Luke 17, Genesis 6, and Jude 1. Does today's world mirror Noah's world?

Stranger than Fiction Conference

Absolutely! That must mean there are giants in the land too. Our good news for the day is from Deuteronomy 3:22: *Do not be afraid of them, for the Lord your God himself will fight for you.*

"So, what has that to do with me and DID, you may ask? Tomorrow morning, we will find out!" Lydia gave a provocative smile and waved goodbye with both hands.

The splat of water and soap fragrance filled the air during small group time as Lydia did a hand wash in her bathroom sink. She then hung the items on the travel clothesline she suctioned to the sides of the shower. Heike, who always volunteered to do laundry, took the remainder of the clothes earlier that morning. Lydia sent an e-mail to Tirza to meet her on Saturday at the Leipzig train station main entrance at 15:10. She suggested they eat abendessen before going to their lodging/conference venue in a renovated castle.

Later that evening, Lydia checked the details for tomorrow's last session at the reception desk. Just then, a short Santa-looking fellow kindly asked if she might like to join the people in the dining room for a beer.

"I would love to, thank you for inviting me," she answered, much to his astonishment.

His eyes twinkled, and his little bow mouth stammered a bit as he asked, "What kind of beer?"

"I like a robust dark beer."

He stroked his long white beard and left. Some time passed before she enjoyed the beer of German culture to the delight of those celebrating life together. Much later, she discovered the hotel supply stocked no dark beer, and several men walked into town to find it for Lydia. One must be true to held values, but to show respect for a culture endears one to the people.

DAY 4 — Transhumanism and New World Order

Coffee aroma met Lydia and Rolf halfway down the stairs to the breakfast room, where Harald, Holger, and the Asian sisters joined them at a table. Most people got little sleep due to so much socializing the night before. Many attendees hustled to bring luggage to the entrance before früstück for an immediate departure after the final morning session. Delicious German rolls with quark and ruby red currant jelly and various cheeses and sausages filled Lydia's plate. Lydia enthusiastically advertised quark as more nutritious than Greek yogurt and happily announced its availability in her hometown. A bitter-sweet conversation ensued as each person privately considered they may never be together again.

The morning session began with much singing and dancing. As much as Lydia loved her chartreuse wool jacket, she set it aside during the joyful praise. Finally, generous applause followed Hannes' expressed gratitude to the musicians. Next, he gave the necessary end-of-conference housekeeping announcements, including a plug for the conference DVDs, CDs, and the book table. Lydia also offered her gratitude to the musicians and the hotel staff for the quality service provided with kindness and smiles. A grateful response followed from the entire group.

Lydia walked back and forth across the stage, talking with her hands as usual. "This is a terrific group of people with which to grow. The small groups functioned with rich amazing input. You produced provocative questions!" A demure smile crossed her face as she asked, "Can you believe this is our last session? Are you ready for this?" Lydia heard different responses throughout the room as she turned to Rolf and asked him the same question.

"I'm ready!" he shouted as he strutted around, comically flexing his biceps. Lydia rolled her eyes and thought, *He is so handsome and fun! I'm fortunate that such an excellent translator and friend compliments my life.*

"Our purpose today is to help you become aware of perhaps the most significant cloaked strategic issue facing the world today. There is a diabolically regimented worldwide plan for the total demise of the human race. This ancient plan proceeds with efficient precision and effectiveness. Part of the plan is to infiltrate the Church, the principal obstacle. The Church is unaware of this strategy for the most part. Even if aware, it appears ineffective to do much against it.

"For at least five years, the religious circles in which I traveled, produced seminars and wrote books on our identity. They stress the absolute necessity to discover, accept and live our created identity to obtain intimacy with God and fulfill our destiny. If you listen to secular information, the buzz is about finding your god-self to be fulfilled, better known as secular humanism.

"The serpent tricked Eve in the Garden of Eden into eating forbidden fruit to become what she already was. Did you ever think about that? satan is the father of lies. First, he told her God lied. Then the ruse, 'If you eat it, you will be like God.' **They were already like God,** created in the His image. Voilà! The great deception! Can you imagine the intelligence and powers required to name every species on the planet? God gave Adam that assignment. After the disobedience, God lovingly protected humankind by cursing them with limitations. He knew the possible devastation of sinful human nature if the incredible potential and power they initially possessed still operated.

"satan despises human beings and busily tries to destroy us any way he can; this includes trying to access the latent power from which God protected us. I think satan is insanely jealous of us. Research identifies satan as one of the most important creations, beautiful, a master musician, and possible previous New Jerusalem building administrator.

God made humans in His image and The Bible records God's many emotions. He wanted a family. When we accept Jesus as our Lord and Savior, we become adopted into the family of God. When we partake of Holy Communion, our contaminated DNA changes into His to empower the commanded exploits. Jesus said, 'As oft as you partake', so He expects us to take communion often, not just at Church or monthly. He also told us that he came to restore all things.

"By the way, the scripture which says *man is a little lower than the angels* is a mistranslation. Some of humankind will judge the angels.

"Now for another great deception… **transhumanism, the new world religion**. Serious research for modifications of the human genome aggressively continued since the 1930s. Current estimates predict that millions of people are genetically changed. It is possible to buy a small kit for less than $500 to target a specific area of a genetic strand for alteration or destruction. Just think a minute of those ramifications. That technology can introduce and pass on unintended mutations to future generations." Lydia paused and posed with her head tilted upwards in deep thought.

"Yes, eliminating disease with genetic engineering sounds terrific. But, mixing our DNA with animal DNA to enhance humans by creating chimeras already happened. Genetically weaponized insects exist. This technology upgrades numerous military personnel while some countries participate and develop super-soldiers."

Lydia felt invigorated by the rapt attention given by the people.

"Admiral Byrd, who explored the Arctic and Antarctica, kept a secret personal journal. As a military man sworn to secrecy by the US Government, his findings never reached the public. However, after his death, his son, not sworn to secrecy, decided to reveal the contents of his father's journal. You can find this on YouTube. Essentially, Byrd discovered another civilization similar to the Third Reich ideology and superior technology with flying machines commonly seen as UFOs. Did you wonder at the Bible's references to 'under the Earth'? The ancients recorded flying machines and serpents hovering over cities in writings and art.

"Hitler steeped himself in the occult. Post World War II evidence strongly suggests that he interacted with alien knowledge to produce the Nazi technology. Contrary to common belief, strong evidence demonstrates that Hitler never committed suicide in 1945 in the Berlin bunker but escaped to South America with the help of the Vatican and others. President Harry Truman asked Stalin at the Potsdam Conference in 1945 if Hitler were dead. Stalin said,

Stranger than Fiction Conference

'No'. Captain Robert Thew said, 'We, the intelligence community, knew that Hitler did not commit suicide.' President Eisenhower reported, 'We have been unable to unearth one bit of tangible evidence of Hitler's death.'

"Post-war photos of Hitler taken in Brazil, Argentina, and Uruguay exist. The small village of San Carlos de Bariloche verified Hitler lived there. In 1960 Eisenhower visited the town, and later presidents Carter, Clinton, and Obama. One might wonder about the purpose of their visits.

"Another photo of Hitler is with Dr. Josef Mengele in Ohio, USA. Do you remember Josef's research in the concentration camps to create superhuman, Arian, and subhuman slave genetics? Mengele's death in 1979 in Brazil became verified in 1985. In the USA, many victims of mind control report Dr. Mengele present during their programming.

"You may be wondering why link Hitler with transhumanism. Hitler hailed Nietzsche as existing principally to prepare the way for himself, such as John the Baptist prepared the way for Jesus. Nietzsche espoused the superhuman as ruthless, exerting unbridled power. He championed strength personified and considered Christianity's virtue weak. He described Christianity as the one great curse, the one enormous and innermost perversion, the one immortal blemish of humanity. Much of Hitler's dream for an Arian superhuman race, *übermensch*, of world rulers became fashioned on this model. Hitler's Youth promised in their oath to become beasts hard as Krupp steel. Hitler criticized the Church as backward and blocked humankind from advancing due to their suspicions of scientific advances. The concept of übermensch survived World War II in the form of The Fourth Reich, which is but one of the organizations which lust to rule the world now.

"Using genetic engineering to create such superhumans is currently vigorously done and introduced to the people as a good thing. **The duping idea is that a human being is not enough but must be modified to be better—transhumanism.**

"Daniel Chapter 2 explains the meaning of King Nebuchadnezzar's dream in which a statue represented the ruling empires of humankind. The head of gold represented the Babylonian Empire, 605 BC-539 BC. The breast and arms of silver represented the Medes and Persians, 539 BC-331 BC. The belly and thighs of bronze represented the Greek empire, 331 BC-148 BC, and the legs of iron identified the Roman empire lasting from 146 BC-AD 476. Finally, the feet of iron and clay, AD 476 to who knows when? The term 'clay' describes humans made of earth. What do you think iron mixed with clay might mean? Daniel 2: 43 states, *And in that you saw the iron mixed with common clay, they will combine with one another in the seed of men; but they will not adhere to one another, even as iron does not combine with pottery.* **Transhumanism combines humanity with a machine and alien entities to create a new race. The Luciferian agenda is to destroy the human race and defeat God's plan.**

"I understand our break this morning only lasts fifteen minutes. Please be back on time because there is more vital information to share. I'll sign books during the break," Lydia concluded.

Lydia began by asking, "How many of you believe in global warming? Can I see your hands? Scary huh? Some people are passionate about global warming, and you probably know many who debunk it. Unfortunately, both groups only did part of their homework."

"In the mid-1800s, Heinrich Moritz Chalybäus, a German philosopher, characterized Hegel's Dialectic into Thesis, Anti-thesis, and Synthesis. The thesis is that man's pollution of the atmosphere is causing global warming. The anti-thesis, in this case, is a fearful and shamefully guilty reaction of humanity to that idea. The synthesis or resolution to the conflict requires regulations and loss of freedoms imposed upon society to reduce pollution.

"This **principle of management** is what the elites of Planet Earth use to speed the implementation of their New World Order.

In 1992 the United Nations Earth Summit with non-governmental organizations implemented comprehensive protection. They use this as an excuse to pull at people's emotions to manipulate them to volunteer their liberties in exchange for safety. That is the choice way to eliminate national sovereignty. It doesn't matter what is true, only if people believe it. In 2016, Bill Gates sponsored a global symposium focused on pandemic control. If an enemy nation manufactured the pandemic sickness and a vaccine loaded with DNA altering and programmable components offered the solution and became mandatory, imagine the fear of the masses!

"The global elite calculate the earth needs billions fewer people. Therefore, childbearing becomes a punishable crime without a government license. Thankfully, Agenda 21 did not pass in 2015 but must be implemented by 2030, according to proponents. The Green New Deal's goal is global socialism and control via taxation on all. **Please research Agenda 21 and The Green New Deal** if you are unfamiliar. You must know that material, but we lack time to address those details.

"It is true that pollution damages our environment but not to the extent of propagandized global warming. Once Warming was not evident, the substituted term, Climate Change, became popularized. Geological, astronomical, and other scientific data show that this gradually happens to our planet around every 405,000 years. The electromagnetic impact of Jupiter and Venus or some other heavenly body's orbit close to the earth cause this phenomenon.

"You see, the global elite, wanting the New World Order, determine most national leaders, financial and criminal oligarchs, many world events, and decide wars. Biblical scholars know that one world domination is the rule of the Anti-Christ. Throughout centuries, satan grooms a Nephilim Anti-Christ ready to be fully possessed by himself if the world stage is ripe. Yes, Nephilim, half-fallen angel/half-human, walk among us genetically altered to look more human and less gigantic.

"Tom Horn reported in his book, *Exo-Vaticana*, that the Vatican built the Binocular Infrared Telescope named Lucifer atop Mt. Graham in Arizona. It is also known as the holy mountain of Native American legend. It tells of a portal for the gods or legendary stargate there. Lucifer's astronomers are anxiously awaiting contact with alien beings. The arrival of these aliens with superior knowledge allegedly solve our problems by ushering in the final world religion making all others obsolete or illegal.

"Aliens from underground civilizations and solar system hives outside ours show extreme interest in human beings. At the end of the age, will they converge on Earth for the final great war, Armageddon, coined as hell-ageddon, to meet at Megiddo?"

Lydia said nothing but intently looked at each person in the room. Pregnant electricity filled the environment. A mixture of awareness, intrigue, fear, and wonder swirled in human thoughts and emotions. Finally, she said, "Our destiny birthed us in the empire of clay and iron. Have no doubt; our Creator gave us everything we need for this time in history to fulfill our destiny successfully. Be relentless in your prayers to God regarding your identity and future on Earth; by all means, guard your genome!

"This information can be devastating to many who do not know how the story ends. We know Daniel 2:44 tells us, *And in the days of those kings, the God of heaven will set up a kingdom which will never be destroyed, and that kingdom will not be left for another people; it will crush and put an end to all these kingdoms, but it will itself endure forever.* Philippians 2: 9-10 informs us, *Therefore also God highly exalted Him, and bestowed on Him the name which is above every name, that at the name of Jesus every knee should bow, of those who are in heaven, on earth and under the earth.*

"Someone may think, that's all in the Bible, and I don't believe in the Bible. I lived a season of doubting Biblical truth and can respect such doubts. During my season of doubt, I searched the world's religions and felt appalled at the origins of most of them. Christianity is the only religion with a God who loves His people and sacrifices for them. All others require sacrifices to a god/s. The fact that forty biblical authors penned sixty-six books in different centuries, which corroborated the whole, demands a master author outside time and space.

"Abundant Biblical references validated by archaeological finds of cities, giants, or answers to scientific astronomy puzzles are compelling. Perhaps most persuasive are the many prophecies in the Bible which came to pass precisely to the day and sometimes the hour.

"Personal experiences of other people and myself with the Holy Spirit leave me with absolute assurance of my choice to live by faith in Jesus Christ, the one who will rule the final kingdom. Intelligence, the Bible, and experience produce belief in the Holy Trinity, resulting in peace even in circumstantial whirlwinds.

"Whether we believe it or not, hard evidence indicates we are at the end of this age and war for the survival of our species. It's time to take our heads out of the sand, wake up and look at our world. satan and other opposing entities use DID programmed humans to infiltrate and subvert the Church to further their agenda. They annihilate the human race, by converting humans into a transhuman super race army to war against Jesus the Messiah.

"This ends the *Stranger Than Fiction Conference*," Lydia shrugged her shoulders, warmly smiled, and said, "I hope it enlightened, provoked, and encouraged you. Please share this information with everyone you know. We own our role to play in this hour. Thank you, Rolf, for your theatrics and excellent translations." The audience clapped and cheered. Rolf bowed, smiled, and briefly did his giant portrayal, followed by robust laughter and applause by the audience.

Lydia concluded, "You are an endearing audience. I hope to see you again." In German custom, the people stamped their feet until the room seemed to reverberate, then stood to offer lengthy applause. Lydia threw kisses as she descended the podium to shake hands and hug the attendees.

Goodbyes over; Lydia took mittagessen with Rolf and Hannes to discuss the conference, tentative plans, and review evaluations. Lydia helped Gerda pack the remaining product and then calculated high finance with Hannes. Finally, Heike delivered Lydia's laundry just as she opened her suitcases to load. *Tomorrow begins another leg of this international tour. A train trip from Kassel to Leipzig takes two hours and twenty-three minutes, with one stop in Eisenach. I'm excited and look forward to time with Tirza again.*

CHAPTER 25

TRAIN TO LEIPZIG

Saturday arrived in gloom and rain. Lydia shouldered her backpack, handed her luggage to Hannes, and followed him to the van. Heike's sweet voice from the terrace turned her head. She and Lydia had a strong connection since counseling several years ago regarding the loss of their child. Heike's eyes filled with tears as she neared and embraced Lydia. She handed Lydia a love-filled lunch. Tears streamed down her rosy cheekbones, "You will come back, yes?"

Engaging her endearing smile, "I hope so and hope to host you in my home someday. God bless you, Heike, and thank you for everything done with such excellence. I feel at home here," Lydia said.

Hannes, a perennial tour guide, drove to Bergpark Wilhelmshöhe and expounded the renowned Hercules Monument statistics in Kassel. Lydia visited it years ago and hiked to the top of the hill, supporting the 8.25-meter-high statue atop a pyramid on an octagonal foundation. At its base, 250 meters of breathtaking cascades emptied into Steinhöfer's Waterfall, rushed under Devil's Bridge and tumbled into the aqueduct. Night lighting created an imposing spectacle. Visitors toured every level of the landmark.

The train station bustled with humanity, unlike the emptiness when she arrived. Hannes' urgent errands required a quick unload of the luggage and departure. *What a relief to manage only two suitcases now. Despite profound fatigue from the whole week, I managed to sleep well. Today feels like a warm fog of softness. I'll sit and watch the world go by without stress with minimal need to interact.* She sat on the Pullman and reflected on the compact days and evenings. Last week surpassed all her expectations for success. The hardness of the luggage handle interrupted reverie and compromised the desire to sit but also exaggerated the week's fatigue.

The Eisenach train change afforded time to use the station toilet, much preferred to the unbalanced weaving and often odoriferous train toilets. She found the locked stall required a coin to open the door. Searched, no change! She remembered a weathered woman clad in a dirty print sitting on the pavement at the entrance. Lydia offered her a euro for change. The woman did not understand Lydia's request to make change but took the euro and turned away. Time ran out for that nature call. The whole scene resembled the third world, certainly not Germany!

The increase in traffic and high-rise apartments replacing fields and forests signaled Leipzig. Lydia found the main station entrance. Wearing the backpack, she piggybacked the carry-on to the Pullman again. She stretched her neck searching for Tirza. A passing auto splashed rainwater. She deeply breathed in the fresh ozone fragranced by trees in blossom. Finally, a "toot" from a familiar royal blue Audi alerted her.

Tirza pointed forward to indicate walking further down the sidewalk. She drove ahead, parked, and popped out to hurry toward Lydia. "I just made it in time; there was a pileup on the autobahn. Sorry, the rain limits our convertible fun, but there will be time for that. Let me put your luggage away. Do you know what you want to eat?"

"I always enjoy Greek, but a crisp wiener schnitzel is also tasty," said Lydia. "Do either of those sound good to you?"

"Let's do Greek. I passed a Greek restaurant near here. I love their salads, hate their ouzo. How was your trip? Can't wait to hear about the conference," Tirza bulleted as she drove away.

Train to Leipzig

Lydia shared the strange experience at the Eisenach toilet. Tirza turned to look at Lydia, "You are going to see even more strange things. Sometimes I fear we are losing our culture."

"The trip was very relaxing actually. How is your mother doing at home?"

"She has always been independent, and that is helping her now. Neighbors help, and nurses and aids visit as needed. All that made it easier for me to come here. I wanted to so much, but family comes first. Mutter's prognosis is good."

"Rolf sends his regards. He missed you," reported Lydia. She shared the storm and other highlights of the conference during the meal. On the way to the castle, Lydia said, "Tomorrow, we relax and prepare for your premier of co-teaching. Are you excited? Nervous?"

Lifting and dropping her shoulders while nodding, "I worked hard for this opportunity and studied and practiced a lot. Sure, I'm a little anxious, but also confident," Tirza answered.

When they arrived, falling darkness blanketed the structure, but they would have plenty of time to explore tomorrow. After Lydia and Tirza crossed through a narrow drawbridge gate, a doorman met them. Other staff offered a friendly welcome but also seemed officious. They perceived their reserved rooms next to each other on the third floor. The recently modernized castle offered private bathrooms and Wi-Fi.

Lydia bade Tirza, "*Schlaf schön* or sleep well… did I say it right?" She then settled in to unpack her luggage. An oak armoire almost seven feet tall with carved doors closeted her clothes. She kicked off her shoes and padded on the thick Persian rug searching around and behind things until she found the Wi-Fi connection near an inlaid French Empire writing table. She plugged in her mobile phone and computer, then quickly accessed her e-mail.

Impact! Stupefied, she stared at the office e-mail while confusion swirled in her head. *Get a grip! Reread it!*

CHAPTER 26

DESTABILIZATION

———◆◆◆———

Slow deep breaths. Lydia struggled to calm herself enough to reread the e-mail. The second reading hammered in the first. A seven-month pregnant client developed eclampsia resulting in an extraordinarily long and complicated delivery. The mother and premature baby were both in critical care.

"Oh God, no!" she wailed, jamming fingers into her temples, pushing apricot locks up in a frenzy. "We carefully avoided deep memory work during the pregnancy to prevent traumatizing the precious little one. It's early. I didn't prepare her for the delivery yet. Why didn't You warn me or tell me to do more? It's too soon! What have I done? God forgive me, forgive me, forgive me! I thought You promised to protect us and to provide for us. Where were You? I knew there would be interference! I should have prepared her earlier!" All night the self-recrimination, wailing, crumbling to the floor, pacing again, and groveling continued.

A warm ray of sunshine awakened Lydia. Initially disoriented, she scanned her surroundings and found herself lying across a made bed in yesterday's travel clothes. She tried to pry her eyes open. Finally in the bathroom, she startled herself. The colossal mirror reflected pallor, streaked makeup, and dark circles under

Destabilization

swollen frog-like eyes. She stood in a quandary; then, remembrance flooded grieved guilt again.

A knock interrupted agony. Tirza's pleasant voice started to greet her and then screeched, "Lydia, what on earth happened to you?" Uncontrollable tears darkened Tirza's blouse as she embraced Lydia's trembling frame. She encouraged Lydia to shower and get into bed. Meanwhile, she would bring their frühstück to the room.

Lydia looked considerably different propped up in her canopied bed with damp hair slicked straight back and features faded without makeup. More tears sogged the nibbled toast. As she reported the e-mail, Tirza sipped coffee while listening intently. Lydia ended with a pathetic stare.

Tirza took a deep breath, set her tray aside, and sat beside Lydia. "You are an excellent mentor. You taught me we are completely accountable for personal responsibilities and those we consented to. Our decisions accomplish this. You decided to protect the child in the womb and your client during the pregnancy based on your knowledge, experience, and skill. Nothing caused you to suspect eclampsia would occur, especially so early in the pregnancy."

Tirza now held Lydia's full attention. "You don't understand, Tirza!" Lydia barked. "I knew there would be trouble at the delivery because when she started to show, a party-animal alter arrived for a session who ranted about the body's increasing protrusion. One of her alters demanded I get the 'dammed parasite out of the body.' She further denied the pregnancy and declared to get even with the mother for doing this to her. She cursed the pregnancy and swore she would not tolerate nine months of limited fun."

Tirza took Lydia's hand in hers and reasoned, "Your clients know you often travel for extended lengths of time, and they need to avail themselves of the help reserved for them by you before you left. I would think she was under the care of a good obstetrician." Tirza gently squeezed the clasped hands, arose, stacked the food trays, and said, "You need to rest. I'll come back at noon."

"No, please, I don't want food," Lydia muttered and turned away.

Knock, knock. Tirza peeped around the door with a huge bouquet of purple, white, and lavender lilacs whose rush of fragrance fully awakened Lydia. "Since you hail from Spokane, the Lilac City, I thought these might brighten your spirit."

"Oh, Tirza, they are gorgeous and magnificently fragrant! Vielen dank!" Lydia exclaimed, rising, and deeply breathing in the balminess.

"How are you feeling? I can almost see your lovely green eyes now. I took the liberty of rescheduling our counseling appointments. We will have plenty of time to get to Munich if we leave after mittagessen. The distance is a little less than driving from Spokane to Seattle and if you are driving!"

"I'm definitely not in the mood for ribbing about my fast driving, but the bouquet was very thoughtful, Tirza. I finally got my wits together to write an e-mail to the office asking some pertinent questions about the status of my client and her baby. I'll call Julie when the time differences don't jar anyone out of bed.

"The translator meeting is scheduled for 1300 tomorrow. You will like Angelica, who served as my first translator. She is a physician fluent in several languages whose advice helped me immensely. She told me I spoke very high English. Most attendees only understood lower English, so I needed to find simpler words for teaching. It can be challenging to understand a language if spoken at the usual speed or fast. Therefore, I needed to slow the speed of delivery.

"Some of my friends asked what country I had just visited because I talked much slower than usual. Most attendees speak Deutsch, but others only understand English. Angelica fluidly changes from one to another, so she translates your Deutsch into English and my English into Deutsch. I can't imagine myself teaching anything now. What do I know? I'm incompetent! I'd feel like a hypocrite! Why am I even doing this work?" Lydia lamented.

Tirza pensively looked around the room and sighed, "You know I greatly respect you, Lydia. I understand and suggest you teach when you recover your confidence. I believe, with the help of the Holy Spirit, I can start the conference, and we can reschedule your talks later in the week. Since we record the sessions anyway, you can still critique mine even though absent. I hope to relieve you of stress by these changes. Do I have your permission?"

Lydia gazed intently upon Tirza as the late afternoon sun haloed her chestnut hair and thought, *look at you, so wise, confident, merciful yet strong. Dearest Tirza, you are ready to fly solo. I see you. I trust in you.* "Yes. Go ahead. That sounds doable. But I don't want to see anyone, and I'm not hungry. But, I'm obligated to respond to my team soon."

Later that evening, Tirza brought chamomile tea and prayed for Lydia with blessings of peace and truth. "Phone me if you want anything. Room service is always available. I'll see you after the meeting with Angelica tomorrow. *Gute Nacht.*"

CHAPTER 27

INTROSPECTION

"Everyone is eager to be with you, Lydia. Angelica is amazing, and she sends her fond regards. Thirty registrants won't be too intimidating for me," Tirza energetically reported. "If people ask, 'You are under the weather' by the way, although you look a bit better today. While I prayed for you, I wondered if I could present some ideas to ponder. Would that be okay with you?"

"I could use some good ideas right now," Lydia dryly remarked.

Tirza straightened and read, "I'll present the ideas and let you think about them after I leave. You are unduly upset with this information, which is not normal for you. Is it possible that you became emotionally involved with this client? Yes, I know you care deeply for your clients but more than that? Is it possible you assumed more responsibility for the client than you should? Is it possible you became more dependent on principles than the still small Voice? I wrote the questions for your convenience. Here. Please don't worry about this event. All seems to be going smoothly. I'll check in tomorrow at noon and brief you on the sessions. Please call anytime."

Tirza bent down to give Lydia a tender hug and left the somber room.

Tirza's positive noon report lifted some heaviness from Lydia. Later that day, Lydia discovered an ornamental grilled door framed

Introspection

her arched window. It recessed onto a stone balcony overlooking a distant lake and beautifully landscaped grounds. The sun stimulated her face and warmed her soul. She spent the morning considering Tirza's questions and realized the perceptions were accurate. She examined past interactions regarding her ill client and other clients but mostly her self-awareness. While soaking up the golden beams, she made peace with God, realizing He didn't cause the problem. She thanked Him for allowing her to identify weaknesses and areas which needed more wisdom through this situation. More tears flowed, but this time in joy. Standing and stretching, she laughed out loud, drank in the beauty, and sank back in the chair to just be. Peace!

"Oh, I dosed! What time is it?" The sun almost disappeared when Lydia rose from her chair, rubbed chilled arms, and reentered her toasty room. A noticeable inner strength invigorated her body because she felt lighter, curious, and hungry! Her watch indicated enough time to get abendessen, so she ordered a tray.

On Wednesday morning, Lydia felt like her healthy self again. She met with Tirza and reported her call to Julie at the home office. The baby lost several ounces, which is normal, and moved to a stepdown nursery. Her client received another blood transfusion but stopped seizing.

Lydia happily entered the event arena, delighted to be with Angelica again, acquainted herself with the attendees, and taught her portion of the program. That evening Tirza came to her room with a basket of supplies. "It's Wednesday night. I brought scented candles, music by great male operatic singers, bubble bath, a bottle of wine, and, oh yes, a goblet."

"You must own a photographic memory, Tirza! I'm sure you never heard me talk about my weekly soaking and loving me ritual more than once," Lydia exclaimed.

Tirza, wide-eyed, said, "Right, but I was so impressed that I copied it for myself! My husband is a non-passionate engineer, sweet, but unable to give what I get from the music."

CHAPTER 28

LEIPZIG APPEAL

The Leipzig seminar repeated the two-day California Seminar Lydia gave two weeks before this tour but lasted four days to allow Tirza to counsel. Tirza conducted herself brilliantly. She and Lydia flowed well together when they taught. The setting presented a perfect opportunity to educate the particular need for a physical Institute. Lydia approached the podium in a golden wool suit, brown heels, and a multi-stranded yellow and brown gem necklace which accessorized her caramel silk turtleneck.

Wide-eyed Angelica smiled a greeting. Then she took Lydia's arm to slightly turn away from the audience, "You look positively stunning, and I love those voluminous brown earrings. I see a glow about you. I'm excited to sense the Lord's presence on you today."

Lydia hugged Angelica and whispered, "I needed that!" She sensed the familiar passion accompanying the Institute Vision surge in her spirit from a simmer to a thrill.

"This morning, it is my honor to present the vision God gave to me in the early 90s before I became well acquainted with DID. Tens of thousands of people are in grave need of a place to heal in safety with explicit services to address their specific needs. There they learn new coping skills and cease the need to dissociate. They find their true identity with purpose, worth, and dignity while gaining new life skills for a victorious life. Onsite services provide education and provision for healthy lifestyles for spirit, mind, and body. To my knowledge, no such facility yet exists which can accomplish these goals.

Lydia initiated a PowerPoint. "Please envision a twenty-acre campus, around eight hectares, in a beautiful rural setting complete with trees, hills, year-round stream, fertile gardens, and an orchard complete with beehives. I can smell the pine and the fragrance of wildflowers visited by honeybees. Feel the gentle breeze? Lush greens, plump tomatoes, and mature produce fill gardens surrounded by heavily laden fruit and nut trees. I see people kissed by the sun and exercised by labor as they learn, teach, and tend.

"A central energy efficient multifunctional structure connects to surrounding buildings by walkways. Harmonious with the land, grapevines, berries, and roses cover the walkways. Benches strategically placed welcome peaceful rest. It houses administration, triage, medical center, classrooms, prayer counseling offices, cafeteria/restaurant, intercessory chamber, combination conference auditorium/gymnasium, and media center. The education and modeling equip lay people, professionals, and dissociative persons about DID.

"Healthy, delicious onsite food service is provided for residents and visitors (professionals, support people, public, and survivors of trauma) who attend educational events. This service also includes work therapy and work experience for survivors once they leave.

"An innovative, novelty-type restaurant is also planned for the public on designated dates and to serve events." Lydia walked back and forth across the stage and returned to the PowerPoint, "Are you tantalized with curiosity about what kind of novelty this might be?" Lydia seductively inquired.

"The media center produces international and domestic educational and supportive blogs, websites, webinars, and podcasts.

"As we consider the contamination and defilement of some survivors, 24/7 intercessory prayer becomes imperative due to the warfare waged against this work of setting the captives free.

I envision the prayer chamber to be high with panoramic views." She waved her arms, twirled around, visually beheld the beauty, then slowly became still. Next, she described flags, dance, worship music, substantial ornate pillows, peace, and joy, then burst into laughter, "Can you see it?"

Lydia stumbled a bit from the heavy anointing on her way back to the screen. "I guess I got carried away," she apologized and steadied herself on the lectern with her left hand to lean over it and hold her middle with her right hand. In continued laughter, weakness, and joy, she looked outward. Most of the audience also shared the holy laughter.

After an interlude of recovery to quiet, Lydia asked as she dabbed any remaining joy tears from under her lashes, "Is that fun or what? I think the Holy Spirit gifts us in that way to break the seriousness of life." She cleared her throat and announced, "Moving on. Are you aware that some people refer to that experience as 'drunk in the spirit'? Be assured there is no hangover!"

She giggled, then announced in a stately tone, "A triage unit assesses unsafe or ill people to prevent endangerment of other residents. Many dissociative people are poly addicted. A medical center to treat the plethora of health problems severely traumatized people suffer requires medical professionals. Clients often suffered difficulty getting laboratory test results because evil organizations positioned their people everywhere.

"Several apartment-like structures with shared living spaces accommodate survivors according to their level of healing. We need to treat entire families from generational satanic cults with facilities adequate for children to thrive and not separate from parents. That requires housing.

"The Institute offers trained staff who don't freak out when a client switches into an alter. Group and individual therapy counselors adequately educated and trained to deal with dissociation reside on campus. One connected building resembles a hotel in design and function. It provides housing for residents and temporary staff, conference attendees, and temporary housing for new patients. Its design offers the necessary division for privacy and safety for each category. The area under the building houses parking and maintenance equipment.

"Revenues from lodging, cafeteria services, restaurant, media productions, counseling, education, produce sales, and healing services all support the Institute.

"Perhaps you know of such a place? If so, please tell me where! Conclusion: There may be costly facilities or facilities that don't offer the completeness of service I believe is necessary for healing.

"When I see most people, they are financially broke from years of seeking healing from every imaginable practitioner, quack, and remedy. Counseling sessions are not enough. People need to be safe to heal, which requires a minimum of three months in-house.

"You are here due to your interest in DID for some reason. I beg you to make this Institute a reality in full rather than just a few counseling offices around the globe. Communicate this need to all you know. I am sure someone or many people do possess the finances and resources to make this a reality for the survival of humanity. Please consult my website for more details. Thank you for listening. May God richly bless you."

The seminar and counseling over, they zipped off to München in the convertible with hair wildly blowing. Lydia chose to drive the distances without speed limits.

"Tirza, you know how languages have words which mean or sound like different things? For example, signs at the off-ramps read '*ausfahrt*' in German. A dear friend who also works in Deutschland rents a car to drive fast. He laughs and remarks at the exit signs, which sound like … all fart in English! You know, a guy thing about burps and flatus. Tirza shook her head and giggled with Lydia at every exit sign for miles. At one point, Lydia uncontrollably laughed as Tirza grimaced.

CHAPTER 29

SOWING AND REAPING

Munich seemed to fill all kinds of seminars. Tirza's final required her to teach all but one seminar segment of *Why Do Bad Things Keep Happening to Me?* She alone coordinated audio, video, and translation.

Lydia's furrowed brow mimicked an unfamiliar translator as he stiffly interpreted Tirza. After the first session, Tirza stoutly announced to Lydia that the substitute translator would be a challenge to overcome.

On Tuesday morning, Lydia hurriedly dressed to allow a phone call to the Book Club at 05:45, the last few minutes of the May meeting. It was good to hear everyone's voice; however, she could not contribute to the discussion since she had not finished the book. The rule. Thi said, "Not to worry, we will be on this book a couple of months."

The week flew by quickly as Tirza taught and counseled while Lydia critiqued. Finally, Lydia presented, "To conclude this seminar, I get to do the fun part. I want everyone to think about three current problems in their life. Come on now, we all have problems. It may be work-related, a relationship issue, a bad habit you can't get victory over, or maybe a health concern. I'll give you three minutes to write them down. Leave some space after each to add

Sowing and Reaping

information later. Okay, go." She scanned the room, amused at the variety of expressions on the faces of the students as they thought.

"Time. Tirza did a superb job of teaching these absolute principles of life." Hearty applause broke out. Lydia turned and nodded towards Tirza, who stood and made a slight curtsey. Then Lydia returned to the podium to activate the screen. "I want to do a quick review before we complete this exercise.

- **Deuteronomy 5:16** is the law of honoring and dishonoring and instructs us to honor our father and mother. That means to try to love, respect, and forgive so that life may go well with you. Authority predominates here.
- **Matthew 7:1& 2** warns us not to judge, meaning to condemn, to prevent the judgment of yourself. This law of judging and receiving means you get in return whatever, and to the degree you judge.
- **Galatians 6:7** says, *Do not be deceived, God is not mocked; for whatever a man sows this he will also reap.* Or as the world says, 'what comes around, goes around'.
- **Romans 2:1** clarifies that you condemn yourself by how and whatever you judge because you practice the same thing. We become like that which we judge.
- **Hosea 8:7** explains that we sow the wind and reap the whirlwind, the principle law of multiplication

"Okay. Now select one of your problems. Please focus your spirit and mind upon the Holy Spirit fully. Then ask when you first experienced something just like this. Remember to capture the first thing of which you are aware. It may be a thought, a picture, smell, physical feeling, taste, or sound. Acknowledge what you get. The Holy Spirit waits to show more once we acknowledge the communication. Write what you receive. We tend to forget these things quickly. You have five minutes."

A door opened in the back of the auditorium, and Tirza's husband, Fredrich, entered. Lydia secretly invited him to the certification ceremony to culminate the seminar. She turned to see Tirza mouthing questions to him in her surprise. The graduating mentee's eyes brimmed with joy as she cast a giant smile Lydia's way.

They listened to the usual body stirrings, sounds of weeping, or nose blowing. "Time's up," Lydia announced. "Would anyone care to share what they discovered?"

The remaining session offered testimonies of original problems and how the roots replicated the current situation. For example, if the issue featured an authority figure, the origin also involved an authority figure like a parent, boss, teacher, et cetera. If the root involved money, so did the current problem. For instance, if the funds were earned and unjustly taken away and given to another, it repeated. The people were mystified at its precision but most amazed that the Holy Spirit knew the information they never shared with anyone else! Lydia thanked the participants for their transparency and blessed them to continue their inner healing with the increased faith and tools.

"And now, we need a drum roll," Lydia proclaimed. "It's your privilege to be here on this golden occasion. Tirza, please come forward." Tirza's heart started to race as she walked to the pulpit, glanced at Fredrich, then fastened her gaze upon Lydia.

"I first met Tirza Piltz in Austria at a conference I led, counseled her, and then found her following me like a shadow whenever I came abroad." Lydia chuckled and turned to give an appreciative smile to her mentee. "That began four years ago, right?"

Tirza nodded, then said, "Yes, but it feels like a lifetime of honor to be with you, Lydia, and to learn at your side."

Lydia fondly put her arm around Tirza and turned again to the audience. "Her excellent English served me well on innumerable occasions and will be an asset as she works with the severely broken of this world. I can speak from personal experience (deep gratitude swelled within Lydia and radiated to Tirza's heart). Observations of client sessions revealed she is highly perceptive,

Sowing and Reaping

compassionate, and able to give tough love as needed. She exercises strong, healthy boundaries, and is very knowledgeable and skilled. Most importantly, she is full of integrity, humility, and greatly anointed for this work." Reaching for a gold and purple document, Lydia turned to Tirza. "You completed all the competencies required to become certified. It is my honor to announce that Tirza Piltz splendidly completed her mentorship and is now recognized as the director of an official branch of this Institute."

Tirza graciously accepted a huge bouquet and took the certificate in hand. Gregarious praise and stomping of feet celebrated her accomplishment. She then hugged Lydia and thanked the crowd.

Lydia quieted the crowd and added, "Fredrich, would you please stand? May I present Tirza's husband, whom I want to thank for his tremendous support and encouragement?"

The audience turned to applaud Fredrich, then slowly exited as he made his way to Tirza. "We need to celebrate! he suggested after giving her a loving embrace and a tender sustained kiss on her forehead. "We may already have reservations for dinner and some surprises.

CHAPTER 30

TRIUNE MOTHER'S DAY

Excitement tingled Naysa as she watched Saqqara emerge from her car. She rolled out of her apartment to reach the door as it opened. "So, how did the triple-header Mother's Day bash go?"

Saqqara styled her hair in a ponytail. She rolled up the sleeves of her T-shirt and wore raggedy jeans and athletic shoes. Her eyes narrowed at Naysa, and irritation ejected as,

"What's it to you, nosey busy body?"

She then turned and bound up the stairs two and three at a time.

A great weight crushed Naysa's heart. She found it strange that her friend used the stairs, but she usually wore high heels. Slowly she maneuvered herself to her table, where she cleared celebration treats prepared earlier with happy anticipation. Saqqara enlisted some of her creative ideas to plan for this stellar event.

Naysa's sleep evinced fitfully, so she slept in, but now the doorbell jarred her awake.

Triune Mother's Day

"Naysa, it's me. Hurry. I'm about to drop our breakfast. The coffee is hot."

It took Naysa effort and time to get out of bed and into her wheelchair. Finally, she struggled into a robe and wheeled to the door.

Saqqara grown tired had finally put the food on the floor to wait with folded arms. At last, the door opened. Saqqara entered and began to arrange food on the table. "Sorry, you are usually up by now, and I thought it would be fun to share a special breakfast while I tell you about yesterday. You do want to know all the details, don't you?"

"I do," Naysa flatly answered. She watched in confusion as Saqqara announced the special breakfast of muesli, yogurt, blueberries, mango juice, and gourmet coffee.

"Well, first-of-all, your idea, Naysa, was to design everything in threes to symbolize the three generations of mothers excelled. A three-peaked pole tent presented a significant symbol.

"The very sophisticated great grandmother, young for ninety-two years, wore a white designer gown to match her white hair. The grandmother, however, looked as though she endured a hard life. She wore a red cocktail dress. The mother wore pink and seemed a bit preoccupied with her ten-year-old. Perhaps she questioned her daughter of a mere twenty-three years capable of pulling off such an auspicious event. Around a hundred guests from around the globe attended. Some real hoity-toity types."

Saqqara stood to put on airs as she licked yogurt from a pinky finger. Coffee, dairy, and sweets pleasured the senses. "They sat at tables covered in white, red, or pink floor-length tablecloths with exotic red, pink and white floral centerpieces. Three bands played dance music of each generation. It was interesting to watch the various age groups get into the rhythm of their genre.

"Of course, there were beautiful streamers and huge floral arrangements in the triune color scheme. We offered three fountains: a white chocolate fountain for the ponderous strawberries, a red tropical punch fountain, and a pink champagne fountain."

SAQQARA

Pressure on her heart lifted as Naysa joined Saqqara's enthusiasm, watched her infectious smiles, and felt the affection of her dear friend. *The Saqqara last night was a stranger.*

"The hostess rocked hot!" Saqqara piped up in a strange tone of voice.

"I prepared a little celebration for you last night. Where were you?" Naysa asked.

Saqqara looked puzzled. She fidgeted and rearranged items on the table. Joy drained from her face, and heat radiated from her cheeks as she wagged her head to confess, "I'm not sure. Something went wrong, I think."

"When you arrived, you weren't dressed in professional attire and didn't seem to know me."

"I always carry grubbies with me in case I help with the teardown... oh Naysa; I think I've lost time again... what happened?" Saqqara broke into bitter anger.

"Well, consider. This same time next week, you will be on your way to Spokane for an intensive week of counseling while I start an intensive week of physical therapy."

Saqqara squealed with surprise, "Do you mean you get to start parallel bars?"

Naysa shrugged, sighed, and said, "At last, I can try to get my legs back. I know it will be torturous, but I want to walk again."

Saqqara ran around the table and enveloped Naysa in a bear hug. "I wish I were here to support you, but, as you told me, I'll be with you in spirit."

The following morning, Nadine joined Saqqara in the office elevator. "Are you getting excited about your trip?" she grunted to catch an escaping legal file from her colossal stack.

"A little, I guess. Naysa greatly helped, especially with the required reading. May is feverishly busy for us. Tiffany and our temp Jillian are separately running two big events on Mother's Day while I fly away. I don't feel like I'm skipping out on them because I singlehandedly coordinated the spectacular international three-generation Mother's Day contract. I'm glad not to be here. My mother keeps leaving these creepy messages, sending stupid gifts and cards. I've arranged for the traditional flowers to be delivered to her Saturday."

"How are you getting to the airport?" Nadine asked.

"Call a cab." quipped Saqqara.

"Let me drive you. My mom's been gone a long time, and I'm not a mom, so it makes the day free for me; after all, I feel a bit responsible for this trip," Nadine offered.

Saqqara gushed, "How kind of you! We'll grab breakfast on the way. I'm not too fond of airline food. I'll e-mail my itinerary, address, and travel mobile number to you today."

CHAPTER 31

CELEBRATE AWAY

―――◆※◆―――

Tirza, Fredrich, and Lydia were greeted with a flurry of congratulations at the upscale eatery. Tirza's three children and their families, her mother, several close friends, and even her brother and family hosted the celebration party. Stories of escapades encountered traveling with Lydia over Europe and Scandinavia ensued, and those exploits at home with Tirza absent. A demonstration of the 'lipstick tradition' after dinner and dessert brought much levity.

The talk also centered around the mother's recent fall and Tirza's plans. Finally, Tirza''s fatigued mother and young children with caregivers called it a day while the others found their way to the Marienplatz Square. They were just in time to experience one of the world's most delightful clocks, the Glockenspiel Clock Tower, with its carillon of forty-three bells. Thirty-two life-sized figures played scenes on two levels from München's history, recounting weddings, jousting, and dancing. It lasted fifteen minutes and ended with a golden bird at the top who chirped three times.

Around the corner, another famous site, the Staatliches Hofbräuhaus, owned by the Bavarian State Government and known as the royal brewery, waited for their destination. The oompah band members dressed in *lederhosen* and elfin feathered hats created a festive atmosphere. The enormous hall furnished long tables where friends and foreigners shared space and conversation. Lydia felt beside herself to

Celebrate Away

see a small house inside the hall. Its walls stacked giant pretzels from floor to the ceiling. Waitresses wearing dirndls and flower wreaths in their hair frequently restocked the pretzels from wheelbarrows they pushed through the pulsating crowds. Their group nearly filled a table. The beer arrived served in at least quart-sized steins and mugs.

Across the way, a group of ruckus young men stacked their mugs and cheered on each contributor adding to the tower of glass.

Lydia leaned into Fredrich's side with rosy cheeks glowing. "Even though I just ate a sizable meal, I'm going to order another pretzel. I may get half of this mug finished, but maybe not," she laughed. Before long, she and some of the women returned to the hotel.

The next morning, Tirza and Fredrich took früstuck in their room. As he slowly drove away for home, she shouted, "I drive Lydia to the airport very early on Thursday morning. I should be home by noon."

After resting on Sunday, the following days brimmed with tedious but necessary organizational creation. Lydia and Tirza drank a lot of kaffe. The last essential review and editing of policies and procedures to satisfy the branch institute's German cultural and legal requirements concluded. They discussed the necessity for consistent communication to ensure success and effective support.

Wednesday evening, packing finished, they met for an early abendessen. Farewells punch such nagging pain. Both worked at eating their meal. Some messages from the heart need no words. Still, Lydia falteringly said, "I can't ever fully express how grateful I am to God for you, what you are going to contribute to the Institute, and how much I respect and deeply care for you as a person."

Tirza nodded, "I know. Thank you for believing in me even when I didn't. I feared that I could never be as resolute as you. I'm much stronger since I saw you are human, as destabilized in Leipzig. I... I didn't mean I thought you weren't!"

"I know what you mean, Tirza. Multiple times in my life, when I tried to tell someone I need something or am in emotional pain, they ignore me because they always think I am soooo strong!"

Tirza waved her uplifted arms to exclaim, "I'm excited to embark on this new chapter in my life!"

CHAPTER 32

HOME SWEET HOME

The trans-Atlantic ticket of Lydia's flight home read upgraded to business class. She liked surprises but not mysteries. "Are you sure? How does this happen without my knowledge? Oh well, I'm happy to take that seat." Lydia responded to the check-in-clerk.

I'm glad and thankful. Bless whomever made it possible, Lord. Her deep thought became distracted when a young man took his seat beside hers. She closed her eyes to enjoy the usual somnolence at takeoff fully. Then, sometime after being airborne, she rallied. The man next to her got up to remove his suit jacket and stow it above in the baggage compartment when the steward offered to hang it up. He nodded and smiled at Lydia as he sat back down and fastened his seatbelt.

Solitude headed her plan for this leg of the journey. The previous days and weeks demanded much on many levels with many people. *I will probably spend the first day home sleeping. After that, I'll sort the mountains of mail, unpack, do laundry, catch up on all fronts and prepare for the new client Saqqara. What an unusual name.*

"Hello. Are you returning home or going away?" the young man asked.

Oh no, a chatty Chuckie and I want to be alone. Lydia looked down and away to reply, "Home."

"Was this a personal or business trip for you?"

"Business." Lydia turned almost nose to nose with her window.

"Me too. I enjoy my work. I worked with several cities in Switzerland to implement recycling waste-to-energy conversion systems. An ROTC college friend stationed in Germany met me in Munich for some R&R. What do you do in your work?"

By now, Lydia was quite annoyed. *If I ignore him, will he go away? I am not being very pleasant right now. Maybe if I'm frank, he will give up.* She deeply breathed, turned around, and looked straight into his eyes. "I make people cry!" she said in a matter-of-fact tone.

Chatty Chuckie gawked with mouth slightly ajar. His Adam's apple fluctuated several times before he dropped back into his seat, glanced at her, and busied himself talking with the steward and other passengers.

By dinner, Lydia felt a bit ashamed of herself and apologized. She shared that after doing four seminars, counseling many people, supervising a mentee, plus dealing with a crisis at home, she needed some alone time. She planned to get it on this flight.

The young man, Justin, demonstrated excellent understanding. He sheepishly asked, "Do you really make people cry?"

Lydia guffawed, "It's unusual if the people I do prayer counseling with do not cry. They do so for many reasons. First, it's a great emotional release. People often enter the office and begin to weep. That can be especially unsettling for some men, but the presence of the Holy Spirit causes that."

"I want you to relax as you planned, but if you want to talk later, it's a long flight; I would like to know more about the Holy Spirit tear maker," Justin said.

Hours later, Lydia energizingly told him many beautiful stories about her triune God and the third person, Helper, Comforter, Holy Spirit's work in lives. He asked if he could e-mail her once in a while to ask more questions in the future. They deplaned together. The long wait at customs accelerated as they chatted about many things and exchanged contact information.

The layover provided adequate time for a good meal and needed exercise. The next nonstop flight to Seattle took five-plus hours. The plane's single aisle made it impossible to make the loop. Sitting lengthy hours made Lydia's bones throb. Her head felt foggy now from the long waking hours. Lydia played games on her phone until her eyes burned.

She ordered spiced tomato juice along with ginger ale. The stewardess observed her mix the two and commented, "I've never seen that done before!"

"It's delicious. Try it!" Lydia urged. Before long, another crew member stopped to say how good it was, then another. Soon other passengers ordered the mixture too.

Lydia welcomed the tight Seattle plane change to Spokane. The short hop over the mountains, desert, vineyards, fields, and forests to home dragged on. *Please let whoever is picking me up be on time. I waited forty-five minutes the last time.*

Lydia hauled the stacked luggage from the terminal baggage claim, feeling quite dull. Then she scanned for a familiar vehicle or face. Cavanaugh's southern drawl called her name. Her spirits rejoiced. He soon embraced a hello and took the luggage. "Gosh, it's great to have you back, Lydia. We sorely missed you. I agree with your family. A month is too long for you to be gone."

PART III

CHAPTER 33

HELLO SPOKANE

The flight steward kindly asked if he could get Saqqara anything as she settled herself in first class. "Red wine, please," she responded, turning to peer out the oval window. *Am I crazy for using a week of vacation time and spending all this money on airfare, hotel, auto rental, and Christian Prayer Counseling fees? Ms. Voight encouraged me to bring a support person! Ha Ha, double expense. Like I want anyone to know what I'm going through, and anyway, who would do that?*

"Oh, thank you." Lifting the wine goblet, Saqqara swirled its contents, inhaled the bouquet, and assessed the smooth taste. She smiled, took a drink, and savored it long while rethinking her decision. *I lacked interest in spiritual anything. My only research on the power of prayer is from magazines. How scientific is that? Dad sat on the church board. Mother eventually converted from Catholicism and often supervised church bazaars. I studied a lot of church history in confirmation. Love of Jesus usually titled the sermons. The youth group always did something fun while treats abounded. Somehow, I perceived it as plastic and hypocritical*!

A middle-aged man seated himself next to her, caught her attention, and offered his hand, "Hello, since we are neighbors, we might as well get acquainted. My name is Nathaniel Kantor."

He presented a stereotypical high-level business type. The expensive suit, pressed shirt, shined shoes, unique cologne, and British accent enhanced his good looks.

"So, is this business or pleasure for you?" he inquired.

"Business," she answered and turned away to focus on a magazine.

"What kind of business, if I may ask?"

"I'm a project manager for many major social events in Chicago."

"That sounds quite interesting. Major, like politics?"

Her azure eyes met his as she answered, "We serve many aspects of society, but yes, a senator commissioned a wedding in June."

"You're American, right? You seem like a person in the know. I wonder if I may ask a pertinent question so many people ask. I've been everywhere, as they say, and anyone I meet internationally who visited your country wants to return. Many want to move here, and the others who know anything about its republic are envious. Why are so many Americans passionate about destroying the constitution and want to create a socialist nation? Anyone who studied history or pays attention to current news knows that form of government eventually fails or erodes into communism, making impoverished slaves of its people. Sorry, that was a mouth full."

Saqqara's long lashes fluttered as she shifted her posture toward him and said, "That is a full question. I try to keep out of disputes; it makes for better business relations. I admit it's confusing to me. The social justice people offer genuine concerns for the underprivileged. They are salt of the earth, good people, for the most part."

"Excuse me, but it is difficult not to overhear your provocative conversation. May I join in to shed some of my understanding?" smiled a distinguished-looking man from across the aisle.

Nathaniel raised his eyebrows at Saqqara as he responded, "Please do. I seriously want to better understand this dilemma. You know as the United States goes, the primary world power, so goes the world." He scooted to the edge of his seat to better see the white bearded gentleman, and Saqqara gave him her full attention.

"Saqqara was it? What an unusual and beautiful name, Dr. Emmet Hargrove here. I agree with you about average citizen social justice people. Their only problem is they hope to substitute government for a righteous God, and we know too well our government isn't righteous.

"Nathaniel, well said. The United States of America is a republic and not a democracy as most people refer to this nation. Many people don't know the difference. A republic is based upon law and its' people democratically decide within the parameters of the law what they want. A democracy is a form of government where the will of the people rule. In that government, emotions and even whimsical thoughts can reign. If the constitution of our nation is discarded, we are a nation at the mercy of human weakness without the strength of principles and its wisdom to guide us. These principles made us perhaps the greatest nation in human history. Well, excuse my verbosity. I'm not giving another lecture."

"No, no, I found what you said very enlightening. What background enables you to be so knowledgeable? asked Nathaniel.

A little shy, Dr. Hargrove reported, some people see him a geopolitical expert on such matters and keep him busy on the speaking circuit. "There are more reasons…"

Just then a delectable snack service interrupted the discussion.

"Dr. Hargrove, you were about to say more," Saqqara prompted.

"Oh yes, a lot of ignorance is at fault. Propogandists make pawns of people with little interest in citizenship but enjoy activities such as financed protests, regardless of purpose. The poor are willing to follow a hopeful line of provision regardless of the source. Then there are the New World Order elitists who own most of the prominent communication organizations to propagandize the masses against the USA's nationalism and capitalism because they are game stoppers for their plan to rule the world. They want them destroyed."

Suddenly, Saqqara turned and plopped back, withdrew from the discussion, pushed the snack away and ostensibly attended her magazine. Dr. Hargrove looked chagrined, scrunched a smile to Nathaniel then reached for his computer. Nathaniel quizzically glanced at both his conversationalists. He shot forward offering a handshake to thank Dr. Hargrave for his informative input, then posed a perplexed frown as he settled into his seat.

Looking out the window upon descent into Spokane International Airport, Saqqara thought it was tiny compared to O'Hare. Nevertheless, the city, located about eighty miles south of the Canadian border at the foothills of the Bitterroot Mountains near the Idaho border, beaconed.

When I called to inquire about an appointment, something strangely comforting happened during the interview. A frequent headache started to press forward from behind my eyes, just like now. Ms. Voight adamantly instructed me to say, 'Step back, please.' After I did, the headache vanished!

"Okay, step back, please," she said aloud. She noticed Nathaniel scowling at her. Cheeks flushed; she waved her hand as if it were nothing but felt a warm rush of satisfaction to be headache free suddenly!

The cab driver loaded Saqqara's three suitcases and asked her destination. Saqqara rolled down her window. Crisp fresh air delighted after being cooped up on the plane. Wafts of sweet fragrance turned her head. "What is so fragrant?" she asked.

"Oh, we're just passing the arboretum. There are about eighty-eight different kinds of lilacs there in bloom now. If time allows, you might enjoy a walk there. Spokane is the Lilac City. Too bad you just missed the festival."

"What is that unusual earthy scent I smell now?"

The driver lifted his head, sniffed several times, and then announced, "Oh, that's tree bark. People use it to landscape." The city center lay ahead in a valley that expanded eastward. City terrain continued rising north and south. Mt. Spokane still flaunted her snowcap in the distance.

CHAPTER 34

THE ENCOUNTER

Day 1—

The waiting room clock announced 9 AM, and the office door opened. Lydia Voight looked the same as the picture on her website. She spoke a cheery welcome and ushered Saqqara into the spacious, well-appointed office. Lydia offered her to sit anywhere after introducing her mentee, Julie Wiseman.

"May I hang up your jacket and get you a bottle of water?" Julie offered.

Saqqara handed off her jacket. She thanked Ms. Wiseman for the water and chose to sit on the teal blue leather couch. A throw with squares of vivid colors edged in lime green draped over its back at its opposite end. Golden walls contrasted with rich walnut French windows.

The mentee called, turning to hang up the jacket, "Please call me Julie."

"And me Lydia."

"Oh, oh yes, and please call me Saqqara. We know it is an unusual name. Sometimes people hesitate to try it," she explained.

"It is a beautiful name. We are so glad to be with you. Your comfort is important to us, so let us know your needs. Tell us about your flight."

"It went well. My neighboring passengers made the time fly with stimulating and informative conversation."

"Great. This week we begin at 9:00 AM and break for lunch at noon. We resume at 2:00 PM for another three hours. I assign homework. Of course, it is not mandatory, but it greatly improves your work here. It's hard work, so please do not fast, but eat healthily. It feels good to exercise after sitting for so long, too," Lydia said.

Rolling her eyes and jokingly, the client said, "The hotel offers a full breakfast and exercise facility, but we'll need to work on a healthy diet."

Noting the 'we'll,' Julie agreed, "Don't we all! Where are you staying, and what is the room number in case we need to reach you?"

Saqqara officiously stated as she handed a business card to Lydia,

> "I thought you would need that information. Here it is and the mobile phone number I use on this trip."

Lydia documented what just happened with an X symbol to indicate a switch. Then, she handed a clipboard to Saqqara. "Understanding the complexity of trauma and the resulting difficulty to make decisions and stay focused, the following rules provide structure to focus and help maintain the decision for counseling. Years of experience produced this form. Please read it and ask any questions. Your signature confirms mutual agreement."

- The session cancels if the client is fifteen minutes late and charged as if the session occurred.
- Breaks occur for all as needed

- The following situations will terminate a session:
  1. Physical abuse of self, prayer counselor/s or ministry team, support people, personal counselor, inner selves, environmental structures, décor, equipment, or technical items.
  2. If a client decides to leave a session, the session ends. The next scheduled appointment expects and welcomes the client back.
  3. There is no toleration of shouting to protect the client's confidentiality and respect of other people in the building. In the event of sustained loudness, the client will leave the building until they can regulate their emotions. They are welcome to return within a short time (5-10 min.).

Different expressions traversed Saqqara's face as she read and signed, "Most of it is clear except the reference to inner selves. I didn't mention before that I sometimes hear things in my head. The history form listed it, but we didn't select it because people wouldn't believe us or think we're crazy."

"It is not insanity but evidence of severe trauma. The term inner selves, refers to aspects of a person's personality that seem alien or other than themselves. We will discuss that later in detail," said Lydia.

"Safety is paramount. For security reasons, I'm asking you to remove the battery from your phone now. It may be better not to bring your phone for the remaining sessions, but that is entirely up to you. Thank you for completing the life history. It's a formidable document which gives me a jump start for preparations and usually starts some deep thinking for the client too."

Saqqara removed the phone battery and replied, "The life history proved hard to finish. We kept going blank to some of the questions. My childhood memories are few. If possible, more nightmares occurred after I started."

Julie informed, "Few memories of childhood may signal a traumatic history."

"I doubt that; my family comes pretty close to a perfect family in comparison to many I know," Saqqara quipped.

"I am sorry to hear of the terrible nights you suffered. Often nightmares that occur after work on the history form represent memories that float into the conscious mind. Dreams, in other words, can be memories," explained Lydia.

"I hope not. They were nasty nightmares!" Saqqara exclaimed.

"Trauma is nasty and often hidden from us, yet causes the symptoms reported on your history form. Were you able to watch the website video about hidden trauma recommended in my e-mail?" Lydia asked while noting that her client did not seem to listen but curiously looked around the room.

"I like this place and the animals in the basket," squeaked a small voice.

Julie hurried a note to Lydia, which asked, Did the client shrink?

Saqqara's blond hair swirled to the left with a jerk as she smiled blankly. "Sorry, what did you say?"

"I think it is appropriate that we begin with prayer," Lydia said as she documented another X.

> "Father God, Jesus of Nazareth and Holy Spirit, we humbly come before You in awe of the wonder of Your creation, majesty, power, and incomprehensible love for us. Thank You for this divine appointment with all of Saqqara. We want to express gratitude ahead of time for healing and fulfilling Your promises to us because only You keep all Your promises. We welcome the seven spirits of God. Please grant us Your Spirit's manifestation. Thank You for the knowledge You will reveal to us, the understanding of it, and the wisdom to know what to do with it. Bless all who

The Encounter

> are praying for this week's work, even though they do not know with whom we are working. Thank You for anointing us with the Spirit of Counsel. We honor the Spirit of the Fear of the Lord and the Spirit of Omnipotence. Thank You for strengthening Saqqara's spirit to be one with You. We request any angelic assistance needed to keep the peace and protect all of us and all people we care about, pets and property. We come boldly before Your heavenly court to request restraining orders against celestial beings with legal rights to Saqqara due to her sins, known or unknown, as well as the iniquity of her generations. According to Ephesians 1, all power in heaven and on earth has been given to Jesus Christ, and He shares that inheritance with those over whom He is Lord. So, in the mighty name of Jesus Christ and the authority of His Holy Blood, we bind all demonic entities who attempt to interfere in this process in any way. I declare them to be totally impotent. If they disobey, they must go directly to the feet of Jesus regardless of legal right. We anticipate Your healing freedom. In the name of Yeshua Hamashuach, Amen."

Years ago, Lydia learned to watch clients as she prayed for any significant clues which might surface during the prayer. Saqqara shivered after the prayer. Lydia then asked, "Saqqara would you like to give your permission to the Holy Spirit to help you?"

She nodded, closed her eyes, folded her hands, and said, "I'm weak in faith in You, God, but I've tried all I know to do, and things are even worse (starting to shake). I'm desperate for some break from this insanity I'm experiencing. Please help me!" She looked up, "I don't know what's wrong with me... shaking like this!"

Julie's eyes brimmed with tears Saqqara suppressed in herself, as she said, "God is here. He delights being with you and wants you healed more than you do. You feel His tender presence."

Saqqara looked long at Julie, then abruptly readjusted her seating and curtly explained,

> "We counseled with many psychiatrists, psychologists, and different counselors but never felt like that before!"

Lydia informed her that she and Julie co-counsel as the anointing shifts from one to the other. Julie will be handing notes to her, the content of which she may or may not share. She also explained the gift of burden-bearing, which Saqqara viewed with Julie's tears. "This empathic ability is perhaps our most important gifting because it comes without judging. It's like knowing someone from the inside as we experience the client's senses, emotions, and sometimes client's thoughts to know what to ask them. How often do you cry?"

"I don't. I can't remember ever crying," Saqqara answered.

Lydia again looked down at the life history form, adjusted her glasses, and looked at her client. "On the life history form, you described your current problems, but please be so kind as to tell us now."

"As I wrote, I sensed the fear of not being able to manage my life. Insomnia plagues me despite pills, white noise, et cetera. When I do sleep, it is fraught with distressing nightmares, which are hard to shake once I get up. It's always hard to get going in the morning. We're definitely not a morning person. Terrible headaches, other pains, and physical problems that doctors can't find a reason for making life miserable at times. We constantly keep busy. I'm self-employed and put in twelve to sixteen hours a day, but it's worth it.

"Months ago, Tiffany, my business partner, told me I ran away from the governor's ball, which we managed, but left my winter coat and purse behind. I remember nothing of what she said and little of that event. The zillions of medications with terrible side effects for all the diagnoses don't solve the problems. I tried natural remedies and realized some comfort, but they didn't eliminate

The Encounter

the symptoms. Sometimes I find things I don't recognize at home and don't even recognize established clients! Decision-making is torturous, especially if the decision requires immediate resolve. It becomes arduous to decide what to wear or order at a restaurant, then the terrible headaches come on, but not only then," Saqqara related, looking fatigued.

"Thank you. That proved extremely informative. Why don't we take a short break?" Lydia stood and pointed to the waiting room door. "The restroom is left of the entrance door. Water, coffee, and a variety of teas are available anytime."

Break over, Lydia continued to read from the life history. "The person to contact in case of an emergency is your business partner, Tiffany? People important to you are Tiffany and Naysa. Who is Naysa?"

"We live in the same apartment building, and she helped me prepare for this week. We read the required books together. She's in a wheelchair from an accident and is currently in physical therapy to regain mobility. I think I see where you are going. No husband or relatives to call in an emergency, a business partner, and one other important person. Pathetic huh? It's simple. I don't trust anyone, not even myself!" Saqqara angrily pushed her hair away from her face with both hands and tried to regain her composure.

"In the event you were traumatized as a young child; you cannot understandably trust. Trust must be earned. It sounds as if you trust Naysa," Julie said.

Shaking her head and pursing her red lips, Saqqara said, "I never realized it 'til now. I guess since she's unable to walk, somehow, she seems less dangerous!"

"That's an interesting choice of words—dangerous," Lydia softly commented and continued to read excerpts from the life history. "You were a wanted baby, parents not having trouble during the pregnancy, you were an uncomplicated full-term delivery, but you don't remember the family telling stories about your birth. In your early years, you had recurring hospitalizations and several later. Were there complications with the tonsillectomy and adenoidectomy? You noted a week hospitalization at age three," asked Lydia.

"We didn't think there were complications."

"A week's hospitalization for a T&A is highly irregular even at that time. Your asthma and broken bones required longer times in the hospital than usual protocol too."

"We never thought about it. You would know; you're a nurse. Maybe our fears of clinical settings are linked to that."

"Your mother, a busy socialite with a problematic marital relationship, isn't someone you confided in—critical, non-affectionate, disciplined with harsh words and isolation. She wanted you to fulfill your destiny, favored your sister, smoked, and probably has an alcohol addiction. She gave you a book about sex when you were twelve. Describe your current relationship."

"It's never been good. We remember Mother took us to all the doctors and dentists. She dropped us off and left to do something during the appointments but never discussed them. She made sure I dressed in the highest fashion and provided supplies for school and extra-curricular activities. I guess she looked like a good mother."

Julie clarified, "It sounds like she maintained you rather than mothered you. That's one reason for feeling empty when you consider her."

"We rarely connect. Probably because work consumes us and there is no time for Mother or anyone. Something bizarre happened, though, after I made this appointment. I kept getting texts and cards from her. I sent her flowers for Mother's Day and felt a little guilty for feeling happy to be flying away instead of being with her."

Julie glanced at her copy of the history form. She glanced up to say, "Let's see, your dad often traveled internationally, was head of the home, and often angry with Mother. You were his favorite; he took you fishing, hunting, and golfing, left discipline to mom, and wanted you to go to college and be successful. But you were not able to confide in him either."

The Encounter

"I sometimes wondered if my parents' discord resulted from Mother's suspicions of Dad's fidelity since he was gone so much. They never talked about sexual things with me. I like my dad, but he may drink too much too."

"Tell us about your sister," Lydia inquired.

"Desiree is different from me. I came along when she was six. Due to the age difference, we share little in common. She and Mother share taste in just about everything. Desiree does everything right. She got a degree from the right university, married, has two children, and is loyal to Dad and Mother if we complain about anything. She, like Tiffany, accused me of lying and all kinds of things I don't believe I did. Mostly, I keep my distance while she lives her perfect life."

"Tell me about your academic history," Julie requested.

"Well, (taking off her shoes to sit on her tucked leg) I received a dual master's degree in business and industrial-organizational psychology. Frankly, I don't remember much about school or college. I can recount that attendance was a big deal at school, and I missed a lot. I don't know why. Dad took me on business trips to Europe and I missed school. Some people know all the names of their teachers. Not me. I don't remember much about broken bones you referred to earlier, other than the fun notoriety as kids signed the casts."

"Did your dad take Desiree on trips, too?" asked Lydia.

"Not as often. Perhaps envy is part of our problem. Desiree once told me she was his favorite and knew so because he told her."

Julie raised her eyebrows with impressed 'oohs' and 'aahs' reading the life experiences page, "Your childhood games and interests were make-believe and reading. My, you were a busy little girl according to all these awards in sports, music, and drama. You don't have a lapse of memory when it comes to your childhood fears: snakes, spiders, the dark, dying, crowds, having to wait and going to new places."

Lydia next commented upon Saqqara's involvement in occult practices such as Ouija boards, tarot cards, fortune telling, pendulums, et cetera. Then, looking up from the form and directly at her, she asked, "Is your father still a Chedebau?" Lydia's heart began to beat fast as the question was out.

"He isn't just a Chedebau, but high up. They do a lot of children's hospital philanthropy. It's all free for the families," answered alarmed Saqqara feeling her heart pounding within.

"When you fractured your bones, where were you hospitalized, and do you remember the duration?" Lydia asked.

"Due to Dad's membership, I went to their hospital, but not all the time. Sometimes I went to the university hospitals. I've felt curious about those times for some reason, but Mother won't talk about it with me, and I can't remember. I'm not sure how long, maybe a week or so? To clarify, I did those occult practices (as you call them) for fun. We even did levitation and broke a valuable art piece and got into trouble." She mischievously smiled and took a long swig of water.

"I see that you drink a lot of caffeine, take a synthetic thyroid, and a variety of sleeping aids. Any other prescriptions or over-the-counter drugs?" Lydia inquired.

"I've stopped all those useless prescriptions. Occasionally I'm tempted to do marijuana for my 'invisible pain,' but the scientific research clinical I read frightens me. It's a powerful precursor to hard drug usage. I'm messed up enough without that problem too. I sometimes enjoy a glass of wine in the evenings to wind down for sleep," Saqqara confessed.

Julie glanced at Lydia to check if her questions ended. "Saqqara, I read here that you were never married. Were you ever, or are you currently in any serious relationship?" Julie asked.

"I lived with Devon off and on my last year in college and through some of the graduate school."

The Encounter

"What happened to that relationship?" Julie continued.

Saqqara rolled her eyes and looked away. She untucked her leg, placed her foot on the floor, took a deep breath, gave a quick smile, and said,

"That answer is quite complicated."

Lydia quickly jumped in to say, "Saqqara, never answer a question if you choose not to. Devon is not a comfortable topic. However, we will revisit Julie's good question if and when you are ready to discuss that relationship.

"Our visit with your valuable history is good work. I see it's time for lunch. Julie will copy the Personal and Family Health portion of your life history to use with this list of symptoms for lunch homework," Lydia explained. She handed a paper and highlighter pen to Saqqara, "I want you to highlight all symptoms which occur on both forms. Any questions?"

> I'm terribly sorry. I usually do things perfectly but didn't have the resources to complete the last page genogram!"an anxious, somewhat variance of Saqqara's voice answered.

"No problem. Most people don't complete it, and it is optional anyway. Remember to eat. A power nap might be helpful if you have time." Lydia opened a door for Saqqara's departure, "A private exit is available through this hallway, or you can exit via the waiting room."

As Julie handed the jacket to Saqqara, she reminded her, "See you at two."

Saqqara listened to the click, click of her heels crossing the parking lot. Then she deeply breathed in the warm fresh air. Lifting her face to the sun, she said, "Well, that wasn't so bad." They put me at ease. Both were thoughtful and kind. They seem to know what they are doing. I wish I did! Strange, feeling what we felt during prayer. I never experienced that! I think I'll grab lunch and take it to the hotel."

Posting

The prayer counselor and mentee returned to their respective chairs to reflect upon the session. "What did you learn from that session, Julie?" Lydia began.

"Well, subjective data suggests she is in denial about her 'perfect family.' Her dissociation and often amnesic to events or time loss cause her anxiety. She is ready for healing in that she owns these issues and tried many modalities. She's lonely and uses 'busy' to block the pain. She presents with the stereotypical minimal memory of childhood.

"Objective data is the life history information. She brought a huge bag, was impeccably attired, spoke intelligently. Saqqara presents conflicted over her family of origin relationships and seemed conditioned not to cry. Her voice quality changes along with her mannerisms. Observation of alters revealing themselves: a young one likes the animals in the basket, a perfect part, Devon's girlfriend, and those associated with the medical side of things. I caught when we discussed hospitalizations; she used the pronoun 'we' rather than the appropriate 'I' and often uses the pronouns 'we' and 'us.'

"Assessments of the data highly suggest dissociation.

"Plan a strategy to help the client become aware of the correlation between the personal history and classic indicators of dissociation. We need to weaken denial coping skills and facilitate dissociative interventions."

Throwing a high five to Julie, Lydia congratulated her. "Just a gentle reminder, be careful with your 'oohs' and 'aahs'. Remember, dissociative persons are usually hypersensitive, and you never know who inside will be offended by your comments or emotions. Presentation of matter-of-fact, cool, calm, and collected mixed with gentle respect is best. Of course, once you are well acquainted, you can become more relaxed and show your emotions, strengthening their learning curve to regulate emotions. I'm hungry. How about you?"

Julie received the homework papers and highlighter from Saqqara and asked, "How was your lunch break?"

"My fatigue surprised me, but it went well. I hope I did it right. The selected symptoms on my life history page matched almost every item on the symptom list. What are they symptoms of?" Saqqara asked.

Lydia explained, "I'm not licensed to diagnose and therefore will not. Frankly, labels are not important to me, only healing. The symptoms on the list are common indicators of a coping mechanism resultant of severe trauma. Our brain protects us by hiding the trauma from our conscious mind, but trauma's pain can 'leak out' and cause many difficulties, especially in our adult lives. Infants and children can use the coping skill called dissociation to survive severe or repeated trauma. Dissociation equals a traumatic childhood. Prescriptions won't work if a biochemical imbalance is not responsible for the symptoms. When symptoms are trauma-based, we must discover and evaluate beliefs which originated at the time of the trauma for healing."

"But I don't remember any trauma!" Saqqara spouted.

Julie reminded her of the usually traumatic hospitalizations, broken bones, and asthma attacks. They would ask and depend upon the Holy Spirit, who knows every detail of her life, for help to discover her beliefs and how they stack up with God's truth. She assured Saqqara they do not practice hypnotism because the Bible considers it 'casting a spell.' They would also not do imagery to change history. She then prayed from a book to bless her with the internal work.

Lydia smiled widely and said, "So then, how do we proceed, you may be wondering? First, I want you to choose to trust yourself. We will ask questions and need you to be a good reporter. By that, I mean, let us know anything which you experience. For instance, a picture in your mind, emotions, odors, tastes, sounds, touch, or seeing something. Let us know if you get a headache, double or blurred vision, or feel as though you are fading away."

"How did you know? That happens often!" frowned Saqqara.

"I would imagine there are many things which alert you to attend when preparing for events. Your reports alert us and soon, you as well, to attend important details," Julie explained.

Lydia obtained a whiteboard from a closet to draw the diagram she taught at the California seminar and explained co-consciousness and amnesic awareness. She stressed prayer counseling's goal is to increase co-consciousness. In other words, Saqqara would know trauma and information held by dissociated alters, which she may be amnesic to at present.

Saqqara leaned toward the board and ran her fingers on the dotted and solid lines. Then she asked, "So, are you saying that some of my lost time or the things people tell me that I do or say, but don't, are the solid amnesic lines, and that's why I don't know about it?"

Lydia returned to her chair and praised, "Yes. Well said. We examine traumatic details to identify belief systems that do not agree with God's words, truth. The lies we believe create the spiritual and mental pain we suffer. We must understand God gave us free will. Even if one finds an ungodly belief, one can still keep it. Of course, the pain it causes will also continue. It's completely up to the person." Lydia briefly rubbed the back of her head in reaction to the occipital headache which suddenly came on. *We're hitting programs!*

"Does all that make sense?" asked Lydia. "By the way, what we think produces the emotions we feel. That's why the Lord tells us in Philippians 4:8 *Finally, brethren, whatever is true, whatever is honorable, whatever is right, whatever is pure, whatever is lovely, whatever is of good repute if there is any excellence and if anything is worthy of praise, let your mind dwell on these things."*

Julie who also possessed a burden bearing gift, passed a note to Lydia to ask if she felt dizzy. Lydia asked Saqqara, "How are you feeling?" Saqqara hesitated then quizzically offered, "I became dizzy when you talked about free will... maybe a little fading sensation.

"Alert me if that happens again, please. We learned that it is efficient and wise to initially deal with the foundational aspects of a person's life because later events often build upon them. I want to do some of that work this afternoon. Please tell me what you know about the Chedebaus," Lydia asked.

Saqqara didn't seem to know much other than her dad's business associates and best friends belonged to the organization. Lydia approached the wall-sized bookcase to fetch a history book of the Chedebaus for her to read during the week. Then Lydia asked if she knew the oath to enter the double triad? Saqqara was clueless but was sure her dad's rank was much higher than that. By then, Julie had retrieved some papers from the lateral file.

"Please read the double triad, Julie," Lydia requested.

When Julie finished, Saqqara threw out her hands and wailed, "They declare satan is God?" But Dad served as an elder in our church and read the Bible! So what are you trying to say?"

"I am not trying to say anything other than present facts. You indicated your father held membership in an organization that requires recognition of satan as God to advance high in rank. You say he held a high position. Why is this pertinent? Because oaths members make directly impact their progeny, natural and legal. Just as God takes our promises and oaths seriously, so does the evil one, as evidenced by the consequences a member agrees to if he ever recants his obligations. Considering these facts, I think it prudent to spend some time this afternoon renouncing oaths to free you from any consequences. Renouncements impact generational involvement in these organizations, negatively impacting you..

"This is so convoluted. Is Dad a satanist? How do you explain him being an elder?"

Julie spoke up, "That's easy, satan already controls those who do not belong to God and needs to infiltrate the Church. satan's people aspire to be in leadership positions of worship, children's programs, and especially prayer because satan knows the great power of prayer."

"I'm feeling again like when you asked me this morning about Dad being a Chedebau."

"Feeling what, Saqqara," Lydia inquired.

"My heart. It speeds up when we discuss this. Okay, sure, there must be something to this. What do I do?"

Lydia leaned forward and offered her hand. Saqqara took it with a bit of wonderment. "Saqqara, never do anything unless you understand it and are sure you want to do it for your wellbeing. We have no desire to control you. It's perfectly safe for you to disagree with us or to say 'no.'" Saqqara sat for a while, fixated on the unfamiliar love coming from the emerald eyes before her. She felt something like light-headed but more like floating. After a short time, she shrugged, pulled her hand away, and placed it on her lap to sit pensively looking ahead. The counselors waited like statues.

"I agree with you that I need to do these renouncements," announced Saqqara. The two counselors smiled; they understood from experience that she emerged from a meeting inside.

Julie asked to sit next to Saqqara. Interestingly, she explained that the renouncer often omitted or added a word that completely changed the meaning of the oath. Julie planned to silently read along with Saqqara's audible declarations to renounce the oaths. If an error occurred, she would alert Saqqara to make corrections.

At one point in the declarations, Saqqara struggled to be audible, but only croaks sounded. Her eyes filled with alarm as her feet moved aimlessly and her hands fidgeted. Lydia quietly did warfare in her prayer language. Julie calmly explained this sometimes happened, then gently assured Saqqara she could speak the words and encouraged her to try until that happened. After several more attempts, her full voice returned to complete the renouncement.

The Encounter

Saqqara grabbed Julie's arm and turned to Lydia to ask in a shaky voice, "What was that?"

"We could call it a spiritual attack trying to impose the oath's consequence. I prayed in the spirit and declared that you chose to be free of that oath. It is canceled by Ephesians 1, which states, ... *all power and authority over heaven and earth has been given to Jesus Christ who shares that authority with His own.* Now no legal right exists to afflict you. The New Covenant made with the Holy Blood of Christ is more powerful than any other.

While doing another renouncement that addressed bareness, Saqqara looked about the room and agitatedly moved in her seat. When asked what was happening, she explained she could not become pregnant, which was part of the Devon trouble.

Suddenly, a purple bruise encircled her neck during another renouncement and vanished when the oath finished. Although the procedure consumed much time, the mysterious effects she experienced convinced Saqqara it was well worth both time and effort.

Lydia exclaimed, "We are off to a great start. Tonight's homework is to buy a journal if needed. Start journaling remembered dreams, especially repeated ones, and those you currently experience. Please take notes and log questions regarding this DVD. It explains how coping with dissociation impacts our adult lives. Here is a DVD player in case you need one.

Opening the private exit hallway door, Julie explained, "We'll discuss it tomorrow. If you are driving, we strongly recommend that you spend time in the reflection or recovery room. It's called reflection because it is highly productive when we reflect on what God did in the session. So much is lost if we wait to do it later. Recovery, because you may be aware of feeling a bit light-headed. Therefore, we want you to get your land legs, so to speak, to regain composure after our session before driving. Have a good evening, and we will see you at 9:00 AM tomorrow."

POSTING

Lydia retrieved a dish of assorted nuts and offered them to Julie as she popped a few to crunch. "I commend you, Julie. You are co-counseling now and doing it well. I didn't respond to your morning note about her decreasing in size. Yes, I saw that too—obviously a little one. Many phenomena are associated with dissociation. One of my interns nearly freaked out when a male client attired in a three-piece suit shrank in the chair and spoke like a young boy.

The note about the dizziness/vertigo was accurate burden-bearing. However, I chose not to address spin programming yet because Saqqara needs more time to adjust to the complexity of her condition," Lydia said.

"I agree. When she experiences it and reports it to us will be a prime time."

"Excellent. Exactly. Then we can instruct how to interact with the spinners. Just before you sent the note, I experienced significant occipital pain. I think we hit a lot of programming when we addressed lies."

"You taught the need to sit next to her for the renouncements well. Your explanation that difficulties sometimes happen consoled her. The gentle coaching during the process increased her capacity. She might become overwhelmed if you cheered her or urged her. Tomorrow, I would like you to do the DVD review. Are we finished for the day?"

After reflection, Saqqara hurried to the auto to get her phone and check messages. She found several notes of encouragement from Naysa, so she decided to take dinner to her room and call Naysa while she ate. It would simulate a meal together at home. Saqqara shared tidbits of the session while they talked without specifics—indeed, not that her father might be a satanist. But in general, she had a lot of insight into her homework assignment, and she looked forward to the next day. Physical therapy fulfilled

Naysa's expectations, and she felt discouraged, not yet seeing much progress.

DAY 2 — NASCENT

Julie and Lydia briefly reviewed the first day and prayed for direction for day two. Saqqara arrived beautifully clad in a turquoise jumpsuit. The stand-up collar of the peach silk blouse framed turquoise dangle earrings with bright orange accents. Orange sandals matched the jeweled bag. "Welcome. You look like a breath of spring! How was your night?" Julie asked.

"I feared that question. I talked with Naysa while I ate supper, listened to the DVD, and remembered I needed a journal to log comments. So, I bought a journal and stopped for cookies and milk on the way back to my room. Quite frankly, I'm not sure about the rest of the evening. I woke up to the white noise machine's roar. Saqqara reached the log to Julie. I wrote some things in the journal. I remember restlessness all night with underwater dreams."

Lydia said, "I'm impressed with your eagerness to do the homework. It shows you are serious about getting healed, a primary to reach your goal. Shall we pray?" Lydia gave thanks for the session direction, the maintenance of spiritual protections requested yesterday and asked for their daily bread.

Saqqara asked, "What do you mean by daily bread?"

"Excellent question, Saqqara. Our Lord never overwhelms us, but we over zealously do beyond necessity or prudence and overwhelm ourselves. This zeal applies to journaling or counseling sessions—the invigoration from memory information flow to heal results in a desire to go beyond the established limit. Wisdom, our daily bread, dictates whether to honor the limit. I strongly recommend you do homework, but limit the daily journaling sessions, lest you become unbalanced and overly tired. Memory work drains. Once you achieve the mental state of communication with your "selves," many people report losing alertness to their environment. Using an alarm clock to end a reasonable time for that activity returns alertness to stop the journaling session. The expected duration adjusts over time as your expertise increases. Begin with a fifteen-minute limit. To end those sessions, thank yourselves for being willing to share. Express your anticipation for togetherness. By doing this, you whittle down denial of the DID and increase strength and confidence in yourself for the excellent work— perhaps the most important work you will ever do."

Julie moved her chair closer to Lydia to share the journal's contents. Several pages displayed different writing styles, grammatical abilities, and themes. One entry of huge shaky print ran across the page. They gave each other looks well-acquainted people recognize to mean a particular thing. The journal entries indicated contributions from several different alters, one extremely young alter for sure.

"Oh, the DVD," Saqqara conducted a vigorous search in the depths of her voluminous bag. At last, produced it and gave it to Lydia. "It's well done. I identified with some of the scenarios, especially the woman who admitted she didn't know when something bad might happen or the church people telling her she lied. Thank you for telling people dissociation is not funny, as so many movies depict, but a coping skill to escape the trauma. That is very clear for me and helped me not feel so alone. I want to know more about triggers. They fascinate me."

"A trigger is like a cue to activate a special thought, emotion, or action. It can be anything as simple as a sound, a specific word, or stimulation of any of our senses. It is our job to discover your triggers. They often happen before lost time, but not always," Julie explained.

Lydia asked questions of Saqqara regarding the principles of sowing and reaping in the book assigned before her appointment. She reviewed the laws and gave several examples of how the principles play out in real life. Lydia told the story of a woman who grew up with an alcoholic father and sowed hateful judgments or ungodly beliefs toward him, married at fifteen to escape. Due to the law of multiplication, she reaped three husbands just like her father, each worse than before. Once able to identify and employ

The Encounter

forgiveness for the sown beliefs or judgments about her father and herself, those painful lies and reaping stopped. She reaped or married a healthy husband.

Julie explained that God makes it easy to recognize our ungodly beliefs because we repeatedly reap with the same types of people, dynamics, and primary topics. She gave an example. "A salesman learned when we sow ungodly beliefs (always lies), bitter roots, or repeated patterns of precisely what we planted result in our lives. He sought a sown bitter root. He worked hard for a bonus of sixty thousand dollars or more. Twice his boss's boss unjustly shared the bonus with colleagues. He feared an impending repeat. As a child, his family lived with his dad's parents. His parents worked outside the home, and Grandma ran the roost. She favored the oldest grandson of three. The middle child, the client, felt unloved but noticed great respect for money, so he decided at age eight to do two paper routes. He delivered papers in the dark at 5:00AM and on evenings in the bitter Minnesota winters. He brought collections to Grandma, who gave some to him, but also her favorite, and kept the rest.

"The elated salesman saw the exact pattern. His boss's boss (Grandma, not parents) kept the major portion for the company and distributed the bonus. Co-worker #1 (peer/ sibling) suggested the potential new client just as his brother suggested a potential newspaper customer. Co-worker #2 (peer/sibling), who also shared a bonus (divided earnings), lent his computer to our client whose computer failed (equipment) like using his brother's bike when he woke to a flat tire. Our client employed the Healing Process and the injustice ceased."

Saqqara mused as she sank back into the turquoise leather, shook her head in amazement, and thanked them for such good instruction. Julie responded by explaining, "Lydia taught me to teach our clients to fish and not give them a fish. We want to empower you with tools which you can effectively use alone with the Wonderful Counselor, and He doesn't keep office hours!" They all laughed.

Together they reviewed the ***Healing Process,*** which Lydia taught in Den Hague to Tabea after her deliverance. "You will know how to do this like a pro when you leave," Lydia assured. Then they took a short break.

When the session resumed, Lydia asked, "Do you remember dreams are sometimes memories? Try to recall the underwater dream. To best assist us, remember to report. You can elevate the footrest to be more comfortable if you like."

"Thank you, but I'm okay. I felt fine being under water, and it seemed I swam with someone else." Suddenly Saqqara's whole body jumped; a scream ripped the peaceful ambiance. Her eyes intent upon an invisible something, she repeatedly beat the air with frenzied slaps. Then, in an instant, she perched atop the couch back and balanced with hands frantically dug into its front and back to furiously kick the air. Julie started to go to her, but Lydia motioned to stop.

Saqqara yelled, "Don't kill me, don't kill me!" She sat motionless with her mouth ajar, then blindly looked around, unaware of her surroundings. "It's all red. Everything is red. Red! Where are you? Where are you?" she called as she slid down the cushions to collapse in a heap. One tear and another striped rouged cheeks as black mascara smudged and flowed. "I'm alone!"

They sat motionless for some time. The one on the couch still in past pain, while the two in chairs in pain of compassion silently prayed. Finally, the client uncrumpled herself with a tipsy clumsiness, straightened, sniffed, and smeared charcoal droplets from her chin with the back of her hand.

"Have some tissues," Julie sweetly offered, then left to get a cool cloth and water.

"Do you know what just happened?" Lydia asked.

Saqqara took a deep breath and tried to smile, then retracted to say, "I think I have a twin brother or did. Is it possible? I think something killed him or took him out of the womb and tried to kill me. I feel so empty and sad right now. Can a baby know something like that?"

"I filed photos of twins holding hands in utero," Lydia said as she rose to open the lateral file and search through the colored dividers. I know twins with fond memories of being in the womb together. The human person's brain finishes developing at twenty-five. Some people are ignorant of the human spirit's Neshamah, which is somewhat mature with memory capacity at conception, though some people poo-poo such ideas. Researchers currently teach foreign languages to babes in the womb. A fetus hears things outside the womb as we hear under water. They feel the pain of being burnt alive or ripped apart in abortions. Here's the photo," Lydia said.

"How darling!" Saqqara squealed and looked up to see a cool cloth and water offered by Julie. "I'm sorry for such bother. The water tastes great. I feel like I ran a marathon."

Lydia nodded, "We told you it was hard work. I now ask Jesus to lift off the fear, shock, and trauma from that experience and to bind any demons which possibly entered at the time.

"For lunch break, please try to get a nap. If time permits, ask Holy Spirit to help you remember repeated patterns in your life and for more understanding of this morning's abreaction, a memory recall of a dissociated event."

"I feel remarkedly better. I appreciate your understanding. A long break sounds great."

POSTING

Julie could hardly wait to post, "I've never seen anything like that before! Do you think our client is a failed abortion? Do you think they didn't know there were twins? Why did you focus on the dream right off?"

"Anything is possible. We need to know the truth of the matter. You will need to study dream interpretation to complete this mentorship. Our dreams are very telling and underwater dreams can be indicative of womb experiences. Since that came up last night, it's best to follow the lead. It certainly is foundational, and *that's a very good place to start!*" sang Lydia to a tune from *Sound of Music.* "There is still much to be done with this trauma. We need to explore the biological parents' relationship during pregnancy and at the time of birth and look for any dissociation which happened then."

"Why didn't you continue with any of those?" queried Julie as she made quick notes in her binder.

"You saw how much the abreaction took out of her. We must consider her capacity. The person is more important than the process. I hope she can take a nap. There will be time to cover those bases. Also, remember not to rush the awareness part of healing. She just faced a mountain of awareness. We need denial to diminish, not increase. Remind me to give her a handout on the Healing Process this afternoon."

Lydia and Julie ate lunch and hurried back for the afternoon session, amazed at how fast two hours could go. Saqqara arrived in a ponytail. Her smooth, fair complexion sported a smattering of freckles without makeup—no glossy red lips. Her azure eyes looked more vibrant without enhancement, or was it the spirited narrowing? She rolled up the sleeves of a T-shirt and wore raggedy jeans and athletic shoes. She virtually burst into the office once the door opened. She planted her feet several feet apart, jammed hands on hips, and let them have it.

"What the hell do you think you are trying to do?" she loudly protested. **Saqqara is never to know about that botched-up blunder. You are to stop, desist! Get it?"**

Lydia gently nodded, smiled, and said, "I'm sorry, but I don't think I've had the pleasure of meeting you. I am Lydia, and this is Julie. Would you care to sit?"

"May I get you a bottle of water?" Julie added.

The Encounter

The women's behavior surprised her. With a confused frown and brusque turn, she took giant steps toward a straight chair along the wall and firmly planted herself with hands propped on distanced knees.

"I'll get my own water... this is not a restaurant, you know. I've worked hard all these years to protect Saqqara from people like you. She's not allowed to tell secrets or else bad, nasty things will happen," she snarled.

Lydia apologized for doing anything to upset Saqqara. "It is obvious you deeply care for her and are good at your job. We find her v e r y nice too. Do you have a name?"

"What's it to ya?"

"Well, I find it unkind to just say 'hey you' to someone. I much prefer a name to honor them, but if you have none, that is okay, or we can give you one," Julie said.

"I have a name! Rory."

"What a strong name. Like you, Rory. I imagine you suffered a lot in the past to obtain your high position. Would you be called Gatekeeper at times?" Lydia asked.

"No, I'm not him. I take care of troublemakers."

"What can we do to help you understand that we are also trying to protect Saqqara? You see, when she was little, when bad things hurt her, she made you, Gatekeeper, and others for help. That is a wonderful plan for a child, but it doesn't work for adults because what you do not know can be dangerous. Saqqara survived and now is an adult. She needs all of you now but differently to be safe. You are a great part of her," Lydia explained.

Rory abruptly stood and looked at both women.

> *"You blind crazy dames. I'm a man! I'm out of here before this gets catching. I watch you all the time. Remember, cease and desist!"*

'Crazy dames' repeated through the waiting room until the entrance door slammed shut. The two women looked lost as they stared at the door. "Well, now what do we do," Julie asked.

"We wait and pray for Saqqara for a half-hour in this case. If the host as we know her or any alter does not return in that time, we end our day. You have enough experience to know what just happened. I don't think posting will be necessary unless you discover new insights," Lydia responded.

After a half-hour, they prayed the post-session prayer and called it a day.

DAY 3 — DEMONS and SHIELDS

On the third day of the intensive week, Saqqara arrived promptly in classic attire with flawlessly applied makeup. After opening prayers, Julie complimented her on her appearance. She commented that women usually stopped doing their makeup at this point.

"I don't understand. Why?" asked Saqqara.

"Makeup sometimes smears if one weeps. You said that you never remember crying, but you did yesterday morning. Do you remember that?" Lydia asked.

Troubled, Saqqara shook her head, searching for the answer. "I...I know that I felt drained afterward and the voices unusually loud."

"What do you remember of the afternoon session or last evening?"

Hefty breathing ensued, Saqqara's face reddened, and she agitatedly searched the room as if looking for the answers. "We've lost time again, haven't we?" She rose, paced the room, then dropped into an armchair.

The Encounter

"Ask the Lord Jesus Christ to help you remember," Julie urged.

"I'm sorry, but I don't have that kind of faith. I don't want to be difficult, but I refuse to be a hypocrite."

"Can you trust in my faith?"

Saqqara directed a penetrating gaze at Julie, "On the first day, I prayed and admitted my weakness in faith and asked for help. I have to!"

Julie proceeded to ask the Lord to bring to memory the work Saqqara did Tuesday with the assurance that it would not be painful. Quiet followed.

Saqqara felt her eyes widen as she met the two women's faces. Then, a fluttering smile came with, "They aborted my twin brother, but somehow, I survived. Is that right?"

"That is what we understand due to the painful and terrifying memories you shared with us," Julie affirmed. "You cried. Did you notice the condition of your makeup after the session?"

"This is so wild. I remember going to the reflection room and looking in the mirror at the streaks of mascara I tried to erase. And... I did lie down to take a nap as suggested. Honestly, I am blank about everything until struggling to get up this morning to arrive here. What pain were you talking about?"

Smiling compassion flowed from Lydia as she said, "We believe your honesty. All emotions are messengers. Pain signals SOS, emergency, act fast. Pain results if you jam your toe into a steel post. There are other causes of pain, like disease processes, et cetera. But, I'm talking about the pain caused by holding a belief system contrary to God's Holy Bible Truth. If the belief system is not accurate, then you believe a lie. All sin results from a lie of some kind which causes emotional pain. Whenever we sin, there is an open opportunity for evil entities and demons to attach to that sin and cause us exaggerated trouble in that area. We need to find the lie and get rid of it and any malicious attachments. When truth replaces the lie, mental and physical pain leaves.

"It's important to revisit the womb to learn what you decided then. There is no reason to relive the trauma. Jesus wants you to remember enough to learn what you decided and what needs forgiveness for your freedom. But, if the memory seems starkly real, you can regain your stability.

"This reality orientation exercise helps you do just that. Think about the warmth under your arms and the floor's pressure under your feet, then identify where you are now. Remind yourself this happened in the past, and you are safe now. Ask the Holy Spirit to help. May I touch my shoe to yours to assure you that you are secure during the recall?"

Saqqara agreed. "I just relax and focus my mind on the Holy Spirit, right?

I loved my little brother, but he left me. She doesn't want me. Nobody wants me. They will hurt me."

"Who is she?" Lydia softly asked.

"Grandmother. She told Mommy they could get rid of the baby... **(trancelike)** *they didn't know we were both there."*

"Saqqara, your twin did not leave you on purpose. He was murdered. Can you find it in your heart to forgive him for his absence?" Lydia asked.

Aware of her environment, Saqqara answered in the affirmative and continued to forgive her mommy and grandmother for not wanting her twin or her. Shaken, she chose to forgive them for aborting her little brother and trying, although unknowingly, to kill her.

"We do not know if anyone else was involved in the abortion, but we can also pray that in the event anyone else participated or agreed to it that you choose to forgive them also," said Lydia. Saqqara nodded and did so.

The Encounter

"Effective spiritual warfare parallels war strategies in the natural. Instead of exorcising only a spirit of murder, we target the top general, in this case, Death, to rid you of any lingering oppressors," Lydia prayed.

> "In the name of Jesus and the power of His Holy Blood, I command Death and all its underlings to now leave Saqqara and go to Jesus' feet."

"Saqqara, are you still convinced that no one wants you?" asked Julie.

"I understand global thinking is rarely accurate, which is a good example. Now I see Devon wanted me to be his wife, Naysa chose to be my friend, Tiffany wanted me as a business partner, and many clients wanted me to serve them. How do I change thinking to see clearly in the future?"

"Repeat after me if you agree, okay?" said Julie.

> "Heavenly Father, thank You for revealing the lie that others will always try to hurt me. Please forgive me for believing that lie, which stole rich relationships from me. I ask for the capacity to discern whom to allow to earn my trust. I choose today to believe that I am wanted and, most of all, grateful You wanted me and created me to be the amazing person I am. In the name of Jesus, Amen."

Saqqara repeated the prayer, after which she wriggled, took a deep breath, and exclaimed, "Wow, I feel light as a feather! Those lies curtailed most of my life. Do you think the abortion explains a distant relationship with Mother?"

"Someday, you may want to bring up the topic with her. You can ask the Lord Jesus to prepare her heart for a divine appointment," Lydia taught.

After taking a short break, Lydia encouraged Saqqara to ask the Holy Spirit when her first dissociative event occurred.

"I sense my mommy was afraid of us... or the father hurt my mommy."

Lydia instructed, "Ask if anyone came to help."

"Did anyone come to help us when the father hurt Mommy?"
"I ACCOMPANIED GOOD SAQQARA SINCE HER CONCEPTION. I HIDE HER FROM THE PERILS OF LIFE. SHE HEARD SHE WAS AN EVIL BASTARD SPAWNED BY RAGING RAPE. THE INNATE GOODNESS IN HER COULD NOT BEAR SUCH SLANDER, SO SHE MADE ME SEPARATE HER FROM EVIL SAQQARA," Shield said.

"It is an honor to meet you, Shield. Thank you for trusting us to talk with you. What do you know about Evil Saqqara?"

Saqqara pushed her hair away from her face and said, "What?"

Lydia queried, "Do you remember the conversation after you asked, 'Did anyone come to help us when the father hurt Mommy?'"

"I felt that 'going away fading sensation,' but no, what conversation?"

Lydia congratulated her on good reporting. "I will update you after I teach you a crucial aspect of your healing. Remember the circles of awareness on the DVD? Some of you are locked or frozen in time as if the trauma is still going on, and you are not aware of them. Things happen without your knowledge, like when you lose time. Hence, you are amnesic to them. That accounts for the mysterious anxiety, fear, and pain. Other parts of you are co-conscious with you. You know about them, but they may not seem so different. For example, the professional who does not recognize established clients, but you are aware of it happening. I want you

The Encounter

to learn how and purpose to stay present all the time to develop total co-consciousness."

Julie glanced at Lydia, turned to the client, and said, "Let me teach a tool if a stage is not scary for you. You did drama as a teen. We are asking you to will not to fade away inside but stay in the wings of the stage when another aspect of you is on stage in the spotlight so you can be aware of everything. We invite all of you to listen."

Lydia continued, "We talked with Shield. He reported Saqqara created his job to separate her from another alter who believes Saqqara is an evil bastard spawned by raging rape."

Grabbing the arms of the chair, Saqqara wailed, "What? We're a product of rape?"

> Her body folded into a fetal position. *"No wonder Mommy didn't want me,"* a tiny voice whimpered.

Julie quickly blessed Saqqara's spirit assuring her that she was no mistake, she prayed.

"God fashioned you in His mind before the earth's foundations were laid. He was thrilled the day you were born. You have always been wanted and loved. Lord strengthen her spirit to believe this and comfort this little one."

In slow motion, Saqqara unfolded herself and gave a dazed look at Lydia, then Julie. "She's so delicate. Jesus reached into the womb, took her out, wrapped her in a soft white blanket, and held her close to His heart."

"Saqqara, can you choose to cherish her and assure her that she was never rejectable?" asked Lydia.

"Yes. I've always had this terrible sense that I was wrong somehow."

"We often see this kind of situation which we call the good/evil split. This split is a primary conflict. Dissociation is all about conflict. **Resolve the conflict, and there is no need for dissociation.**"

"I thought I told you to cease and desist!" popped out Rory.

White knuckles clenched the wooden chair arms, "I'm trying to stay, but I'm going inside to somewhere!" alerted Saqqara.

"You are setting things in motion which will put her in danger. Get it?" Rory stormed across the room, pointing back and forth at the prayer counselors.

"Just like you, Rory, we only want to help her be safe. When we don't know what can hurt us, we are in danger. Perhaps you can help us understand what you think is so dangerous. I imagine you suffered much for your current position. I am so sorry," Lydia offered.

He stopped, sat down, and asked in stunned intonation, **"How did you know that?"**

"I had the privilege of working with hundreds of severely broken people, and most made a protector such as you as part of themselves who suffered to get the job. Do you remember the body's age when you came to help her?" Lydia asked.

"I've seen him before! I can't exactly remember how or when," Saqqara mused.

"That means you are somewhat aware of a male protector alter named Rory. He came to yesterday's session in your place to threaten us to stop working with you to prevent you from knowing what he thinks will cause you harm. In other words, on some level, you believe it would be dangerous for you to understand all your history. I hope to become Rory's friend and help him heal by eventually learning the origins of that belief system, but now it is lunchtime.

"I think the wee one stuck in the womb whom we met today may have integrated, so you may find yourself unusually tired."

POSTING

During posting, Julie said, "We must have great prayer support for so much to happen so fast. I feel the anointing."

"Yes. And she definitely wants to be healed. That is key!" Lydia stressed.

The afternoon session began with Saqqara reporting a strange text from Dad today with two small rose drawings at the bottom instead of a single rose. She received a weekly note from Dad since leaving home to live on her own. Somehow, she felt uneasy. They prayed for understanding and for the uneasiness to lift.

Julie asked, "What do the notes say?"

"Oh, not much of anything, just weather or his golf game," said Saqqara.

"We covered a lot of ground this morning. Any questions?" Julie asked.

"Are you kidding? My head is full of them!" Saqqara spouted.

"Let's ask the Lord where He wants to begin," Lydia suggested. They listened.

"I was extra tired. Tell me more about integration," Saqqara finally requested.

Lydia said, "Great idea. My understanding from the Lord is that He wants all alters together with the OP, just like before the shattering of trauma. Twenty scriptures exist about a double mind, but the most familiar is James 1:8, which says, *...being a double-minded man, makes him unstable in all his ways.* Jesus integrates when it is best, so don't be foolish and try to do it yourself. He wants all the parts/alters healed and cleansed before combining with the OP or integrated. He will do it when it is a good time for you. God is considerate, loving, and practical. Integration is real. There is always a degree of fatigue, more if the alter played a major role, but it rarely lasts more than forty-eight hours. Sometimes a group of alters or fragments all resulted from a single trauma. Often, they will be merged or fused before integration with OP. People frequently pat themselves as if discovering something new—more substantive than before. Some report movement in their head as Creator God makes new neuralpathways.

"I worked all day with a major alter, Ramona. The next morning of the intensive week, the client arrived with a latte. She asked if I thought Ramona integrated. I told her I could not be sure of those things and requested why she asked. She lifted the cup, took a sip, raised her eyebrows, and said, 'I don't like coffee, she did, and this is not bad.'

"That is one kind of clue. Your attire will finally become less diversified. It will not take as much time to process a question or decision. Now it is like going through a Rolodex to find information. With integration, all is available to you rather than some information known only by another part of you.

"A client couldn't balance the checkbook until she discovered an alter created in the first grade to hold all the math skills. After integration, the checkbook was a cinch."

Saqqara squirmed and said, "That is enlightening, comforting, and scary."

"Did you hear from anyone inside at lunch break?" Julie asked.

"Just the usual noise but nothing succinct."

Julie chuckled, "That's another sign of integration; no voices inside— it's quiet."

Lydia said, "Saqqara, you said you didn't hear the conversation with Shield. Shield alters are usually benevolent protectors of the OP. Rory is also a protector but not aware his 'protection' is currently blocking your healing. Shield's job is to separate your OP from an early split with a part of you who believes she is evil. Don't answer now, but quiet yourself and ask the Lord to help you remember when you were aware of darkness or wicked thoughts."

"What comes to mind are the terrible nights when I awaken with weight on my chest as if paralyzed, unable to breathe, and the idea

The Encounter

that someone just raped me—horrifying nightmares! We rarely admit that."

"That description fits an incubus spirit. A person who desires intimacy consults an occultic practitioner for a 'love potion' but is ignorant that the products and consultation conjure up a demon of lust. The demon has legal rights to harass the person due to their participation or generational activity with ungodly sexual contact with other men, women, or animals. They cause frustrations with marriage attempts, marital discord, barrenness, and sexual organ diseases. They deeply lodge in sexual organs, hands, fingers, anus, and tongue. There are many references to generational sin in the Bible. Occultic rituals can be an open door also. Shall we pray against that spirit?"

Saqqara gave full attention and said, "So my ancestors could cause this as well as me. Yes, I'll repeat after you."

> "Father, in the name of Jesus, I ask forgiveness for myself and my generational line for any fornication, incest, adultery, sexual addiction, pornography, homosexuality, bestiality, or sex for money. Also, forgive me and my generational line for consulting witchcraft for 'love potions' and then sexual relations with evil spirits and demons such as familiar spirits, incubus or succubus (who attack men), and Mara.
>
> "I renounce and break all covenants or dedications to Nephilim, Baal, Belial, the harlot spirit, and the Demon Queen of Heaven. Forgive us for seeking comfort from these evil spirits and trusting them to fulfill our needs and desires. In the name and blood of Jesus, I renounce and break all ungodly spiritual, soul, and bodily ties, false love, lust, hatred, impotence, frigidity, and diseases caused by these spirits. I break these spirits from my tongue, hands, fingers, breasts, sexual organs, and anus.

> "I repent for allowing these spirits to reduce and control my will. No longer will I serve these demonic spirits. I stand in authority as a believer in the Lord Jesus Christ according to Ephesians 1 and renounce and demand all incubi/succubae, Eldonna, and Mare, leave my body, mind, and spirit levels.
>
> "Father, I forgive my ancestors. I ask You to forgive, wash and cleanse me. Restore my innocence. Please increase my love for You and give me ability to be faithful to You and seek my comfort from the Holy Spirit. Thank You, Jesus, for making this possible. Amen"

"I heard nasty screeching at one point in the prayer. When I asked for cleansing, this rush of warmth waved through me. I know I've said it before, but I feel lighter," said Saqqara.

"We hear that often. I would like you to familiarize yourself with this handout on generational curses for homework. If you identify other ones in your life, feel free to pray the renouncements just as today. You might want to share this information with your friend Naysa and do some renouncements together.

"Do your best to journal with Shield and Rory. But, remember not to edit, judge, criticize, correct or defend what you hear at this point. You are just gaining understanding now. Instead, warmly welcome their conversation and offer appreciation for their contributions," Lydia instructed.

"Tomorrow is the last day, be sure to bring your questions about what we accomplished so far," Julie encouraged.

Saqqara took advantage of the reflection room. *I can't remember ever feeling like this. A heavy shroud is gone! So, I suffered the night terrors from demons who got there due to generational and personal sexual ungodly acts. My mother conceived me due to rape—there's an ungodly act—and I'm illegitimate. Those demons are gone now. My twin brother, whom I loved, was aborted, but I survived. I dissociated the attempted murder and created a shield to protect me from the part of me who believed the lie that I was an evil bastard. I thought my twin deserted me, that no one wanted me, and people wanted to hurt me. Those lies are corrected. Whew! I've got to call Mother to check this out.*

POSTING

Lydia and Julie reviewed the previous sessions and prayed for continued protection and enlightenment for their client. They asked for direction and anointing for the next day, and finally, for the end of session cleansing and release prayers.

"I hope Saqqara continues with prayer counseling because I believe we just scratched the surface of her trauma. She is determined, and that is the major factor for success in anything," Lydia commented to Julie as they ended their day.

DAY 4 — NEW STRATEGIES

Lydia and Julie excitedly looked forward to Saqqara's last day of the intensive week. They unearthed critical foundational information and found major belief obstacles which inhibit the quality of life. She received deliverance of some nasty entities. When she arrived, one could sense a heaviness. The usual chit-chat followed with a prayer request for elongation of time to accomplish all the Lord wanted to do.

Saqqara sat forward, straightened, and widely smiled. "News flash. Last night I slept uninterrupted for the first time that I can remember! No nightmares, rapes, no need to change sweaty PJs, trouble getting back to sleep, getting up exhausted—it's wonderful!"

The three rejoiced together. "We especially thank God for the deliverance," Lydia said.

"But, Saqqara, I sensed you were a bit down when you arrived. Did I misread something?"

"You don't miss much, do you? Neither does my mother. I imagine I felt piqued after calling her last night. We hardly said hello when she started sweetly drilling about my whereabouts and activities.

"I gave her vague responses and then asked, "Why didn't you tell me I'm illegitimate? My head flooded with other questions, but she instantly shouted, 'Where did you ever get such a ridiculous idea? Are you accusing me of infidelity? I don't need to put up with such insolence!' and hung up. I don't need to tell you how confused I am right now. The sleep confirms whatever we are doing here is real. Reflecting on the sessions, I believe the revelations are true. So why would she lie?"

"Your conception may be a dark secret. If it comes out now, it could cause tsunami waves in the family. That topic is full of shame, guilt, and fear. Trust due time to answer that question. Now let us direct your energy on your purpose here and not allow that encounter to rob you." Julie said.

"I'm pretty good at blocking out unpleasant things. Thank you, I agree," Saqqara nodded.

Lydia asked, "Were you able to journal?"

"I told the front desk not to put through calls for an hour. I turned off the mobile, radio, television, and fan and put a do not disturb sign on the door. I set the alarm for thirty minutes. I got comfortable, asked the Holy Spirit to help, and told myself that I wanted to talk with Rory and Shield. Nothing. I read once that if blocked, to start writing anything. Sometimes something will come to you, so I did—nothing. It's hard talking to myself. Crazy! I almost quit but decided to put in the half-hour. At the last minute, I distinctly heard a child say, 'We're afraid of integration. Please don't send us away.' Hearing that felt a bit creepy. What a waste of time!"

"No, no, Saqqara, you journaled well. You prepared excellently and honored yourself by waiting. Your system may not trust you yet, but we'll talk more about that. You got a critical piece of information about your goal—they fear integration.

"I want all of Saqqara to listen carefully now. Saqqara, do you want to lose your nose, feet, heart, eyes, or hands? Of course not.

The Encounter

They are vital parts of you, just as the human alters are. Right now, their jobs or functions may or may not be beneficial to you as an adult. Once you know their beliefs, you can determine how to promote them to better participation in your life. None get eliminated in any way. No one needs to fear integration. Julie, please explain earning system trust."

Julie taught that a host alter (possibly a group or rotating hosts), usually recognized as the managing me, protectively guards who decides which alter gets 'out' or executive control of the body. "That is power. Some alters may resent your authority. On the other hand, you said you didn't want them, denied their existence, and begged God to take them away. That would hurt my feelings. So, the solution is to eat humble pie. While journaling, explain that you were clueless about trauma and dissociation. Tell yourselves that you are sorry for anything you did to hurt their feelings and ask forgiveness. Explain that you want to become friends and invite them to talk with you. Don't make journaling difficult. Just talk to yourself as you would to another person. You know, introduce yourself, ask what they do, ask if they have friends, where they live, et cetera. Thus, you build the trust needed for the capacity to face facts of your history."

Lydia gave Julie a high five, "Excellent teaching!" Then, she turned to her client. "In this stage of healing, you are getting to know yourself via addressing alters and their functions. In truth, you become aware of your conscious and unconscious beliefs about life, your history, and how you coped. Denial and confusion predominated your ways of thinking. There is no need to be afraid of human alters; they are you. The number of alters usually indicates the amount of trauma suffered, but all are wonderful you. Of course, once dissociation becomes a coping style, alters can be made to serve non-traumatic purposes too. Complex? Yes, but once understood, manageable. That is our focus today…system management.

"My clients tell me a fruitful way to learn about interior life accelerates by taking advantage of quasi time. Take the same steps as for journaling, but this time lay down and relax to get yourself into a near-sleep state. Often voices can be heard inside. Rise and journal what you heard, then follow up on that content when you next journal with yourselves."

Saqqara intently listened, then commented, "So that's what I sometimes hear but may not fully comprehend.

> Oh yes, I think I understand you saying that no matter what I hear, even if it is nasty, threatening, disrespectful, or inappropriate, to listen gratefully, thank them, and let them know they and I are the same person.

"What? Did you ask me a question?"

Lydia's emerald eyes flashed as she said, "You were telling us your understanding of how to relate to alters."

> Almost interrupting, Saqqara said, "Oh yes, I think I understand that no matter what I hear, even if it is nasty, threatening, disrespectful, or inappropriate, to listen gratefully, thank them, and let them know they and I are the same person.

"What? Did you ask me a question?"

The third time Saqqara repeated herself, it became clear to Lydia that a mind-controlled alter blocked Saqqara's thoughts. "Saqqara, are you aware that you repeated and interrupted yourself three times?"

Saqqara's face contorted. She shifted and grabbed her head. "I... all I know is my head is killing me. Excuse me; I must take medicine," she said, hurrying to the door.

"Wait, first try this," Lydia pled. "Take your authority now. Say, 'You are welcome, but I need you to watch from a distance now. Please step back because my head hurts.' Repeat it, if necessary, with a greater tone of authority."

The pressure inside clashed against her nails digging into her skull. Strands of hair irritatingly tickled her face. She looked up and around, gradually dropped her hands to push her hair back. Her face relaxed. She returned to the couch to glance quizzically at her companions.

She remembered her amazement the first time this happened.

Lydia smiled and said, "Well done. Now each time this happens, I want you to ask inside, 'Who is there?'"

"Who is there?" Saqqara asked.

"You may or may not get an answer. Proceed with 'I want to understand what you need.'"

"What is your concern about what I was saying?" Saqqara complied. Although she met with silence, she strongly sensed a group had run away.

Julie consoled, "Eventually, a reply happens. Then proceed with the conversation." Soon patterns of triggers that evoke certain parts of her to function or come out would evolve. Triggers listed in the journal made for easy access as pointers for memory work.

"Saqqara, it's a delight to work with you. You are progressing well. I know this is not easy. During your lunch break, I would like you to view a short DVD that demonstrates how a dissociative system works. I think you will enjoy it. We can discuss it this afternoon. We'll not be doing memory work in the last hour today. In that time frame we will discuss plans.

POSTING

"Julie, what do you think we should cover this afternoon?" Lydia asked.

"The degree of achieved containment proves difficult with dissociation. Strategies may settle the one present, while others inside may be in chaos, but containment is key."

"True, but on the other hand, it is amazing how a client may work long hours here and seem exhausted, while other parts are upset, yet another part reserves energy to go out all evening. I wonder if the interrupting one is the Perfect part we met during introductions. Unpleasant memories mar a perfect life, but her strength will prove a significant asset for the OP. She seems to comprehend journaling and headaches. The life history review provoked productive questions for her consideration and the denial surprisingly minimal."

Julie smirked, "The conception part proved critical and a great beginning, but we haven't hit the nasties yet! At least Rory didn't interfere today. It's too early to try to free him. What about mapping? I know spending much time with alters is passé, but necessary to some degree to understand how she functions and why. Should we tackle spinning?"

"Only if she is bothered by it today. Mapping (drawing perceived dissociated parts in relationship to each other) is a good idea for homework discussion in the intensive follow-up call. How about a buffet? I'm starved!"

Saqqara seemed in high spirits after lunch. "I'm glad I followed your advice and booked my flight home tomorrow. I'm exhausted. I think I am beginning to sense when parts are close. A lot of comments and questions swam in my head during the DVD. Here it is, thanks."

Lydia explained, "The stuffed animals in the DVD represented the different types or categories of alters commonly found in a level of alters known as a system. People potentially devised multiple systems with different kinds of internal environments. The whole phenomenology is whatever the victim thought could survive the moment. That idea could be theirs or suggested by another source during the trauma."

"What were some of the comments?" inquired Julie.

"Well, someone said they weren't a clothed bunny," laughed Saqqara. "The baby's dead part hit a nerve. From my vague sense of Rory, I venture to say he may identify with Tiger. He's great. A small voice asked if we were real animals. Frankly, we were captivated."

Lydia offered, "The website features articles on the different types of alters, this DVD, and other helpful products." She

The Encounter

encouraged Saqqara to avail herself of those resources while withdrawing a client's handwriting from the lateral file. "Do not be surprised if your handwriting takes on different characteristics; you may already be aware. These samples are lovingly permitted to share with the hope they help another.

"That reminds me, Saqqara, since you now know what you are dealing with, it is reasonable that you may want to research it. Please hear me. Dissociative people are highly suggestable. It would be best to discover your inner world before research to prevent assuming false beliefs. There are many sites on the internet to lure in survivors for nefarious purposes. I will recommend reading materials, but the same principle applies to books. Enjoy beneficial internet and books later. I am not trying to control you. I only want this to be a safe and smooth process for you. Does that make sense?"

"Yes. Thank you, Lydia. I feel that genuine care and concern. Time here proved an extraordinary life experience for me. It feels like I just beached on a strange island after being adrift, never knowing when a wave would dash me asunder."

Lydia felt tears swell as she expressed her heartfelt satisfaction from Saqqara's words and reminded her that the Lord's care and concern are excellent and always present. Lydia encouraged her to purposefully develop an ongoing conversation with the Wonderful Counselor, enjoy His companionship, make requests, and receive wise guidance to help her identify the island and finish the needed integration.

Julie introduced Saqqara to the concept of mapping alters. "Assemble unlined paper and various writing tools before choosing an hour of undisturbed time. Truly, it's intuitive. Thinking hard won't work. Rather, ask the Holy Spirit to help draw your map. Just select whatever tool comes to your mind and draw. You will know when it concludes. Maps are unique and interpreted by the owner. It will be helpful when talking with alters. They can point themselves out, and you can discuss their positional relationships."

Lydia shared, "In the hour follow-up session included in this fee, a map can be an appropriate homework discussion. You could e-mail it to us before the phone call. Since we worked together in person, future sessions are now possible by telephone or visual media. It's not guaranteed confidential, but it's better than nothing. As an established client, you may talk with me for ten minutes free of charge on designated days. What are your thoughts and feelings regarding goals based on what you learned this week?"

"That's a difficult question because there is a swirl of them. It's like fall leaves grounded in stale earth and caught up to dance in all directions beautifully. I feel stale and fresh, free but unsure where I'm going, afraid the leaves will dash back to the ground, or I'll fly too far and be alone."

"Poetically stated. It sounds like you got stuck in past seasons but enlightened by revelation. Now, as you joyfully touch trust and intimacy, you know fear will not last," interpreted Julie.

"I'm impressed and privileged to be in this poetic company. What a succinct interpretation, Julie. For human beings to thrive, they need intimacy and hope. Saqqara, I see beauty as cultivating a feeling of self-worth. You perceived yourself as unwanted and chose to love and accept yourself as a person created for a purpose. Only after we love ourselves can we love others. That sense of benevolence engenders hope, enabling us to risk the trust necessary for intimacy. You are now free to fly to find true meaning in life. We must deal with our past to enter the future. These past days, you demonstrated courage to do just that."

Julie's eyes flashed at the clock. "We must be having fun because time flew. Now, I'll prepare the communion." Ethereal music soon dwarfed the sounds of cupboard doors and tingling glassware. The fruity fragrance of the white grape juice quickened Saqqara's senses. Julie carried an ornate tray with three goblets and an unfamiliar matzo cracker on white linen.

"It's celebration time!" Lydia happily proclaimed. "As priests and kings, we come in gratitude to You, Father God, for the gift of Your Son, Lord Jesus Christ, who gave us Holy Communion. Luke

22:19 instructs, *And when He had taken some bread and given thanks, He broke it, and gave it to them saying, This is My body which is given for you: Do this in remembrance of Me.*"

"Saqqara, this is unleavened matzo with brown spots to remind us of Christ's bruises, and the lines represent the stripes of beatings which heal us." Lydia broke the matza and gave a piece to Saqqara, Julie, and took one herself. They ate with satisfaction and smiles. Then Lydia continued. "Matthew 26: 27-28, *Then he took the cup, and after giving thanks he gave it to them saying, Drink from it all of you for this is my blood of the covenant, which is poured out for many for the forgiveness of sins.*" They each took a goblet and drank with solemnity.

"Isn't this an amazing privilege?" Lydia's smiling eyes radiated light. "Holy Communion symbolizes the miraculous forgiveness of all our sins. It reminds us that Jesus cleanses, heals, delivers, and empowers us as a transformation of our spiritual DNA into His. We praise you, Holy Spirit! We request that all the Lord has done will now be sealed. We bless your spirit with strength, Saqqara, with the truth which sets us free, protects us, and gives us the capacity to continue this healing journey." Lydia then anointed Saqqara's forehead, hands, and feet with the sign of the cross. The stimulating fragrance of the oil, music, Holy Spirit, or maybe all three, embraced Saqqara's spirit in downy peace.

Julie's voice brought her back to the reality of ending this week. Intensive indeed—but good. Lydia scheduled Saqqara's follow-up appointment, conducted high finance, and bid good-bye. Prayer counseling is an intimate experience and intimacy affords pain.

CHAPTER 35

WORLD VIEWS

———◆◈◆———

Lydia looked forward to tonight's book club. Since Cavanaugh picked her up at the airport, they had dined a couple of times. She had enjoyed a quick lunch with Natroya to catch up on her husband's recovery since his heart attack, but she missed contact with the others.

Everyone gregariously chatted until Thi announced, "Time to get serious. We all read the book. In May, we discussed it generally but found it so provocative that we decided each would select a view and give bullet points of each. Distillations probably leave much more to be desired compared to this extensively fine academic work. This review may require more than one meeting, but what the hey, let's get started and see how far we get.

"We've been reviewing *The Universe Next Door* (Fifth Edition) by James W. Sire. For review, this set standards for clear, readable introductions to worldviews that have competed with Christianity for thirty years. First, I'll paraphrase my understanding of Sire's definition of a worldview: *A world view is defined as an orientation of the heart (consciously or subconsciously, possibly true or not) that we hold about reality which is the foundation on which we live our lives.*

World Views

"Next, I direct you to this chart with eight primary components of a worldview," he indicated with his left index finger but quickly stood to adjust the tilted whiteboard. Now that's better. There are eight primary foci of a worldview.

1. What is real?
2. What is the nature of the world?
3. What constitutes a human being?
4. What happens when we die?
5. Why is it possible to know anything?
6. How do we know the difference between right and wrong?
7. Is human history meaningful?
8. What personal core commitments are consistent with a view

I think you took theism, Yacov. Take it away!"

"The chart you provided as an outline for us, Thi, made it quite succinct. **Judaism, Islam,** and **Christianity**, all theists, believe in one God who is infinite, personal, transcendent, imminent, omniscient, sovereign, and good. Human beings are the pinnacle of God's creation. Death is a transition between our earthly life and eternity. All people receive judgment to determine whether they spend eternity in paradise or hell.

"Judaism and Christianity believe in an open system where God intervenes. Christianity and Judaism believe in man's free will. Islam believes nothing happens in the world outside of Allah's divine decrees.

"There is a purpose and a future for our lives. God made people able to know the truth, the world around them, and life itself. He communicates with us. God's character determines ethics, making them transcendent. God is good, so we should be good too.

"History is linear to fulfill God's purposes for humanity. I wasn't aware the three held so much in common. Then I reflected upon our last book and the evidence that Islam borrowed much content from the Bible."

"Thank you, Yacov," Thi said and turned to acknowledge the elegant social justice professor. "Now, Natroya, please explain deism."

"Deism coined the great isthmus between theism and naturalism, is the first step away from theism but is still prevalent in the belief that God is a force. Each person is free to reason their view of ultimate reality. However, each is on his own without hope of an afterlife.

"Deism evolved from the original into warm and cold divisions. All current separate views with similar foundations believe in an impersonal god. This God created a cause-effect closed system, meaning there is no opportunity for miracles or revelation. Early deists saw the world like a clock with a linear history and a future determined at creation. People are part of the clock. Locked into the closed system, we become insignificant because we can't change anything. God is not interested and will not change anything.

"Humans can only know from data (empiricism) and thought (rationalism). Ethics come out of nature; whatever is, is correct. Humans are personal with a sense of morality and can choose to do evil, but it is not due to a fallen nature. We have a capacity for creativity and community without connection to anything higher.

"John Locke proclaimed himself a warm deist. Also, Benjamin Franklin believed in the soul's immortality, one God who is the creator of the universe who governs by his providence and requires worship.

"Cold deists believe that God is a transcendent force, not a person but foreign, an alien not to be worshipped. This force does not love its creation nor care for it. The force is pure monotheistic but never incarnate.

"Sophisticated philosophic deism is lukewarm which believes God models classical theological attributes of a good foundation for human morality. Whereas sophisticated scientific cold deists such as Albert Einstein and Stephen Hawking view a "higher power" in science and mathematics. They want to maintain reason in a created world. Science mostly abandoned the clock idea because sub-atomic particles and electrons do not behave like machines."

Thi expounded, "I'm definitely not a machine." Everyone agreed with enthusiasm.

Natroya continued, "Modern deism sees God as sheer abstraction, and in conclusion, popular deism sees God as a big happy face who is always around to talk to and guide us. He makes no demands upon us to be good and always forgives us."

Cavanaugh purported, "I think many people who call themselves Christians are actually popular deists."

"This is very clarifying for sure. Thank you, Natroya, for a detailed feminine review," Thi praised.

"I find the absence of detailed feminine views makes life most uninteresting!" retorted Natroya, whose anger distorted her lovely face.

Looking chagrin and offering his hand, Thi apologized, "Natroya, I meant nothing diminutive. Women naturally provide more details than men. You gave an excellent report. Perplexed, other members of the club frowned. Natroya's uncharacteristic retort revealed the strain of her husband's illness upon her life.

"Naturalism evolved next," Thi said energetically to lighten the mood. Then, he adjusted his seat to face the opposite side of the table and said, "You are on, Desmond."

Desmond lifted his notes to read, "In **naturalism or atheism**, God ceases to exist. Instead, there is only matter which exists eternally within a closed system. Values are totally subjective. People have no spirit but are mysterious animals of highly complex machinery with chemical and physical properties presenting as personality. Extinction of personality and individuality occurs at death.

"People learn from logical reasoning, which is the only criterion for truth, but that may not be reliable. Data provides learning too.

"History is a stream of meaningless events, aimlessly linear with cause and effect.

"Some naturalists believe in **singularity**. A universe originated from space-time curvature, density, pressure, and temperature, which becomes infinite. Carl Sagan and René Decartes were naturalists. Most are determinists, but many also argue it does not remove our free will."

Thi enthusiastically commended Desmond with, "Great job."

"A nihilist believes nothing is real and there is no meaning to life," Thi exuded his personable laughter, which revealed perfect dentition, then said, "I took the easy world view but am anything but nihilistic. This worldview is incomprehensible to me. I can't remotely imagine how people get there, considering life experiences.

"Well, here goes. **Nihilists believe God is dead**. If that were true, I can see how the previous would be real and true. Humans are mud without meaning. Our demise is irrelevant because life is hell and death. We don't know anything, so history doesn't exist, and we can't know right from wrong. Therefore, anything goes because nothing is immoral."

The group applauded. "A clear and succinct description, Thi, 'nothing' is a short topic," Yacov cheered.

"Thanks!" Thi offered and proceeded. "Next, Cavanaugh will tell us about secular humanism. Do we need a short break first?" Negatives boomed around the table. "Great, we are good to go then," Thi raised a teacup and then chugged to the last drop.

Cavanaugh raised his coffee cup, imitated a toast, took a drink, and began. "Basically, **Secular Humanism** is naturalism but differs with an emphasis on the significance of the human being. Nature is God in everything, but man is the supreme being for man.

"There is a natural flow into Marxism that summarizes human existence's dilemma around the reality of economic and social forces that control human existence. Humans are part of the cosmos, which is somewhat determined and closed.

"Extinction of personality and individuality in death is not important.

"We know the truth by innate and autonomous reason; however, for social and economic liberation (which is all that counts), we may need insights of Karl Marx. People need to work to satisfy material needs.

"Ethics emerge out of human need and interests. Greed, competition, and envy of inequities of a capitalist society engender evil. Property rights are the ultimate source of evil. Good relates to overthrowing the class society based on evil capitalism.

"History's goal is the final revolution to inaugurate a classless society of abundance from human bondage and emergence of the new humanity to advance commitment to communism."

"Wow, that was great, Cavanaugh! Now we do need a break. Let's take five," Thi declared.

After everyone enjoyed Viviana's strawberry rhubarb pie and small talk, refreshed from the heavy academic reports, they proceeded.

Lydia gave the account on **existentialism**. "Secular humanism's roots in naturalism flow into Marxism. Existentialism also exhibits its' roots in naturalism with a twist. The naturalists say the objective world is real, and the subjective is merely its shadow. Atheistic existentialists see reality in two forms. They see the subjective world as galaxies, atoms, and quarks. Those structures stand against human beings and appear absurd. The cosmos is a structured or chaotic matter determined by inexorable law or chance. It makes no difference. I feel confused and hopeless simply reporting this," Lydia expressed as she shook her head in disbelief, wearing a sad expression.

"People are complex cosmic machines. What makes us human is that we choose to govern the subjective. Therefore, each person is free to decide their nature and destiny.

"The meaning of bold subjective choices ceases at death, seen as the ultimate.

"We know objective truth by the scientific method and our reasoning. The truth of the subjective world is whatever we choose. Good is whatever a person chooses out of their subjective self. Core commitment is only to self."

"Fascinating difference, Lydia. Thank you. You are on, Viviana with **Eastern Pantheistic Monism**!" smiled Thi.

"Pantheistic Monism believes that everything in the universe is one undivided reality. God is the one, infinite-impersonal, ultimate reality in every atom of creation to be pursued, called Brahman. Brahman is beyond good and evil. The distinction between good and evil fades to nothing.

"Time is unreal, and history is cynical without meaning unless meaningful today. All else is an illusion. Reality is a hierarchy of appearances, with some things more than others. Matter is at the farthest reaches of illusion. "The core commitment varies widely among different types, but all exhibit one consistent commitment. The goal is to eliminate desire, thus achieving salvation or oneness with the One or Void.

"The cosmos is always perfect. Experiencing oneness with the cosmos is to pass beyond personality. Personality and individuality mean nothing. A unique human life is without value.

"We only know by realizing our oneness with the world. The value of knowledge is its utility to move us in the right direction. No doctrine can be true. A lie or myth can be beneficial.

"We do good to attain unity with the One, not help others. There is no value in helping alleviate suffering since we will suffer later." Viviana reported the same way she conducted television news programs.

She stood, picked up her note file, gave a little hip swing and sighed deeply, then read, "There are many variations on this theme, but I listed a few types.

"One, **Pantheism** identifies the universe as a manifestation of God, but each person is God himself.

Two, **Hinduism** identifies freedom from the material world by purifying desires and eliminating personal identity. There is no central authority or creed. There is an immortality of the soul but not personal. Death ends personal existence but does not change an individual's nature.

Three, **Buddhism** espouses that life is full of suffering caused by desire. One can halt an endless sequence of births and deaths by avoiding desire through meditation for spiritual enlightenment. A soul never passes out of existence but finds its' way to the One via multiple reincarnations. The Void or Emptiness is a Buddists' ultimate reality. Viviana concluded with a voluptuous bosom shift followed by a scan of the other members for hints of approval or criticism.

No one said or did anything. At last Cavanaugh said, "Many people who espouse any of these world views would be fascinated by what they claim to believe in full. This book proved insightful and quite demanding intellectually."

"Yes, responded Thi. "Interesting, Viviana, there are so many variations on the theme of Eastern Pantheistic Monism. Whew, are the rest of you tired as I?" Thi solicited. "I found it difficult to get my mind around some philosophies. What is the consensus? Do we spend more time on this book, or do you think we garnered enough? Desmond, you were especially interested in world views. Did this book satiate your curiosity?"

"Desmond?" Thi, in puzzlement, repeated.

"Huh? What was that?" a faraway look in Desmond's eyes vanished with a blush. "Oh, yes, yes, the book more than satisfied my interest with detailed information." Heads nodded agreement around the table, accompanied by requests for a new book since they spent two meetings on this one.

"Good. Any suggestions for our next read and who would like to lead the review?" Thi queried.

Yacov responded, "I think it is Lydia's turn to lead, and I request a lighter read. Any ideas?"

Lydia piped up to accept leadership and suggested, "We are tired this evening. Please send your ideas by Friday, and I will select what I can best moderate from the suggestions. You will get the necessary information via the e-mail that evening." Lydia and Yacov left last.

A pat of Italian leathers on cement echoed in the parking garage as Desmond hurried toward Lydia's vehicle. Whispers hugged the passenger window as it disappeared into the door, Lydia stretched over the seat to ask, "What's up?"

"Do you have a minute? Can we talk?"

"Sure. Step into my 'office." Her joke smile soon vanished. A frown replaced it as Desmond got in and searched her face. He lowered his head before sad eyes lifted to give a piercing stare.

"What is it, Desmond?" she asked, reaching for his hand. His shoulders slumped tightly as a flood of tears wetted his silk shirt. She waited and silently prayed.

Haltingly he began. "I'm sure you know my orientation, but you always treat me with respect despite your doctrine. I'm HIV positive! I got the lab results today. My partner and I checked out negative at the beginning of our three years together. We talked about marriage. Monogamy isn't exactly a strong point with gays. Betrayal! Death and betrayal, what a great life!"

"Oh, Desmond, I'm so sorry! How can I help?" Lydia urged.

"I always attend sexually transmitted disease (STD), clinic for testing… incognito. They don't treat this."

"So, does your primary doctor know?" she queried.

"Only my ex-partner."

"I strongly recommend an appointment with that physician as soon as possible. To get in soon, tell them you are in pain. Pain seems to be a magic door opener. But it is true; you are reeling in emotional pain. Ask the doctor about their experience treating this, and if none or little, ask for a referral. Your doctor will know the next step and resources for you. The sooner, the better."

"The clinic gave me a pamphlet with health rules," Desmond offered as he pulled the crumpled publication from his pocket.

"Desmond, I realize this is a terrible shock, and life feels wobbly now. However, a friend outlived his predicted life expectancy with AIDS and is still going strong. We continue to pray and hope for a cure soon. New medications continue to improve health and longevity. You are not poison," Lydia stressed as she gently stroked his arm. Thank you for trusting this news with me—it's secure. May I pray for you?" she asked. Seeing a nod, she asked the Holy Spirit to lift off the fear and shock and replace it with peace and hope.

Desmond's face lightened as he remarked, "Maybe there's something to that stuff. I feel a lot better."

"Don't hesitate to call if you want to talk again," Lydia called as he walked away to his auto.

CHAPTER 36

CHICAGO, MY WONDERFUL TOWN

Saqqara slept well despite the usual airline punctuality stress. The uneventful flight ended pleasantly with Nadine's bubbly welcome and superficial chatter as she drove Saqqara home. Always discreet, she asked no questions. Naysa's silhouette appeared at her window as they rounded the familiar corner.

In the time it took Saqqara to unload, thank Nadine and come inside, Naysa wheeled herself into the hall. After warm welcome hugs, Naysa said, "It feels like you stayed away a long time. I missed you. It's late, so I won't keep you. I'm excited about the surprise tomorrow. Please meet me here at ten."

"I almost forgot the time difference. Ten it is. Thank you sooo much for all your support during the intensive week of counseling. We can recap tomorrow," Saqqara called over her shoulder as her stilettos walked her into the elevator. "Oh, I do trust you, but not because you aren't dangerous." A mystified expression spread over Naysa's face as she returned to her apartment.

A huge basket with a profusion of spring flowers met Saqqara at her apartment. She deeply inhaled their fragrances. Inside, she read the floral note from Tiffany, "Welcome home. I hope things went well. See you at 9:00 AM on Monday." Saqqara filed through the answering machine messages. *Why is Mother calling so much?* The last message from Dr. Chenoweth's office instructed her to call ASAP.

Naysa flung open the front door of the apartment house when the elevator doors opened.

To Saqqara's surprise, a van parked at the curb. "We're going for a ride," Naysa happily announced. The driver loaded the wheelchair and his fares. "We're off to Grant Park. Can you believe that I live here and have never seen the world-famous Buckingham Fountain? It resembles a wedding cake in a rococo artistic style inspired by the Latona Fountain at the Palace of Versailles. It symbolizes Lake Michigan. The park offers excellent food, so we are free of preparation fuss. It sounded as though you lost your heart to the natural beauty in Spokane, with the crystal-clear lakes, daylight forever, and no sticky humidity. I thought it might be good for you to see that you also live in a beautiful place. We can catch up on the bad stuff of life surrounded by beauty at the park.

"Mornings are less crowded," Naysa explained as they entered the park and looked for the perfect site for their time to share. A dimpled childlike face full of enthusiasm entreated Saqqara. "Over there, under that ancient weeping willow tree! What do you think?" They found a sizable flat area suitable for the wheelchair where gentle breezes swayed curtains of green, creating a secret garden atmosphere.

"If you look in the pouch on the back of my wheelchair, you will find a nifty folding chair and a blanket if you want to sit on the ground. I didn't want to be looking down on you all the time. Now, what did you learn?"

"I think I'll enjoy both provisions. First you, Naysa," Saqqara urged. "Tell me about the physical therapy."

"They weren't kidding when they said it's arduous. Before I arrived in Chicago, I worked on upper body strength building, balance with eye exercises, and core work. When I came here, I could get myself up and into a wheelchair. We also did preventative foot drop exercises. My vision checked out great. I want to walk independently.

"Most spinal cord injuries majorly heal in the first six months. After twelve months, the damage is considered permanent. Initially, they removed bone fragments in my spine. Next, they suggested I may need several rods and screws placed in the future. Then I discovered this new research using direct brain control and spinal electrical stimulation implants. Every option entailed months of physical therapy.

"Now I'm harnessed up, so my upper body supports me on the parallel bars while I think a link with my legs. I command them to move. Eventually, stand-and-step training will follow. This neuroplasticity practice or rewiring the brain is the mental part. I experience extreme temperature changes such as now. Whew, I'm burning up," Naysa said, frantically fanning herself with her hand as perspiration rolled down her face. "Could you hurry and get some ice at the food stand and maybe some chocolate eclairs to go with some iced coffee?"

The feather-light chair tipped over as Saqqara rose to run the errand. It seemed like a long time to Naysa, but the request returned in less than seven minutes. "Thank you so much. I'll be freezing before the morning is over. To continue, if all fails, a spinal stimulator implant to walk and get feeling in my legs is an option. Attitude! That is the key. The therapists say I'm doing exceptionally well for only one week. I monitor my blood pressure more now. It's a lengthy process. Now, please tell me everything! Oh! What did you mean last night about me being dangerous?"

Saqqara laughed aloud as she dropped onto the blanket to enjoy the treats. "We discussed my total distrust of people when Julie, the mentee, said it sounded like I trusted you. I thought about what she said and replied, 'Since she cannot walk, she seems less dangerous.' Lydia jumped all over the 'dangerous.' Like I said, being with Lydia and Julie transported me into another world of peace, safety, compassion, wisdom, and humor at times. Even in times of shock and confusion, I felt the softness. At last, I'm sleeping and don't even need the white noise machine or earplugs. I told you about the homework to sit in silence for twenty minutes. Well, I couldn't do it. I flunked because keeping constantly busy blocks the emotional pain I tried to escape all these years, and who wants to feel that? With the new understanding and tools I now possess, it is possible for the healthy life balance you encouraged me to plan."

Leaning intently forward, Naysa asked, "Now what?"

"I booked a follow-up phone call in two weeks to evaluate how things are going. Now that Lydia worked with me in person, we can schedule long-distance sessions. I can do much of the work talking to myself with the help of the Holy Spirit." Saqqara leaned back on her hands and laughed infectiously. They laughed together until tears rolled down Naysa's cheeks. "What is really spooky is that I answered myself." They guffawed even more. "Apparently, multiple selves conducting business accounts for the capacity to work so much. Of course, that is damaging my body." Irritated, Saqqara rose from the blanket. "This is too weird to discuss!"

"You seem different in a good way, Saqqara. I don't think you're weird, but a courageous woman searching for her truth. I'm happy for you. When we laugh at ourselves, we're getting healthier. Let's take a stroll after we finish our snacks."

Following the stroll, they watched the fantastic fountain and concluded the surprise with a scrumptious open-air lunch. The French onion soup succulently tantalized the olfactory sense. At the same time, the croissant sandwiches' buttery flavor enhanced the variety of meats and imported cheeses. A minted green tea accompanied the enticing red raspberry sundae drenched in real whipped cream.

Naysa quickly tired but persevered to enjoy the lunch thoroughly. Saqqara affectionately smiled at her nodding friend on the ride home. They both enjoyed the full morning but now Saqqara felt anxious to get home and work on plans for the senator's wedding.

CHAPTER 37

SHORT TRIP

On Monday morning, Tiffany welcomed Saqqara as they joined Millie and Jillian in the office to focus on the senator's wedding status, less than three weeks away. For huge events, Tiffany and Saqqara usually divided the responsibilities and personally supervised their portion during the actual event. Tiffany engaged Jillian to stay on staff until after the wedding to assist them both. Tiffany and Jillian decided to administrate the wedding and Saqqara and Jillian the reception. Millie worked the office, not the events.

Preparations came together more elaborately and quickly than they dreamed. This event potentially featured the business on the international societal map! Understanding how things worked, they made special notes of honoring personal assistants and security people along with the celebrities. Next, they excitedly reviewed the enormous number of completed preparations to identify loopholes or omissions, then they detailed the steps and timelines to meet before the event.

Immediately after the meeting, Saqqara called Dr. Chenoweth's office. To her amazement, he answered. "Hello Saqqara, you know your mother and I are long-time friends, and I have been the family doctor since before you came along. She's concerned about you. So, I made an appointment for you with a most respected leader

Short Trip

in his field to help you where I'm not able. He's in Boston, but you are a world traveler, so that won't be a problem. I'll switch you to the front desk, and they can give you the details. Let me know how things go. Good to talk to you, Saqqara." *What does Mother think she's doing meddling like this?*

Saqqara efficiently worked with Jillian. She interviewed her to learn her preferences for reception duties and assigned those duty plans to her to enable ease and complete knowledge of her responsibility at the event. Of course, everything needed to be reported to Saqqara when she left town.

Saqqara arrived at the airport on Thursday morning, an hour before her two-hour 8:03 AM flight to Boston. The appointment site at the prestigious university elicited a sense of déjà vu as she approached the building. She departed the elevator and walked to the suite with large signage of 'Chief of Staff.' No one occupied the office except a voluptuous young woman wearing an extremely low-cut suit jacket.

"The doctor is expecting you, Ms. Fain, this way," she said and opened an enormous door. Saqqara stepped in and onto a multicolored Persian carpet. Ponderous furniture, statuary, the smell of leather, and expensive cigars filled the imposing office.

A distinguished, obese man stood tall and leaned over a massive desk to shake her hand. "Nice to meet you, Ms. Fain. Please be seated. Dr. Chenoweth and I go back to our college days. He sent a medical history briefing but tell me in your own words about your concerns."

Saqqara related the symptoms, trial medications, hospitalizations, loss of time, night terrors, and undiagnosable bodily pain. She ended by telling him of her recent visit to Lydia, where she realized she suffered from childhood trauma and dissociation.

Leaning forward from a previous relaxed drape over his chair, he gazed at her directly. He compassionately said, "Dear Ms. Fain, I am so sad to tell you, but you've been had. Lydia, or whatever her name is, is a fake, a fraud. I would imagine it costs a lot to go there. Definitely, there is no such thing as Dissociative Identity

Disorder. Yes, the DSM mentions it but does not mean what you understand it to be."

Saqqara sat open-mouthed in dismay while a sinking feeling overcame her until the physician's peppy voice jolted her.

"You came to the right place. I have just the solution." He took out the prescription pad and wrote on it. "We just came up with a new promising drug. Here is the prescription," he said. Then he leaned forward, handed it to her, and said, "Jill, Humpty Dumpty had a great fall." He rose, unzipped his pants, walked around the desk, and sat on it before her while a lascivious grin smeared his face.

Saqqara lifted her head from the bistro table and looked around. Aromas of chocolate and vanilla filled the room. She looked at her watch, 4:23 PM "Oh no, my plane left at 2:30 PM!" Confused, she hailed a cab for the airport. The airline clerk offered her a 6:40 PM direct flight to Chicago (with a sizable change fee).

An older woman took a seat across from her while waiting for the plane. "Dearie, I would want someone to tell me, so I'm telling you. Your blouse buttons are all whamperjoled," she reported with disgust. Saqqara looked down at her blouse to find the third button in the second buttonhole. She self-consciously corrected the alignment as she smiled at the woman and thanked her. *I'm meticulous about my attire. How and when did that happen?*

She noticed some discomfort in her left arm as she rebuttoned her blouse. She went to the restroom to examine her arm to find a slightly swollen, possible injection site. She resolutely went home hopeless and in total denial of her dissociation.

CHAPTER 38

WIVES UNVEILED

Lydia instructed, "We needed that extra time to pray before Clarice and Seth arrive, Julie. I predict a breakthrough session, but it won't be easy. Keep interceding. I'll bring them in."

"It's so good to be with both of you. It's been over a month since I met with each of you.

We are excited to see what God planned for you today. Let us pray.

> "Thank you, Lord, for this divine appointment. You are Truth. We appeal to You for Your strength, wisdom, and compassion for all of Clarice and Seth. We thank You for Your anointing and continued binding of evil. May the words of our mouths and the meditations of our hearts be acceptable to You. Amen.

I want to begin with some catch-up reporting to help Julie and me be on the same page with you. Who would like to start?"

Holding hands and looking at Clarice, Seth volunteered to start. "Great news! There were no nightmares since you three worked with the little girl, and Clarice is getting adequate sleep, maybe for the first time since early childhood. I'm getting more sleep too."

Clarice chimed in, "No more sleeping pills, and the bothersome white noise machines are not required. I am weaning off the anti-depression prescription. Lydia, it was so kind of you to talk with my doctor to advocate for me. It's difficult for me to ask for my needs."

"You are welcome, Clarice. I believe it is wise to work as a healing team. Each discipline has its value and deserves respect. Part of your healing will be participating in some community classes about co-dependency. Co-dependency says, 'tell me what to be, and I'll be it; just tell me how to behave, and I'll behave that way; tell me what to think, and I'll think like that.' That is why it is so hard to ask for your needs. You require more coping skills to actualize your true worth. Remember, dissociation is a maladaptive or harmful coping skill for an adult. It works well for childhood survival but causes a lot of trouble in adulthood. A sexual abuse support group will also be helpful. Still more integration is needed to prevent triggering, potentially resulting in embarrassment.

"In an earlier session, we worked with the alter representing your biological mother, who kept the demeaning litanies going in your head. Her job ensured you remember how worthless you are. We kicked out a mocking and a lying spirit which inhabited her. What does she think of her new job?

"She is thrilled we no longer resent her and scream for her to 'shut-up'! We studied the handouts of positive words and feelings and read the two books about identity in Christ. Oh, here they are. I don't want to forget to give them back. Oh yes, my forgetting is less! I want to buy the book on forgiveness you assigned early on. Understanding forgiveness made it easier to choose to forgive my mother. It does such a great job of clarifying all the wrong ideas we hold about forgiveness. That is the key, isn't it?"

"I finished a seminar on inner healing. A man introduced himself as a psychologist. He shook his head and said, "Are you trying to tell us that forgiveness is the key to emotional healing?" He contacted me about six months later to report that he employed the forgiveness tool. Long-term patients no longer needed him, and new patients were getting well so fast that he wondered if he could run out of work. I assured him that would not happen because tens of thousands of broken people are in the world. He expressed delight to see patients finally get well.

"Without unconditional love, you learned to be performance-oriented, trying to earn your love by being a good student, good athlete, and performing arts person. Much like…"

> "Me…, Lydia, you said we could reveal ourselves today. I am one of your wives Seth," announced Mother sitting straight and proper.

Watching Seth inch his way to the end of the couch, staring wide-eyed at his wife, Lydia intervened, "Mother, it may be more comfortable for everyone if Clarice tells Seth what we discovered before any introductions."

Clarice's body relaxed as she turned to face Seth. She smiled apologetically. "We experienced conflict in our marriage over the way the house is maintained… or not, the budget, making a parenting plan we did not always follow, the physical intimacy problems, and so much confusion. Oh, Lydia, help!"

"You were doing just fine, Clarice. Seth, this is a great day because the confusion is going to evaporate. You manifest wonderfully mature in all this discovery. We discovered the reason for the conflict. Although all marriages encounter conflict, your special case, to some degree, resulted from Clarice's functioning in a compartmentalized way. Sometimes she appeared only as your adoring, amorous bride. The proper, nurturing mother made sure the children came first, not you or the home when it came to the children. An efficient woman ran the important demands of home management without interest in the children and absolutely no romance.

Due to abuse, Clarice lacked the skills to concurrently run a home, cope with the children or participate in a normal sex life with her husband. Do you see that when each of the wives heals and integrates into the OP God created, all the strength, knowledge, skill, caring, and experience will, at last, be able to function fluidly? Voilà… much less confusion!"

Lydia witnessed the silence and felt their anxiety, so she asked, "How about a short break?" The couple hustled out separately without speaking.

"We need to pray," urged Julie. They thanked the Lord for this time of awareness and the power of truth, which produces freedom. They thanked Him for strengthening the couple's spirits. Then, they requested angels of wisdom and peace to minister to them.

Clarice returned first, wearing a distressed expression, and slowly sank into the couch. Seth returned with a smug look on his face. "God always gets my attention in restrooms. Maybe that is the only time I'm not too busy to listen. Huh! God told me not to fear. He gave me a Proverbs 31 wife to cherish. Together we will be a testimony to others in similar situations. He is turning these ashes into beauty," Seth said as he fell to his knees and gathered Clarice in his arms. They wept and laughed together in joy.

Julie handed a note to Lydia. *I feel like we should leave. What a holy moment!*

"I think I can do this now; after all, I am already well acquainted with my wives," sighed Seth. "On with the introductions!"

A curl gently fell over Clarice's left eye. A devoted sweetness in her tone conveyed,

> "I'm first because I love you so much, Seth, and thank God for you in my life. I wanted to be all you wanted in a wife, but so many times when intimate, the little girl triggered, came out, and I went inside. Then you know how she always cried and kicked or just went limp," explained adoring Bride.

"That was so hard on me. I want my wife to want my body, all of me. I never want to harm you. It was demoralizing to make love to you and feel like you weren't there with me or, worse, hear that horrible crying or whimpering. It got to where I would rather forget about the sex and take care of myself another way."

> "Oh, Seth, I am so sorry. I didn't know how it was for you. I felt so discarded by you when you were not interested, even though I would plan special times. You see, Clarice made me for the wedding night because she knew she could not consummate the marriage on some level, but we wanted our children with you and to grow old with you," she pled.

"I love you too and look forward to normal, compatible enjoyment of each other."

> "You are a wonderful father, Seth. Clarice made me when she started kindergarten. I loved school. It felt safe and encouraging. I wanted to be the best, so someone would love me. Now I know striving is unhealthy. My Creator adores me. I realize that God fully loves me, and I cannot lose His love. Hopefully, I will drive you less crazy trying to be someone or something I am not and learn to be me. Moreover, I will be less hard on the children to achieve and teach them how to be themselves too. As Mother, I want my children to rise up and call me blessed. For homework, I made long lists of all the lies I believed about myself, not measuring up and replacing the lies with God's truth about who I am."

"I see the changes and rewards of your journaling. You used to be a walking apology," Seth acknowledged. "I have to admit my frustration with you not co-operating in the house chores and forgetting to make the monthly statements at times."

> "It's my turn. I'm Cinderella. Clarice's mom worked out of the home and expected finished housework when she returned. Her husband did not help, but

he yelled alot at the mom over the messy house and unprepared meals. Little Clarice tried to help, but no one taught her the skills. She only got us into more trouble. I grew up with Clarice. I went next door whenever I could. Mrs. Martinetti had four kids and kept a clean, well-ordered, pretty house, and boy could she cook! I closely watched how she did things and decided to be like her. I am. I am a hard worker and expected to provide a nice home for all of you without notice and not much help or respect. This family is like it was at home with Clarice's mom and dad. I worked just as hard as Mother to list the lies I believed. I forgave that family and yours. I understand that with integration, I can share in the rewards and appreciation that Bride and Mother receive."

"Please forgive me, Cinderella; as you know, I have been clueless. I want you to know I appreciate all the effort you put into keeping an ordered house for our family. A well-managed home is important to me, especially if I want to bring business clients to dinner or the kids bring friends home. Also, I am sorry if you felt offended if I thought you were Bride."

Lydia explained, "I asked you to read the book about relationships—the sowing and reaping principles. Do you see how Clarice/Cinderella sowed seeds of expectation that she would maintain a home without any praise from her parents? Then she reaped the same in her primary family. It is also interesting that you have four children, like Mrs. Martinetti. Yet, you two weathered this time with so much grace. For homework, it would be good to make time to sit down together and organize your lives based on the information you received today.

"Clarice, you are a master at journaling, so continue to identify any more ungodly decisions your wives made and work the healing process. Don't be surprised if you experience integration once a wife alter is healed. Seth, I think you would benefit from some journaling instructions from Clarice. Then you can work through any lies you believe or judgments you make. It is helpful to read the sowing and reaping book again together. It isn't the two of you against each other; it is: "Let us go together and work our bitter root garden."

After they left and during the session review, Lydia said to Julie, "What you addressed in your note about a holy moment is the great benefit we get to experience with our dear clients. When a person calls me for help, they are usually broke. They spent years and a lot of money on all kinds of physicians, counselors, drugs, quacks, hospitals, and spiritual care which didn't offer what they needed."

CHAPTER 39

THE WEDDING

Long workdays without breaks ensued. Saqqara canceled her follow-up intensive counseling appointment with Lydia. She neglected to make time to "talk to her selves," but they did not fail to talk to her. "Stop!" she shouted as she pounded her desk. Pushing hair away from her face with both hands, she sighed, "I need to work and don't have time for you now!"

They hoped and now felt ignored and rejected. In other words, she overworked herself and thereby neglected herself and those healthy activities identified in the counseling as necessary for her healing. The incubus attacks ceased but resurfaced insomnia compromised energy, patience, and immune system. She awoke with a fulminating cold on the wedding day.

Tiffany texted a glowing report of the wedding to Saqqara and several details to scrutinize. After winding up the wedding venue, she declared exhaustion and looked forward to relaxation at home. Jillian arrived at the reception site well before the guests and commenced her duties.

Saqqara's tasked upfront surveillance activities and alerted Jillian to fix anything which may be awry. She gorged herself with cold medicine and gorgeously floated among the guests in a full-length yellow organza gown with iridescent highlights. Fluidly,

The Wedding

she guided the principles to their respective places of honor upon arrival and announced guests of distinction. She welcomed some with brief venerable chatter; she memorized the extensive guest list, the research pictures, and social history. All guests arrived.

Several minor toasts concluded when Saqqara, distant from the entrance, noted another arrival. An unusually tall, imposing male party crasher. Mentally evaluating how to deal with the situation, she started toward him. Within hearing distance, she detected his Russian accent. Suddenly she felt dizzy and nauseous—the room whirled. *Run! Run! Run!*

On the opposite side of the enormous venue, Jillian also noticed the late arrival when swift peripheral movement caught her attention. Saqqara raced towards the kitchen with hair and billowing organza flying. Jillian struggled to know whether to engage the party crasher or attend Saqqara. Priority. She enlisted a security guard who headed toward the uninvited guest. Just then, the senator's brother approached the man and led him to a table. Jillian gave a 'no problem' nod to the guard. She discreetly proceeded to the kitchen by a different route from Saqqara. The kitchen staff only knew Saqqara sprinted through and out the door. An empty alley filled Jillian's searching eyes. A cat jumped off a dumpster bringing her awareness of her solo administrative role. She quickly refreshed herself in the ladies' lounge, took a deep breath, and decided to be amazing.

CHAPTER 40

THE LAST STRAW

Warm afternoon air wafted through her window to awaken Saqqara. Organza swished when she turned over. Her hand clutched her forehead, and with a frown, she stared at the clock just as the phone rang. She frantically searched for the mobile, then recognized the landline.

"There you are. I called and called since you came home yesterday morning, but no answer," Naysa rebuked.

The answering machine blinked Monday and full. Saqqara asked, "What day is this?"

"Monday afternoon. You asked me to pray for you when you left for the wedding reception early Saturday morning and returned home Sunday morning. You repeated the blue afghan scenario. A cab drove you home without keys to get in. No, you wore both heels this time. Helga dressed you down for your despicable lifestyle."

"I can't talk now, Naysa. I'll call you later." Saqqara sank onto the sofa, then rose and activated the answering machine. Most calls came from Tiffany and Naysa. None made sense except the last one which awakened her. Tiffany sternly announced a meeting at 10:00 AM Wednesday at their attorney's office and demanded that she be there with all legal business formation papers. *So, what is that all about? Was I so exhausted that I slept in my dress? Why can't I remember the reception?*

Saqqara worked alone at the office on Tuesday. The wedding probably wore everyone out. No matter, Saqqara kept herself constantly busy.

On Wednesday morning, when she met Tiffany at the attorney's office, she was startled to find Jillian there. Tiffany hardly looked at her, and Jillian busied herself with a magazine. Once called into the appointment, the attorney began by saying, "These situations are regrettable but do happen, so let's get on with it in a congenial manner," *What in the world is he talking about?*

Tiffany began, "I am terribly sorry, Saqqara, but even though I deeply care for you, I cannot and will not endure any more catastrophic humiliations doing business with you.

"I found Jillian amazingly competent and compatible. I want nothing to do with our business anymore. Jillian offered that I share a partnership with her and reactivate her business, *Exuberance*, which holds a stellar reputation. I asked our attorney to completely remove me and all interests from our corporation and draw up a reasonable financial distribution of funds. He advised that can be accomplished within thirty days at most."

Saqqara pieced together events at the reception within the next few days with Jillian's and Naysa's help. She or some part of her ran again and lost time. The realization of her life in shambles slowly subdued her. She cancelled all previously scheduled events and scheduled no new ones. Saqqara was puzzled when she reflected upon the bizarre Boston appointment. Her sensibility informed her the drug would not work. However, everything she learned during the intensive prayer counseling made sense and significantly improved her condition. Lydia told her people moved there to get needed prayer counseling. Saqqara decided to call Lydia to ask if she could structure a bi-weekly counseling schedule if she moved there for a season. *I'll take a sabbatical from the business or what is left of it. I'll miss Naysa, but now I'm not suitable for anyone, not even myself.*

CHAPTER 41

DESMOND'S VISIT

Lydia's face lit with surprise to find book club Desmond at her office door. Desmond strode in with hands exaggerating his speech and announced, "I just kept hearing you say if you need to talk, I'm here for you, well here I am. I'm furious at myself for setting myself up for a possible disaster or facing a death sentence. I'm so confused. I guess I always felt that way. I'm fighting myself, blaming myself for going into this lifestyle. I need someone to sort this all out for me.

Lydia motioned to a chair and said as she sat across from him, "I am so sorry you feel so much pain and confusion now. There are many treatment advances for HIV today, and one can expect to live a relatively normal life. I doubt I can sort it all out, but I'm sure Jesus can." Desmond watched Lydia look up as she pled,

> "Lord, we need You now. We are confident there is no condemnation in You. We thank You for your grace, mercy, correction, direction, and peace. What does Desmond need to know and understand now?"

Desmond's Visit

"Thanks for the prayer, but you know I'm not a Christian. The Bible describes homosexuality as an abomination to God. Why would He make me for an abomination to Him?" Desmond frowned.

"I know of seventy-six scriptures listing abominations, and homosexuality is only one of them. Primarily, God hates everybody's sin but loves each sinner beyond our comprehension. First of all, Desmond, God does not create homosexuals. He creates marvelous males and females who naturally desire each other for sexual satisfaction. There is absolutely no solid scientific evidence to prove homosexuality is genetic. So, you were not born that way. People decide to reject their created gender."

Desmond shook his head and mentally threw questions with a furrowed brow.

"Yes, I know hermaphrodites exist, for whom we hold compassion. Something went wrong with genetics, but this is not our topic. Psychology books previously listed homosexuality as insanity, a total break with reality, or common folk would say 'crazy.' However, a preponderance of scientific data reveals something important. A child's experiences, indoctrination by family, friends, and culture train a child to think something. Significant indicators show wounding causes a child to reject their gender, and there is only one gender left.

"Some ridicule the idea that people are born homosexual. That is not ridiculous. It is possible to reject one's gender in the womb. Why? Babies hear well under water. We are spiritual beings, and our spirit seems quite mature at conception, able to sense rejection.

"Defilement affects the mother and the fetus when involved in rape or evil occultic sexual rituals. The result is the same as that after birth. Is that clear?"

Desmond shook his head and exclaimed, "Amazing!"

"Humans are amazing, agreed Lydia, which brings me to sexual abuse, a major cause of homosexuality. I never worked with a homosexual free of sexual violation. Hatred against the abuser grows to total rejection of that gender. Women sexually abuse as well as men you know. So, if the pedophile is male and the victim is female, she may totally reject males and only be interested in females. The same dynamic is true of the little boys. Pedophilia, incest and otherwise, always damages the child differently depending upon the lies fed them by the perpetrator and the circumstances of the crimes."

"Okay, but some cultures deem pedophilia more holy than a wife, especially with boys."

"Just because a culture or person believes an idea doesn't make it so. Holiness and evil stand on their results. Malicious threats such as, 'If you ever tell, your puppy or mommy, et cetera, will be killed,' fill the victim with fear and compliance. The child is vulnerable to candy seduction, shame, guilt, or being told, 'You are special, and this is our secret, so never tell.'

"A powerful desire for the same sex springs from a child's rejection by the same-gendered parent. Ronnie was fourteen, with a younger brother and two younger sisters. His attorney father left the family without any warning and divorced his wife out of the blue. His departure devastated the family. But, six months later, the father crept into the house and snatched the younger son. Ronnie presented as a normal healthy male very interested in the girls at school. He even wore an earring to let the world know he was not gay until the brother's abduction. Then his life swelled with confusion, a great desire for his father's love, and a constant rejection agony. His heart screamed, 'Why didn't he take me?' Overnight he sought male companionship, which quickly degenerated into an unnatural, unhealthy attraction for sexual intimacy with males. He reported multiple daily encounters with anyone. Finally, at eighteen, he contracted aids and died at twenty-one—such a tragic story but common. The same dynamic is true for lesbians. These are precious girls who deserve the love of their mothers. But, for some reason, real or imagined, they believe they are unacceptable to their mothers and try to fill that vacuum in their hearts with sexual intimacy with females.

"For over twenty years, I enjoyed working with many men and women confused into believing they are gay or prefer another gender. All were sexually immoral in that confusion. Many confessed they hated the pestering desire and disgusting situation in which they found themselves. They sought counsel due to the guilt and shame.

"Others proudly reported their conquests and escapades, absolutely confident of the legitimacy of their lifestyle and haughtily expressed disrespect for anyone who disagreed. They sought counsel for another reason. But, a healing of the lie usually happened, and when it did, everyone usually collapsed in great sobs of relief and release as they identified the bitter root cause for their wrongful belief that they were always 'this way.'"

Desmond followed with an honest litany of the same negative feelings the client types above expressed.

"High-level confusion is part and parcel of homosexual thought. A person could be wounded and captive to the lies in all the above situations, which compound the stronghold (a firmly held belief system) in their life. We must also realize demons look to live in people. They attach to sin in a person's life and greatly energize it, resulting in other forms of immorality."

"My theatrical studies included classical works, which included demons. Wow, Lydia, I feel like a quaking leaf alone on a tree that realized the gale stopped. Your voice and the information produced a calm in me. Thank you so much for your time. I'm aware of your packed schedule. I identify succinctly with a lot of what you just said. I think counseling may be beneficial for me; what do you think?"

Lydia reached over and took his hand, "Definitely. I know you too well and love you too much to help in that way, but I'm happy to recommend three people whom I consider a good fit. Have you seen your physician yet?"

Desmond answered, "Yes, waiting for test results, and he's referring me to a doc specializing in AIDS. Hey, I'm off. Thanks a million." He smiled as a tear lifted to flow.

CHAPTER 42

THE MOVE

The travel agency booked Saqqara's road trip and lodging from Chicago to Spokane, Washington, to coordinate with scenic and historical sites. The distance of around 1,780 miles or 2,870 kilometers required three days if she drove eight-plus hours and covered six hundred miles each day. A more flexible plan added sites, miles, and days to her journey.

At the start of the route, the terrain looked similar to Illinois, other than thinning traffic, small towns, private homes, and fewer large buildings. The course touched the tip of Wisconsin and continued through the heartland of Iowa's expansive cornfields. At one point, a cloudburst culminated in a double rainbow. North into South Dakota, trees grew less dense. The Black Hills produced dramatic landscapes of multicolored layered Badlands with deep canyons and towering pinnacles that rose out of nowhere. She shared the genius sculpture of Mt. Rushmore with summer tourists, which added a lighthearted sense of adventure.

Next, the event planner visited many Native American historical sites. The tour passed a herd of buffalo in Wyoming reminiscent of the wild west before she entered the forever flatland of eastern Montana. The big sky country highway stretched hundreds of miles straight ahead to end like a dot at the horizon to make certain areas of unlimited speed of one hundred miles per hour feel like thirty. Weather twisted isolated cedars dotted the landscape. Gradually land appeared with rolling hills, lush valleys, and forests. Her auto easily pulled a 5x7 trailer to pass lumbering semi-trucks as they ascended the dramatic summits of the northern Rockies.

Scars on mountainsides in Idaho evidenced great mining bygone days. At last, on the evening of the third of July, she descended the Bitter Root Mountain Range to view the shimmering expanse of Lake Coeur d'Alene, Idaho. Saqqara stretched into the steering wheel and scanned the terrain, exhaled a giant sigh, and loudly declared herself tired. Thirty more miles before her destination. No one expects me today. My first appointment is Monday, and I'll have time to settle in after the owners leave. I'll lodge here.

The hotel buzzed with activity centering around tomorrow's flotilla and best-ever fireworks display. The friendly front desk clerk asked if she visited their fair city to celebrate this national holiday and needed a place to lay her attractive head.

"Yes. If there is a room in the inn," Saqqara joshed. "In the past, I've either coordinated an event or fell into bed with exhaustion without seeing the fireworks."

"Actually, we do because I just took a cancellation before you stepped up to the desk," he clucked with self-satisfaction.

Saqqara checked in, found a safe parking spot, and sauntered downtown, relieved to feel stiffness from driving release to lighten her steps. Festive decorations entertained, and the aroma of outdoor cooking tantalized her taste buds. It lured her to enjoy a juicy hamburger with all the trimmings, including Walla Walla sweet onions and a gigantic portion of famous Idaho potato fries. She chose an outside deck on which to dine and feast on the lake's beauty. A blazing orange sunset filled the sky well after she slept.

The next day the beach beaconed a barefoot stroll. White sandals in hand, the hot sand cooled if her toes dug deeply, and her arch flattened into it. She waded the lukewarm shores of the clear water. She noted quartz sparkling from the bottom rocks. Sounds of distant motorboats and playing children filled the air. The wind whipped her long hair while she stopped in a cool current of knee-high water and pondered. *I'm alone in a distant place. Lydia kindly arranged housesitting while I'm here. Responsibilities to supplement my time apart from the counseling and homework assignments make for a busy day. That is prime*!

Some flotilla participants showed off solo throughout the day but later joined the flamboyant performance. Saqqara assented to a blue butterfly face-painting to add frivolity to the celebration. She joined the throngs to gather on an expansive boardwalk. Around 10:00 P.M., daylight finally gave way to a cloudless night sky. Children's shrieks of pure delight at the beautiful lights or for fear of banging bursts punctuated the crowd's oohs and aahs. West and behind a small mountain, smatterings of fireworks showed themselves from the town of Liberty Lake. Amazed at the dual display, people suddenly winced as gigantic lightning bolts repeatedly streaked the sky above the mountain. The thunderous heavenly light show dwarfed the light of fireworks and muffled their sound.

Saqqara and Naysa had prayed for two signs to confirm a wise decision to move. She shivered a little to realize the celestial light show and double rainbow delivered two signs. A smile of satisfaction lingered as she shuffled through the crowd to her hotel. *I must tell Naysa! Oh, it's after two in the morning in Chicago. I'll text.*

Ben and Sylvia belonged to Lydia's support team. They offered to rent the apartment above their garage to Saqqara while on a mission trip through December. The opportunity included home maintenance plus care for lawn and pets. The gentleman mused about seeing a trailer arrive with the tenant. Of course, Lydia only gave essential contact information for Saqqara. Still, since they participated in her work, he assumed the new tenant was dissociative, and that said it all. They met her at the curb, and Ben introduced his wife and himself. "I'm a bit challenged about where to put all the trailer contents," he said.

"It's all boxed. I'll manage to make it work. Thank you," Saqqara soothed. He helped her back the trailer into the drive to unload and carry the boxes upstairs to the modest apartment.

The Move

While he rested his aging body from labor in the day's heat, Sylvia oriented Saqqara to the house. Sylvia handed Saqqara an extensive typed instruction sheet of everything she told her and a tablet to take notes.

When Sylvia finished, Ben led Saqqara to the garage to introduce her to lawn care. The pungent odor of lawn fertilizers, old grass, and oil hit her. Her family always hired lawn care, and she knew zilch! But, unlike his organizer wife, Ben did not prepare instructions. Saqqara's pen flew across the notepad as perspiration beaded across her face. Snowblower and unique oil mixture!? Ben noticed her anxiety and inquired about her lawn care experience. "You know, I probably should give the backyard a quick touch tomorrow before we leave. Why don't you join me? I'll let you help out. How about 7:30 AM before it gets too hot? By the way, Cody and Grace in the yellow house across the street will be happy to help you with anything," he knowingly offered.

The semi-arid morning air felt cool. Ben demonstrated how to work the weed whacker then he handed it to Saqqara to manage not to throw grass into flower beds. Next, they started the mower by taking turns adjusting the choke until she got it to start. Ben reminded her that she might experience the same issue with the snowblower, "One needs to prime it five times before pulling the rope." By the time they finished, she felt too stressed to accept the invitation to join them for their last breakfast. Soon after, they bade farewell to interested neighbors, and friends drove them to the airport.

It felt good to be alone. Saqqara heard the dog in the house whining after its owners. She decided to nap, explore the town a bit later and buy groceries. She planned to walk the dog in the evening, unpack more and settle in until Monday—then it begins!

CHAPTER 43

THE 9TH OF JULY

―◆―✕―◆―

Varieties of conifers rose to the clouds and gently swayed with occasional breezes. The fragrance of summer flowers and cedar bark welcomed Saqqara's subtle approach to each manicured lawn. She felt elite with only one dog on a leash as she passed current neighbors who smiled or waved.

Her Chicago neighborhood vibrated a cacophony of noise. People mostly avoided looking at each other as dusty wind gusts messed up hairstyles. Pet walkers usually handled at least four animated leashes.

In a way, she wished for invisibility, especially from the effervescent woman across the street from her apartment. Although she gave a brief return wave, she busied herself with the leash to avoid conversation. She disliked the canine responsibility, but the well-trained dog behaved well enough to tolerate it.

The usual challenge of mornings forced Saqqara to push through to veil the struggle and resistance which reigned inside. Nevertheless, she felt grateful for the conveniently scheduled afternoon appointments only a few blocks away. Lydia's office offered a mysterious comfort.

The 9th of July

On her first return appointment, Julie met Saqqara. She led her to Lydia, who arranged a bouquet that matched her long floral skirt. It flowed as in a dance when Lydia twirled, assumed a expression of pleasure, and enthusiastically greeted, "It is so good to be with you again, Saqqara. Please make yourself comfortable and catch us up. We felt disappointed and concerned when you canceled the follow-up appointment and pleasantly surprised when you called to arrange a season of ongoing prayer counseling."

"I included what you might call a brief vacation driving west and enjoyed gorgeous areas and history of our great country. Ben and Sylvia seem like stellar people. Thank you again for the suggestion of such a perfect arrangement for us. Ben appeared dubious the apartment would accommodate the 5X7 trailer of belongings, but we got it all upstairs. I've managed to settle in. I'm happy to say most of my things match the decor quite nicely. I saved the boxes in the garage for when we leave and need to pack again... still labeled."

Julie sent a note to Lydia: *Her system must have diversification if she needed a trailer for so many items.*

Lydia glanced at it and nodded a smile, then she prayed.

> "Loving Heavenly Father, we thank You for enjoyable, safe travel for Saqqara and all the provision. We remind You of the restraining orders and boundaries set for all evil entities regardless of level. We welcome the seven spirits of God to manifest. We request angelic assistance as needed, direction, and anointing all for the work at hand. In the name of Jesus, Amen."

"Tell us, Saqqara, what transpired after you left and returned home?" inquired Lydia.

Saqqara's long lashes fluttered as she drew in a long breath. She kicked off white diamond-studded sandals and sat on her folded leg to begin. The pleasant expression as she reported Naysa's surprise faded to solemnly. She shared the tale of rejection by her business partner, her mother's interference, and the Boston psychiatrist who debunked DID and disparaged Lydia's integrity. "That's why I canceled the follow-up. He is a renowned therapist!"

"Oh, Saqqara, I am so sorry!" said Lydia offering a hand.

"Me too!" said Julie. "It must be quite destabilizing to leave here and bump into such denial of dissociation from an expert. However, I commend your factual conclusion to pursue your dissociation healing and to refuse the always present denial."

Lydia took pen and tablet in hand and said, "The loss of your business and Tiffany's friendship must be agonizing. It sounded like a thriving concern, and you worked so hard. I'm confident good will come out of this, but that is in the future. Our focus now is to get your Humpty Dumpty put back together. She paused to get a cue from her client as she observed a tranced stare come over Saqqara's face and a change of position. "Hello. May I help you?" she asked this other Saqqara.

Nothing.

Saqqara returned to her leg sitting position and continued to relate the saga of events following and leading up to the present. Finally, she stopped, slouched, and deeply sighed again. "Then I took stock of the life changes that transpired during and due to working with you."

The body took the previous sitting position on the edge of the teal couch. The same stare reappeared, after which the alter became aware of the two ladies in the unfamiliar room. She looked around.

"I only do men. How did you know how to call me?"

Lydia sat still to observe body movements and pupil size intently, then weighed each word. "We didn't, but perhaps we said a code

The 9th of July

word to call you out by accident. Saqqara and we work together. Do you know her?"

"No. That's a strange name. Where are the men?"

Julie responded, "No men are here, but we are interested in you. Do you have a name? When you came to be, how old was the body?" A noticeable lapse of time ensued before Jill gave her name and reported remembrance of some memories at age three. "Would you mind sharing some of those early memories with us?" Julie asked. Sensing Jill resembled experiencing a rag doll. She felt very flexible and malleable, willing to comply and please. She presented a delightfully youthful countenance and bounced happily on the cushion as she began to share times when her daddy and she took trips. Everyday child experiences described the first few trips, but a morose cloud quickly infected them.

Jill scooted back on the seat to settle in, surveyed the room again, and resumed her tales,

> "Daddy and me always flew first-class, and everyone commented on my cuteness. We stayed at and visited pretty places with famous people and sometimes even royalty. A special mother who did not live in our house in the United States always met us wherever they went in the world; it could be China, Europe, South America, private islands, or of course, the United States. This mother made sure that I dressed just the right way for the events and arrived at the right time. Daddy went to many business meetings without me and with me. The mother always oiled and massaged me whenever I went with him, especially my pee-pee, before going places. She trained how to act with each person or group. I never complain unless they want me to, but the whole point is to do whatever they ask. Sometimes I help only one man, or there could be a whole bunch of em. It is important to let them know how much I enjoy it... or exaggerate how much I don't!"

"You said that now we must focus on what?" Saqqara asked in a dreamy tone.

Lydia inquired, "Are you aware that we engaged in a conversation with Jill?"

"No, but I did experience that 'going away feeling' again. Are you saying that I have an amnesic alter named Jill? This idea is so hard to deal with. I suppose I should want to know about her, right?"

Julie explained, "We want to help you be co-conscious with Jill. All of you need to know your history just as a person who is not fragmented. The key here is to choose to know your history and learn what you decided about it. Remember, DID is a coping skill children use to escape real or perceived traumatic experiences. You did not want to remember what happened, but what you do not know is causing great problems in your life now. You can only resolve this conflict by being fully aware."

"I don't understand the trauma piece; I spent a happy childhood. This is so hard!" Saqqara whined as she bent low to hold her head in her hands and weave back and forth. "Okay, what just happened?" she abruptly asked, straightened, and pushed blond locks away from her face.

Lydia's emerald eyes met Saqqara's, "You may find it beneficial to take journal notes during the sessions to use as a reference for your private journaling times. If you didn't bring it today, you could use this notepad. I want you, Jill, and all of you to listen to what we are talking about now. I unknowingly said a code word, a trigger, which called Jill out to take executive control of your body, Saqqara. That is when you faded away amnesic to Jill. Your lost time works like that.

"In some cases, initially, only the client knows their triggers. In others, the people who traumatized the child also know them. At the time of the planned trauma, they install and record the trigger or cue to be used in the future to 'call forth' that alter to use for their purposes. This procedure is known as mind control. From what Jill shared today, it seems this may be in your history."

Saqqara's eyes widened with alarm as they darted back and forth at Julie and Lydia. "Are you telling me that I'm a mind-controlled slave? I heard news reports about that kind of stuff recently. This is too absurd!" she anguished. Wringing her hands, she stood to walk the room, then felt her head spin. She stumbled into a nearby table but straightened as she felt the strength of supporting hands on either side leading her back to the couch. Her head sank into the soft leather as voices from afar called her name while she floated into silent blackness.

Saqqara shot forward, instantly aware of her surroundings. Cold sweat beaded her face as she weakly mumbled something in clumsy embarrassment. "You fainted. You're fine now, relax a while," Lydia explained. She carefully covered Saqqara with the couch afghan and offered a pillow.

"I hope you like peppermint tea, Saqqara. It's nice and hot," Julie's spritely voice called as she set a small tray near the couch. A pleasant interlude with soothing music ensued before Saqqara rallied to sip the tea. "Tea and honey. It warms all the way down. Thank you, both of you, so much. I experienced that severe vertigo for years for no reason, although today's news could shock anyone for sure."

Lydia explained, I did not tell you that you are a mind-controlled slave, but if that is confirmed, on some level, you always knew it. All alters are you and what they know is your history—denial walls off information.

Still quaking inside, Saqqara urged Lydia to tell her about Jill. "I realize I fainted, but I made sacrifices to come here for healing. I am strong."

"I believe you, Saqqara, but my current responsible assessment indicates you have minimal capacity for more work today. Believe it or not, you provided an excellent beginning. I honestly sense Jill's contribution is the Holy Spirit's anointing of you to be able to trust us to do this work. Trust is minimal now. I think it wise to allow you to communicate with Jill through journaling first. On Thursday, you can bring the journal, and we can discuss this more. Okay?"

Lydia encouraged Saqqara to write her homework assignments, and Julie encouraged her to journal with the intent to learn more about Shield, Rory, and Jill. Lydia provided reinforcement to listen and ask questions without judgment or criticism. If Saqqara encountered frightening information, she should jot a reminder of the topic and ask Jesus to hold it until a counseling session to provide support during memory retrieval. Since dreams often surface as memories, they encouraged her to log them in her journal or keep one at her bedside. After recording the dream, she needed to ask the Holy Spirit to enable her to sleep again.

"Did you do the system map homework for the follow-up session?" Julie inquired.

"No, but I think I remember how to do it," Saqqara replied.

"Please be sure to interrupt me or ask me to slow down so you can write homework and information important to you. As you know, it is easy to forget some things," Lydia explained, reaching for her appointment book. I will be able to see you from 2-4 PM on Mondays and Thursdays except for the second and third weeks in August, the third week in September, and Thanksgiving Day. I will notify you in advance of intensive weeks, which take priority over weekly appointments. Other days in other weeks can make up for missed appointment sessions. I shall assign extra homework for those times. The office closes on December 21 for the year. Questions?"

"No, you spoke slow enough for me to write it. Sounds good. Thank you," shrugged Saqqara as she rose to leave.

Lydia Lifted the trusted book of spiritual blessings and said, "Before you leave, we want to bless your spirit to restore and strengthen your capacity." Julie and Lydia rose, blessed her spirit, offered a prayer of thanksgiving for the productive session, and requested a comfortable adjustment to her new home away from home.

POSTING

"It will be interesting to see the map," Julie noted.

"Many therapists no longer do maps or interview alters. I find those activities early in the process powerfully demolish the denial needed to reach the trauma. Once the denial is mostly out of the way, the client can accept the alters are projections of themselves. What are your thoughts regarding Jill, Julie? She demonstrated a significant aspect of dissociation for us?" the mentor requested.

"I'm not sure to what you refer. Jill presents the typical enslaved sex personality."

"Yes, but think about her behavior, bouncing while she talked versus her emergent persona."

Julie shifted her whole body and directed her eyes at the bouquet in deep thought until, at last, "I'm sorry, I am blank. Maybe I don't know what you are thinking."

"Do you remember talking about alters who get stuck in age, time, or experience and those who develop and mature over time? I think the bouncer is a younger aspect of Jill, the adult. Really the same mindset but changing behavior to some degree with age. Once one heals, all those Jills integrate."

"Fascinating! Yes, I noticed but gave it no significance, but her extreme reaction to the mention of mind control gives it strong relevance to her history."

"We need to prepare for the next client, but she needs a healthy schedule, social interaction, and spiritual sustenance for maintaining balance while doing this work. Another priority is to check for retrainers and saboteurs to protect her and the work. We can address the spin program since she is now aware of the frequency of vertigo," Lydia concluded.

CHAPTER 44

UBA

―――◆※◆―――

Smiling in satisfaction, Saqqara hurried into the office and opened her oversized bag on the table, "I had a bit of fun doing the map. It just flowed as you said. Before we knew it, we did it. I got magazines at the thrift store and found pictures to match my impressions of parts on the map and their emotions. I realize when I say nice things to myself, I get co-operation. I mean, we sense or hear input or questions. The journal looks a mess, but here it is," handing it to Lydia.

"Thank you. I am anxious to see it. May we make copies of the map and your journal as we see fit?"

"Oh yes, whatever will be most helpful."

Lydia handed the journal to Julie, "We need all contents so far. Would you be so kind as to make copies? I see obvious differences in handwriting and printing, even color choice of writing instruments. Some delightful little ones not yet skilled in writing made their strokes in loops and jabs. Well done, Saqqara! Alters are co-operating. Shall we sit?"

After the opening prayers, Julie copied the journal and returned to ask, "I see that Shield is giving you comforting and wise words about adoption. Do you know why?"

– 306 –

"No. But Shield reported Rory is angry at me and won't talk. Jill is confusing. When I sense her personality, I feel small and childlike but an adult at other times. She talks a lot about how much she loves her Daddy due to special secrets which make Mommy mean."

Jill rose and retrieved Bunny from the stuffed animal basket.

> *"Sometimes I am supposed to be afraid, or act like I'm in pain or hate men... like a play."*

"I got that! I felt her. Jill spoke, didn't she?" gasped Saqqara.

"Excellent, Saqqara; yes, Jill explained her job. Good work, Jill!" said Lydia. "Saqqara, in the past, Jill came 'out,' and you automatically went inside somewhere, but now I want you to determine to know what Jill is saying…what you are saying. Remember the stage; stand in the wings while she is in the spotlight. Okay?" encouraged Lydia. "Now, Jill, did you visit Boston recently?"

> *"Sure. I go to the east coast a lot. I satisfy many of the big wigs in government, finance, and entertainment too. Why?"*

"Do you mind telling us what took place then?" asked Julie.

> *"The egg heads hang out in Boston, the brains of society with letters behind their names. I did a quick blow job on a big psychiatrist. He requested me for years, but he always asks for somebody named Uba when he finishes with me."*

"Who is Uba?"

"Enough! I told you to cease and desist," belted out Rory and went inside again.

"My head is killing me," Saqqara squinted. "I know. I know. Step back, please."

The pressure eased. "That really works. Thank you. What do you need? I don't sense or hear anything. Do you think Uba is the runner? I want to understand the runner issue."

Lydia explained that Rory tried to protect information about Uba and probably blocked the communication. He did his job well. She went on to ask if anyone knew Uba.

"The back of my head hurts, and I feel dizzy," reported Saqqara. "There are flashes of many rooms, doors, and kids, all ages... everywhere. They look so sad and frightened. I'm one of them. This memory work is all so crazy. I get the impression that I won't be hurt if I help."

"Help who?" asked Lydia.

"I must hurt the children like the... I don't know what they exactly are. They have big oval black eyes and wear no clothes. They use electric prods on us."

"Can you describe your environment?" probed Julie.

Saqqara scanned the room in a trance-like state but described rapid travel underground to a technical setting, walled in metal with dangerous machinery. She began to tremble and shouted, "No, no, please!" then came to herself in the office. Breathing heavily, she mopped her brow and announced "I'm feeling sheer terror! Is it possible that I created Uba then because, at the end, I sensed another me who felt fearful but heartless?"

Lydia explained, "You expressed what sounds like a programming station for children. The child will first be traumatized for dissociation to occur, to install a program. You described an alien race known as Grays, who serve as grunts for higher echelons.

"I made myself disbelieve they came through my walls and took me away at times."

"We live in a multitude of dimensions which most of us do not understand," said Julie.

They thanked the Lord for the memories. Then prayed trauma off of them, bound any demonic attached to Saqqara during that trauma, chose to forgive all who contributed to the trauma, and prayed to heal DNA. Finally, the three enjoyed a cup of tea while Julie taught the Healing Spiral.

"Once we pray through a trauma and belief system, it is healed. If I find a similar one later, I am not to get discouraged but know it's higher on the healing spiral and closer to complete healing," reviewed Saqqara.

"Yes, events repeat but often result in different beliefs, which brings me to homework. Remember we must turn one-hundred-eighty degrees away from any ungodly belief for healing," said Lydia. "Even if Jill is not co-conscious with Uba, she may be easy access to her. Ask the Holy Spirit what He wants Uba to know and then tell her. We need to know what she decided in the trauma. If that journaling feels unsafe, ask Jesus to be a buffer between her and you until we can work together."

Saqqara opted not to reflect and hurried home to walk the dog. *What's wrong with me? Why do I recoil at the thought of this animal?*

Posting priority focused on Rory getting healed and being able to truly protect Saqqara.

CHAPTER 45

SETH AND CLARICE

Seth happily reported as he and Clarice entered the office and assumed their usual places on the couch. "Our lives make much more sense since she told me about the different wives and their jobs. I admit, at first, that discovery wigged me out. It took about two days, wouldn't you say, Clarice, for me to work that out, and then like I said, it all started to make sense."

"He's amazing. We gave him space, reassured ourselves that we were not crazy, only fragmented, and then we started to talk—I mean, all the wives—there weren't more. Seth genuinely tried to understand the parameters of their function to eliminate unrealistic expectations and frustrations of the past. He requested the wife he needed at the time. He did it real nice, not in a commanding way, and never in front of anyone. Thank you, Seth. I doubt I could do this without you," her eyes pled as tears streamed down her face.

"I'm amazed. It's common for some irritation to arise if a spouse calls out an alter," Lydia said.

Looking warily at Seth, Clarice explained there were some snafus. "We didn't appreciate being jerked like a puppet on a string. We tried not to show our irritation. We knew he tried."

Julie sent a note to Lydia, *Did I just detect Cinderella?*

– 310 –

Seth took note but went on to share, "Yeah, but after the first integration a lot changed, especially the house's condition. Clarice mentioned you talked about a vacation for her."

Lydia responded, "Cinderella demonstrated the first stage of burnout. I described a vacation, and we discussed its benefit."

Clarice scooted forward and excitedly said, "Actually, we are pretty sure Cinderella and Mother integrated. We felt profound fatigue several times, and after each, we never heard them in my head again. Just like the mother inside quit putting me down, but positive thoughts occur in my head now."

Lydia showed them the last note Julie passed to her, "Nice confirmation of integration. You see, no one is ever lost or eliminated! You need all your humanity. We still see and appreciate who you are in all the facets of your personality. Integration gains much unity without loss. Even after full integration, we will need to help you adjust to your new way of thinking."

Seth agreed and admitted the support group helped him to do just that. "The dissociative support group is terrific. The other guys gave me helpful suggestions. I almost felt ecstatic to be with others educated about this coping disorder and genuinely interested in sharing the facts to give hope to those strung along so long as we. Journaling is provocative. The best part is experiencing the help of the Holy Spirit. I confess this is all new to me. I guess I thought like a cold deist, not a Christian, you know, I believed in a creator God but not a personal Savior who knows details of my life, desires, and does help me."

"How are the children doing?" Julie asked.

"They are calmer. There were no screams at night to scare them; Clarice is off those medications that made her so lethargic. Now there is more energy for them. I'm a nicer dad and a happier married man," Seth smiled coyly.

Lydia ventured, "Since Cinderella and Mother integrated, how about an appointment at your home to assess and give you some pointers on how to co-ordinate mothering and maintain a gracious home? You know, solve the 'messy' problems."

"That sounds terrific," Clarice said. "I'm enrolled in the community college class for assertiveness. It begins in two weeks. Could you visit after it starts? The co-dependent class follows it."

"Please call me next week to schedule the best coordination appointment with the classes. Also, since the integrations and free of psychotropic drugs, greater energy is available, but Clarice, you worked diligently for healing. Consider rewarding yourself with two or three days away from the family alone just to be and relax. Your Cinderella self needs to understand a vacation. How about celebrating all the Lord accomplished with Holy Communion?" Lydia offered to close the session.

CHAPTER 46

VACATIONS

Fluffy bubbles tickled Lydia's chin nestled in a soft neck cushion. The steamy fragrance of lily of the valley bubble bath joined the bouquet of gardenia candles whose gentle glow caressed the room. Under the blanket of foam, a soothing Epsom Salts bath began to churn in a noisy frenzy when Lydia hit the jet button. Bubbles puffed above the tub's rim and greatly soothed Lydia's throbbing muscles. Wednesday traditionally involved love thyself physical care, but this Wednesday concluded two weeks of hiking the gorgeous northwest mountains with a forty-pound backpack, heavy due to her medical designation. Touch and the room fell silent except for tiny bursts of minute rainbows.

Her mind aimlessly floated from one subject to another. Her senses relived trudging precarious heights, relief from taking off the backpack, melting snow to brew a hot drink, and sights of pristine alpine lakes.

She sniffed aromas of freshly caught fish frying in bacon drippings for breakfast with the superior coffee brewed in a blue enamel pot.

They descended into hot August pine forests, drank tiny green bugs in the water jug, bedded in fragrant cedar groves, and bathed under stimulating crystal-clear waterfalls amid lacey ferns.

Saqqara's counseling before the vacation developed more trust. She now volunteered at the soup kitchen three times a week, often jogged the Centennial Trail or cycled with Sylvia's bike for exercise and proved highly dedicated to her healing by doing the homework assignments even when sure she could not. She finally warmed up to Grace, who lives across the street, and joined her Bible Study focused on identity in Christ.

Years before, Lydia juggled family, home, garden, food processing, and profession, making summer grueling. But it was wonderfully interrupted with the joy of family and friends camped together at Priest Lake. They harvested huckleberries in the morning and frolicked in the expansive lake in the afternoons. They swam, built rafts, and floated to the nearby store or canoed to a distant island. Their combined children shared the glorious outdoor vacations in earlier years, but as adults, far away, were sorely missed this year. Evenings always chilled, but the crackling sparks of the campfire, sing-alongs, chocolatey s'mores and hot apple cider welcomed the snuggle into eiderdown sleeping bags to drift into the next day.

The last five years after Lydia's husband Michael's plane crash in the Middle East, Ben and Sylvia, Grace and Cody, and Cavanaugh and Lynn never gave her any reason to feel like the odd one out. However, she still felt lonely, especially when they sang around the campfire. This year Grace requested Cavanaugh play *Love Divine, All Loves Excelling*. A little shock shot through Lydia as her eyes locked with Cavanaugh's. He dropped his head to focus on the guitar strings and slowly strummed as a tear slid down Lydia's cheek. Lynn's vibrant voice sang in heaven this year as her husband strummed her favorite hymn.

The bubbles dissipated, and Lydia chilled. She slid further under the water after activating mentee Julie's last recorded session for a critique. Her independent phase indicated most of the clients progressed well. Before she shriveled into a pickle, Lydia drained the bath and toweled. Generous full-body lotion applications and a pedicure finished the weekly ritual.

Vacations

Julie busily brewed coffee as she shared, "I'm so glad you scheduled this morning for review and planning, Lydia. I sorely missed you, but your stunning tan hints at a grand vacation you so richly deserve. All was quiet on the home front. Saqqara or some parts of her made more than the usual nightly phone calls. I think she needed the security of your voice. Maybe you should prioritize creating that CD of your voice, reminding the clients of their tools, singing, and reading scriptures. I added two new clients to my caseload."

"It was easy to leave this time because you proved so competent. I reviewed your last session with Clarice. I agree that she healed enough to benefit from the sexual abuse group. You might want to schedule a family session to take the temperature because her changes, even though healthy, could present difficult adjustments. Humans naturally resist change. What is the plan for Saqqara's appointment today?"

"In the review of appointments before your vacation, there are a few options. Once Saqqara identified daily communications from her father reinforced certain programs, she decided to delete them immediately or destroy them upon receipt and since experienced fewer time losses. We learned she nearly starved in a basement cage and ate like an animal as punishment for seeking help from the school counselor and made Rory to protect herself from telling the "secrets." Once those memories healed, Rory's new job aided rather than blocked visits to the "secret "memories, then along with the associated alters he integrated. She is blocked less, former bulimic urges waned, but hatred of the dog in her care increased. I think the dog situation is a God set-up to reveal some trauma. Jesus rescued four retrainers (alters programmed to retrain programs if removed) from boxes full of spiders and snakes. We removed synthetics (demonic constructs) associated with them. They need integration after inside vacations. Remember when she vomited before two sessions but kept the appointment anyway, and that hostile alter popped out to demand she leave here? I think she is a key saboteur. Oh, we need to find Runner."

Lydia gave a high five and asked, "So, in your opinion, which option affects most of her life?"

"The hostile part of Saqqara is trying to sabotage her healing, but we need to armor up to target that one. She is loaded with demons."

They spent the next hour praising God for His pure love for all of Saqqara and desire for total healing. They thanked Him for spiritual weapons, angels, and protection of the Blood of Christ. The requested wisdom and knowledge proved vital when Saqqara burst in ahead of her appointment and verbally blasted Lydia for abandonment, tearing her away from family and interfering with matters much too complicated for her mini-brain to comprehend.

Saqqara wore an expensively tailored summer suit and steel blue heels to match. The pearl earrings and necklace smacked genuinely. She coiffed her hair in intricate twists which angled along the right side of her face and ended behind her ear. Her authoritative voice pierced the air with mockery and arrogance. Saqqara's face appeared older and stern. She made her way across the room to sit in Lydia's chair.

> "I told Saqqara that her time here is over. Important engagements with responsibilities beckon me to a higher, finer lifestyle than living over a garage in this boring excuse for a city. You will not hear from her again! I despise wasting my time talking to you, you too, (she nodded toward Julie) **but I considered the need to remind you of confidentiality vows if you want to keep your license and reputation. Forget you ever knew Saqqara. Am I clear before I leave?"**

She rolled her shoulders, crossed her legs, and menacingly glared with narrowed eyes at Lydia.

Lydia and Julie silently prayed in the spirit. Lydia smiled and said, "Excuse me, but I don't' remember a formal introduction and realize that formality is appropriate to cultured individuals. I

Vacations

think you briefly contributed to some sessions, but we never had the honor of meeting you."

Stiffness faded as the other Saqqara uncrossed her legs to bend forward and offered a handshake to announce,

"My name is Evtwin."

Lydia shivered as she sat back on the sofa. The woman's eyes appeared black instead of azure blue. "It's always a pleasure to meet humans, but I'm sure that you are not human, so in the name and blood of Jesus Christ, I bind you and your underlings to be totally impotent until removal of legal right for you to inhabit Saqqara," Lydia calmly declared and rose to get coffee for all.

Evtwin appeared limp while she slowly looked around the room. She watched Julie assist Lydia with a tray set before her, then suspiciously lifted her cup of coffee,

"What just happened?"

Lydia sipped her coffee and spoke reassuringly, "A demon was impersonating you and trying to trick us, but it is shut up and shut down now until we discover what sin opened the door for it. If you choose to repent, then it must leave."

The leap to Evtwin's feet sloshed her coffee,

"How dare you interfere in my life!' Do you have any idea what I suffered to get demonic power? You sit here in this chair, act calm, and want everyone to think you are powerfully wise and helpful. Well, let me set you straight. You don't know squat! After all these hours with Saqqara, you have no idea who I am and the power I exert in this world or the places I'm privileged to prepare. You are such an ignoramus. You don't even know such sites exist. When the NWO, you don't

even know those acronyms, NEW WORLD ORDER, is established, I'll get more riches and privileges with power unimaginable."

Seemingly spent, she glided back into Lydia's chair and noticed the coffee stains on her suit and carpet.

Lydia assured her not to worry because they could manage the carpet. Julie offered a stain remover tissue for her suit. "When you mentioned places you are privileged to prepare, does that mean you assist Saqqara with event planning?"

Incensed, Evtwin rose to shake the tissue and yelled,

"I am the event planner extraordinaire, not that sniveling Saqqara. I'm the one who knows the movers and shakers of this world. I am the one who strictly provides which slave profile the connoisseurs of prime pleasure desire. I travel the world to design the events needed to procure the necessities of world domination. Blackmail always gets what it wants. I work side by side with the gods of this planet, the elite, bankers, and high-tech industrialists. Then, of course, we have extraterrestrial colleagues. My demons obey me because I paid the price!"

Lydia's natural look of contrition and words surprised Evtwin, "It must be painful to Saqqara's world to be ignorant of your superior existence and power. She often restricts you from coming out to do your job, and that must be greatly frustrating because, as we know, there are serious repercussions if you are not fully compliant."

Evtwin shook herself out of amazement at the astute kindness and resumed her in-charge demeanor.

"Your caring act does not impress me. I willingly perform my duties! What do you know about repercussions?

Vacations

"A lot. I worked with people who suffered severe trauma for several decades. I listen to their stories of punishments... torture... when they stray from their programmed assignments that support the Elite and their Nephilim leaders in destroying humanity via the NWO."

Evtwin's lips quivered,

"You are not supposed to know about the Nephilim; it's a secret known only by the privileged."

"I serve Jesus Christ, omniscient and very generous to share his knowledge with his friends. He just informed me that you had the high honor of helping plan the last international meeting of rulers of the world system at a famous grove in California near Shasta Mountain. You nearly got caught when you sneaked out with another female to watch the sacrifice during the final ritual."

Evtwin sat motionlessly, eyes droopy and mouth ajar.

"No one knew that except my co-worker, Marissa, who feared for our lives.

"Evtwin, I intended no alarm. Please forgive me. This is not a power contest. My omnipotent Creator is compassionate and gentle to those He created. He sent His son, Jesus Christ, to pay for all humanity's sins with His Holy Blood which can cancel the conviction of all illegal or immoral activity in which a person engaged for eternity if that person accepts that pardon. Of course, there may be earthly penalties because there are consequences to our actions."

Julie felt painfully exhausted while she prayed and observed the client. So, she informed Lydia with a note which interrupted Lydia's deep synchronization with Evtwin.

Lydia smiled a knowing nod towards Julie and announced, "Evtwin, you are part of Saqqara and not separate. I know this is shocking news and perhaps unacceptable, but true. I am asking Saqqara if she heard our conversation to report that to you now."

Time passed.

The end of the twisted hair fell from behind Saqqara's ear as silent tears streaked down her cheeks. "She's the one who caused me so much trouble, isn't she? In what am I involved? Where is she anxious to take me?"

Julie reached out and held her hand, "Saqqara, you experienced a breakthrough today. Evtwin's demons are bound. She will be different now. I encourage you to befriend her. Decide to embrace and love all your humanity, regardless of their responses. God will give you that love and compassion. There is nothing to fear. Evtwin holds answers to your questions and is now experiencing the same confusion as you upon learning the dissociative phenomenon."

"I think I heard most of today. Evtwin just sort of vanished at the end, but I can still feel her. I have plenty to journal for our next appointment. Thank you so much! I need to get home and walk the beast."

POSTING

"Julie, I am so proud of your reassurance at the end. She needed that. Thank you for lifting me out of my synchronization to alert me to her fatigue. Your burden-bearing gift helps me too because I am freer to hear the Holy Spirit and connect with the client."

"Thank you, Lydia; your affirmation is crucial to me. The words of knowledge amazed me as well as Saqqara/Evtwin. I pray to hear as clearly. I may already, but I am a coward to speak it out in case I'm wrong. Do you suspect Evtwin is an early split?"

"Yes, possible during gestation or soon after birth. I'm excited about our next appointment—Evtwin mentioned slave profiling, and I wonder what Saqqara discovers? We will find out. Her early arrival this morning instead of the scheduled afternoon appointment presents an opportunity for a late lunch. Ready?"

All spiritual disciplines require risk and practice. As a result, you will become more confident!

CHAPTER 47

RUNNER

No rain for weeks made the hot sidewalk radiate through the bejeweled sandals. Saqqara surveyed stately homes with sounds of chirping sprinklers offering relief from the August blast. Her heart felt like it might burst. Her legs felt like melted rubber while panting slowed for her sandpaper mouth to utter, "Where am I?"

Julie poured an icy lemonade to break from the prayers and waiting. "Where do you suppose Saqqara is? How will she get back? She tore out of here and left all her things. It's over a hundred today. This run is the second time she switched to Runner. I ran after her; she was so fast that it seemed she had evaporated into thin air. It's been over two hours this time. Do you believe her story about being snatched away in the night and transported to China, and returned the same night? Or today's abreaction of zipping across the country for programming in underground labs with this mysterious Russian guy who keeps showing up at VIP events? It all sounds unbelievable to me, but her terror while relating these memories is convincing."

"Thank you, Julie, this hits the spot," said Lydia, who sipped the fresh citrus brew. Saqqara's discoveries in previous weeks mimic the memories of hundreds of other victims. One thing is clear now. The Russian speaker is probably a principal Nephilim (genetic human and fallen angel hybrid) programmer for Saqqara. Apparently, she managed to create a runner alter and escaped the programmer at some time; hence, his appearance triggers her to run. To answer your questions, she will probably switch from Runner when she perceives she is safe. All these survivors are brilliant, so she will figure out how to return to a regular routine. Her phone is here, but she will contact me to retrieve her things. I hear you. I found such information hard to believe at first. Still, after multitudes of similar stories from clients around the globe and authentic documents from whistleblowers, I now believe. Airplanes and underground trains, which travel at unbelievable speeds, were used for a long time. We, Earthly peons, are not privy to such access. Many people do not want to believe it either.

No one in sight, Saqqara bent low to cup her hands near a sprinkler head to gather several long drinks. Then she swatted it to produce a full body spray of chilling refreshment. She walked along and recited Psalm 94:19 to herself, *"When my anxious thoughts multiply within me, Thy consolations delight my soul."* High traffic fossil fumes replaced the freshly mowed grass fragrance. The teen clerk at the convenience store didn't know the answers to her questions, but an elderly customer graciously pointed out directions for her desired destination. *The counseling office is now closed. I can get into the apartment with the hidden key.*

Grace called from her garden pool, "Why on earth did you walk to a session on a blistering day like this? I see your car isn't in the drive. Is it in repair? Why didn't you call me for a lift?"

She's not nosey, just interested and kind. "Hi, Grace, called Saqqara and crossed the street to chat. I experienced a little complication during the session. I left rather abruptly, and now my keys and phone are in the closed office and my car in the parking lot."

Grace compassionately noted significantly overheated red skin, sopped hair, and dark circles under her neighbor's eyes. She dawned a bathing suit cover, then poured Saqqara an iced tea, "You relax while I call Lydia to resolve this little complication."

CHAPTER 48

GONE

"Where is Saqqara? She's always punctual and never misses a session? Did she mention anything about this Thursday's appointment?" Julie asked Lydia.

"Nothing. I anticipated this time to learn the changes with Rory not interrupting but helping her to remember." Lydia hung up the telephone, "She doesn't answer. Maybe she misunderstood the schedule and went on a sightseeing trip. Well, our afternoon's free. This will give me more time to pack for next week's seminar." They prayed for Saqqara's safety and enjoyment and went home.

"I'm glad you picked up, Lydia; this is Grace. I realize you just returned. I didn't want to disturb you at the seminar. Do you know where Saqqara might be? Last Monday, I gardened near the street and heard Sylvia and Ben's dog. I accessed a key to their house, investigated, and found Horatio almost starved. I cleaned up, exercised him, and fed him and the fish. I am not a nosey neighbor or spy, and I know you cannot give me any information. Saqqara's auto is not in the garage," a worried Grace reported.

"Oh no! Thank you, Grace. Please continue the good neighbor work until we solve this mystery." Lydia quickly called Julie to inform her to pray.

Lydia meditated on the situation with Saqqara. *When Evtwin came out, she mentioned needing to go places and their time here was over.* Lydia felt inspired by the Holy Spirit to reflect upon the power of spiritual decree and spoke aloud, "Saqqara, wherever you are, please come back and be safe. Dearest Holy Spirit, help her switch to her OP."

In a far-away place, luxurious hotel trappings impressed attendees of the *International Pharmaceutical Horizons, Weather Control, and AI Strategies Convention.* Brass luggage carts pushed by uniformed staff wove silently through the symphony of languages orchestrated by expensively garbed people. An exceptionally tall man stood out as he entered the expansive glass doorway and searched over the crowd. He quickly identified a tall, obese man who approached him with an unlit cigar in hand. The rotund man motioned to go outside into the beautiful gardens to talk. "I hear there is an increased demand for infants and younger children this year," he stated while lighting the cigar. "Ahh, nothing like a Cuban!"

"The taller svelte man spoke in a Russian accent, "Yes. First, Evtwin excellently administrated orders, and now Uba is in charge. You know her methods are exacting due to my flawless programming skills. She arrived over a week ago to fulfill the orders and even now supervises the care for the candidates, many babies, and younger kids for hire."

Uba conducted last-minute checks on the rooms holding the ordered sex trafficked people. She gave threatening stares and words to those caring for the babies and toddlers to keep them shut up.

Out of a windowed area on the ninth floor overlooking the garden, the blond Caucasian woman with a collapsible cattle prod in her pocket watched the two men. Suddenly, Uba swerved and almost lost her balance. She crossed to the hall and held onto the wall to stabilize herself. Her head felt like a volcanic explosion. She grabbed it with both hands and slid down the wall in agony.

Relief at last, except for the prod poking her thigh, Saqqara stretched out to grasp the prod and reacted when she saw it. "Where am I?" she asked and looked up and down the hall. Vaguely she remembered hearing Lydia's voice and suddenly filled with terror.

At times it felt like flying around the stair flight exchanges. Lack of air conditioning in the stairwells soon found her drenched in perspiration. In her fright, she missed the main floor and ended up two floors underground in the laundry. Her abrupt arrival caused workers' heads to pop up, glance, and quickly return to their work. Saqqara swayed to a stop and weighed her situation. A rack of pressed clothes stood before her. She grabbed a hanger with clothes her size and ducked into a restroom. During the change, she discovered a money belt around her waist with a passport, cash, credit card, car key, and airline ticket to Boston. Interestingly, she immediately located the auto for the key and left to find an airport.

The next morning, Lydia was thrilled to hear Saqqara's voice on the message machine, "I listened to your voice calling me in my spirit to come home. I am really muddled right now. It feels as though I just woke up. My watch informs me I lost a week at least. I'm not sure where I am but driving a rental BMW. I think I'm okay. I'll keep you posted and apologize for the inconvenience."

CHAPTER 49

EVTWIN

"It took two more flights from Boston to get back here," said Saqqara. "So many things are clearing up in my mind now. Glimpses of island memory indicate that I participate in a human trafficking ring. How hideous!" Saqqara began to furiously beat herself and collapsed in a heap of wailing contrition.

"I'm so glad you came directly to us, Saqqara," said Lydia. "You are safe now."

Saqqara's body straightened, and Evtwin shouted,

> "Maybe now but not soon, you bitches. Do you know in how much danger you put me? You took me away from an historical event that required years to prepare? Heaven knows what calamity that produced!"

"I'm sure it does and is rejoicing," commented Julie. Lydia gave a rebuking look to Julie.

Evtwin angrily turned toward Julie and yelled,

> "You don't know anything. In 2019 a pandemic simulation held in New York City convinced the new world order hopefuls such a plandemic could successfully

control the demolition of the global economy. The collapse ushers in the blockchain systems worldwide to certify and authenticate all financial transactions. Everyone must receive the quantum dot tattoo on their forehead or hand to buy or sell. Of course, it will also deliver, shall we say, poison to DNA which will eventually reduce the populations."

Lydia interrupted Evtwin, "You need not continue; many knew about this secret for many years because Biblical Revelation details it. I also know where we are in the timeline. Revelation also tells us those who receive this purchasing power mark are condemned for eternity because to receive it requires worship of only satan. I'm now asking the Holy Spirit to reveal the traumatic dissociation that created you."

Julie sent a note to Lydia stating the thought which came to mind and waited with her for Saqqara to share.

"My Shield told us about an evil bastard spawned by rape. From what I know now, that alter would be easy prey for programmers. I think that alter is Evtwin," recollected Saqqara.

Lydia showed the note to Saqqara, "Confirmed. Evtwin, you are a wonderful child of God created in His image, and the method of conception is separate from your identity."

"Grace's Bible Study on *Identity in Christ* gives me strength for this. I am Evtwin and Uba," declared Saqqara, who spent the next hour asking forgiveness for the crimes against humanity she committed. "Should I give myself up to the police?" she asked sheepishly.

"Do you possess hard evidence for them to prove what you did?" inquired Lydia.

"They drill us to leave no evidence," answered Saqqara with a frown.

"In that case, police will probably catalog you as a fruitcake and send you home."

"What now, then? Those people are ruthless. Have I put all of us in danger?"

"Death threats are not new to my family or me. I ask Father God for the Blood of Jesus to cover us and protect us and all about which we care. Christians who obey God are not to fear man but live with power and a sound mind according to IlTimothy 1:7. You can do that too. I'm confident that the Holy Spirit helped you escape unnoticed.

After the session, a much lighter Saqqara visited Grace, thanked her for pet care during the hiatus, and resumed her distasteful duties.

CHAPTER 50

MAGIC

Lydia asked, "Where do you want to begin, Saqqara? It's courteous to inquire inside if anyone wants to talk now."

"That sickening dizziness occurs more frequently, and I am ashamed to report increased dog hatred. I jerk its leash often and kick it into the house after a walk. It whined for what seemed forever, drove me crazy!"

"Who inside knows why Saqqara is mean to the dog?" asked Lydia. Silence followed.

Saqqara seemed to shrivel, whined, then barked.

"I think dogs are important because they help humanity in so many ways. What do you think of dogs?" inquired Lydia.

As Saqqara pointed to her behind, the shriveled creature exclaimed,

"I'm a bitch, scum of the earth, worthless, and good only for this! I hate dogs!"

The session discovered magic surgery performed at pre-school resultant of fighting attempted sodomy. Because Saqqara "misbehaved," the programmers made her watch them decapitate a dog. This trauma caused her to dissociate and created the atmosphere for successful magic surgery. The high suggestibility of children enables criminals to convince a child they removed their head and replaced it with the dead dog's head. The child then naturally endures sodomy without fighting. The alter's self-identity declaration revealed the programming. The counselors called upon Jesus to correct the situation.

Saqqara emerged in awe to report watching Jesus crawl to the little girl on her level. First, He told her she never needed to be a dog again because He performed miracles. Then, He asked if she wanted her head back. As soon as she said 'yes,' a human head whose face Saqqara remembered in pictures of herself at five replaced the dog head.

Another alter emerged who described parties in which children engaged in sexual activities with trained dogs while the people made bets and chortled. Saqqara chose to forgive the programming perpetrators and all who took advantage of it, including those who put her and the animals in harm's way. The counselors read many scriptures which described identity in Christ and gave the list to Saqqara. Lydia prayed for the healing of Saqqara's anus and lower bowel and prayed off the severe shock sodomy creates in the brain. They delivered demons of sodomy, bestiality, and illusion. Saqqara renounced hating her perception of herself as a dog and forgave the animals who defiled her.

Saqqara announced, "Grace's Bible study on Identity in Christ will help cement the truth of my identity and its great worth. What kind of monsters do this to innocent children? I already feel a kinder attitude towards my canine charge. The dogs are victims too."

"You are so right! Without the restraint of the Holy Spirit, all of us could be as evil," said Julie.

Saqqara hurried to the apartment and found the dog. She went down on one knee, called to it, and addressed Horatio by name for the first time. A steady wary gaze met hers. He approached slowly, tilted his head, and gently rested his chin on her knee as he watched her with doe-like eyes. "I think you sense my contrition," Saqqara said haltingly, then affectionately stroked his head. A thumping tail made Saqqara laugh, "I love that sound and I'm so sorry for my abuse. We need an enjoyable walk together!"

CHAPTER 51

ABSOLUTION

Lydia wondered at the knock on the door. Who is here now? "Viviana, what a pleasant surprise!"

"I know you do telephone calls on Tuesdays and are sort of free. I need to talk with you. Could I please? I...would you be…"

"You are so welcome, Viviana. Please come in and take a seat. I am about to drink a cup of coffee. Would you like some too? As Lydia hugged her, the strong perfume took her aback.

"Sure, you know me, Java Jane."

"What's so urgent. Have you been ill? You look so tired.

Viviana's hot pink mini skirt inched higher as she crossed her tanned legs and studied her jeweled heels as if seeing them for the first time. After taking a sip of java, she began. "I parked my car, and as I stepped onto the curb, an elderly couple standing on the sidewalk greeted me and offered a card to me. I barely glanced at it as I looked up to see them smile and say, "We are praying that God will give you wisdom today." I told them, "That's nice." I read the caption, which stopped me dead in my tracks when I saw the picture. A tiny baby is pictured sucking its thumb. Thumb sucking—a sign of a healthy fetus at three months.

I don't know how long I stood there before I shook myself alert and entered the clinic. The staff treated me kindly and professionally. Up in stirrups, suddenly, pictures of the baby in the picture flurried in my mind. First, I saw the little thumb flip out of its mouth as an arm tore from its tiny body and floated up. The butchering continued until all was red and ripped from my body. I received counseling, and the procedure went fast but was not as easy as counsel. 'That's it. All done' said the nurse and ushered me to the cubicle where my clothes waited." No more words, Viviana sat staring into space.

A tear marked Lydia's salmon blouse before she could dab it. She sat still, silently praying while waiting for the processing of Viviana's mind to end.

Viviana abruptly tossed her blond locks, shrugged her shoulders, and enjoyed more of her java. "Lydia, you know, I'm a modern, well-educated, liberated woman. When I discovered the pregnancy, I responsibly analyzed the situation and decided the pregnancy was utterly inconvenient. My career looks ducky right now. Maybe a transfer to San Diego is not far off. So, I chose abortion, pure and simple. I'm confident that it was the best choice for me now."

Lydia reached out and touched her hand with eyes searching Viviana's face, "So why are you here, talking to an anti-abortion person?"

She pulled away, notching back, and said in an astonished tone, "Why, it's the picture. I was three months pregnant with a healthy fetus who could suck its thumb!"

Lydia responded, "You mean Creator God blessed your womb to nurture a precious new human life, and you destroyed that sacred trust?

Viviana's eyes widened and nervously blinked while she wrung her hands.

Lydia asked, "You don't need to answer me, but who is the baby's father?"

"It's okay, Lydia; I'm not sure."

Absolution

"So, the baby's father offered no participation in the decision to end his child's life?"

Viviana clutched her abdomen as she leaned left to bend forward, reeling to and fro. Her flushed face blanched white as she wretched. "No, I'm fully responsible. It's my body. It was only the product of conception. It was a fetus."

Lydia inched closer," I'm so sorry your decision brought you to despair and heartache. Everyone makes bad decisions at times. It's impossible to make wise decisions based on false or twisted information. I'm a medical person, and yes, we gave medical terminology like 'fetus' for a precious developing human person whom we will call a newborn baby after birth. It's easier not to respect the life of 'products of conception' or 'fetus.'

"Those terms depersonalize a baby and make it easier to do it harm. Our culture idolizes free sex. I remember working in a pre-natal clinic and talking with women who used all sorts of birth control and sometimes multiple types simultaneously but still got pregnant. People enjoy sex without new life coming forth. You probably heard of the sorrow of couples who cannot conceive. Only God is the source of life. He gave us moral laws to protect us and provide abundant life. The virtue of purity and other virtues seem hidden away and replaced with hedonism in our culture. Life is full of twisted words and false information now. Enough teaching on how we make significant mistakes. How can I help you?

"I don't know." Her chin quivered as tears pooled, then hurried to her chin, where they gathered until heavy enough to run into the skin folds in her neck or onto her dress. Is abortion murder? Have I killed someone? Oh God, I just couldn't be saddled with a kid now! What did I do? BURP. I think I'm going to be sick."

"Take a deep breath. Just lean back and rest your head on the couch," Lydia said. She wetted and neatly folded a linen cloth on Viviana's forehead tenderly. "Can you put a word to what you are feeling?"

She sat forward, peeled the cloth from her forehead, and said, "Guilt, I guess, and shame too, although I believed I had a right to do it if it is legal."

Lydia offered a mint and said, "You believed lies which led you to events which brought shame and guilt. Jesus is real, Viviana. Please ask Him for the next step."

"You mean to pray to someone I don't even believe in?"

Lydia sweetly smiled knowingly, "He's here. Just talk to Him."

"What am I, what am I supposed to ask him? Oh yes, what's the next step?" Viviana rolled her eyes up and around, searching the room expectantly. "Oh my God!"

The shout startled Lydia, who watched Viviana's hand quickly cover her mouth as short giggle sounds escaped while her body danced in place. Prolific tears jumped off her glowing countenance.

"Oh my God, I saw this man in a white robe and blue sash holding a baby. He said to be at peace because he is with Me."

Lydia explained, "Jesus is the son of the God who took on human flesh to come to earth and live a sinless life. He willingly gave His holy lifeblood for the remission of ALL our sins. He rose from the dead and lives today and asks us to give our guilt, shame, hate, anger, bitterness, pain, and sorrow to Him, so we do not carry them. Such conditions destroy us. He did and does all that due to His eternally deep love for us—for you, Viviana. Would you like to give your guilt and shame to Him now?

"How?"

"If you agree with what I'm saying, you may repeat after me."

"I like that idea." She repeated,

Absolution

> "Dear Jesus, thank You for your sacrificial love for me. I choose to offer my guilt and shame for choosing to end the life of my baby boy. I ask You to forgive me for that decision and action. I ask You to forgive me for my sexual immorality. Please show me how to live a righteous, abundant life. In Jesus's name. Amen."

Afterward, Lydia said, "You are forgiven in the name of Jesus, and your sins are as far as the east is from the west." She then asked if she wanted her little boy to know anything. She explained that we are not to talk with the dead, but we can ask Jesus to give someone a message.

Composed and meditative, Viviana cooed, "Jesus, I want you to tell my precious baby boy that I'm so sorry he will never know more of this life because I murdered him for my selfish convenience. Please tell him I truly love him. I really do!" Racking sobs consumed her entire body.

Lydia rose and knelt in front of her with open arms. Viviana melted into them. Her sobbing ebbed, her body relaxed, and peace enveloped the two women for some time. Finally, Lydia carefully freed herself to sit back on her heels and said, "I think Jesus wants to give a message to you."

Viviana straightened, cocked her head, closed her eyes, and listened. In her spirit again, she saw the man with the baby. He didn't speak audibly, but she knew what he said, "Yurgan Jr. forgives you and wants you to know that he loves you and always will." Again, she fell into Lydia's arms and cried with joyful tears, "Yurgan must be his father!"

Lydia rose quickly, "I'm so sorry, I forgot to switch calls into voice mail when you arrived." She hurried to her desk to transfer the call. "It is unusual for no calls to ring. So, I see this as a divine appointment.

"This experience seems unreal to me. I feel so light and sense this, like solace inside. Thank you, Lydia. You weren't critical or blaming, but so understanding, kind, and loving. I always knew you as nice from our time in the book club, but this is over the top."

"Thank you for your sacred trust with this information. May I offer a suggestion? Make friends with Jesus. He's always with us and loves to help guide us. Here is a Bible. An excellent place to start is in the back of the book with Romans. You may also want to visit some churches to learn more about Him and accept Him as your Savior.

Viviana looked at her watch. "Oh my gosh! I've got to be in the studio in twenty. Thanks again." She ran to Lydia, gave her a quick hug, and ran to the door shouting "bye-bye" from the hall.

CHAPTER 52

UNFINISHED BUSINESS

October usually triggers victims due to Halloween when satanic rituals occur worldwide. However, Saqqara purposefully spent more time reading the Bible, playing Christian music, and staying with Christian friends on the evil holiday, which celebrates evil and death.

One of Saqqara's mother's nosey texts, which she usually ignored, caught her eye. *Your father suffered a massive stroke, and we do not expect him to survive. If you have a heart or sense of decency, return to your family immediately.*

At first, an array of emotions overwhelmed her, then she called Naysa, "What will I do? Those people are not safe, at least not yet. I'm still dissociative, and there may be alters loyal to them, and heaven knows what they or I will do." After praying together, they decided to honor her dad with a truthful visit but, if possible, avoid the family. Her counselors applauded her decision and promised to pray for a godly outcome in safety.

As the taxi stopped at the hospital, Saqqara remembered Naysa called this unfinished business. The taxi door barely opened when she spied her mother and sister descending the hospital steps. Saqqara ducked back into the vehicle until they were well out of sight, relieved not to engage them.

Hospital odors engulfed her determined walk along glassy floors to his room. Side rails caged her dad's large frame draped with perfectly folded bed linens. Still, he lay with his eyes closed. Saqqara recalled stories about comatose people understanding what they heard while unconscious.

She reluctantly stepped close, took a deep breath, and spoke with increasing force, "Dad, I know who and what you are. I know what you did with me, you son-of-a bitch!" Her heart pounded, and white knuckles clutched the railing. A cacophony of fearful and angry voices throbbed in Saqqara's head. She turned away and sternly told herself, "We are here on an important mission; I am in charge now, so everyone steps back. I am your advocate now! No. You, dear Jesus, are the advocate, and I sense Your presence now." Her voice softened as she turned back and said, "Because of you, I greatly suffered, and worse. I caused others to suffer and die. I gave all that guilt and shame to my Savior, Jesus Christ, and I received forgiveness. I decided to forgive you, too, so hatred and bitterness don't destroy me. In other words, I gave my right to get even with you to Jesus. The Righteous Judge will vindicate me. You're dying anyway, so how could I get even?"

Her dad's right arm jerked, and his eyes shot open to stare at her. She unflinchingly continued, "I don't know where you will spend eternity, but somehow, I sense severe abuse created the monster in you. If you can, I hope you will come to your senses and acknowledge Jesus as your Lord and Savior before it's too late."

A tear emerged to pool in his ear. Saqqara left.

CHAPTER 53

HOPE

Once Saqqara mainly shed her denial, the memories came quickly for healing. No, it was not easy. The pain stabbed every detail, but her prayer counselors' wisdom, love, and compassion helped her get to more integration.

Several Bible Study ladies invited Saqqara for Thanksgiving. Still, she chose to serve a feast to the homeless at the shelter where she volunteered. Her mother expressed fury when she did not go home.

Grace, Cody, and Saqqara celebrated with friends before the Christmas Eve candlelight service at church. Christmas Day found Saqqara at the shelter helping the broken people.

Saqqara booked the same hotel in Coeur d'Alene in which she lodged on her way to Spokane six months earlier. She reserved the same room overlooking the lake. This New Year's Eve, she felt safe, secure, not alone, and titillated by the beauty of the giant fireworks display. Loud bursts of explosions reverberated against the mountains with distant thuds. Soon after, huge puffs of smoke like fleecy clouds moved quietly and quickly overhead as she peered through the slider glass.

Celebration over, she mused for a considerable time. *This is a new year with hope, sleep, energy, and security, even though*

SAQQARA

nothing is certain. It's time to return to Chicago. I wonder if it's possible to conduct my business free of evil elements and survive, or if I'll need to relocate or completely enter a new career? Did grumpy ol' Helga honor my deposit to hold the apartment until I return? I wonder if I'll seem different to my old friend...friends, Naysa or okay, Nadine. Maybe more friends now that I am willing to trust more and know that I'm not some weird bird.

She stepped out onto the balcony into the stillness of the night. A snowflake floated by and drifted away. Another, then more, and soon the sky filled with glittering jewels of purity, and the fragrance of freshness silently covered the earth. It felt so good to feel clean, free of night terrors, at peace with herself and empowered to return home knowing who she had been and why she had been so confused. Granted, although not fully integrated yet, she skillfully held the tools for completion, started to love herself/her selves and most importantly, knew whose she was.

Saqqara pondered Romans 8:38-39. *For I am convinced that neither death, nor life, nor angels, nor principalities, nor things present, nor things to come, nor power, nor height, nor depth, nor any other created thing shall be able to separate us from the love of God, which is in Christ Jesus our Lord.*

THE END

Go into God's world, expect always the unexpected, anticipate miracles, knowing that with God, all things are possible.

Reverend David Peterson

GLOSSARY

Alter– the term for a distinct part of a dissociative person. Think of the person as a broken vase; each piece (alter) is a vital part of the whole.

Amygdala– part of the human brain situated next to the hippocampus, mainly processing fear related emotions and memories. Trauma is held in exact detail here.

CIA– acronym for the central intelligence agency.

Demons– evil spirits whose forces enlarge or make worse our sins. For example, a person can be angry, but a demon will enlarge that emotion to rage.

DID– acronym for dissociative identity disorder, previously multiple personality disorder.

Dissociation– psychological disorder caused by trauma. The disconnect usually begins in young children and results in problems with identity and sense of self, sensory experiences, thought, memory, perception, and behavior.

Hippocampus– has two parts located in each cerebral cortex of the two temporal lobes of the human brain. Its primary function deals with memory. Think of it as a vast library.

Integration– process and goal of healing trauma in every broken aspect of the human being. Integration unites the part or alters together as a whole person.

Mind control– process of inputting a belief system for the programmer's benefit at the victim's expense.

NWO– acronym for New World Order, a goal of multiple opposing groups to rule the entire world.

OP– acronym for the original person God the Creator made at conception.

Prayer counselors– do not minister as secular counselors, therapists, psychologists, or psychiatrists. Nor is a prayer counselor a Christian who does secular counseling. Principles of psychology that originated from Biblical Principles are honored by the prayer counselor. Christian prayer counselors do not use hypnosis or guided imagery but use prayer and depend upon the Holy Spirit for guidance.

Programs– what people are trained to believe.

SRA– acronym for satanic ritual abuse.

Trauma– shock of a profoundly distressing experience that can involve the mind, emotions, body, spirit, or any combination thereof.

Transhumanism– new religion for enhancing human beings by combining them with machines and demons.

MAJOR CHARACTERS IN THE BOOK

USA

Ben and Sylvia– Saqqara house sits and rents their Spokane apartment

Birgit Malloy– hostess for California seminar, counselor

Cavanaugh– book club, a friend of Lydia

Clarice– client; Alters: Bride, Cinderella, Mother

Desmond– book club

Dr. Emmet Hargrove– geopolitical speaker on the airplane with Saqqara

Grace and Cody– neighbors across the street from Ben and Sylvia

Horatio– Ben and Sylvia's dog

Jillian Woodard– the temp

Julie– Lydia's USA mentee

Lydia Ouray Voight– protagonist prayer counselor

Marley– client

Millie– Saqqara's employee

Nadine– paralegal in Saqqara's office building

Nancy– SRA caller

Nathaniel Kantor– businessman on the plane with Saqqara

Natroya– book club

Naysa– Saqqara's neighbor and friend

Saqqara Alexandria Fain– protagonist client of Lydia;
  Alters: Shield, Rory, Perfect, Sweet, Little Innocent, Small Voice, Jill, Evtwin, Uba, Shield, Devon's Girl

Seth– Clarice's husband

Thi– book club

Tiffany– Saqqara's business partner

Vivana– book club

Yacov– book club

EUROPE

Asian sisters– Lydia's conference followers

Bernhard Fährmann– Belgium client; Alters: Erotica, Quarry

Brunhilde Hetz, Ph.D.– the former client; Tabea's psychologist

Fredrich– Tirza's husband

Günther Grundman– Netherland's seminar host, husband of Kirsten

Hannes– hotel proprietor; Kassel, Germany

Harold and Holgar– suitcase recipients for Romanian orphans

Heike– Hannes's wife

Justin– Lydia's airplane seat companion to USA

Kirsten Grundman– Netherland's seminar hostess, a mentee of Lydia

Rolf Gehrke– a translator in Netherlands and Germany

Tabea Schichan– a Netherlands client

Tirza Pilz– Lydia's European mentee

RESOURCES

The last century produced many excellent listed resources. Look at how long we slept! Let us wake up to honor the survivors and aid their recovery.

Sandra

Anderson, Neil T. *Resolving Spiritual conflicts*, The Workbook, Part II, Freedom in Christ Ministries, LaHabra, CA, 1992.

Ankerberg, John, and Weldon, John, *Secret Teaching of the Masonic Lodge,* Moody Press, Chicago,1990.

Ballard, Tim, *Operation Underground Railroad, https://ourrescue.org*

Bohart, W.H., *Operation Mind Control,* Dell, New York, 1978.

Buys, Amanda, Kanaan Ministries, P.O. Box 15253, Cape Town, South Africa.

Campbell, Ron G., *Free from Freemasonry,* Regal Press, Ventura, CA,1953.

Clark, Terri M., *More Than One, An Inside Look at Multiple Personality Disorder*, Thomas Nelson Publishing, Nashville, TN, 1993.

Condon, Richard, *The Manchurian Candidate*: Movie (old) Newer Version 2003-4.

Cox, Paul L., *Come Up Higher*, The Joy Books, Libertyville, Ill. 2010.

DeCamp, John W., *The Franklin Cover-Up*, AWT, Inc., Lincoln, NE,1992.

Dizdar, Russ, *Expelling the Darkness*, Russ Dizdar, www. Russdizdar.com.

Estulin, Daniel, *The Bilderberg Group*, TrineDay LLC, Walterville, OR, 2007.

Finck, Charles F., *As We Forgive Those*, Liberty Cross Ministries, Liberty Lake, WA, 2013.

Friesen, James G., *Uncovering the Mystery of MPD*, Here's Life Publishers, San Bernadino, CA, 1991.

Gunther, Sylvia, and Burk Arthur *Blessing Your Spirit*, Cornerstone Fellowship, Frederick MD, 2005.

Hawkins, Diane, "Why God?", Restoration in Christ Ministries, POB 479 Grottoes, VA 24441-0479.

Hawkins, Tom R., "A Pastoral approach to Dissociative Identity Disorder," Restoration in Christ Ministries, POB 479 Grottoes, VA 24441-0479.

Henderson, Robert, *Operating in the Courts of Heaven*, Robert Henderson Ministries, 2014.

Horn, Tom, and Putman, Chris, *Exo-Vaticana: Petrus Romanus, Project LUCIFER and the Vatican's Astonishing Plan for the Arrival of an Alien Savior*, Defender, Crane M, 2013.

Horton, Katherine, https://stop007.org-home

Kurath, Edward, *I Will Give You Rest*, Divinely Designed, Post Falls, ID, 2007 (Workbook available).

Knight, Cheryl S. et al., *Care-Giving: The Cornerstone of Healing* (A manual for supporting and caring for satanic ritual abuse survivors).

Marks, John, *The Search for the "Manchurian Candidate" The CIA and Mind Control*, Times Books, New York 1979 and reissued by Dell in 1988 with a new introduction by Thomas Powers.

Méndez-Ferrell, Ana, *Regions of Captivity*, Destiny Image, Shippensburg, PA, 2010.

Resources

Missler, Chuck, and Eastman, Mark, *Alien Encounters*, Koinonia House, Post Falls, ID, 2003.

Miller, Alison, *Healing the Unimaginable*, Karnac Books, Ltd., London, England, 2015.

Mitchell, Kriss, *Identity-What It Means to Be You*, Amazon Publishing, 2014 (workbook available).

Morrissett, Rob, *Pray Through It*, Big Blue Skies Publishing, Hayden, ID, 2006.

Pearcy, Nancy R., *Love Thy Body*, Baker Books, Grand Rapids, MI, 2018.

Power, Elizabeth, *Managing Ourselves*, 1992 (Contact: POB 2346, Brentwood, TN, 37024-2346.

Riggs, Doug: https://www.dougriggs.org.

Ryder, Daniel, *Cover-Up of the Century*, Ryder Publishing, 1996, 225 Crossroads Blvd. #415 Carmel, CA 93923.

Ryder, Daniel, *Breaking the Cycle of Satanic Ritual Abuse*.

Sandford, John, and Paula, *The Transformation of the Inner Man*, Victory House, Inc. Tulsa, OK, 1982.

Schetlin, Alan, W. and Opton, Edward M. Jr., *The Mind Manipulators*, Paddington Press, London, 1978.

Schore, Alan, Dr., *Affect Regulation of the Origin of the Self*, Lawrence Erlbaum Associates, Inc., 365 Broadway Hillsdale, New Jersey 07642, 1994.

Sessions, Deborah, *My Mom Is Different*, Sidran Press, 1994, 2328 w. Joppa, suite 15, Lutherville, MD 21903.

Seymour, Patricia, *North Texas Dissociative Disorder Study* Group, 1 July 13, 1992.

Shoebat, Wahid with Richardson, Joel, *God's War on Terror*, Top Executive Media, NY, 2008.

Sire, James W., *The Universe Next Door, 5th Edition*, Inter-Varsity Press, England, 2009.

Thomas, Gordon, *Journey into Madness: The True Story of Secret CIA Mind Control and Medical Abuse*, Bantam Books, 1989.

U.S. Government, *Final Report of the Select Committee to Study Governmental Operations*, U.S. Senate, April 1976.

Watson, Peter, *War on the Mind: Military Uses and Abuses of Psychology*, Basic Books, Inc., New York, 1978.

Whitfield, Charles L., *Memory and Abuse, Remembering and Healing the Effects of Trauma*, Health Communications Inc., Deerfield Beach, FL,1995.

Wilder, E. James, *The Red Dragon Cast Down*, Chosen Books, Grand Rapids, MI, 1999.

Willson, Angel, *Over the Rainbow: God's Eye for the Gay Guy*, Amazon, 2017.

ABOUT THE AUTHOR

The author is an international speaker, mentor, and Christian Prayer Counselor focusing on dissociation associated with severe trauma. As a Registered Nurse graduate of Mount Carmel School of Nursing, she pioneered Intensive Care Nursing at Ohio State University Medical-Surgical Hospital. Later she earned an AA Degree from Spokane Community College and a BSN from Gonzaga University.

As founder and C.E.O. of A.C.A.C.I.A. LLC., Sandra passionately desires broken people to achieve the abundant life promised in the Holy Bible by providing a common understanding of dissociation by "normalizing" it. She lives in the beautiful northwest of the United States of America.

A.C.A.C.I.A. INSTITUTE VISION

It is my honor to present the vision God gave to me in the early 90s before I became well acquainted with DID. Tens of thousands of people are in grave need of a place to heal in safety with explicit services to address their specific needs. There they learn new coping skills and cease the need to dissociate. They find their true identity with purpose, worth, and dignity while gaining new life skills for a victorious life. Onsite services provide education and provision for healthy lifestyles for spirit, mind, and body. To my knowledge, no such facility yet exists which can accomplish these goals.

Please envision a twenty-acre campus, around eight hectares, in a beautiful rural setting complete with trees, hills, a year-round stream, fertile gardens, and an orchard complete with beehives. I can smell the pine and the fragrance of wildflowers visited by honeybees. Feel the gentle breeze? Lush greens, plump tomatoes, and mature produce fill gardens surrounded by heavily laden fruit and nut trees. I see people kissed by the sun and exercised by labor as they learn, teach, and tend.

A central energy-efficient multifunctional structure connects to surrounding buildings by walkways. It houses administration, triage, medical center, classrooms, prayer counseling, offices, cafeteria/restaurant, intercessory chamber, combination conference, media center, and auditorium/gymnasium. The education and modeling equip lay people, professionals, and dissociative persons about DID. The walkways covered with grapevines, berries, and roses have benches strategically placed welcome peaceful rest.

Healthy, delicious onsite food service is provided for residents and visitors (professionals, support people, the public, and survivors of trauma) who attend educational events. This service also includes work therapy and work experience for survivors when they leave. An innovative, novelty-type restaurant is also planned for the public on designated dates and to serve events. Are you tantalized with curiosity about what kind of novelty this might be?

The media center produces international and domestic educational and supportive blogs, websites, webinars, and podcasts.

As the contamination and defilement of some survivors are considered, 24/7 intercessory prayer becomes imperative due to the warfare waged against this work of setting the captives free. I envision the prayer chamber to be high with panoramic views. Can you see it?

A triage unit assesses unsafe or ill people to prevent the endangerment of other residents. Many dissociative people are poly addicted. A medical center to treat the plethora of health problems severely traumatized people suffer requires medical professionals. Clients often suffered difficulty getting laboratory test results because evil organizations positioned their people everywhere.

Several apartment-like structures with shared living spaces accommodate survivors according to their level of healing. We need to treat entire families from generational satanic cults with facilities adequate for children to thrive and not separate from parents. That requires housing.

The Institute offers trained staff who don't freak out when a client switches into an alter. Group and individual therapy counselors adequately educated and trained to deal with dissociation reside on campus. One connected building resembles a hotel in design and function. It provides housing for residents and temporary staff, conference attendees, and temporary housing for new patients.

Its design offers the necessary division for privacy and safety for each category. The area under the building houses parking and maintenance equipment.

Revenues from lodging, cafeteria services, restaurant, media productions, counseling, education, produce sales, and healing services all help support the Institute.

Conclusion: Facilities don't offer the completeness of service I believe is necessary for healing. When I see most people, they are financially broke from years of seeking healing from every imaginable practitioner, quack, and remedy. Counseling sessions are not enough. People need to be safe to heal, which requires a minimum of three months in-house.

"If you are reading this, I suspect interest in DID for some reason. I beg you to make this Institute a reality. Communicate this need to all you know. I am sure someone or many possess the finances and resources to make this a reality for the survival of humanity. Please consult my website for more details. Thank you for listening.

May God richly bless you.—Sandra

acaciaministries.com